THE
CROSS
AND THE
CURSE

THE BERNICIA CHRONICLES: II

MATTHEW
HARFFY

Muile

Hii

DÁL RIATA

N

HIBERNIA

IRISH SEA

ALBION
AD 634

PICTLAND

DÁL RIATA

BERNICIA
Bebbanburg

DEIRA

Eoferwic

ELMET

GWYNEDD

MERCIA

WEST SAXONS

Cantwaraburh
CANTWARE Hithe

FRANKIA

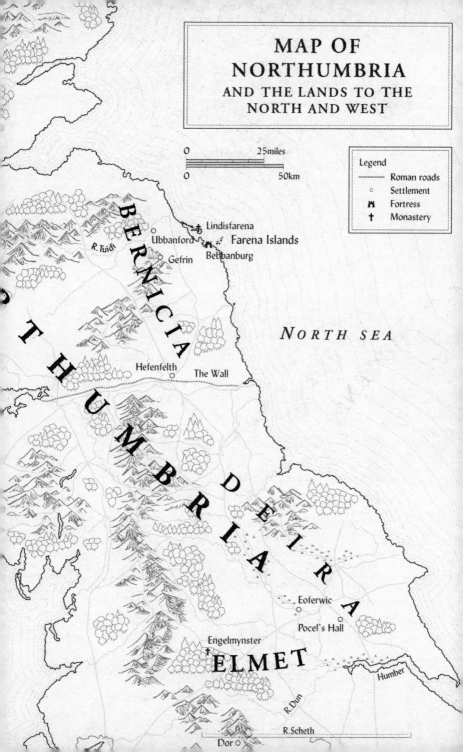

MAP OF NORTHUMBRIA
AND THE LANDS TO THE NORTH AND WEST

0   25miles
0   50km

Legend

- - - - - - -   Roman roads
  o   Settlement
  ᛗ   Fortress
  ✝   Monastery

BERNICIA

R.Tuidi

Ubbanford

Gefrin

Lindisfarena

Farena Islands

Bebbanburg

NORTH SEA

NORTHUMBRIA

Hefenfelth

The Wall

DEIRA

Eoferwic

Pocel's Hall

Engelmynster

ELMET

Humber

Dor

R.Dun

R.Scheth

For my parents, with love.

Place Names

Place names in Dark Ages Britain vary according to time, language, dialect and the scribe who was writing. I have not followed a strict convention when choosing what spelling to use for a given place. In most cases, I have chosen the name I believe to be the closest to that used in the early seventh century, but like the scribes of all those centuries ago, I have taken artistic licence at times, and merely selected the one I liked most.

Albion	Great Britain
Bebbanburg	Bamburgh
Bernicia	Northern kingdom of Northumbria, running approximately from the Tyne to the Firth of Forth
Cantware	Kent
Cantwareburh	Canterbury
Dál Riata	Gaelic overkingdom, roughly encompassing modern-day Argyll and Bute and Lochaber in Scotland and also County Antrim in Northern Ireland

Deira	Southern kingdom of Northumbria, running approximately from the Humber to the Tyne
Dor	Dore, Yorkshire
Dun	River Don
Elmet	Native Briton kingdom, approximately equal to the West Riding of Yorkshire
Engelmynster	Fictional location in Deira
Eoferwic	York
Frankia	France
Gefrin	Yeavering
Gwynedd	Gwynedd, North Wales
Hefenfelth	Heavenfield
Hibernia	Ireland
Hii	Iona
Hithe	Hythe, Kent
Lindisfarena	Lindisfarne
Mercia	Kingdom centred on the valley of the River Trent and its tributaries, in the modern-day English Midlands.
Muile	Mull
Northumbria	Modern-day Yorkshire, Northumberland and south-east Scotland
Pocel's Hall	Pocklington
Scheth	River Sheaf (border of Mercia and Deira)
Tuidi	River Tweed
Ubbanford	Norham, Northumberland

Prologue
AD 619

"We do not need your new god. He is weak. Was he not killed by men?" The raven-haired beauty turned to her audience with a savage smile. But the eyes of the men and women who glared back were dim and dark, like deep meres from which no warmth came.

"What god can be slain by mortals?" the woman sneered.

"I do not seek to battle with you," the thin, hawk-faced man before her said. "I am simply bringing the word of the one true God to you and your people. Edwin King has granted me the right." The man's words were difficult to understand. His strange accent garbled the sounds, but the meaning was clear enough.

Some weeks before, a pedlar had ventured up the valley for the first time since the snows thawed and had told tales of fabulous things afoot in the land. King Edwin's bride had brought a holy man with her from her homeland of Cantware. But this priest was from even further away, if such things could be believed. It was said he was from the land of the giants who had built the Great Wall, but that was ridiculous. Everyone knew they were all dead now.

And this man was no giant. Yet he did carry himself as one sure that others would follow.

"One true god?" she spat. "Only one god? You are mad. What of the sky, and the water? Battle, and the crops of the earth? Each has its own god, we know this." Again she looked to the villagers, but stony silence met her gaze.

"There is only one God," the slender priest said, speaking as a father explaining something to a small child. "He sacrificed, Jesu Christ, his only son, so that no man should know death, but have everlasting life."

The woman recoiled as if he had struck her.

"Mother?" A boy stepped close to the woman, reaching out hesitantly to touch her arm. He was a swarthy youth, at that awkward age close to adulthood, yet not quite a man. Tall and strong, but without the bulk that came with age.

He knew that his mother would never willingly allow this stranger to speak of his god to the villagers.

She would kill the priest first.

The boy looked at the warriors who had come with the priest. They stood nervously holding their horses' reins. They were grim-faced. Killers. Light glinted from sword hilts, and burnished byrnies of iron. His mother's magic was strong, and she might kill the priest, but her own death would follow close behind.

"Mother," he repeated.

"Silence, Hengist," she hissed, pushing him away.

She turned her face to the sky and let out a piercing shriek.

Startled, the horses shied and snorted. The warriors tugged on the bridles.

"Leave this place!" she screamed, her beautiful face contorted into a mask of fury. "Begone and do not return! Take your weak god and his son and go back to the land you came from." A strong wind blew down the valley suddenly, whipping her black hair about her face. Her dress pressed to the contours of her body.

She began to tremble and shake. Hengist had seen her do this countless times. She always did so when the gods spoke through her. He shivered. The gods were preparing to speak and he was frightened of what they might say.

A broad-shouldered man with greying hair and a stern jaw stepped forward, shaking off the hands of his wife, who tried to hold him back.

"Wait, Nelda," he said. "I would hear what this man has to say about his god. A god that does not demand sacrifice and promises life rather than death. This is a god I would hear tales of."

For several heartbeats Nelda glowered at the man.

"Do not think to tell me what to do, Agiefan," she said, her words full of contempt.

Then, with a cry even louder than the first, she spun to face the dark priest once more.

"No! You bring lies to poison our minds. Lies!" She reached into the leather pouch that hung from her belt and drew forth several small items. Without hesitation she flung them at the stranger. He flinched as the small objects, white against the dark wool of his robe, hit him and fell to the ground. They were human finger bones.

The priest touched his head, then his chest, then each shoulder, in a magical symbol of some kind.

Nelda screamed in words of a tongue none there could comprehend. The wind tugged the words from her mouth and shredded them. A great flock of rooks flew overhead, black against the darkening sky. Stinging grit from the path spattered into Hengist's eyes. The air itself crackled with the promise of violence. Mothers pulled their children away, shielding their eyes. Nelda wielded the power of the gods in her voice and all there stepped back from where she stood.

All except the priest.

He was unmoving, with eyes closed. His lips moved, but he spoke too quietly for the onlookers to hear.

His lack of response seemed to enrage Nelda even further and her voice began to crack, her throat tearing with the force of her arcane words.

One of the warriors stepped forward, drawing his sword. The priest, sensing the movement, held out his hand for the man to halt.

Nelda's cries and exhortations to the gods continued for some time, until at last, the words dried in her throat and she stood before the stranger, panting and wild-eyed, foam flecking her lips.

He opened his eyes then, this man who spoke of a new kind of god, and held out his right hand towards the witch. In his left hand he clutched a silver amulet that dangled from a thong about his neck. Hengist saw that it was similar in shape to the hammer of Thunor; a cross, like the sign the priest had made over his chest.

Nelda's shoulders heaved from her exertions. For a moment there was silence, only broken by the rush of the wind that now howled in the valley.

Then, in a clear voice, the priest said, "In the name of our Lord Jesu Christ, I, Paulinus, command you to leave this place, that these people may know the true word of God."

Nobody moved. The ferocity of the wind lessened. A calm settled on the valley. Nelda's mouth began to twitch into a smile. It seemed this stranger's god would not speak.

And then, with a sound as loud as mountains collapsing, the

shadowed vale was lit with the white brilliance of lightning. The bolt crashed so nearby that people screamed out, in fear for their lives. It was as if the sky itself had fallen. Women threw themselves to the ground, protecting their children with their bodies. Several of the warriors' horses broke free and galloped down the valley track, eyes white-rimmed with terror.

The thunder-crash was deafening. The air was rent with a ripping sound, followed instantly by a hammer-crash blow of god-like intensity. The echoes rolled down the valley. Was this a display of Thunor's anger? Had he heard Nelda's screams of defiance at this new god?

The clouds churned black and terrible above them. Nelda's smile broadened. The gods were furious.

But Nelda's expression changed to a look of anguish as she saw where the lightning had struck.

To one side of the valley stood the sacred ash tree. This was the symbol of Woden, All-Father. The tree where the rites to the gods were performed. Where sacrifices were made.

The tree had been split asunder. Part of the massive canopy came crashing to the earth in a jumble of broken branches and wind-whipped leaves. The remaining section of the tree's bole was aflame. Great sheets of fire leapt into the sky, fanned by the wind.

No more lightning came and no rain fell, but the wind continued to scream down the valley, and the sacred ash burnt.

People began to recover from the sudden shock of the lightning. They cowered in tight groups, as if by proximity they could protect themselves from the wrath of the gods.

Agiefan spoke then, his voice loud and hard.

"This new god has shown himself. Look, the sacred tree is shattered. The old gods' power has waned. And what have they brought us but death and pain?"

Nelda's face was pale as frost. None there had ever seen her thus.

Afraid.

Gods had been pitched against each other, and Nelda's had lost.

"No!" she said. "You do not understand the signs of the gods. I have been there to guide you all for years, I have helped you bring your babes into the world, I have—"

Her words were cut short when a gaunt woman, sallow skin stretched over sharp cheekbones, stepped in close to Nelda and punched the witch solidly in the mouth. Nelda staggered, but did not fall. She spun to face the woman, raising her hands, ready to fight her, but the villagers crowded in. Nelda held herself in check.

"Do not speak of bringing babes into the world, Nelda," spat the woman. Her eyes were dark and sunken, as one who has witnessed horrors that can never be scoured from memory. The woman seemed set to strike again, strong in her rage. But then her shoulders sagged, and she said in a thin voice, "Never speak of helping us, witch."

The villagers knew of the woman's pain; the darkness that had consumed her since the coldest days of winter. They shared some of that pain. And they knew that they were partly to blame for it. They remembered the blackest night of Geola, when they had turned to the cunning woman. Nelda had promised them an end to famine, and they had listened, accepting in their desperation the sacrifice she had demanded.

They had accepted her price. Yet the cost of it weighed heavily on them all.

And now the witch's gods had deserted her.

As a fire will burst suddenly into life when a tiny flame is blown upon in just the right way, so the anger, resentment and shame of the villagers sprung into life.

Another woman stepped forward and slapped Nelda hard, splitting her lip. A man shoved the witch. She tripped and fell to the earth. The villagers swarmed around her, kicking and spitting in their sudden-found ire.

Hengist let out a roar that stilled the crowd. He surged forward, pushing men and women aside. He was strong and his fury lent him power. More than one man fell from the onslaught of the boy's rage.

"Get back from my mother," he screamed, standing over Nelda's huddled form.

Agiefan took a step forward. Without thought, Hengist lashed out, striking the older man squarely on the nose. Blood sprayed and Agiefan staggered back, caught in the arms of other villagers.

"Hengist," Agiefan spoke from behind the hand that sought to staunch the blood-flow from his nose. "We have no fight with you. But your mother is not wanted here." He spat blood onto the gravel of the path. "She must leave this place." Agiefan flicked a glance to his own son, Hengist's best friend, who stood looking on aghast. "You are welcome to stay here, Hengist. But she must go."

Hengist looked at the people gathered around them. Folk he had known all his life. Friends and enemies. Old and young. Agiefan's son looked on with pleading eyes. Hengist's gaze fell on the glowing beauty of the girl, Othili. She was as pallid as the rest, but there was no hate in her eyes. There was something else. Excitement?

Then Hengist met the stare of the strange man, Paulinus, the priest who had come from a faraway land. The priest's eyes were dark and hard, like caves hewn of granite. For a moment, Hengist felt his rage screaming to be unleashed. He could leap at Paulinus. Rip out his throat or snap his neck like an autumn twig.

His mother's hand on his leg stayed him.

To kill Paulinus would serve no purpose. Hengist would be struck down by the warriors who protected him. But Hengist scowled at the priest. He would have vengeance over this man and his king.

He pulled his mother to her feet.

"Help me to pack my things," she whispered to him.

He swallowed, unable to speak for a moment. He would not weep before these people.

They walked away from the crowd. The scent of wood-smoke was pungent in the air. The snapping sounds of the burning ash followed them.

"I will come with you," Hengist said.

"No," Nelda turned to him, a savage glint in her eye. Blood trickled from her lip and her face was bruised, but Hengist did not believe he had ever seen a more beautiful woman. "No, my son, you will stay here and you will be great! You will serve kings, like your father did. And you will bring them down, Hengist." She clutched at his arm so tightly that it hurt. "Stay and topple these worshippers of the soft Christ god."

He was ashamed at the rush of relief that washed over him. The thought of fleeing their home terrified him.

"Your father was a thegn of renown," she continued. "You will be greater. You will serve kings, feeding the wolves with the gifts of your slaughter. Oh my son, you will cast terror into the spirits of your enemies. You have been touched by Woden, who goes by many names and guises. But the name that suits you best is Frenzy."

She pulled his face close to her own, smoothing his dark

hair back from his forehead with her lithe fingers. Her touch both thrilled and unnerved him. Her breath was metallic.

"Remember," she said, spitting blood into his face from her bleeding mouth, "you are Frenzy. Woden-touched."

Hengist stared back at the dark Christ priest. Behind Paulinus stood the sacred ash that was now a towering torch of flame and smoke.

Yes, he would stay. But he would never forget the day the new Christ god came to the village. Hengist would never forget and he would see to it that Paulinus and his king, Edwin, would remember him when their time came.

ANNO DOMINI NOSTRI IESU CHRISTI
IN THE YEAR OF OUR LORD JESUS CHRIST
634

PART ONE
THUNOR'S FURY

1

"**G**et your hands off of my woman, you whoreson!"

Beobrand felt his ire rising at the sight of the grizzled warrior pawing at Sunniva. The older man looked up, but kept a firm grip on Sunniva's slim waist. She struggled, her golden hair spilling from its plaits in a shimmering wave, but the man's arms were gnarly and strong. The rings on those arms attested to his prowess as a warrior. Years of training with shield and spear had made them as unyielding as tree branches.

The hubbub of the hall died down the way a fire will when doused with water. There were hisses and whispers as the men on the mead benches jostled for a better view. A fight was always a thing of excitement.

Beobrand spoke again, this time in a quieter voice. "I said get your hands off of her." His words carried around the hall, the promise of violence clear.

"What are you going to do about it, half-hand?" The warrior squeezed Sunniva again. She squirmed, but did not give him the pleasure of making a sound.

Beobrand looked down at his left hand. His shield hand.

The smallest finger had been severed only weeks before, along with a large part of the next finger. The wounds were still red and raw. He clenched his disfigured hand into a fist. The recently healed skin stretched and cracked. Blood oozed from the wound and the pain washed up his arm in waves. But he did not flinch. The wound had almost proved fatal. Fever had set in and he had been close to passing on beyond this middle earth. And yet Beobrand's spirit had clung to life and he had not followed the rest of his kin into the vale of death.

"The mighty warrior Hengist took my fingers, yet I still live and he feeds the ravens," Beobrand said. "I only need half a hand to kill the likes of you, you bag of piss."

The mood in the hall changed. Talk of killing reminded them all how serious such minor disputes could become. They were not allowed to bring weapons into the great hall, but eating knives could kill as well as a seax or sword.

"Kill me, would you? I am Athelstan, son of Ethelstan, and I have killed more men than I can remember." Athelstan pushed Sunniva away and stood, jaw jutting and frost-tinged beard bristling. He was a large man, broad-shouldered and imposing, but Beobrand still needed to look down to stare him in the eye.

"It is a sad thing to see when the memory departs in greybeards," said Beobrand, the slight smirk on his face not reaching his cool blue eyes. "Perhaps you were once a warrior of renown. Now you are just old. Sit back down before you get hurt."

A ripple went through the hall. Men were both impressed with the bravado of the younger man and wary of the reaction from Athelstan. He was known to many as a man quick to take offence and slow to back down from a confrontation. He was also famed as a deadly fighter.

"Old, am I? We'll see about that! I'll rip your heart out and then pleasure myself with your girl before you're cold!"

Athelstan lunged towards Beobrand, swinging his huge fist at the young man's face. There was terrific force behind that punch. Athelstan's bulk and strength made the blow a terrible thing; a crushing hammer that would fell Beobrand.

If it connected.

But Beobrand had the speed of youth. He was not yet fully recovered from the injuries he had sustained in the shield-wall in the shadow of Bebbanburg, but he was a natural warrior. The cold of battle had descended upon him now and Athelstan seemed to move like a man wading through a bog, slow and clumsy.

Beobrand deflected the brunt of the attack on his left forearm and stepped in close to Athelstan. In the same motion, using his forward momentum and that of Athelstan combined, he raised his right knee and dealt the older man a crippling blow to the groin. Such was the force that Athelstan was lifted from the rush-strewn floor.

A collective wince ran through the hall. All the fight and breath rushed out of Athelstan in a sighing groan. He crumpled over, clutching himself.

"I'll... I'll..." he gasped.

"You'll what?" said Beobrand. "Bleed on me?"

Laughter in the hall.

Athelstan fought to regain composure and control. "I'll kill you!" he croaked, his face red with rage. He pulled a small knife from his belt, brandishing it before him.

Silence fell on the hall again. Death was in the air.

"There'll be no killing here today." The voice of Scand, Beobrand's lord, rang across the hush of the room like a slap.

All eyes turned to stare at Scand. He stood at the head of

the hall. He had been seated at the high table, but now he towered over the room. The light from the torches and the fire in the central hearth lit his silver beard with flickering gold. His lined face was craggy and dour in the gloom.

"We are all sworn to the service of King Oswald. Do not forget yourselves. There will be time enough to fight soon. The Waelisc are violating our lands and Cadwallon's forces amass near the Wall. Beobrand, you will be glad of Athelstan's strength when we stand in the shieldwall again. And you, Athelstan. You are old enough to know better than to touch a young man's woman. Especially if that young man fights as well as Beobrand, son of Grimgundi."

Beobrand glanced at Scand, then back to Athelstan. He could feel the danger drifting out of the air, but his fury was still pumping round his body, making him tremble.

Athelstan straightened and looked Beobrand in the eye. He lowered the knife.

"Put the knife away, Athelstan," Scand said. "And apologise."

Athelstan hesitated, but then seemed to see no alternative. He sheathed his knife and lowered his gaze.

"I seek your pardon," he mumbled.

Beobrand quivered with pent-up rage. He loathed men who used their strength to bully others, especially women. His fists were still clenched and it was all he could do not to pummel Athelstan's drink-slack face into a bloody pulp. Behind Athelstan, Sunniva was gazing at Beobrand, her eyes shining in the firelight. She was without question the most beautiful thing in the hall. Her hair was like molten bronze and her face seemed to glow with an inner light. Amongst the warriors in the hall she was like a single fine flower in a field of rocks and mud.

And she was his.

Neither Beobrand nor Sunniva had any living family, and they each filled that gap in the other's life.

She seemed to sense he was preparing for more violence and she shook her head, almost imperceptibly. He could not bear to make her unhappy. He swallowed down the angry words he wished to shout.

"You have my pardon, Athelstan. It was the mead that spoke your words for you."

Athelstan smiled ruefully and rubbed his crotch, still struggling to remain upright. "I wish you had realised that before crushing my balls."

The tension vanished from the hall. A few men chortled.

Athelstan collapsed back onto the bench and reached for the mead horn once more.

"You have an interesting way of making friends, Beobrand." Acennan guffawed and slapped Beobrand's shoulder. Acennan was considerably shorter than the young man from Cantware. He had a round face that was quick to smile, but he was a warrior to be reckoned with. They had stood shoulder to shoulder in the shieldwall, and there was nobody Beobrand would trust more in a battle. Beobrand looked at his friend's face. Acennan's nose still bore the scars from the beating he had received at Beobrand's hands when they had first met.

Acennan had been drunk and had threatened Beobrand. He had lived to regret his actions. For a time afterwards there had been animosity between them. But shared experiences had led them to a mutual respect, which had become the bond of friendship. Shield-brothers. Beobrand smiled back at Acennan, the cold wind blowing off of the North Sea stinging his eyes and making them water.

"Well, it worked for us, didn't it?" Beobrand said.

"True. After you showed me you were not too useless in a fight," Acennan retorted with a grin.

Wyrd was impossible to fathom. If anyone had told Beobrand he would be friends with the stocky warrior after their first meeting in Gefrin, he would have thought them mad.

They were standing on the eastern palisade of Bebbanburg, the slate sea stretching into the distance. The brooding shadows of the islands to the south could just be made out. In the other direction lay the larger island of Lindisfarena. Now protected by the waves on all sides, but at low tide it would once again be accessible from the mainland of Bernicia.

The two friends often stood here. Sometimes they talked. Many times Acennan joked. Frequently they just enjoyed each other's company. The fortress was bustling and noisy. It still housed all of the survivors from Gefrin, in addition to King Oswald's retinue and those stewards, thralls and servants who had remained after King Edwin's death. It was overcrowded and the wall was one of the few places where peace was a possibility, even if just for a few moments.

"You are lucky Scand stepped in when he did," said Acennan. "That Athelstan is not someone to cross by all accounts. You'll have to watch your back."

Beobrand pictured the old warrior touching Sunniva and suppressed a shudder. "I know. But I could not just stand by and watch him."

"Your temper will get you killed one day."

"Well, so far, it doesn't seem to do me much harm."

Acennan touched his nose gently. "No, it doesn't do you much harm." He hawked and spat over the palisade. The wind caught his spittle and flung it back towards them. A gull wheeled close, trying to snatch the morsel from the air.

"I suppose my nose looks better now. Like a real warrior. I was too handsome before." Acennan laughed.

Beobrand grunted. He was in no mood for jesting. The confrontation with Athelstan was still fresh in his mind. His hand ached where he had cracked the scabs on his fingers. He was still angry. Tense with contained violence.

"How long till we march south?" he asked.

"Not long now," answered Acennan. "I know Oswald says we should wait for the warbands from the north to come, but I cannot see how we can tarry much longer. Cadwallon is not idle. With each day that passes, more settlements are destroyed. More Angelfolc put to the sword or enslaved."

King Oswald had sent messengers north in search of aid from Gartnait, the king of the Picts. But no news had returned yet. The warriors trained, but each day they grew more restless. News came almost daily of death and destruction at the hands of the Waelisc host in the south. Oswald would not be able to afford to keep this many men at Bebbanburg indefinitely. Supplies were already running low, but with the threat of Cadwallon's force harrying the populace of Northumbria, he couldn't disband the warriors.

Beobrand said, "Do you think we can raise enough men to beat Cadwallon?"

"Only the gods can know. But we've been outnumbered before and we are still here."

Beobrand remembered the clamour and terror of the shield-wall. The twists of wyrd that had allowed them to escape with their lives.

"Facing the Waelisc once on equal terms would be a welcome change," he said.

"Aye, but who wants an easy life, eh, Beobrand?" Acennan snorted and slapped his friend on the back. "Our tale will be that much greater in the telling when we face Cadwallon once more against greater numbers and crush him in the field."

Beobrand wondered whether there would be anyone left in Bernicia to tell their tale, but he kept his doubts to himself. He had spotted something out on the Whale Road, still far to the north, but heading towards them.

It was a ship. Riding the waves swiftly on the stiff breeze.

The two warriors fell silent for a while, watching the vessel approach. Sea birds careened in its wake. The sleek bark came on quickly, sail full and straining at the mast and stays. They watched as the ship rounded Lindisfarena and sailed towards the moorings on the beach below Bebbanburg.

"Perhaps Oswald's calls have been answered," said Acennan. "That ship looks full of men."

The hall was crammed with people. Oswald was going to speak and everyone in Bebbanburg wished to hear his words. The men were keen to learn whether they would march. They wanted to be on the move. Some longed for battle. For glory and slaughter. Others secretly prayed they would be spared the shieldwall. But all were tired of the confines of the fortress. The women were thin-lipped and tense. They knew the lives of their men rested in the hands of this new king, returned from exile after many years. Their lives had been thrown into disarray in the last year. The peace of King Edwin's reign had ended abruptly at the battle of Elmet far to the south. Many good men, husbands, sons and fathers, had perished that day. In the months that followed there had been a welter of blood-letting throughout the land at the hands of Cadwallon and the accursed native Waelisc. No family had been untouched by the slew of violence, which had culminated in the destruction of the royal steading of Gefrin and the murder of Oswald's brother, Eanfrith.

Now war and death once more threatened their land and the men would march. It was their duty. The women wished there was some other way to protect their homes. But they knew of none.

The hall's beams were soot-darkened. A fug of smoke and sweat made the atmosphere hazy. The rush lights guttered. The hearth fire blazed. Those near the flames were sweltering and drenched, but unable to move away, such was the crowding in the room.

Beobrand, with Sunniva and Acennan on either side, stood at the end of the hall, far from the high table where the king and nobles sat. They watched as King Oswald, slim and pale, yet with a commanding presence, raised himself from his seat and spread his arms over the crowd that thronged the hall. His long chestnut hair was brushed back from his forehead, framing intelligent eyes and prominent cheekbones.

Slowly the chatter died down. Oswald stood there, arms outstretched for a long while. The tension in the room built. The watchers leaned forward expectantly. All talk ceased.

Silence.

At last, the king spoke. But not in the declaiming tones of a warlord or a scop recounting a tale of battle-play. Instead he spoke in a hushed voice. The audience shuffled forward in an attempt to better hear the words of the man who could decide how the weft of their wyrd was woven. Many held their breath.

"Men and women of Bernicia. The good Lord God has answered our prayers. King Gartnait, brother of Finola, has responded to my appeal for aid and sent some of his finest warriors to bolster our numbers against the heathen Cadwallon."

Finola, widow of Oswald's brother, Eanfrith, sat demurely to Oswald's left. After Sunniva, thought Beobrand, she was the next most beautiful woman in the hall. She was pale, fragile of build, with a long river of flame-red hair washing down her back. She sat immobile, resigned it seemed, to be used as a strategic piece in the deadly game of tafl played by kings. There was no love between the Angelfolc of Bernicia and the Picts. Eanfrith had married her to secure an allegiance, and now Oswald was taking advantage. Perhaps she, and her young son Talorcan, were little more than hostages of noble birth. Behind Finola, the silver-bearded Scand stepped forward, and placed a reassuring hand on her shoulder. She reached up and tenderly patted the old thegn's hand.

Oswald paid no heed to Finola or Scand.

"We will march. The fyrd has been summoned once more to protect the land."

Sunniva's small warm hand found Beobrand's. He clasped it with a reassuring squeeze. He remembered being in this same hall only a year before. King Edwin had sent for the fyrd then too, and promised to rid the land of Cadwallon. How many would come to this new king's call? But even if all heeded the summons, after the previous year of bloodshed and battle, there were fewer men able to take up shield and spear in defence of the realm.

The Pictish reinforcements were welcome, but Beobrand and Acennan had counted only a couple of dozen men in the ship that afternoon. They had both stood shield to shield against Cadwallon's host before and it looked increasingly likely they would once again be outnumbered by the Waelisc. If they survived the upcoming battle, their tale would be great indeed.

Oswald continued: "I have prayed and the Lord has told

me we will prevail over our enemies. I have been exiled these many years from this fine land of Bernicia and I will not allow anyone else to stand between me and my birthright. Many of you stood by me through those years," his gaze swept the room and he met the eye of several warriors, his closest retinue, his comitatus. "Your loyalty to me, your bravery in the battles in Hibernia and your faith in the one true Lord will now be repaid. I will be a good king. None of you shall want." Some of the men stamped their feet or clapped their hands.

"To those of you who know me less well I say, 'Keep faith with me and God, and you will have your reward, both in this life and the next.' We will march into battle under the shadow of the Holy rood and we shall sweep the pagan Waelisc before us."

Acennan nudged Beobrand and whispered, "If he can fight as well as he talks, we'll have nothing to worry about."

"Why must you leave so soon? It is not right. You are barely healed." Sunniva could hear the tinge of despair creeping into her voice. She tried to keep her anguish to herself, but it was ready to burst forth, like a banked forge blown by a bellows back into roaring, searing life.

"You know I must go. I can do nothing else," answered Beobrand. His tone was coloured by his exasperation with the conversation. They had been skirting around it for days, but since Oswald's announcement, Sunniva could ignore it no longer.

"I know," she said quietly. She leaned back against the wall and closed her eyes. They were seated on the ground in their makeshift quarters in the corner of the store building that had been given to Scand for his men and their families. Like all of Bebbanburg, it was overcrowded and noisy, but they had done what they could. Sunniva had crafted a partition from cloaks and withies that provided a semblance of privacy, though they were well aware that it did nothing to conceal sound. There could be no secrets in the cramped building.

All of their possessions lay piled as neatly as she could manage in the small space between the withy-cloak barriers and the outside wall. Each night they lay together, whispering, kissing, exploring each other's bodies. They clung together in the dark, neither wishing to let go for fear of being lost. In those moments when they coupled in the gloom, breathing each other's breath, she could almost forget the reality of their life. She was content in those night-time moments. Happy to hide from the world in this small home-space she had made for them.

But in the light of day, she remembered all too keenly her mother and father's passing. Her mother had succumbed to a coughing fever the previous winter. Her father, Strang, smith of Gefrin, had been savagely murdered. Beobrand had avenged his death and had come back to her. He was all she had now. Only weeks before he had been on the edge of death and the memories of the vigil at his bedside haunted her dreams. And now he was marching south to war. Against a superior force. And the worst thing of all was that he looked pleased.

Sunniva opened her eyes and looked at Beobrand. His eyes glimmered in the glow of the rush light that burnt in a small earthenware holder on the ground. The shadows distorted his face, making his features hard.

"Why can't we just leave?" she implored him. "We could find someone in need of our skills. I could smith and you have your sword. There is always need for strong men."

Beobrand sighed. "You have said it yourself. I have my sword. What good is a strong arm and a fine blade, if not used? I am Scand's man now. We are oath-sworn to Oswald. I cannot break my oath." He reached out and stroked her cheek with his fingertips. "You would not love me if I were an oath-breaker."

She nodded. It was the truth. She loved him because of who he was, not in spite of it.

"Then swear an oath to me that you will return and wed me," she said.

Beobrand grinned in the darkness. His teeth gleamed in the dim light. "Nothing would please me more. I promise you this, I swear by Thunor's hammer," he gripped the carved whale tooth amulet that hung on a thong at his neck, "that I will fight to come back to you with all my strength and when I return, I will marry you. And you will give me a fine son!"

He reached for her and pulled her to him in a strong embrace. In doing so, his arm caught the fragile cloak partition, unseating it from its precarious position. It fell over the two of them. The rush light sputtered out.

Sunniva's joy at his words and his touch curdled into woe. The gods had heard Beobrand's oath and had answered by blowing out the light. A bad omen.

"What have you done?" she shrieked, panic welling up from where it had been lurking just beneath the surface of her feelings.

Others in the building stirred from their slumber. Someone hissed, "Shut that wench up, by all that is holy!"

"It is nothing, just the cloak," said Beobrand, trying to placate Sunniva. He picked up the rush light in its holder and stepped carefully over the prostrate forms, towards a large tallow candle that burnt at one end. He re-lit the taper.

In silence they replaced the partition. All the while tears streamed down Sunniva's face.

He would never return to her. He would die. The gods had spoken and it must be so.

He reached for her, tenderly now. She clutched at his kirtle and crushed herself to his muscular form, as if she could prevent him leaving by using her own sinewy strength to hold him close.

He smoothed her hair and kissed her neck. Slowly, her sobbing subsided. They lay down together, warm and close.

"It was nothing," he whispered. "Just my clumsiness."

She could hear the forced smile in his words. Perhaps they were both cursed.

"I should not have asked you to swear an oath," she replied, her voice hollow and desolate. "You should not tempt the gods."

"Nonsense," he kissed her. "Thunor will watch over me and I will return to you. And we will be wed."

She snuggled into his chest.

She had behaved like a frightened child. Overreacting. Whatever their wyrd, time would tell. Surely a falling cloak and an extinguished flame signified nothing.

Beobrand caressed her back. Sunniva felt herself relaxing.

"We will be wed," she murmured. "And I will give you a fine son."

Beobrand's lips brushed hers as he shifted his position and blew out the light once more.

The next morning dawned blustery and cold. The sky spat spitefully at the men who gathered on the beach below Bebbanburg to train. King Oswald had tasked each of the thegns to prepare for the battle. To that end, Scand took the survivors of Gefrin down to the moist sand to spar. The men knew each other, they had stood shield to shield at the ford of Gefrin and had lived. There was not one amongst them who was untempered by the fires of battle. They were grim. The elements and the certainty of battle weighing on them. But soon, after a while of shoving in the shieldwall, sweat loosened their muscles and their tongues. The jests began and laughter drifted on the wind to those who stood watching on the ramparts of the fortress.

Beobrand joined in with the others, but his mind was clearly elsewhere. They had all seen him fight. He was formidable in combat and none could easily stand against him. Yet today, he lost half of the bouts he fought, many quickly and to vastly inferior fighters.

Scand raised an eyebrow at Acennan after Beobrand suffered a particularly vexing defeat at the hands of a man twice his age. Tobrytan, a squat, sombre man, was torpid and his style was blunt, all his attacks clearly signalled. Normally, Beobrand would have dispatched him in a blink. Today he let Tobrytan get under his guard and deal a bruising blow to his ribs. Beobrand clutched his side, nodded to the man and trudged away, shoulders drooping in defeat.

Acennan followed him to where he sat in the shelter of a dune. The marram grass whipped and whispered in the wind.

"What ails you?" Acennan asked, seating himself next to his young Cantware friend.

Beobrand raised his mutilated left hand. He clenched it into a fist and shook his head.

"Nothing. It is just this hand. I cannot hold the shield boss as I should. My grip is weak."

"Is that all?" Acennan grinned. "You are a fine warrior and we cannot have you feeling sorry for yourself just because of a couple of fingers. Think of them as sacrifices. One to Woden and half for Thunor!" The stocky warrior laughed at his own wit. Beobrand did not smile.

"We'll get some leather and strap your shield to your arm. It will mean you'll need to practise some more. It will make punching with the boss tricky, but a natural like you will manage." Acennan clapped Beobrand on the shoulder. "And Woden and Thunor will not allow the man who gives them fingers to die!"

"Do not talk lightly of such things," snapped Beobrand. "I swore an oath on Thunor's hammer that I would return from the battle and wed Sunniva. But the light blew out and now she is sure I will die and I am cursed. Perhaps I am."

Beobrand had slept fitfully after the incident, his dreams full of his father's violence. In the dream he had been a small child again, but his brother, Octa, had not been there to protect him. Their father had rained down blows on Beobrand, clubbing him with his fists and when he fell, kicking him in the face and ribs. Finally, the dark shade of his father had stepped close and stamped on his left hand, making him cry out loud. He had awoken with a start. He was lying on his hand, and the scabs had opened again.

How could it be that his father still frightened him from beyond the grave? Would he never be free of the man? He had thought his father's death would end the man's power over him. His mother, sisters and brother had already left this world. He hoped that their father was not tormenting them in the afterlife. No, it could not be so. Octa had gone before him, perhaps to protect them from Grimgundi's violence as he had in life.

Beobrand shivered. They were close to Octa's grave. He was buried in a sacred place just beyond the dunes. Last time he was here he had vowed to avenge Octa's death. He should return to tell him he had kept his word.

"Cursed, lad? You?" Acennan shook his head at Beobrand's foolishness. "I do not jest when I say you are blessed by the gods. You have battled against Hengist, one of the meanest sons of a whore to ever walk middle earth and all you lost were a couple of fingers. You survived the elf-shot fever. You have a sword fit for a king and a woman men would kill for. Not to mention wonderful friends." He winked.

"So you have promised you'll marry, Sunniva. That will not prove a hardship now, will it? And if you do not return? Well, you'll have more important things to concern you than that broken oath. Perhaps Thunor blew out the light to show you he had heard your oath. Who knows?" Acennan shrugged.

Beobrand nodded. Acennan was right. He should not think such dark thoughts. Wyrd would take him where it would. He stood and reached a hand out to Acennan, pulling him to his feet.

"Thank you, my friend," Beobrand said. "I was forgetting myself. I have been blessed, as you say." He thought of all those he had lost in the last year and struggled to keep his smile. He pushed the memories away. Squared his shoulders.

"Come, show me what you have in mind for my shield," he said.

Together they returned to the warriors on the beach.

2

Beobrand said his farewells and tried to believe they were not final; that he would not die in the battle. But the omen of the snuffed out flame had unsettled him. Do what he might, he could not shake the nagging feeling of doom that clung to him. Sunniva seemed to sense that he would not fight well with this cloud over him, for she did not mention it again. Perhaps Acennan had said something to her. Beobrand had caught them whispering and looking in his direction as they broke their fast with the rest of Scand's retinue, his gesithas and their womenfolk. When they had seen Beobrand staring at them with his cool glare, they pretended to be engaged in conversation of no consequence. Beobrand knew them both too well.

Before taking his leave of Sunniva, Beobrand decided to visit Octa. He was not eager to go to the place of the dead, but he wished to set his brother's spirit at ease. He could not bear to think that his murder had left Octa unable to move on from this world of the living.

He rose early and made his way south. It was not far and he knew the way. The morning air was cool and still.

It would be warm once the sun was up high. But in the shade of the dunes it was still cold. Trudging through the sand and marram grass, his mind turned to Bassus, his brother's friend, who had brought him first to his brother's resting place. He wondered whether he would ever see the giant warrior again. When they had parted company, Bassus had been setting off to return to Cantware. To Beobrand's homeland. Yet it was somewhere he could not return. His father's shade loomed too large there.

He shivered on reaching the place of canted marker stones and raised barrows. The dead had been laid to rest here for many generations. It was silent. Peaceful. The stillness of those who breathe no more.

He picked his way between the graves to where he remembered Octa lay. In the year since he had stood here last, everything had changed. And yet, here he was, once more on the verge of heading to battle. And again talking to his dead kin.

The ground had settled somewhat in the intervening months. Grass and a few flowers had seeded in the turned earth. Beobrand's shadow fell over the grave, dimming the glistening beads of dew.

"Well, I promised I would avenge you," Beobrand said. He felt uncomfortable breaking the silence. He did not wish to wake those who slumbered here. Still, he knew he must ensure that Octa could rest.

He spoke in hushed tones. "I killed Hengist. And I took back Hrunting from him." He slid the sword from its wooden scabbard. The sun caught on the fine, shimmering patterned blade. It shone like a lake in winter sunlight. Brilliant, yet cold. As always, Beobrand was moved by the beauty of the weapon.

"It is the most noble of blades and I will do my best to

honour it and your memory." He paused, unsure of what else to say. His feet were cold, his leg bindings and shoes soaked through from the dew on the long grass.

"Be at peace, brother. Watch over mother, Rheda and Edita." He waited. There was no sign. No omen. No answer. What had he imagined? Octa would be nothing more than rotting flesh and bones now. Beobrand suppressed a shudder.

He stood there for a few moments more, the morning sun warming the back of his neck. He nodded once at the grave and returned to Bebbanburg. To the living.

Beobrand was surprised to note that he felt a lightening of spirit after his visit to Octa's grave. His step was less heavy. When Sunniva cleaved to him in a tremulous embrace, tears flowing down her cheeks, he was able to summon up a smile.

"Pay no heed to what happened in the dark," he said, stroking her hair. All around them others were bidding their loved ones farewell. Many goodwives kept their faces blank, expressionless. But not a few of the younger women joined Sunniva in shedding tears. The fortress was abustle with preparations.

Oswald's host would march before the sun reached its zenith.

"The night-time is a place for fear," Beobrand continued, "but the day is warm and bright. I am strong. I have Hrunting, a good helm and iron-knit shirt. My new shield will protect me now. Thanks to you." Acennan had told her what was needed and Sunniva had flung herself into the task of fashioning leather straps that would aid Beobrand to hold the linden board in place, rather than having to rely on his damaged hand to hold all of the shield's weight by the iron boss.

"And Acennan will stand at my side. I will return to you. I swear it."

Sunniva stifled her sobs. Beobrand could feel her weeping

moistening his kirtle. She mumbled something. He could not make out the words, so he pushed her away from him gently, to see her face. It was tear-streaked, blotchy. But she was still lovely; her hair radiant in the bright daylight.

"What?" he asked.

"Then we will wed and I will give you a fine son," she said.

Late summer was a time for collecting the harvest and preparing the fields for winter. As they marched south, Oswald's warhost passed ceorls and thralls working the land. They saw a great flock of birds, fluttering in the wake of an oxen-drawn plough. The birds tumbled and dived, plucking insects from the freshly turned soil. The ploughman stared at them with blank eyes.

It was a reminder to the marching men that their own fields were untended. If they did not return to their homes soon, they would not be able to sow their winter barley. A victory in the shieldwall could still lead to a lingering death from hunger in the months that followed.

As they moved south many homesteads and settlements were deserted. Whether the people had fled at the approach of the column of warriors, or fearing attacks from the bands of Waelisc who had ravaged the land, they could not tell. Some homes had been destroyed, consumed by fire. At one such place, a large farmstead on a hill overlooking the straight Roman road, the hall and the outbuildings were charred husks. The beams jutting in silhouette against the bright sky like the skeleton of some huge beast. Oswald sent a group of mounted thegns up to the buildings to investigate. They returned grim-faced and sombre. They had found human bones amongst the ashes.

Oswald ordered the host to halt while the people were given a burial in the way of the Christ followers. One of the dark-robed monks who travelled with Oswald spoke magic words over the graves. Oswald looked imperiously on. Many of the warriors touched amulets and charms. Some made the sign of the cross. Beobrand touched Hrunting's hilt and spat.

"We won't get very far if we stop to bury everyone we find on the way," said Acennan, shaking his head. "All Cadwallon has to do is kill a few ceorls and leave them in our path if he wants to get away."

"Maybe he doesn't want to get away," said Beobrand.

Yet they made good progress. There were more ruins, stark reminders of their enemies' movements with impunity throughout the land, but they found few bodies. The weather too, seemed to smile on them, as if the gods themselves wished them to reach their destination and confront the Waelisc.

Beobrand studied this new Christ-following king and the host that marched behind him. Oswald sat stiffly on a large white horse. He looked neither comfortable nor at ease, but he did look as if he belonged at the head of a mass of men. He led them with quiet self-belief and none of the bluster of some war chiefs. And the men followed.

There were men who had been in exile with Oswald in Dál Riata. Some were old, like Scand, others were younger, perhaps the sons of those who had served Oswald's father and accompanied the athelings Eanfrith, Oswald and Oswiu into exile in the west. There was a small contingent of Hibernians, allies from that western isle. Beobrand had heard that the athelings had fought on the island, and apparently they had attracted some followers there too. Then there were some Waelisc, natives of Dál Riata. They dressed in the way of their people with colourful, decorated braughts over their tunics and armour. The brighter and more richly tasselled the braught, the more proud and haughty the wearer.

Lastly, there was the group of Picts, sent by Gartnait. These men looked formidable with their long lances and clutches of short throwing spears. They wore simple tunics and cloaks, but the flash of silver torcs and fine brooches spoke of their standing amongst their people. They strode bare-legged and apart from the rest of the host and did not engage in conversation if approached.

On the second day, word came to them of the whereabouts of Cadwallon and his host.

There had been a constant trickle of people travelling in the opposite direction to them, heading north, away from Cadwallon. These refugees had come in small groups. Families, or a handful of travellers who had joined forces on the road.

Then a glut of people approached them from the south. Several dozen men, women and children pushed before the Waelisc warbands as game is driven before the beaters in a hunt. Exhaustion and despair were etched on the dirt-streaked faces of those hapless survivors of Cadwallon's desire to destroy the Angelfolc.

The column halted. King Oswald and his most trusted thegns gathered to talk with those leading the refugees.

Beobrand unslung his shield and massaged his neck where the strap had rubbed his skin raw. He dropped the sack of provisions he carried and slumped to the ground. Beside him Acennan flopped down and began untying his leg bindings.

"I have a blister the size of a fist, I'm sure of it," he said. He cast a glance at the head of the host, where Oswald and the others were deep in conversation. Oswald had dismounted and stood straight as a spear while all those around him appeared hunched. "Let the nobles stand to talk. They've ridden all the way here. I would sell my left ball to have a soft bed and a warm woman right now."

All around them, Scand's gesithas were making themselves comfortable. Hopeful of a respite from the gruelling pace.

"A woman and a bed would be pleasant," sighed Beobrand. "But right now, I'd be happy just for the bed. This byrnie is as heavy as a dead horse." Before this he had not travelled any real distance wearing the iron-knit shirt that Acennan had stripped from a body at the ford of Gefrin, and his back ached from the weight of it.

"It is hard work being a warrior of legend, Beobrand." Acennan slapped him on the back. Attor, a slender warrior with a thin, straw-like beard, laughed, the scratching sound mimicking the rasp of the whetstone that he dragged along the edge of a vicious-looking seax.

"It looks like you may get the woman sooner than you'd like," Acennan continued, "though I wouldn't leave Sunniva for that wizened old hag. But I suppose it is as they say, and any furrow is good to sow when the sapling is ready to plant!" More laughter.

But Beobrand did not join in the mirth. He looked at the object of Acennan's comment. A woman, old enough to be his mother, head covered and stooped, walked towards him. Recognition gleamed in her eyes.

She was followed by a young man, who glared at Beobrand, menace evident in his every move.

They stopped in front of the reclining warriors, their shadows falling over Beobrand.

"Beobrand, son of Grimgundi, are you hale?"

Beobrand stood, and to Acennan's surprise, he reached for the woman and pulled her into an embrace. The young man

26

at her side tensed and Acennan sensed violence in his posture. He pulled himself quickly to his feet, one foot bare, ready to defend his friend should it come to that.

But the man did no more than stare with open hatred at Beobrand.

Beobrand pushed the woman back gently and held her shoulders. His eyes glistened, wet with unshed tears.

"Wilda, goodwife of Alric, it is good to see you. But I fear the news you bring is not good."

"Never mind my story, Beobrand," Wilda said. "That is sad enough, but tell me: where is my elder son? Where is Leofwine?"

The men around them shifted uncomfortably. They had stood in the shieldwall at Gefrin with Leofwine the scop. He had been a fine bard. His fingers could pluck beauty from the strings of his lyre and his voice was like golden honey, sweet, smooth and healing. He was brave; had taken up shield and spear in defence of the land. Yet the bravery of the blond, youthful teller of tales outmatched his skill in battle. His wyrd had ended his tale on the blood-soaked bank of the river at Gefrin. Many more had fallen that long hot day, but none was a sadder loss.

The warriors looked down. They could not look upon the mother of the valiant singer of songs.

Beobrand did not meet Wilda's gaze.

She needed no more. Her fears were confirmed and she let out a howl of utter dismay. "God has forsaken us!" she screamed. She pulled away from Beobrand and collapsed into the arms of her other son, Wybert, the man standing at her side.

Wybert held her close. She shuddered and raged against his chest. All the while, he glowered at Beobrand.

"This is your doing," he said. "You have brought nothing but death and sorrow to us all, Beobrand."

Beobrand recalled the last time he had seen Wilda and Wybert. Alric, Leofwine and Wybert's father, had told him to protect his son.

His failure burnt his eyes and throat as he choked back tears. Acennan placed a hand on his shoulder, but he shrugged it off.

Beobrand learnt the story of the end of Engelmynster as Oswald and his retinue plotted and schemed. The king thought up strategies to counter the Waelisc threat while Beobrand heard of the death and destruction that had been wrought on the defenceless.

Beobrand, Acennan and several other warriors sat, listening raptly as Wilda told the tale.

She began: "That day had dawned like any other. There was nothing of note about it to presage the death, darkness and despair it would bring."

Those who had listened to Leofwine recounting tales recognised the same spell in the words of his mother. She too had the gift of story-telling and they were enthralled.

She told of the warning sounds of the horns, echoing around the clearing, shattering the peace of a late summer's morning. The men had quickly gathered together, ready to defend their settlement from one of the bands of brigands who roamed the land. But they had not been prepared for the thicket of spears and armour that descended on the small monastery. This was no small group of miscreants. This was a warhost. Light glinted from shield bosses and helms like the scales of a monstrous dragon. There was nothing they could do to prevent the destruction of Engelmynster.

Wilda's eyes misted as she spoke of how Alric, her husband

and head man of the village, had told the women, monks and children to flee.

"Alric turned quickly to his brave son, Wybert," Wilda placed a hand lightly on her son's arm. "'Wybert, you must take your mother, the other women and the monks and head north. To Bernicia. To King Oswald.'"

The men, entranced at the tale, leaned forward. There was strong magic in the honour of sacrifice for loved ones. They did not know Alric, but they felt proud of his actions.

"Wybert protested. He wished to stand and fight along with his father, but he saw the finality in Alric's eyes. Heard the stony resolve in his voice. He must do his duty and protect those entrusted to his care." Wilda looked at Beobrand, her eyes full of sorrow.

The listeners nodded their approval. A son should do his duty and obey his father. Beobrand squirmed inwardly.

"Father and son shared a brief embrace. Each certain they would never meet again in this world. There was no time for long farewells or speeches. Wybert led us from our home, while Alric stood with the other men, holding back the Waelisc to allow us time to escape."

There was silence at the ending of Wilda's tale. Not a few of the men had tears in their eyes or on their cheeks. Many more had gathered around during the telling and now Wilda sat at the centre of a throng of avid listeners.

"Goodwife, your story is the same as that heard throughout the land," a voice spoke out into the silence, clear and assured.

All eyes turned to look upon Oswald. He stood, serious and sad, yet emanating strength.

"I am Oswald, king of this land of Bernicia, and I offer you and the others who come with you succour in my kingdom."

Wybert, Wilda and the other refugees bowed their heads.

Oswald continued: "I have heard tell of how Cadwallon's host has continued north, harrying the land of Deira to the south and is now close to the borders of our lands. We will hurry south, to the Great Wall and there we will defeat this Cadwallon and bring slaughter to his host. This we will do in the glorious name of our Father in heaven."

For a moment, Beobrand imagined his own father in the heaven of the Christ. You had to lead a good life to go to heaven, so surely Grimgundi would not be there. Alric had been more of a father to him in the weeks he had known him. He would surely be in his Christ's heaven.

Oswald continued to talk to the crowd. He raised his voice to reach the members of the fyrd who had joined his host in the last days, his retinue and the gesithas of his closest thegns and the newly arrived, displaced inhabitants of Deira and Bernicia.

"We will head off Cadwallon's host before they can cause further harm to our land or our people. We will crush them against the Wall and Christ will bring us a victory to be sung of for generations to come."

A voice spoke close to Beobrand's ear. "Well, it is good to see you following a good Christian king, Beo."

Beobrand spun round. Next to him was the smiling face of Coenred, the young monk he had befriended at Engelmynster. Coenred had grown in the months since they had last met. His face was more angular, his shoulders wider. He would never be broad and strong like Beobrand, but he was no longer a boy. He had grown into a young man.

Despite the painful memories of Leofwine's death and hearing of Alric's sacrifice, Beobrand could not help but grin. Coenred had saved his life after finding him in the forest, wounded and feverish. Like him, Coenred was alone in the world, an orphan. His sister had died while Coenred had been protecting Beobrand. Coenred had never blamed him for her death, but Beobrand was acutely aware of what the novice monk's aid had cost him.

"Oswald looks to be the perfect king for us," said Beobrand. "A Christ follower to keep you happy, but one who wishes to wage war and destroy his enemies in battle. What more could we ask for?"

Coenred looked into his eyes for a long while before eventually smiling a sorrow-filled smile. "It is good to see you, Beobrand. You look well." Coenred looked him up and down, taking in his fine helm, metal byrnie, sword and shield. "And prosperous. War suits you."

Beobrand winced. He should not have made light of battle and death. Coenred was not one of the men who had stood with him in the chaos of the shieldwall. Coenred despised violence. He could not begin to understand what drove Beobrand to fight. To seek revenge for crimes. To right wrongs at the point of a sword.

Beobrand could no more understand Coenred's devotion to the forgiving Christ god than Coenred could fathom Beobrand's belief in the old ways of strength and blood to confront obstacles.

But one thing Beobrand knew for certain. The threads of their wyrd were intertwined.

Coenred was a true friend. And he was pleased to see him.

They rested long enough to eat, but they did not light fires and set up camp. They were close to the Wall now and Wilda's story spurred the men on. Her sincere, poignant account of the demise of all she held dear moved them all.

The Waelisc were coming and the Waelisc would pay.

Oswald had sent out word for fyrd men to meet to the north of the Wall. On a hill known to all as Hefenfelth. There they would congregate and form ranks, stopping Cadwallon's force from passing the Wall and gaining access to Bernicia.

The pace was exhausting. A renewed urgency had fallen on them all. The day was warm and they sweated and panted their way along the furrowed and cracked road built by men who had left these lands in a time beyond memory. It might be crumbling and uneven, but it was still the best route to follow for a large group of men marching apace to battle.

"Cadwallon will be travelling up Deira Stræt towards us," Acennan panted from Beobrand's side. "It is the only way he can move a host of that size. If God is smiling on us, we'll arrive at the Wall before him. Then we'll be in with a chance. Not much of one, I grant you, but a chance all the same." He punched Beobrand's arm and let out a laugh.

How Acennan could be so happy when they were heading towards almost certain doom was beyond Beobrand's ken. He could not imagine ever being happy going into battle. Yet deep within him he did feel the first quickenings of excitement. A spark deep within a forge blown into life by a gust from the bellows. The shieldwall was terrifying. A place of sickening fear and pain. But also of exhilaration. He could not deny it. He was not content to be battle-bound, but part of him was eager for the thrill of it.

That is what separated him from Coenred. The young monk was truly perplexed that Beobrand welcomed the chance to test himself once more against the foes he had faced already three times in the last year.

Beobrand had tried to explain it to him before they had parted ways once again, Coenred heading north to the safety of Bebbanburg, Beobrand continuing south with Oswald and the fyrd of Bernicia.

"These are the men who killed Tata. I will avenge her death," Beobrand said.

If he had thought by mentioning Coenred's sister that he would gain his approval, he was sorely mistaken.

Coenred turned pale and screamed at Beobrand, "Do not speak her name! More death and killing will not bring her back to me. She…" Coenred's eyes brimmed. "She…" His words caught in his throat. "She is dead. I want no more death on my soul." He rubbed his hands over his face, scrubbing at his eyes. Men who had turned to stare at the monk's outburst looked away. Coenred continued in a calmer tone. "Defend the land, Beobrand. That is noble. Do not use Tata's murder to justify your own lust for blood."

His words had stung Beobrand. Is that how Coenred thought of him? Craving violence and death the way bears crave honey? Once they have the scent of a hive they can think of nothing else and no number of stings will stop them. Beobrand looked down at his left hand. At the stumps of his two last fingers. He pictured Leofwine's face as it had been in death. Pallid and muck-spattered. Could it be that he sought battle, whatever the cost?

Wybert certainly blamed Beobrand for his brother's death. Wybert had always disliked him, but now, without Alric's calming influence, his hatred bubbled freely. Beobrand had approached him as the warriors prepared to march on.

"I am sorry for Leofwine's death," he said. It was the simple truth. "He died bravely."

"Bravely?" Wybert spat. "He was no warrior. He would not have been at Gefrin if not for you. Your dreams of glory spoke to the poet in Leofwine. He went north because of you.

You might as well have struck him down with that fine blade of yours."

Beobrand reeled under the heat of Wybert's fury. He could offer no defence. Leofwine was dead and he had failed to protect him. Nothing could change that now.

"I am sorry." Beobrand swallowed the lump in his throat and took his place amongst Scand's gesithas, next to Acennan.

The warriors allowed Beobrand to join their ranks without the usual jesting and jostling. If he had just received a beating at the hands of another warrior, they would have teased him without mercy. But they had seen the encounters with Coenred and Wybert. They had heard Wilda's tale too. They were subdued and sombre.

Beobrand's pain was no matter for laughter.

Some wounds were more easily dealt with than others.

3

Scand ached. He placed his hands in the small of his back and stretched. The throbbing pain subsided slightly but was replaced by a tingling, numb sensation in his right leg. Gods, he was old. His body had barely recovered from the gruelling battle at Gefrin and the punishing march to Bebbanburg. His torso still bore the marks. The bruises from blows he'd received had faded, but were still visible. At the time, in the heat of the action, he had not felt anything. It had always been so in combat. He would lay about him with his sword and shield, allowing his metal shirt to soak up any strikes he could not deflect.

His frame was not what it had once been. Years ago, before his hair had turned the colour of hoar frost, the bruises and aches would disappear within a couple of days of a fight. Now, weeks passed and he still suffered. He was no longer young, it was true. He wondered how many battles he had left in him. Well, he could not sit by the fireside telling tales of his exploits just yet. He had sworn his oath to Oswald, and his oath was iron.

He looked over at the young king. Oswald resembled his

father, Æthelfrith. He had the same intensity in his gaze. The same clarity of vision. Æthelfrith had been a brilliant leader of men. Oswald had inherited his father's charisma. Scand had known Oswald since he was a mere youth, fleeing in exile into the west, with his brothers and their mother. Scand had been sworn then to Oswald's older half-brother, Eanfrith. Eanfrith had also had charm and a keen mind. Men had flocked to serve him like carrion crows clouding the corpses after battle. But despite Eanfrith's ability to have men follow where he led and his undoubted prowess in battle, his blind ambition was tinged with a recklessness that saw his demise only months after his triumphant return from exile.

During the long years in exile, Scand had often wondered whether it would be Oswald who would succeed in reclaiming Bernicia. Even as a child he had always carried himself with a calm assurance. There was a cunning behind his cool eyes. And a ruthlessness too.

He would be a good king. If he could secure his place with a defeat over Cadwallon here, at the Great Wall.

The massive structure, built by long-dead rulers of this land from grey slabs of stone, stretched to the horizon to the east and west. One of the fortified gates, that stood at intervals along its length, loomed near. The rocks that formed the edifice had been cunningly fashioned and placed together. None living knew how to build such things. Whenever he saw the Wall, or any of the tile-roofed buildings or stone bridges that yet stood throughout Albion, Scand felt a sense of awe and unease. People talked of giants having wrought these things, but Scand was no fool. The doorways and stone-hewn steps of the buildings were made for men, not giants. But how could men who ruled the land so absolutely have taken their leave of these lush shores? Had they all died?

It was a quandary he would never solve, so he pushed it from his thoughts.

Scand turned his attention instead to the young man at Oswald's right. Oswiu, the youngest of the sons of Æthelfrith. He'd been only four years of age when they had fled to Dál Riata. Now he stood, straight-backed and proud, but always in the shadow of his brother. He had the same chestnut hair and thoughtful eyes as Oswald, but he was more solid somehow; broader and shorter, closer to the earth. Oswald was like a strong oak, looking down on all as the winds of his wyrd moved him. Oswiu was more akin to a boulder, unmoving and unyielding. Scand disliked the boy. He was unsure why that was. Too young, probably. He was too full of anger for his liking. Still, he was a fine swordsman and would stand strong when the time came to face the Waelisc.

Oswald broke the silence that had fallen on the small group of thegns who were gathered in the shade of an awning made from cloth stretched over a wooden frame and secured with cords.

"You say we are outnumbered. Give us news we do not already know. Where is Cadwallon? What number of men does he have with him? Do they have horse guards? Are they on the move, or camped?" Oswald spoke to the scout in a soft voice, which made all of the listeners strain to hear over the background hubbub of the several hundred-strong fyrd amassed on the hill around them.

The scout had just ridden into the camp and was covered in dust and sweat. The day was still hot, but muggy and heavy with pent up rain. He beat some of the dust out of his clothes and wiped his face and straggly beard with the inside of his cloak. He accepted a flask of water from Scand and drank thirstily before answering the king.

Oswald remained still and outwardly patient, but Scand knew that he would be furious with the small affront to his authority. The scout, Attor, was Scand's man, and Scand would not have him bullied after he had bravely volunteered to ride close to the enemy force.

Attor nodded his thanks to Scand and spoke at last. "They are camped a short march to the south of the Wall. The force is more than double our number." A sharp intake of breath from the listeners. "I recognised the banner from Gefrin's ford." Scand grimly acknowledged Attor's effort to remind the king and others that he was one of the few who had stood before the mighty warlord Cadwallon and survived. "The banner still bears the skulls of fallen foes. King Eanfrith's head is there still." Attor looked down, unable to face Eanfrith's brothers with this gruesome fact.

"If the murderous heathen believes he can cow me with skulls on a pole, he will be sorry. He has yet to fight a true Christ follower." Scand decided it best not to mention that Edwin had converted to follow the Christ and had ordered all his men baptised, before being defeated by the alliance of Cadwallon and Penda of Mercia.

"We should not be scared of his standard, but he has double our number of warriors," said Scand. The other thegns nodded. Such odds were inconceivable. They could not hope to triumph.

"That is true. But I tell you again, we will destroy the Waelisc. We will march under the rood of our Lord Jesu and we will bring destruction on our enemy." Oswald surveyed the men on the hill, lounging close to the crumbling Wall. He furrowed his brow, as if trying to understand something, then his face lit up.

"Let me tell you how we will crush Cadwallon and his rabble." Oswald smiled, confident and relaxed.

Scand and the others listened intently to their king. Their faces showed the anxiety they all felt.

Oswiu's expression was unreadable. Perhaps he had an idea of what his brother planned. Perhaps he didn't care.

Beobrand clumsily unwound the wraps from his legs. He was still not used to the lack of the best part of two fingers on his left hand. His feet hurt from the march and he wanted to let some air onto them. He was sure he had blisters. Perhaps he could pop them and then they wouldn't hurt so much.

"My feet are killing me too," said Acennan, from the prostrate position he had slumped into after it became clear they would be setting up camp on this hill by the Wall. "It's the worst thing about war. The aching feet."

The men around them groaned their consent.

"My feet are paining me more than my hand. I'd quite happily cut them off."

"Be careful what you wish for," said Attor, as he flopped to the ground beside them.

"Welcome back, Attor," said Acennan. "What news? Are they close?"

"Too close for my liking. We will fight on the morrow." Attor repeated what he had told Oswald.

"Just as we suspected then," said Acennan. "Outnumbered with our backs to the Wall."

"The king has a plan to use the land and the Wall to help us. He will assemble the men at sunset to tell them to prepare for battle."

"If we can get Cadwallon to attack into the gap between the Wall and the hill, it is not a bad plan," said Beobrand. "But it relies on Cadwallon attacking where we wish him to."

A light drizzle began to fall. The moistness in the air cooled the weary warriors. The sun was still bright, shafts of light streaming through breaks in the clouds.

Beobrand leaned back and turned his face to the sky. The welcome smirr of rain soothed his hot face. He opened his eyes and looked at the men around them. On the brow of the hill, under the canopy shelter, stood Oswald, Oswiu, Scand and some others. They were deep in conversation. Below them, on the hill's skirts, were scattered groups of men. Some had lit fires already, and smoke was rising lazily into the damp, warm afternoon haze of rain and sunlight.

A couple of men were busily chopping at an ash tree that grew half-way down the slope. The sound of their axe blows reached Beobrand a moment after he saw them connect.

On the Wall itself, wardens had been posted. They stood with their backs to Beobrand, looking out over Deira Stræt to the south.

Light and dark dappled the clouds in the sky above them. Beams of light pierced the leaden clouds and then, like a sign from the gods themselves, shone a perfect arc of colour. The rainbow stood out in brilliant glory before the gloom of the rain-laden clouds.

Some men pointed. A ripple of comments and gestures rolled across the resting warriors.

A sign, some said. An omen.

A distant rumble of thunder filled the sky. A flock of birds flew overhead.

A hush fell on the warhost. The gods were speaking. But who could understand their signs?

"Perhaps that is Thunor reminding you that he'll watch out for you in the battle," whispered Acennan. Even he was subdued by the portents in the sky.

Beobrand thought back to the darkness of the room in Bebbanburg. His oath. The fallen cloak. The snuffed out rush light. Sunniva's fears. He closed his eyes, remembering the sudden gloom.

What if it hadn't been an omen after all? Perhaps it had been a message.

Beobrand leapt up and started up the hill.

"Where are you going?" called Acennan. "You've got nothing on your feet."

"Never mind my feet," replied Beobrand. "I must speak with the king."

"What is the commotion there?" Oswald looked up from where he sat. Where the canopy had protected them from the heat of the sun, now it gave them shelter from the light, yet soaking, rain.

Scand stood. "It is one of my men. Beobrand is his name." He rose and made his way down the slope to where two of Oswald's gesithas remonstrated with the young man from Cantware. They clearly had no intention of letting Beobrand pass and the headstrong warrior was getting increasingly frustrated. Scand shook his head. The man needed to learn to control his temper. He would get himself killed one day.

"Beobrand, be still," Scand commanded, using the tone that served him so well in battle. All three men desisted in their arguing and turned to face him.

"Now, what seems to be the matter?" Scand asked. "I hope it is important. The king is discussing plans for the battle tomorrow." There was an edge of ice in his tone. A caution.

"It is about the battle that I wish to talk. I was telling these two fools that I needed to speak with the king, but they would not listen." The two men bridled. One of them dropped his hand to the hilt of the large seax that hung from his belt. They were all allies here, but men of pride and honour could not be insulted and let it pass unanswered.

"Enough, Beobrand! You are my man and you bring dishonour to me with your insults. Now, apologise to these men."

Beobrand burnt with the light of the ideas in his head. He had to tell the king. He was sure of it. But he looked at the stern face of Scand and saw the disapproval there. Scand had given his life meaning. He had believed in him when no other would. He was a good man. Wise and just. And he was his lord.

Beobrand dropped his gaze. He swallowed.

"I am sorry for my outburst. I meant nothing by it. I merely need to speak with the king. It is urgent."

The tension eased and Scand stepped close to Beobrand. He placed a hand on his shoulder.

"So, what is it that you so urgently need to speak with your king about?" said a voice from behind them.

They turned quickly, and saw that Oswald, apparently intrigued, had walked down the hill to where they were talking.

"I apologise, my king," said Scand. "It is one of my men. He never seems to know his place." Beobrand felt Scand squeeze his shoulder painfully. A clear warning.

Oswald looked Beobrand up and down. "Ah, the mighty Beobrand." Was there a hint of sarcasm in his tone? "I have heard tell of your exploits. So tell me," Oswald glanced down, "what is so important that you approach your king uninvited and barefoot, like a thrall?"

Beobrand was trapped in the calm gaze of the king. He could feel the cool grass on his bare feet. The rain dripped from his eyebrows into his eyes, like tears. His mouth was suddenly dry.

"I..." Why was it so hard to speak? He coughed and swallowed the lump in his throat.

Oswald waited patiently.

Beobrand was afraid that his thoughts would sound ridiculous to this man of power who stood resplendent in his purple cloak. The bejewelled scabbard at his side glimmered. The golden brooch at his shoulder shone.

Beobrand felt shabby. Dirty. He was acutely aware of his bare feet and dusty britches.

He forced the words past his lips.

"I think I know how we can defeat Cadwallon," he said at last.

The rain still fell and the sun fought to show itself through the heavy clouds when Oswald addressed the men.

He stood before a rough cross, made from the large tree he had ordered felled earlier in the afternoon. It was three times the height of a tall man. The crossbeam was fashioned from some of the thicker branches lashed to the vertical with braided leather ropes. A deep hole had been dug at the top of the hill and the king himself had held it in place, embracing the wood while it had been raised and secured. It had taken the strength and ingenuity of several men to pull it into place.

Silhouetted against the crimson sky-glow of the setting sun, it reminded Beobrand of the yew tree where he had hanged Dreng, Artair and Tondberct. It was a dark memory. At that moment, the corpses twitching at the end of a creaking frayed rope, he had understood what it was to bring justice. Tondberct had been his friend, but in the end, Beobrand had given the order to kill him along with the others. His crimes were unforgivable. Such were the decisions a leader must make. Watching the king standing in the shadow of the wooden edifice, Beobrand wondered what hard choices he had made to bring him to this place. And what decisions he was yet to take that would affect all of their lives.

The warriors jumbled on the slope of the hill, shuffling to get a glimpse of the king. They could all see the cross. It dominated the horizon.

Oswald raised his hands as Beobrand had seen him do before in the great hall at Bebbanburg. A hush fell on the men gathered there.

"My friends. Bernicians. Angelfolc, Hibernian and Pict. I am Oswald, son of Æthelfrith, known by the Hibernians as Lamnguin, Whiteblade. By right of blood, I am king of Bernicia. You all know what we have come to do." Oswald raised his voice in order for it to reach all those who listened on that damp afternoon. Beobrand realised it was the first time he had heard Oswald speak in anything but a quiet tone.

"We have come to rid this land of the scourge of Cadwallon and his accursed pack of Waelisc defilers. Perhaps some of you have heard already of the size of the host we are to face. It is true that they are greater in number." This was news to none of the listeners. Word had spread around the camp quickly after Attor and the other scouts returned.

"But it is also true that we have the power of the Almighty Christ on our side. You have all seen the sign of his power in the sky. The rainbow is his promise to his followers.

"Last night I had a dream. I had been wondering about the battle to come. Like all men, I know doubt and I was questioning. How could we defeat Cadwallon and his host?" Oswald paused. Letting it sink in that he too was vulnerable. Beobrand wondered at the wisdom of it. Surely the men would prefer to believe that their king was infallible, god-like in his abilities. He looked around him and was surprised to see many men nodding. Solemn understanding on their faces. It seemed Oswald understood his audience better than Beobrand.

The king continued: "In my dream, the holiest of men, Colm Cille himself, founder and abbot of the island of Hii came to me. He was bathed in light and he spoke to me.

"He told me to construct a rood; a tree like that on which the Christ sacrificed himself for all men, so that we might live forever. He said that all who followed me into battle should bow before the rood and be blessed. 'The power of the blood of Christ will be upon them all,' he said.

"'Be strong and act manfully. Behold, I will be with you. This coming night go out from your camp into battle, for the Lord has granted me that at this time your foes shall be put to flight and Cadwallon your enemy shall be delivered into your hands and you shall return victorious after battle and reign happily.'

"And so it will be as he foretold. You will all be blessed in the shadow of the rood, and then, in the darkest, deepest tract of the night, we will go forth. We will march with stealth and we will smite Cadwallon at his camp. We will destroy him there and peace will be ours thereafter."

There was a murmur of dissent amongst the warriors. They were strong, doughty in battle and brave in the face of spear and shield. But the night held fear of a different nature. At night shadow creatures crept and slithered. Elves and goblins lurked ready to pounce on the unsuspecting traveller. Fires could keep those things at bay, but stealth would not be possible if they carried brands. They would need to walk in the raven-wing blackness of the night. Towards armed foes and surrounded by unseen enemies from the otherworld.

Some of the men spat. Others touched amulets or the iron of their weapons. Those who already followed the Christ God made the sign of the rood over their chests.

The light in the sky was dwindling to a dim afterglow behind Oswald. He raised his hands again. The host quietened.

"Be not afraid of the things that haunt the night. Darkness and death are no match for Christ. He was hanged upon a rood such as this and then, on the third day, He rose from the dead. Never to allow death to defeat man again. After you are blessed here this day, you will not die. Everlasting life in the halls of God awaits us all."

Oswald seemed to sense that he was close to losing the audience. If the plan was to work, he would need all the men there to march into the night. To fight to the death before the rising of the sun.

This was the plan Beobrand had told to the king. Or was it an omen? A message from the gods? Or the Christ, as Oswald said? The idea for the night attack had come to Beobrand fully-formed. The snuffing of the rush light had not been an omen of doom. It had been a signal for triumph.

Beobrand cared not whether the tale of the king's dream was true. He believed that attacking in the dark would provide them with the best chance of success and he had told Oswald as much. Oswald had listened intently before dismissing him.

Now the king caught Beobrand's eye. He stared straight at him for a moment and then, in a loud ringing voice, he said, "Who will kneel with their king and pray under the cross? Who will take the fight to the heathen in the darkness? Who is with me this night?"

Silence fell over the camp. The crackle of damp wood burning on the fires could clearly be heard.

Oswald looked out over the men. Beobrand sensed the

nervous anxiety in the air. The men were willing to stand and fight in the shieldwall, but this was more. Oswald asked them to trust in him and the Christ. To march into the darkness against far superior numbers.

Somewhere a man coughed. A horse snickered.

Beobrand took a step forward and spoke into the silence. "I am with you, Oswald King. I will kneel with you, and march into the night at your side." His voice rang out. He was surprised at the assurance there. But even as he spoke, he relaxed. He was not sure of the power of the Christ, but he believed in this plan.

And more importantly, he believed in Oswald.

4

A warhost, bedecked with the trappings of battle, cannot move with stealth.

The chink of armour, the rattle of spear against shield, the whispers of nervous men, all seemed to be amplified by the silence of the night. Even the footfalls of hundreds of warriors in battle-harness created a slow, rhythmic thrum that reverberated in the darkness.

"Are you still pleased you stepped forward?" Acennan whispered. "The Waelisc will hear us long before we reach their camp. A herd of horses would make less noise than this rabble."

Beobrand couldn't help but agree with his friend. He knew he was largely responsible for this night raid. He had given the idea to Oswald and it was only after he had spoken up in support of the king that the others had followed. In his mind, the plan had been simple. They would march quietly to where the enemy slumbered and there they would cut them down like so much barley being harvested. Now, with the terrifying blackness of the night pushing around them, and the men traipsing along the old paved road, jostling and jingling like a train of merchants on their way to sell their wares, he was less assured of success.

"Well, they will hear our approach if you keep yammering on," he hissed. The unease gnawed at him. The tension of the men was palpable. They had waited until after midnight. Huddled around the fires that hissed and cracked in the rain. Weapons had been sharpened. Armour had been donned. The men grumbled at the rain. It would rust their blades. Those who wore metal-knit byrnies cursed. If they survived the night, they knew that much toil would be needed to rid the chain links of rust. First they would toss the armour in sacks filled with sand to rub the ochre-coloured patina from the iron. After that, when their arms burnt from the effort, they would rub in fat, coating the riveted links to fend off moisture. None of them welcomed the thought of this work, but the alternative – that someone would clean the armour after stripping it from your corpse – was less appealing, so they gritted their teeth and prayed for the night to be dry.

Shortly before they set out southward, the rain had stopped. The men's hearts had been gladdened. They'd grinned at each other, flashing teeth in the gloom, pleased to be marching without the added discomfort of being drenched.

Now though, Beobrand wondered if rain would not be a good thing. It would keep any watchers sheltering. Wet guards were not the most observant. Rainfall would also cover much of the noise they were making.

Beobrand looked up at the sky. He could not make out the moon, just a slight silvering in the thick clouds. Little light reached the rain-slick ground.

They had been walking for what seemed a long time.

Sometime before, they had crossed the wide river using

the huge bridge that had been left by the same people who built the Wall. Even with the anxiety of impending battle, Beobrand could not stop himself from marvelling at the construction. It was made of massive blocks of stone that, using some cunning or magic, were placed together to form giant arches carrying the road high over the dark water. One of the arches had collapsed at some time in the past, and was now bridged by stout wooden planks. The men had crossed this slowly, unsure it would take their weight after the solidity of the stone. But it had held, the sound of the men's passing loud over the quiet flow of the river.

Beobrand hoped he could return in daylight to see the bridge. He smiled grimly in the darkness. For that, he would need to survive the night.

Surely they would be upon the Waelisc soon. They must have fires that they would see long before reaching the enemy encampment. Peering into the night Beobrand only saw shadows and darkness. He could barely make out the shapes of the men in the rank in front of him. Could it be that the Waelisc had moved their camp? Or perhaps they had decided against lighting fires. Were they expecting a night attack?

Beobrand's stomach clenched. He had been unable to eat much that evening. His bowels were in turmoil. He recognised the feeling of dread that always settled on him before battle. His mouth was dry. His throat rasped. He wished he could stop to drink, but that was out of the question. Oswald's host continued south along the Deira Stræt. Now that the decision had been taken to march at night, nobody else seemed especially concerned about the darkness.

A needle of doubt pricked at Beobrand. Could his idea be flawed? Had he misread the signs that the gods had placed before him? He was not even sure they were signs. The events that led up to this moment could have been nothing more than coincidence. Or perhaps the gods were once again laughing.

Was that a flash of light in the sky? He could not be sure. A deep, slow rumble roiled over the warriors, like mead benches overturned in a brawl in a distant hall.

Thunder.

Thunor. Beobrand pulled on the leather thong at his neck to free the whale tooth hammer amulet that hung there. He gripped it tightly.

The gods were there in the dark. He had sworn his oath to Thunor and now Woden's son was talking.

Another flicker of lightning lit all of the men for an instant. For several heartbeats the image was burnt into his vision. Helms, shields, a forest of spears, frozen in the eye-blink quickening light of Thunor's fire.

The road sloped down before them. In the distance, the red glow of campfires became visible.

As if driven on by the thunder, or perhaps by the sight of their enemies' camp, the warhost surged forward. Beobrand stumbled, his footing unsure on the cracked, slippery stones of the road. He trotted forward, pushed on by the pace of those around him.

If they rushed down like this, they were sure to be heard by sentries who would alert the camp. Another flash of lightning could show any watchers the approaching mass of warriors.

The afterimage from the lightning faded. Sunniva's face came to his mind. Her lustrous hair. The curve of her neck. Her scent. He had sworn he would return to her. He prayed to Thunor not to have him go to his death as an oath-breaker.

Then the skies opened.

Torrents of water fell from clouds as swollen as gravid mares. With the rain came a cacophonous roar. In an instant every man was soaked. Clothes and armour were no protection from the vicious force of it. The clouds spewed rain in a tumult. The ditches at either side of the road flooded in moments.

The men slowed. Stunned by the vehemence of the elements.

But Beobrand urged them forward. This is what they had been waiting for. The gods had provided them with the cover they needed. There would be no watching warden who would detect them in this. They could move right up to the camp, as invisible to the Waelisc as spirits.

If the rain held.

The host came to a halt.

Beobrand pushed past men. He could not see who, but he elbowed and shoved his way through the lines. He was dimly aware that Acennan was keeping pace with him.

Another stuttering flash of lightning lit up the host before him. He had almost barrelled into Oswald in his eagerness. The king had stopped, perhaps unclear how to proceed. Thunder boomed.

Beobrand clutched at Oswald's arm. It was covered in chain armour, cold and hard. Oswald spun round. It was difficult to make anything out in the water-filled blackness.

Strong hands shoved Beobrand back. He slammed into Acennan, who pushed him upright.

"Get your hands off of your king," said the man who had interposed himself between Beobrand and Oswald.

Beobrand could not see his face, but he recognised the voice. Athelstan. He could feel his anger suddenly coursing through him. He held it in check. Now was not the time for fighting. That would come all too soon.

"Don't be a fool, Athelstan," he said. "I mean no harm."

Athelstan placed both his hands on Beobrand's chest and

pushed. Hard. Beobrand was forced back, but Acennan stood strong and held him in place.

"Go back to your lord. You have no right to fight at your king's side. You have not earned it."

"Enough of this," Oswald stepped forward and placed his hand on Athelstan's arm. His words were almost lost under the roar of the rain. "Is that you again, young Beobrand? What troubles you? The enemy is in sight… but this rain…"

"My lord." Beobrand stepped in close, ignoring Athelstan. He placed his face close to the king's so that his voice would be heard. Their helms almost touched. "We must attack them now. While the rain lasts."

More lightning. Recognition on Oswald's features. Yet still indecision.

They had to take advantage of this downpour. Of that Beobrand was certain.

A crash of thunder.

He had to make the king understand.

"The Christ has sent the rain to provide us cover," Beobrand said.

At last Oswald moved, shaken from his inaction at the mention of his god. "Bless you, Beobrand," he said, though it was hard to hear the words. "You are right. With this God-given rain we will purge the land, as in the time of the great flood of Noah."

Oswald's words meant nothing to Beobrand, but he nodded. "Yes. We must strike now."

"Athelstan, pass word through the ranks. We will run to the camp and attack on the agreed signal. Speed is of the essence now." The huge warrior nodded stiffly, his features hidden in the night. Then he was gone, pushing Beobrand to the side.

"Godspeed, Beobrand," said Oswald, and Beobrand could not be sure, but it appeared as if the king was smiling.

Athelstan did his king's bidding and word spread through the host.

The sky flared again. Acennan grinned at Beobrand's side.

"By Woden, Beobrand," he said, "you really know how to pick a good fight." Thunor's hammer echoed over them again with a resounding smash. "This is going to be like a battle in the underworld. But never fear. Stick close to me and I'll see you safe!" He punched Beobrand on the arm and then unslung his shield.

Beobrand smiled in the darkness. He was glad of Acennan's presence at his side. He pulled his own linden board from where it hung on his shoulder and fitted his left hand into the leather straps Sunniva had fashioned for him. It felt heavy and unbalanced on his arm, but he would not drop it.

Perhaps the gods had given him signs to follow after all. He prayed he would live to see the sunrise. And Sunniva.

But death and darkness lay before them that night. Before the broadening light of morning.

With a shout, shredded by the roar of the rain, Oswald broke into a run.

The men surged behind him. They charged, slipping and sliding towards the Waelisc camp.

Beobrand pulled Hrunting from his scabbard. The heft of it reassured him. He let his ire at Athelstan loose. The men in the camp had killed Leofwine, Alric and countless more. Now they would pay.

The campfires were clearer now, shining through the sheets of rain.

Then the long note of a horn sounded. It cut through the noise of men and the elements.

Like dogs who had been held, straining at the leash with the scent of a stag on the wind, King Oswald's Bernician warhost let out a deafening roar and rushed screaming into Cadwallon's camp.

The thunder had woken Sunniva.

For a time she had lain in the dark listening to the breathing of the women, children and old folk who had not marched south with Oswald. She found Beobrand's kirtle in the darkness and brought it to her face. She breathed deeply. The smell of him lingered. She had given him her father's kirtle to wear, saying it was less threadbare. She had not told him the truth: that she wanted something with his scent. At night she was so alone. So frightened. It helped to have a part of him to hold. Once she was warm under her cloak, she could close her eyes and almost imagine he was with her.

She was not sure what had made her stir, but then she heard it again. The distant rumble of thunder.

Would they have already joined in battle?

Thunder again. Long, deep and distant. Was Thunor speaking? Was this the omen playing itself out?

Was Beobrand alive?

Someone giggled in the darkness of the room. It was an eerie sound in the black of night. Sunniva shivered.

She did not want to be here in the gloom. Alone, but surrounded by others each feeling their own fear as their husbands, fathers, brothers were with the fyrd.

She stood, moved the partition to the side and picked her way over the sleeping forms.

The cold outside shocked her. Wind buffeted her. Her cloak

slapped about her. The smell of rain was in the air and the ground was wet beneath her bare feet.

She shuddered. She should have dressed. She would not be able to stay out for long in this chill.

A wall-ward recognised her as she stepped up onto the southernmost palisade. His name was Anhaga and she had often seen him watching her while she went about her chores. He was young and polite. Not like that old goat Athelstan, or some of the other warriors. Despite his youth he had not travelled south with the warriors of the fyrd. He had a deformed leg. His right foot was twisted which left him only able to walk slowly with a pronounced limp. He would never walk with warriors into battle. Never stand in the shieldwall. She knew not what had caused his affliction. Perhaps a childhood illness. Or an accident. Whatever the cause, part of her felt for him. Unable to fight, he must feel less of a man.

She knew she had to be careful without her father or Beobrand there to protect her. She had decided many days before that Anhaga was not a threat.

But now, in the windy night, Thunor's wrath lighting up the sky with flashes to the south, she felt vulnerable. Again, she cursed her own stupidity for not dressing before leaving the hall. She was all too aware of her bare feet.

Anhaga stepped close to her, clumsy on his twisted leg. He offered his hand. His gaze flicked down to the pale curve of her ankles. The light from the brazier on the palisade glinted in his eyes.

She didn't take his hand.

"Couldn't you sleep?" he asked.

"The thunder woke me." She wrapped her cloak tightly about herself, against the cold and to prevent the wind blowing it aside. She did not wish to give Anhaga's eager eyes anything to fix onto.

"It is a cold night," he said. "Step close to the fire here. It's not so bad then."

She didn't move.

"Do you think they have already fought the Waelisc?" she asked.

He shrugged. "Only the gods can know. We have heard no word." He looked out into the night. Lightning flickered. For a moment his face was white, stark against the black sky.

Sunniva followed his gaze. Had Beobrand already been taken from her? Were the gods laughing? Or rejoicing? Were the flashes in the sky the souls of men feasting in Woden's corpse hall? Or angels of the Christ god?

"Perhaps the gods are angry."

"Perhaps," Anhaga said, his voice distracted.

Sunniva turned back to him. His eyes were roving over her. Lingering on her legs. The curves of her form beneath her cloak. Their eyes met.

Anhaga quickly looked away.

Sunniva felt a wave of loneliness. Beobrand had sworn he would return to her. He would not break his word to her. He would not.

But what if his wyrd had a different path?

A few drops of rain fell, sizzling into the embers of the brazier. Sunniva looked up and felt drops on her face. Like tears.

She stood for a moment like that, face uplifted with the rain washing down her cheeks, then she turned abruptly. She would not stand here fearful for a future she did not know. Beobrand would return to her. He would.

"I had best get in, out of the rain," she said. Her voice sounded harsh and jagged to her own ears.

Anhaga stiffened.

"Aye, that would be best," he said. "Watch your step on the ladder." He turned his back on her and did not offer his hand again.

Sunniva was at once relieved and saddened by his lack of attention.

She made her way quickly back to the hall. There she removed her wet cloak, wrapping herself in everything she had available. It took a long while for warmth to return to her body.

She clutched Beobrand's kirtle, breathed of his redolence and prayed for his return to any god that would listen.

Scand gritted his teeth against the pain. His back throbbed and the tingling in his right leg had transformed into a jabbing sensation in his knee. Every step was agony.

The warhost ran headlong towards the Waelisc camp. The rain fought their progress, but they pushed through it. Towards their prey. Just enough light spilt out from the dampened campfires for the Bernicians to guide themselves.

Scand hobbled along as best he could. He drew his sword, revelling in the perfect balance of it, despite the discomfort he felt in his back and leg. The blade was a gift from King Oswald, as recognition for his oath-swearing. It replaced the sword that had shattered in Gefrin. That had been a great blade. It had slain many men and even in its moment of destruction it had served him well. A shard from the broken blade had injured Cadwallon, causing the Waelisc to retreat. Scand hoped this new sword would serve him as well.

The front ranks reached the encampment. Shouts and screams. That was the king's own retinue, his most trusted thegns. Like a pack of wolves loose in an enclosure of sheep, they were wreaking havoc.

Scand slipped on an uneven stone, almost losing his balance. His ankle was close to turning, but he righted himself with a grunt. Stumbling, he moved on. He could not see the look of unease on the faces of the men who ran with him. But he imagined it. They would be concerned that their lord was no longer the warlord he had been in his prime. Gods, he was as concerned as anyone!

These were his men. Trusted. Battle-hardened. He was proud of them and they had once been proud of him.

He vowed they would be proud again. This night he would show them who they followed.

He was Scand, son of Scaend. Mighty in battle. Bringer of death to his foes. Songs were sung of his exploits in Albion and over the sea in Hibernia.

He may be old, but this wolf still had teeth.

Raising his sword in the air with a flourish he screamed in his battle voice, "Onward, my gesithas! Remember the ford at Gefrin. Remember the faces of those who fell. They were our brothers and these are their slayers." His voice was potent and it pierced the clamour of the battle easily.

"For Bernicia and Oswald!" Scand sprinted forward into the fray, aiming for one of the camp fires that lay some way off to the left. His men cheered in the dark and followed him.

He was dimly aware of the pain in his knee, the ache in his back, but he pushed the sensations away. Now was the time for swords to sing, not to whimper and moan of cramps like a gum-sucking longbeard.

His retinue formed up to his right and left. A moving, pointed shieldwall, with Scand at its apex. He smiled, savagely pleased at his men's training paying off. They moved as one.

Around them all was chaos. The rain still fell heavily. Shadows moved, silhouetted before the fires. A flicker of lightning lit the scene. Men were stumbling from shelters into the night. Some were armed, but Scand could see no armour.

A small group of men sensed the danger, or perhaps spotted Scand's shieldwall approaching by the flash of light in the sky. They turned to face them, trying to form their own wall.

Too late. Scand crashed into them, all his bulk behind his shield boss, the men beside and behind him driving him on. He shoved one man aside to the left while lashing out to the right with his sword. He felt the blade connect, and black blood splattered his arm. Its warmth a sudden contrast to the cold rain.

They surged forward. Scand trampled the men who had fallen before their wedge of shields. A hand gripped his cloak, slowing Scand. He yanked his cloak trying to free it from the clutch of the fallen man. But he would not let go.

There was no room to swing his sword at the man, without a good chance of hitting his comrade to the right. So Scand hammered his sword's heavy bronze pommel into the man's knuckles. He crushed the fingers against the anvil of his byrnie-clad thigh. Scand hammered twice, thrice, before the grip loosened and the ruined hand fell away.

They moved on, but the shieldwall had lost its momentum.

"Halt!" shouted Scand. His men obeyed him instantly.

"Form up. Shieldwall. Three deep." His gesithas moved into positions they had practised all that long hot summer. They formed a square of warriors. Those at the front held their spears forward. Scand stood in the leading rank, his bloody sword dark and deadly in the gloom.

The rain was easing. Another burst of lightning, this time further away it seemed. It shone its light on the battlefield for the merest instant. Scand saw that Oswald's host had been scattered. The smells of death – piss, blood and shit – rose from the wet mud. It was strewn with corpses. But Cadwallon had many more men than Oswald, and they were now beginning to react.

The moment of brilliant light had shown where the Waelisc were forming on their leader's standard. They were some way off, and in numbers that Scand could not hope to beat. He needed to reunite with Oswald and the rest of the fyrd.

"Turn to the right and keep an eye out for Waelisc creeping up on us," he said. The shieldwall shuffled and turned until they were heading in the direction Scand hoped would lead them to Oswald.

The footing was treacherous. Some of the fires had been kicked out. Others had been doused by the torrential rain. There was almost no light.

Scand's foot caught on a fallen spear. He stumbled, a jolt of pain lanced up his leg. He grunted, steadied his shield and walked on.

The rain stopped. The sounds of battle seemed suddenly louder. Screams and the clash of metal on metal indicated where the fiercest of the fighting was under way. Scand adjusted their course.

The embers of a campfire gave just enough light for Scand to pick out the slumped body of a warrior. It was good that he had not tripped over the corpse. He was not sure he could stand another jarring of his knee. Scand stepped over the fallen warrior.

He shifted his attention to their destination. They would reach the fighting soon.

A sudden searing pain seized him. He cried out in anguish. Looking down at the source of his agony, he saw that the warrior was not dead. In his hand he held a long knife which he had buried up to the hilt in Scand's groin, beneath his byrnie.

Scand hacked down onto the man's head, splitting it with a wet sound. The man's hand fell away from the knife handle, flopping to the mud.

Scand reached down and pulled the blade from his body. Blood gushed. He let out a groaning gasp, and collapsed to his knees.

His men formed around him protectively. One warrior, a bearded man, named Derian, flung himself to the earth beside his lord. Scand fell back and Derian cradled his head in his lap. He removed Scand's helmet.

"Derian?" Scand asked, his voice unnervingly frail.

"I am here, my lord. As I have always been."

"Yes." Scand gripped Derian's hand.

For a fleeting moment Scand wondered at how peaceful everything had become. The sounds of battle subsided. The pain in his back vanished and then, he understood the truth of it. The chill of death was already upon him. He hoped that he would see his beautiful Morna again in the afterlife. He had missed her so all these long years.

"I am killed, my friend," said Scand, clutching Derian's hand firmly one last time. "I always told you to watch for the knife under the shieldwall. Stupid…" His voice trailed off.

Derian had no words for the man who had always provided for him. His hlaford. His lord. Scand's grasp on his hand was loosening by the moment.

Derian could see the dim light from the cloud-cloaked moon glimmering in Scand's eyes. After a time, he saw that Scand's eyes were unblinking and Derian knew that after all the years, all the mead halls, all the stories, all the gifts, all the shield-walls and all the killing, Scand, son of Scaend had left him.

★

The rain thrummed against Beobrand's iron helmet. The cheek guards, each topped with a bronze boar emblem, obscured his side vision. But in this darkness it was of little matter.

The night and the rain rendered him as good as blind and deaf.

He could sense the weight of warriors behind him. They had kept pace with Oswald, screaming straight into the camp towards the centre, where the largest fire burnt. Acennan was at Beobrand's left with Athelstan to his right. The king was positioned on the other side of Athelstan.

Beobrand would have preferred to have his friend on his right. He did not relish relying on Athelstan's shield for protection in the shieldwall.

A flare of lightning picked out figures moving towards them. They looked confused, unprepared for the sudden attack. Beobrand fixed the position of one of them in his mind and threw himself forward. An instant later his shield collided with a flailing assailant. In the darkness the man swung an axe blindly. The axe head glanced off Beobrand's helm with a clangour that merged with the crash of Thunor's ire in the sky.

Dazed and unbalanced, Beobrand fell. His shield boss caught the man in the chest and they both crashed to the muddy earth. The straps holding the shield in place encumbered Beobrand. Laden with armour and sodden clothes he struggled to right himself. He could feel the man beneath him squirming in the mire.

Beobrand rolled his body to the left, removing his own weight from atop the shield, then, lying on his back in the mire, beside the man, he lifted his shield and slammed it down with all his strength onto the axeman. He felt the boss connect. His fingers hurt where the scabs split.

He raised the board again, glad now of the straps that allowed him to use the strength of his whole arm, and smashed it down. Bones crunched under the boss. Over and over he battered the iron boss and linden board into the man.

Was it the Waelisc's screams or his own he could hear through the roar of the rain?

At last his foe lay still. Beobrand sat. Another sudden flash of light revealed Acennan grinning before him. He was reaching out, offering his hand.

Beobrand grasped it and Acennan pulled him to his feet.

"There will be time enough for resting after the battle," shouted Acennan with laughter in his voice.

"We must rejoin Oswald. Do you know the way?"

"Follow me, and try to keep up," replied Acennan and ran into the night.

Beobrand sprinted after him, keen not to be lost on this battlefield that was like no other he had seen. All battle was a confusion of sound and smells. Fear of death weakened some men and emboldened others. But in this rain-soaked gloom, it was hard to tell friend from enemy. Attack could come from any quarter. It was impossible to gauge the progress of the conflict. Was the attack successful in breaking Cadwallon's force, or were the Waelisc now regrouping, forming up to repel the Bernician host?

And should they all die in the screaming maelstrom of the stormy night, Beobrand knew that he would be to blame.

He ran on, barely able to make out Acennan's bulk before him. He stumbled over the dead. A flicker of light burnt images into his mind, where they stayed, like the carvings on some gift-stool of nightmare. The steaming, uncoiled entrails of a young man, kneeling alone, an expression of surprise on his face. The ruined mess of a smashed skull, ichorous ooze dripping into open, sightless eyes.

Sunniva had been right to fear the omen. It was madness to attack at night. And it was a madness that Beobrand had passed on to Oswald. What had possessed him? Was it his wyrd to die here and to be the downfall of Bernicia?

Acennan drew to a halt. There was more light here. Beobrand could make out Oswald's helm. His brother Oswiu and the massive Athelstan in the middle of a shieldwall. Their backs were turned from Acennan and him. The light came from a large fire. It smoked and steamed in the rain, but threw a fitful light over the attackers and the Waelisc defenders.

Those of Cadwallon's warriors who had not fled into the night or been killed by the initial Bernician onslaught were in the process of forming lines. It appeared that Oswald's host had faltered, failing to push home the advantage.

"Where are Scand and the others?" asked Beobrand.

"I cannot see our lord," replied Acennan. "They must have been separated from the main host. But we'll never find them in this. Not till morning. He has a better chance of finding us here."

"Come then, let us join the shieldwall."

Moving close behind the ranks of warriors, Beobrand shouted, "For Oswald and Bernicia!" Some men spun around, their faces shadowed. Anxious. "Friends. We are friends," said Beobrand in a strong voice.

The men sized them up and then parted to allow Acennan and Beobrand to step into their ranks.

"We need all the friends we can get," said the man to Beobrand's right. "Whoever talked the king into attacking at night should have his neck wrung."

Beobrand swallowed. His throat was dry. "He had a dream of a holy man, didn't he?"

"Holy dream or not, those damned Waelisc still outnumber us, and we can barely see." The man spat. "I think the gods enjoy watching men die and this is just a new way for us to do it. In the dark and the rain."

Beobrand grunted. He did not wish to talk more on the subject. He feared the man was right. Perhaps he was the gods' instrument in this.

The Waelisc had coalesced into a strong line of men. They began to crash weapons on shields. A chanting rose from them. Beobrand felt the back of his neck prickle. The confidence of them was unnerving. They had been awoken by enemies in their camp in the heart of the night. Lightning, rain and thunder battered them. Confusion had reigned and many had died, cut down in the dark. Yet they had rallied around their leader. And they still believed they were invincible.

At the centre of the Waelisc line lofted the standard of Cadwallon. Beobrand had seen it at Elmet and Gefrin. From it hung skulls and scalps. Its most recent totem was the erstwhile king of Bernicia, Eanfrith. The scant light from the fire was insufficient to show the emblems of the standard clearly. The objects were just shadowy shapes, but Beobrand could not suppress a shudder.

As if sensing his rising state of panic, Acennan said, "Do not fear, Beobrand. There is light here now. And what we can see, we can kill."

The two shieldwalls stood for some time, staring at each other over a spear's-throw of muddy scrubland. The Waelisc continued to chant. Beobrand did not understand the words, but the sound was eerie. The smoke from the fire hazed and blurred the shadows of the enemy warriors. He knew they were only men. Flesh and bone. But his mind screamed at him to flee from this host of night creatures.

One of the holy men who travelled with Oswald began to recite his own spell. Beobrand recognised the language as that used by Coenred and the Christ followers in their rites. The holy man's voice was weak. Lost against the soaring chants of the Waelisc. Beobrand could sense the strength sapping from the Bernicians. A warband's mettle is a fragile thing. It is bound up in each man, but must be forged with a common purpose. The Christ man's words were meaningless to most. Perhaps there was power in his magic that would aid them, but the men needed more. They needed to remember why they fought. Who they fought for.

Beobrand began to shout, "Oswald! Oswald!" Acennan picked up the call. Then others. And with the speed of a fire in dry grass, all of the men – Angelfolc, Hibernians, Picts – were screaming their own chant. The holy man's prayers were drowned out.

The name of the Bernician king resounded across that field and gave the Waelisc pause.

"Oswald! Oswald! Oswald!"

The chant built to a climax. Then a flash of lightning rent the clouds and lit the scene in a harsh white light.

Thunor's hammer-blow of thunder seemed to signal the attack, for both shieldwalls charged forward at the same moment. They met with their own thunder. The bone-crunching crash of shield on shield.

5

Coenred pulled his coarse woollen robe about his shoulders against the cool night air. Another flash of lightning flickered in the south. A storm was raging over the Wall. The wind picked up, tugging at the hem of his robe. The boulder-grind of thunder rolled over the land. Rain would follow soon.

Others stirred in the camp behind him. He was not the only one who could not sleep. A child cried out. A woman hushed it.

His slumber had been tormented by shades. The spirits of dead loved ones.

He had seen Tata, as she had been in life. Bright, full of mischief and happiness. She had skipped away from him, giggling. Beckoning over her shoulder she had run through a dark doorway into a building.

In the dream, Coenred had been eager to follow his sister. And yet somehow he'd known that he did not want to see what was inside. With a start he'd recognised the chapel at Engelmynster. He had stepped forward, unable to stop. The doorway loomed, dark and foreboding. He did not want to enter. Yet his legs carried him on.

"I don't want to see," he sobbed. "Don't make me look."
But nobody answered and his body refused to obey him.

Trembling, he stepped into the cool dark of the interior.
For a heartbeat he could see nothing. Then, with a crash the
scene had been lit with a brilliant light.

Tata was naked. She was sprawled on the altar at the end
of the small chapel. Her knees were raised, the firm young
flesh of her thighs was white. In her hand she held an object,
which she was savagely thrusting between her legs. With each
push she lifted her hips and gasped. Whether in pleasure or
pain Coenred could not tell.

She pushed harder, more frantically. Grunting like an animal.
Blood splattered her thighs, ran in rivulets from her crotch
down her milky buttocks. He could not drag his eyes from the
object in her hand. Then, in a moment of exquisite disgust he
realised what it was. It was a golden rood. A gem-encrusted
likeness of the tree on which the Christ had been slain.

The wrongness of the scene hit him with a physical force.

Tata turned her face to him and smiled.

Coenred screamed.

He could not shake the images of the dream from his mind.
He had dreamt about Tata before since her murder, but never
like this. He shuddered.

Abbot Fearghas said that dreams of women were sent by
the devil. Thoughts of lust, he said, were trials for young
monks. Coenred sometimes had woken aroused after seeing
visions in his sleep of women. He always felt hollow and lost
after such dreams. Dirty. Sordid.

But this dream of Tata was worse. It was not a temptation
for a young man. It was evil. Dark. Sinister. Horrific.

Another stab of light in the sky. A grumble of thunder.
Perhaps the devil rode on the storm.

Beobrand was down there in that storm. Had they already joined in battle with the Waelisc? Was Beobrand alive or had he fallen; struck down by a warrior certain of the righteousness of his own actions? Just as Beobrand was of his?

Coenred knew that Beobrand was a man of honour. But the ease with which he killed filled him with dismay. Seeing him again had brought back the loneliness he had thought gone. The horrors of the last weeks filled his mind. Death stalked him it seemed. So many he had known and loved were dead. He yearned for the closeness of the friendship he had felt with Beobrand for a time the previous winter. While he recovered from his wounds, Beobrand had been happy to sit and talk to Coenred. They had talked of all manner of things. Gods, life and death, family. Those days had been good. But as Beobrand grew stronger, his mind had turned once again to war. To vengeance. To killing.

Coenred wondered if they would ever know that closeness again. It seemed that wherever Beobrand trod, death followed.

The wind picked up and rain began to fall in roaring sheets. The sleepers were woken by the sudden downpour. Their shrieks and yells could easily be mistaken for the screams of the dying in a shieldwall. Or of those they had left behind in Engelmynster.

Coenred drew his robe about him and hurried to find shelter.

The rain had stopped. Light seeped into the eastern horizon and still they fought.

This was no night-time skirmish that would snuff out Cadwallon's hopes of conquest. After the initial Bernician rampage through the camp, his host, battle-skilled and organised, had mounted a staunch defence.

If the Waelisc resolve was intact, the same could not be said for their numbers. Oswald's first desperate charge had slain many. The odds were evened. Yet the battle raged for longer than any would have imagined possible in that hellish night.

Beobrand's sword arm ached. Each swing was difficult. His shield dropped low on his left side. He allowed the straps to hold the weight of the linden board, only pulling it back up when needed. It was a dangerous tactic but he was too exhausted to care. How many men had he killed? He had lost count.

The man he had talked to before the fight had fallen in the first moments after the shieldwalls met. A spear had pierced him just below his collar bone. He had screamed out and Beobrand had seen him no more.

Beobrand had splintered the spear with his sword, then slid his blade along the ash haft until it had met with the fingers of its owner, a wild-eyed Waelisc warrior, looming in the darkness. Hrunting was sharp and severed much of the man's hand instantly. He screeched, letting go of the spear. He tried to cover his body with his small circular shield, but Beobrand feinted at his face, then, effortlessly gutted him. The Waelisc wore no armour, and Hrunting's patterned blade cut through him as easily as if he had been made of smoke.

After that first clash, with the weakest and unluckiest dead, the battle became long and bloody. Acennan shifted round behind Beobrand to take up his position on his right. As at the battle of Gefrin, where they had stood for the first time together, they made a formidable union. They slashed, parried, blocked, charged and retreated, as if they were of the same mind. It was uncanny to watch. Those from the Bernician ranks who managed to step back and draw breath watched in admiration as the tall Cantware warrior and the stocky gesith enacted the deadly battle-play. They slew all who stood before them.

Those who watched from the Waelisc lines saw two mighty warriors stepped out of legend. Their blades glimmered in the firelight. Their battle-knit shirts, shield bosses and fine helms shone. All along the line men shoved and heaved. Hacking, battering with shield, axe, sword and seax.

These two alone seemed elevated to a higher form of combat. The shieldwall could not contain them. Their music was the sword song. And it played to their tune. To approach them was to die. But to falter or retreat was to be marked a craven. So on they came.

And fell in the gore-drenched mud.

Screams, whimpers, curses.

Dying men are not eloquent. They tremble and puke. Soiled by the fear-shit of their impending doom. They will grasp to anything that might hold them for another moment on to this fragile world we call middle earth. And they will lash out and strike anyone who comes close enough.

Death is a lonely voyage and a fallen warrior will always seek to take someone along with him if he can.

Which is why Beobrand and Acennan killed those who stood before them as efficiently as those ceorls they had seen scything barley in the sun. If their foes were not dead soon after they fell, they sent them on their way with a savage thrust of blade, or downward smashing blow of shield edge.

And so it had gone on. Until everyone was spent. Panting and gasping for breath and all wishing they had never come to this place. Battles are glorious in the mead-hall tales. Gold spun from the lyrical kennings of scops. But in that muck-splattered night, there was no glory. Just death, fear and above all else, tiredness.

*

Battles rarely end with one side wholly defeated, killed to the last man. What ends each battle is always different. Sometimes it is the death of a leader; with the head severed, the serpent can fight no more. Other times it is exhaustion; men simply throw down their weapons in apathy. They can see their end is in sight and they cannot find the strength to rail against their doom any longer.

In some confrontations, there is an unspoken communication that seems to flow between the men. First one, then another, and soon the whole host turns and flees in a flood like a breaking beaver dam. The reason for this is often hard to understand, with no apparent weakness on the side that crumbles.

In the dawn light that morning, after the long, bloody night of death, it was the routing of the horses that pulled the first pebble from the dyke that shored up the Waelisc's will.

Following the death of his lord, Derian had been leading Scand's men towards the large fire and the heat of the battle when one of his men caught the sound of whinnying on the wind. Knowing that the Waelisc favoured mounted raids, and fearing Cadwallon would use his mounts to flee should the battle go badly for him, Derian quickly decided to chase off the Waelisc's steeds.

The horses were corralled to the south of the encampment, but Derian's band found no resistance as they cautiously picked their way past empty shelters and over corpses. As they edged further into the camp, they saw no more bodies. Oswald's force had not penetrated that far south. They skirted around those few dead they did see. They were all keen not to make the same mistake as Scand.

A fenced enclosure had been built to hold the horses in place, but the storm and the fighting was driving them mad. The horses huddled in a seething mass of muscled terror. Their eyes rolled white. Their ears pressed flat against long skulls. They shone and steamed in the darkness. The handful of thralls and warriors who had been left to guard them had been forced to turn to the animals. Calming them was clearly impossible. All they could do was use sticks and spears to prod them back from the fences. All this did was enrage and terrify them more.

Derian saw all of this in the dim light from nearby spitting fires. The horses would break free soon, that much was clear. But he could help them on their way.

"For Scand!" he screamed, and the warband surged forward, hungry for vengeance for their lord.

There was no fight there at the horse enclosure. The thralls and guards were slaughtered in moments.

Derian's teeth flashed in the dark. "Pull down the fences."

Two of the men hacked at a section of fencing, pulling and heaving at the wattled withies until it collapsed. An angered mass of horseflesh and flailing hooves finished their task. The fence gave way and the horses stampeded from the enclosure. They streaked into the night, a deadly equine wall of fear.

The Waelisc seemed to sense something before Beobrand saw or heard anything. The shieldwall quivered and then men took a few steps back. Some flicked a glance over their shoulder.

The Bernicians did not press forward. They welcomed the respite from the battering assault.

Then Beobrand heard it. At first he thought it the sound of Thunor's chariot, but the rain had ceased. The storm had passed.

The Waelsic turned and began to run, then Beobrand saw

what caused the noise and their retreat. A rush of wild-eyed horses galloped towards them. Certain death lay under those hooves. The Waelisc shieldwall fell apart like barley gleanings blown by the wind.

The Bernician host was beginning to see what was happening and would soon follow the Waelisc.

Cadwallon's grisly standard dipped and then fell to the ground. Dropped from hands that had held it bravely in the face of shield and spear through the long night, but would not hold before a wave of animal rage and terror in the grey dawn.

At the last possible instant, the horses wheeled and turned, as if on some hidden signal. They veered south and disappeared into the grey-smeared dawn gloom. All save three. Maybe they were driven mad, or did not heed the signal followed by the other mounts, but three fine steeds continued on through the centre of the disintegrating Waelisc line directly towards Oswald.

One careened into a Waelisc warrior. The warrior fell, his red cloak dimly visible against the mud and churned grass. Beobrand had seen that warrior before. That same helm and that scarlet cloak had been worn by Cadwallon ap Cadfan, king of Gwynedd. The horse, as if feeling remorse at having toppled its king, skidded to a halt, pawing the turf with its hoof and dipping its head.

All this Beobrand saw as he roused himself from where he had rested a moment to suck in long, ragged breaths of cold morning air. Before conscious thought permeated his mind, he was already sprinting forward. He ran onto the ground between the two forces. It was corpse-strewn and treacherous, but he leapt with a nimbleness that belied the aches in his limbs. The horses were storming towards Oswald and Oswiu. Beobrand watched as the scene slowed for him. He saw gobbets of mud lifted from the hooves. One of the horses stumbled on a fallen shield. Its fetlocks buckled and it tumbled. It fell in a thrashing heap of hooves and screams.

The other horse, a black stallion, all rippling power under sleek hair, galloped on. Beobrand had worked with animals all his life until coming to Bernicia the year before. Back on the farm in Hithe, he had seen horses spooked. Once, a mare had been bitten by a viper that had lurked in bracken. She had let out such a screech, like a baby being gutted, Uncle Selwyn had said. The mare's panic had spread to the other horses and they had stampeded towards the men who had been pollarding the ash trees in the lower pasture. Beobrand remembered what Selwyn had done in that bright, sunlit summer day and he repeated the action here on this dismal, murk-filled morning.

Beobrand stood firm with his back to Oswald and held out both his arms, like the Christ god on his rood. Neither Selwyn, when he had done this back in Cantware, nor Christ when he had been pinned to his death-tree, had a shield strapped to his left arm and a blood-drenched sword in his right fist. But, if anything, these objects helped to dissuade the horse from its course.

"Woah! Woah!" yelled Beobrand.

All eyes on the battlefield were on him.

For a moment, Beobrand doubted the horse would halt. Its eyes glowered in its black face. Its lips pulled back from wicked, long teeth. Its hooves pounded.

Beobrand stared into its eyes. He stood his ground. The host ceased breathing.

At the last possible instant, the stallion flicked its head and dug its hooves into the earth. It skittered and slid towards him.

It came to rest almost touching Beobrand. Its hot breath billowed in the chill morn. The moist warmth of its panting enveloped Beobrand's face. He let out his own pent up breath. They stood that way for a long moment. Sharing the same air.

As slowly as possible, without breaking the fragile spell between them, Beobrand let his shield fall. He shook it from its straps. Kicked it away. The stallion shied from the movement.

"Easy now. Easy boy." Beobrand dared not turn away his gaze. He reached out with his left, half-hand and stroked the long snout. He fumbled to sheath Hrunting with his right hand. Eventually, he risked a quick look down, and slid the blade slowly into the fur-lined scabbard. Some distant part of his mind berated him that the blood would ruin the lining. He brought his full focus back to the stallion. He did not want to lose control now.

With both hands, he smoothed the trembling animal's neck. He took a good hold of the thick mane and then, with a sudden, fluid motion, he swung himself onto the horse's back. It wore no saddle and had no bridle. And it was petrified from the lightning, the battle and the stench of fresh blood and death. But it was also a warhorse. A steed bred and trained for war. It must surely have been the property of one of the nobles in Cadwallon's force. Perhaps it even belonged to Cadwallon himself.

The stallion gave two bucking kicks, then a sudden side-step. Beobrand held on tightly with his thighs and clung to the coarse, greasy hair of the mane. When it was clear he would not be dislodged easily, the horse settled. It shook its great head and snorted.

The onlooking host let out half a cheer before seeming to realise that this might well cause the horse to throw its new rider.

"Beobrand! Look!" Acennan's voice cut through the ragged cheer. Beobrand followed his friend's pointing finger to where Cadwallon was also astride a mount. The Waelisc king had pulled himself onto the horse that had knocked him down. The horse turned a complete circle twice, as if allowing Cadwallon to survey the ruin of his warhost. The king's red cloak billowed. The Waelisc were running. The herd of horses was vanishing into the south, followed by the warriors who had lost the stomach for this battle.

Cadwallon got the horse under control, dug his heels into its flanks and galloped off south and west.

Beobrand looked down to Oswald. The king's face was pale and splattered with blood and mud. His helm sported a large dent. Their eyes met. Oswald nodded.

"You have done well, Beobrand, son of Grimgundi. Now go, and bring me Cadwallon! I would have him face justice here this day."

"Your bidding, my king," said Beobrand. He wheeled his mount around and raked its flanks. The stallion jumped forward.

Grim-faced, Beobrand sped after the king of Gwynedd.

As soon as he started riding, Beobrand could see that Cadwallon was a better rider than him. The Waelisc king sat proudly on his horse, matching the rise and fall of the galloping mount with ease.

Beobrand clung on to the black mane of his mount until his hands cramped. Already fatigued, he struggled to squeeze the horse's sides tightly enough with his thighs. But somehow he managed to stay on the back of the stallion.

In the murky distance, he could see the rest of the horses showing no signs of slowing their fear-fuelled stampede.

Waelisc warriors were all around him. They had scattered when the horses charged and they were still dispersed. Beobrand rode past small clumps of warriors. There was fear in the eyes of some. Anger in the faces of others. One must have realised what was happening and who he was, for a spear streaked out of the gloom and thudded into the sodden earth a few paces to his left. The stallion tossed its head, but did not break its stride. It was a warhorse and it was not so easily frightened.

Despite his precarious position, Beobrand began to revel in the power of the beast. He could feel the thrum of each hoof's impact. The horse's breath steamed and tattered in the wind. The speed was intoxicating. Never had Beobrand ridden such a horse. It would be easy to allow the sensation of potency to wash over him. To lull him into a state of calm.

The night had sapped him of all his strength. Now, he felt the familiar lethargy that followed combat threaten to settle on him. He shook his head. Not yet. He had survived the night, but it was not over. Rest would have to wait.

As if to emphasise this, a group of Waelisc warriors formed a small shieldwall before him. Beyond them Cadwallon's horse leapt a small brook easily and galloped on into the scrubby, gorse-spattered heathland. The king's red cloak flapped in his wake like a banner, or a parting wave. He was getting away.

The shieldwall numbered but five, but Beobrand could not risk charging. Should his steed be injured he would lose all hope of running Cadwallon down.

He scanned his surroundings.

The ground to the left was marshy. Rushes tufted between pools that reflected the first rays of the morning sun. To the right was a slope, crested by a tangled stand of birch and hawthorn.

Beobrand cursed. There was no alternative. He turned the horse to the right and kicked its ribs savagely.

"Come on!" he screamed.

The horse pounded up the slope towards the shade of the wood. The Waelisc on the road shouted and another spear arced towards Beobrand, but fell well short.

The small wood was a thick jumble of low-hanging branches. He drove the horse forward, but how they would get through the copse, he did not know. He would be lucky not to be blinded by the twigs and sharp thorns. But there was nothing for it. Sense would have him dismount and lead the horse through the foliage, but the men below were too close. As he came near to the trees Beobrand dug his heels in once more and lay down along the length of the stallion's neck. He wrapped his arms around the neck and closed his eyes.

Branches scratched and scraped his face and hands. The horse whinnied. Something crashed against Beobrand's helm with a deafening knell. Snagging fingers pulled his cloak.

Were there elves here in this wood? Were those voices, whispering of his death in the leaf mould? He squeezed his eyes tightly shut to protect them from the undergrowth and kicked the horse once more.

"Fly! Fly!" he cried.

The air was dank. Sinister and dire. The taste of bile rose in his throat. There was an evil presence here. Some forest spirit clinging to the night, not yet banished by the sun. The horse was slowing. Its breathing was ragged. Was that the breath of another being, hot and rancid? The horse too seemed frightened. Its neck trembled beneath Beobrand's arms.

Beobrand thought of the rush light blown out. Sunniva's tears. His oath. Was he to fall here? His bones rotting into the roots of a spirit tree?

No. He had sworn a vow to return. And first he must capture Cadwallon. So many had died. Their faces swam before his mind's eye. Leofwine, Alric, Eanfrith, so many others. Cadwallon must be stopped and no eldritch phantom could hold Beobrand back.

"Easy now, boy," he whispered, his face near the ear of the stallion. "Take us out of this dark place."

The horse shuddered and snorted. Then moved forward. Beobrand could still not bring himself to open his eyes. But he was less fearful now of the twigs and branches that had torn at his face and clothes. He was certain something unspeakable lurked in the gloom. To see its face would mark his end.

More burrs and brambles tugged at his armour as the horse walked on. But the atmosphere had changed. Birdsong rang out, warbling and joyful of the morning light. At last he looked around him and saw they had come though the copse. Before them lay open scrub and in the distance, with nothing but gorse, heather and long grass between them, was his quarry.

Beobrand shivered and patted the horse's neck.

"You are a brave one," he whispered. The stallion's ears twitched. "You brought us through the shadows." Beobrand did not look back for fear of what he might see in the murk beneath the trees. "Now you must run once more."

With a kick of his heels they set off in pursuit of the king of Gwynedd.

Beobrand followed the king's red cloak across the low, rolling hills for some time. The sun burst through the clouds to their left, its light dazzling from the finery of the Waelisc's war gear.

Cadwallon threw a glance over his shoulder. Beobrand was lagging far behind and it must have been clear to the Waelisc king that he had little to fear from his pursuer.

Beobrand was no horseman, but he was allowing himself to settle into his steed's rhythm once again. The horse had shaken off the terror of the wood and now seemed keen to place as much distance as possible between them and whatever dark entity lurked beneath the trees. Beobrand felt his muscles loosen. He still held tight to the black mane, but unclenched his fists slightly. The stumps on his left hand throbbed as the blood returned.

Beobrand watched as Cadwallon lengthened the distance between them. He resigned himself to a long chase. Probably failure. He could not compete with the nobleman's skill on horseback. But he would strive to bring him to ground. Perhaps Cadwallon's horse would tire first. Even as he thought it, Beobrand knew it was not likely. His black stallion was a battle mount, muscled and hale. It was not built for the chase. It was already blowing hard. If he pushed it too far, he would kill the horse.

Beobrand gritted his teeth. It would be a sad end to such a fine beast, but he must continue. Seizing the Waelisc king would end the bloodshed that had washed the land with death. This northern kingdom was now his home and he would do all he could to bring peace to it. He gave the stallion its head and the great hooves thundered across the bush-strewn turf.

In the end, Cadwallon's pride in his horsemanship was his undoing.

Beobrand had fallen into a waking reverie. His exhaustion seeped into his bones as the horse's rolling gait rocked his body. Cadwallon drew ever further away. The taste of defeat was in Beobrand's mouth. To come so close, only to see the ruler of the Waelisc escape into the hills to the south-west of the Wall was galling.

Then, as if swallowed by the earth, Cadwallon and his horse disappeared. For a moment Beobrand was unsure what he had witnessed. Cadwallon had been riding easily down a slight slope and then he had gone. Beobrand shook his head, bringing himself fully awake.

He rode on, cautious of some treachery. Perhaps Cadwallon meant to ambush him.

He cantered down the incline and the sound of screaming reached him. But these were not sounds made by man. The hairs on Beobrand's neck prickled. He slowed to a trot. Then the scene became clear.

The slope ended in a burn. Its waters, swollen by the storm, were brown and churning. Cadwallon's horse floundered in the stream. It was on its side, thrashing and screaming. Cadwallon was waist-deep in the water. The scraped furrows in the nearest bank attested to where the horse had skidded. Apparently Cadwallon had thought to leap the burn, but his horse had baulked, slipped and thrown him. Both horse and rider had ended up in the burn. It seemed the horse must have broken a leg for it was moaning pitifully and could not right itself. Its violent thrashing placed Cadwallon in danger of being crushed or kicked.

He waded dazedly out of the brook. He was not kingly now. Loam-smeared and bedraggled, his cloak a sopping rag, he dragged himself out of the mire.

Beobrand pulled his stallion to a halt and in one smooth motion leapt from its back. For a fleeting moment he worried that his horse would run off, leaving him stranded here. But it was on the edge of collapse. It drooped its head, snorting hard and trembling.

Cadwallon dragged his sword from a mud-drenched scabbard and faced Beobrand. His teeth flashed from the dirt-dripping face.

"Well, boy," said Cadwallon, in the tongue of the Angelfolc, "it seems you have finally caught up with me. Just as well for you that my horse was clumsy and had no heart for the jump. You ride like a sack of turnips!"

Pulling Hrunting free from its scabbard, Beobrand stepped forward. The blade was blood-encrusted and dim. He had not stopped to clean it after the battle.

"So, do you mean to kill me, boy?" said Cadwallon. "Do you think the likes of you could best me?"

Beobrand thought of all those who had died as a result of this man's ambition. So much blood. So much death. It would all end today.

"I have killed many men this night, and more before. I have stood before you three times now, though you have not seen me. I stood at Elmet. We broke you at Gefrin, but never have we met on equal terms. As men."

Despite Cadwallon's bluster, Beobrand could see the fear in his eyes. His hand darted up to touch the scar on his cheek where the shard of Scand's blade had scored a deep furrow.

"You are alone now, Cadwallon. You have no retinue. No hearth warriors to cower behind."

"Very well, Seaxon. We will end this here. I will kill you, take your horse and as you die know this: Cadwallon ap Cadfan will kill every last one of your goat-swiving race."

Cadwallon leapt forward. He was skilled with a blade, and the suddenness of the attack took Beobrand off guard. He took a step back, leaning away from the swing that would have taken his head from his shoulders.

Neither man carried a shield and Beobrand was mindful

of Hrunting's fine blade. It was already nicked and chipped from the battle, and he would save it more damage if possible. Taking another couple of quick steps backwards, Beobrand drew Cadwallon in. He watched Cadwallon's feet. He was nimble and skilled. His footwork good. His sword point darted at Beobrand's face. Beobrand was forced to parry and sparks flew from the collision.

Beobrand feinted at Cadwallon's neck, then sent a blow arcing down towards his adversary's leading foot. Cadwallon read the move easily and stepped back lithely.

The king grinned. "You will not beat me. You are a clumsier swordsman than you are a horseman."

It was true that Cadwallon was skilful and strong. It was his hubris that was his greatest weakness.

Beobrand kept his face impassive. A mask of concentration.

Cadwallon sent a flurry of attacks at him. He parried them all, but allowed himself to be forced back, on the defensive.

Another thrust swatted away as Beobrand took a further pace backwards.

Then, seeing his opportunity to strike the killing blow, Cadwallon sprang forward, sure that his sword would find the Seaxon's throat.

But Beobrand was no longer there. He deflected the probing blade and stepped inside Cadwallon's reach. With all his weight and height behind the blow, Beobrand hammered Hrunting's pommel into the Waelisc king's face.

Teeth shattered. Lips ripped and blood burst forth in a crimson bloom. Cadwallon's knees buckled. He staggered, and fell to the earth.

Beobrand kicked the sword from Cadwallon's limp fingers.

"I am Beobrand, son of Grimgundi, and you would do well to fear me and my race."

"Go on then, kill me, you Seaxon scum," spat Cadwallon. Blood dribbled down his chin.

"No."

Confusion in Cadwallon's eyes. A glimmer of hope?

"Never fear. You will die. But your death belongs to another."

With that Beobrand stepped close to Cadwallon's kneeling form and thundered another blow with Hrunting's pommel into the blood-streaked face of the king of Gwynedd.

6

The sun was high in the sky and past its zenith when Beobrand rode wearily into the remnants of the Waelisc camp. The clouds had scattered on a brisk wind and the day was bright. The black stallion plodded under the weight of two men. It was as tired as Beobrand, but still held its head proudly. Beobrand patted its neck and whispered soft words of encouragement to the horse. It was a fine beast.

Cadwallon sprawled over the horse's broad back.

It had been a struggle to get the unconscious king up onto the horse, but Beobrand had stripped him of his armour and then manhandled him up. Like a sack of turnips. The irony was not lost on him and he'd smiled grimly to himself despite the exertion. He'd used strips of the red cloak to bind him hand and foot. Cadwallon had begun to moan, just as Beobrand was passing a strip of cloth under the horse's belly tying his wrists and ankles together. The steed had grown skittish then. Nervous of the noisy, restless burden. It was already spooked by the crying of the fallen horse in the burn. The injured horse had finally managed to right itself, but could not climb up the bank out of the water. Its right foreleg was broken. It hung limp and pathetic. The once noble mount hobbled and staggered away down the course of the stream. Beobrand let it go.

He stroked the stallion's flank. Its trembling subsided.

"This is no way for a king to ride," said Cadwallon. His words were slurred from the broken teeth. He spat blood onto the turf.

"You are no longer a king. You have been defeated. But you will keep your mouth closed or I will bind it shut." Beobrand had contemplated letting Cadwallon ride seated before him, but the chance for the king to cause mischief and escape was too great.

Cadwallon glared at him. His eyes were sharp and bright with hatred. They glowered from the mask of mud and blood that caked his face. But he kept silent.

They had ridden back at a slower pace. They saw groups of men, but none threatened them. They all seemed content to slink away. They wanted nothing to do with the mounted warrior, clad in fine metal-knit shirt and polished helm. The armour, weapons and mount were all of great value, but to confront such a strong opponent would require organisation and bravery. The ragged men they saw were clearly broken. Death had come in the night for them and they had survived. Their eyes were hollow. They had seen the end of the glory days of their people. They had been broken by iron and steel. And all the while lightning had flashed and the gods themselves laughed in the heavens. They had been abandoned by their king at the end, as well as the gods. The signs were there for all to see.

This new king of Bernicia had divine favour. Now was his time.

And so the survivors from Cadwallon's invincible warhost

fled south and west. They never stopped and posed no threat to Beobrand.

The encampment was not a place of celebration, despite the victory. Ravens and crows circled already. The carrion birds helped guide Beobrand back to the place of battle. The corpses of the Waelisc had been systematically stripped of all valuables. Clothes, shoes, belts, hats, pouches, as well as weapons and armour, were all taken, unless damaged beyond any chance of repair. The fish-pallid bodies were heaped together at the south of the encampment, downwind of the Bernician host. The whole area stank like a midden pit. The charnel miasma of spilt bowels, congealed blood and vomit, hung like doom over the battlefield.

All of Oswald's force wished to leave this place of death. The night had been filled with terrors that were too recent to be forgotten. In the bodies of their enemies and their own dead they saw themselves. No man knew why the spear thrust found his friend's neck but spared him. Why one shield breaks, allowing a killing blow through, while another board remains whole. Why does a metal shirt choose that moment to fail, allowing the bite of a sword between the ribs? It is madness to think of these things, yet every warrior who survives a conflict ponders the imponderable. Why should it be that he lives while so many died?

Later they would drink and feast. The horrors of the shieldwall in that thunder-rent, scream-laden night would fade, the way dreams fracture and disappear on waking, like gossamer webs brushed aside from a forest path. In the light and warmth of the fire-glow, with the heat of mead in their bellies, they would tell tales of the battle. They would sing of their dead. Praise their valour and talk of their own prowess and exploits.

But now was not the time for song. Now men wished to be gone from this place that reminded them of how they had killed. How they had lived to see the light of day because that was their wyrd. They lived when all around them was death and for that they were glad.

But they could not be happy for it yet.

They waited, for that was what their king ordered. They waited to see whether the young warrior from Cantware would return. Would he bring back the king of the Waelisc; the man whose name struck terror into all the inhabitants of Deira and Bernicia?

They waited to discover whether the head of the serpent had been severed.

Upward-turned faces stared as Beobrand and Cadwallon rode slowly through the camp. Some men seemed not to notice the identity of Beobrand's prisoner. Perhaps they were too exhausted to understand. Or care.

But others roused themselves from where they sat or lay and followed the stallion on its plodding path. By the time Beobrand reached the leather tent at the centre of the camp, there was quite a procession in his wake.

Someone called out from the crowd, "Is that Cadwallon?" Beobrand ignored the voice and continued until he was in front of Oswald's wooden cross standard. It was much smaller than the tree structure that stood at Hefenfelth, but it was clearly the same symbol of the Christ god.

Oswald stood beneath the standard. He looked every part the noble warlord. His hair was sleek and brushed. His clothes had been cleaned and his purple cloak hung elegantly over his left shoulder. His byrnie gleamed and his silver-crowned helm shone in the afternoon light.

Beobrand blinked the sleep from his eyes. He looked

around and saw that all eyes were on him. The faces were expectant. Eager. He spied the rounded features of his friend, Acennan, and his spirits lifted to see him well. Yet a needle of uncertainty pricked him. Acennan did not return his smile, but glowered from beneath sullen eyebrows. Surely he must be as tired as Beobrand. No wonder he was not happy. They had all been awake for two days with a march and a battle in that time.

Beobrand looked back to Oswald. The king was scowling. It would be wise to break the silence. The watchers knew not of what had befallen him and the king of the Waelisc.

He dismounted. Careful not to lose his balance. His legs quivered but he kept upright with an effort. Moving swiftly Beobrand drew his seax and sliced the bonds that held Cadwallon to the horse. He pulled him down, giving him a push as his feet touched the ground, sending the king sprawling to the mud.

A smattering of laughter from the onlookers. A stern look from Oswald. He clearly was not a man accustomed to being kept waiting.

Beobrand cleared his throat. "Oswald King, I bring you your enemy and the slayer of your brother, Eanfrith, son of Æthelfrith." He looked down and saw that Cadwallon, his ankles and wrists still tied, could not easily rise from a kneeling position. He was muddy, bedraggled, bloody and beaten. "Kneeling before you is Cadwallon ap Cadfan, king of Gwynedd."

For a moment there was silence. Oswald's face gave little away of the emotions he felt as he stared at the man on the ground before him. With the vagaries of war and allegiances, Cadwallon was largely responsible for Oswald returning to claim his place as the ruler of Bernicia. Had he not killed

Edwin the year before, the sons of Æthelfrith would still be in exile. By also slaying Eanfrith, he had opened the way for Oswald's ascension to power.

Cadwallon was also responsible for killing many innocent men, women and children. He was a cruel killer who had sought to destroy all of the Angelfolc. He was sworn to eradicate their race from the island of Albion.

"You have done well, Beobrand, son of Grimgundi. You have proven yourself to be true and faithful. Your service will not go unrewarded. But first I must see this Cadwallon."

Oswald stepped forward, close to his defeated enemy. The onlookers quietened. They jostled and shoved to get a good view of the encounter between the two lords.

"Cadwallon ap Cadfan, you are before me today as an enemy of Bernicia," Oswald said, his voice ringing clear over the warhost. His words would be heard. And remembered.

From where he knelt, Cadwallon looked up at Oswald, squinting into the light. He spat a gobbet of bloody spittle.

Oswald continued, "You have destroyed our settlements. Violated our womenfolk. Defiled our holy places and slain innocents. What say you?"

Cadwallon spat again. Hate-filled eyes burnt from the grime-caked face.

He lowered his head and Beobrand wondered if he would not answer. The scene was as still as a carving and Beobrand would always remember it. Two kings, facing each other at either end of their reigns. One victorious and shining in the sun, the other defeated, kneeling and broken, head bowed. The eggshell blue sky framed the tableau. The warm afternoon sun seemed to give Oswald an aura of light around his head, such was the brightness of the reflection.

The stillness was broken by Cadwallon.

"Innocents?" He coughed out a cracked laugh. "Innocents, you say? Your kind have fallen on our land like a scourge. It is your kind that has despoiled our land. Taken our women. With fire and iron your father destroyed everything that stood before him."

"I am not my father," replied Oswald. His voice was sharp and cold, like shattered winter streams. Beobrand started at the words. He heard the echo of his mother's dying breath. "You are not your father's son," she had said to him, as she lay racked with fever. He still did not comprehend her meaning. Was it always thus, even with kings? The shadow of the father falling over the life of the son?

Cadwallon looked calmly up at Oswald. "No, you are not," he said. His face split in a smile. "Neither are you your brother. You are no fool and you still have your head."

There was no sound throughout the watching warriors. Oswald and Cadwallon held each other's gaze.

Eventually, Oswald turned to his brother. "Oswiu, hold him. We must avenge our brother and the people of Bernicia. This man's blood will begin to quench the pain of the land. His head will adorn my hall at Bebbanburg."

Oswald's tall young brother stepped forward. Oswiu bristled with rage. He grasped Cadwallon's shoulders roughly.

"Wait, my lord." One of the dark-robed holy men who had travelled with Oswald from the island of Hii spoke out in a tremulous voice. Oswald turned to him with a withering stare.

The monk swallowed and said, "This man should be tried with proper ceremony before God. Men should be assembled. A Witan of thegns…" His voice trailed off in the face of Oswald's furious gaze.

"I am king here," Oswald's voice was strong and hard as steel. "Cadwallon ap Cadfan is guilty of too many crimes to list. He is condemned in the eyes of the Lord. He is the enemy of Bernicia. The enemy of the Angelfolc. And the enemy of God. I will not suffer him to live any longer."

Oswald dragged his sword from its scabbard. He leaned in close to the kneeling man and whispered something. It was inaudible to Beobrand. Oswiu could clearly hear his brother's words, for his lips curled in a wicked smile.

Cadwallon tensed and lowered his head.

"Now step back, Gothfraidh," said Oswald, "unless you wish my sword to take your head this day also."

The monk scurried backwards so quickly that he stumbled and was caught by his brethren. At any other time this would have made the warriors laugh. But the weight of this moment sat heavily on all of them. It was not every day you saw the end of a king's life.

Oswald took the hilt of his sword in both hands. He held the patterned blade high. It shimmered and shone. Its shadow lay over Cadwallon's neck. Oswald nodded at his brother. Oswiu released Cadwallon's shoulders and stepped back in one smooth motion. As if rehearsed, at the same instant, Oswald swung his sword with great vigour.

It landed where its shadow had lain a moment before. There was the briefest of sounds at the impact. His blade was sharp and his arm guided it true. The metal sliced through sinew and bone and Cadwallon slumped forward, crumpled to the earth. The head did not roll free, but lay at an impossible angle. Blood gushed, pumping from the raw neck. It splattered Cadwallon's chin and hair and soaked into the ground.

Beobrand was transfixed. The king's head had twisted around and seemed to be staring at him. The crimson life surged from the body as the eyes blinked twice, and then they blinked no more. The light left them and the king of Gwynedd was gone from middle earth.

Oswiu stepped forward and used his own sword to cut the last threads of flesh that held Cadwallon's head to his torso. He looked to his brother, who seemed dazed. Perhaps stunned at the enormity of his action.

Oswiu touched Oswald's arm. "Brother," he said in a voice none save those closest to the king could hear.

Oswald stared at him for a moment. Shook his head, as if to clear it of dreams. Then nodded.

King Oswald, son of Æthelfrith, picked up Cadwallon's blood-drenched head and raised it aloft for all to see.

"Cadwallon ap Cadfan, king of Gwynedd, defiler of our land, is dead!" he shouted.

The warhost erupted in a tumult of cheers.

Beobrand stared down at the body lying in the muck. Blood still pumped feebly from the neck.

History was being made here in the brutal death of the Waelisc king. He knew that. But he could not take it in. His hands began to shake and it was all he could do to remain on his feet. He steadied himself against the warm solidity of the stallion. The rough hair of the horse was real. The rest of this day seemed like a waking dream.

"Scand would be alive if it weren't for you!" Acennan roared. His round face was contorted with rage. Beobrand recoiled from the heat of his anger. It burnt like the maw of an open forge fire.

Acennan's voice carried over the noise of the men who drank and ate. They were all too exhausted to celebrate. That would wait for when they returned to their halls. For now, on the hill of Hefenfelth, away from the stink of death, they were content in the knowledge that the Waelisc threat had been silenced.

Beobrand had sought out Acennan and the rest of Scand's retinue as they had made their way back to the Wall. But his friend had avoided him.

Beobrand had learnt of Scand's demise from Derian and the death fell heavy on him. His face had drained of colour at hearing Derian's tidings.

"I know you looked up to him, Beobrand," the bearded thegn had said, grim-faced. "We all did." His words fell like chiselled rock, sharp and hard.

"He was a great lord," Beobrand choked on his words. "I owe him everything." Scand had taken him in and offered him a place in his gesithas when all seemed lost. He had known him for less than a year, but he now felt his loss keenly.

Derian had patted Beobrand on the shoulder and nodded. He understood. They all felt the same way.

Scand's gesithas had walked with heads bowed, down-heartened despite Oswald's victory. Their future was uncertain and many of them had served with Scand for most of their life. His death was a sore blow.

"It is not easy to accept the death of one so beloved," Derian had addressed all of Scand's gesithas as they trudged back to Hefenfelth, "but Scand was a warrior. It was a good death. A lord's death."

The men had nodded, eager to hear words of comfort to soften the aching in their hearts.

"We too are warriors," Derian had continued, "and one day we will fall in the shieldwall. If the gods allow it and our wyrd is spun that way."

Tobrytan, one of the oldest warriors, had said, "Better to

be slain in battle than to die toothless and crazed like some longbeard who's outlived his usefulness. I would rather die with honour, a death worthy of song, than live out my last days as another drooling mouth to feed."

Derian hoomed in his throat and the warriors had walked on, battle-weary and saddened at their loss.

Acennan appeared to be the only one who blamed Beobrand. His anger hurt all the more as they were the closest of friends.

And because Beobrand agreed with Acennan. If they had not attacked at night, Scand would not have been caught unawares by a wounded foe.

Beobrand looked at Acennan's furious features and wondered if this small conflict between friends amused the gods. After the countless dead the previous night, the heaped bodies feeding the carrion birds and beasts. After the death of a king and a great old lord like Scand, perhaps this was a welcome diversion for gods. Or did they not care?

"He was as a father to me," replied Beobrand. His voice was flat. He wanted nothing more than to sit and share a horn of mead with Acennan. Every sinew of his being was tired. Tired almost beyond thought. But he could not turn away from his friend now. Their friendship rested on a seax edge.

"You barely knew him," thundered Acennan. "I was his man for ten years. I knew him all my life. Once, in Hibernia, he saved my life in the shieldwall..." The anger drained from his voice then, replaced by an aching sorrow that made Beobrand's heart wrench. He had never seen Acennan weep, but now the stocky man's eyes welled with tears.

"Oh, my lord..." Acennan said, his voice quaking. He drew in a ragged breath and cuffed the tears from his eyes. "Do not speak to me of this, Beobrand. It was you who led the king to attack at night. And you who left Scand's side at the start of the battle." Acennan's face was as dark as the thunder clouds of the storm. "If only I had not followed you. Scand could still live."

Grief washed over Beobrand then. Acennan had the right of it. His folly had caused Scand's death.

"Do you think I do not know that?" Beobrand said. "I would blame the gods for sending me the signs. But it was I who chose to follow them. Perhaps it is my wyrd to see all those I care for die. I would have given my life to save Scand's, if I could."

"If only you had," muttered Acennan.

Beobrand turned his face from Acennan and took a step back, as if slapped. He could not see the look of anguish and remorse on his friend's face as he walked stiffly away from the camp into the night.

7

Sunniva jostled for a good position to see the men returning. The palisade was crowded with womenfolk and children. After the arrival a few days before of straggling groups of survivors from Cadwallon's scourge of the land there had been no news. Until the previous morning. A rider had galloped into the courtyard of Bebbanburg shouting the joyous tidings that Oswald was victorious. Cadwallon was killed.

The atmosphere in the fortress shifted. Thralls and servants rushed to prepare for the king's return. Vittles would be needed for a feast. There would be more people descending on Bebbanburg before they could expect any peace. A victory of this magnitude would be celebrated with thegns and ealdormen from all the shires of Bernicia. Wise women and holy men also made their preparations. They would be needed to tend to the bodies and spirits of those warriors who would return wounded.

Bebbanburg was all abustle.

There was a change in the spirits of those who had bid their menfolk farewell. But the air was not yet filled with jubilation. Women went about their chores efficiently enough.

Floors were swept. Fresh rushes laid in the great hall. Animals were butchered. Bread was baked and ale was brewed in vast quantities. There could never be too much ale at a feast and every available pot was put to use. The scent of boiling and fermenting barley and gruit permeated the whole fortress. The barrels of sweet mead would be saved for the warriors of highest rank.

But all the while the women's eyes held a distant look. Would their men come back? Would they soon be sewing a shroud while others feasted on the food and drink they now prepared?

Sunniva tried not to think of what might be. She had suffered the burden of such thoughts too frequently of late. She wished to believe that the snuffed out rush light had been nothing more than the wind. That it was not an omen presaging the death of her man in battle. Yet try as she might, she could not dispel the fear that had worked its way into her very being.

The constant shade of worry enveloped her like wet sackcloth. It weighed her down and chilled her. She was exhausted by her anxiety.

In an effort to draw her mind away from the darkness that clouded her thoughts, she attacked chores with gusto. The other women, many of whom she had known since childhood, welcomed her into their midst. They liked the pretty, hardworking girl. They knew of her losses. They saw the despair threatening to engulf her. But she was strong, like her father and mother. The womenfolk looked upon her with affection. And prayed that Sunniva would not have to face another death so soon.

"Careful there! Get down!" An elderly man shouted up to two boys who had clambered up to the highest point of the palisade. They stood precariously on the parapet of one of the turrets that supported the wall.

The boys' mothers' voices were added to those of the man. The lads looked angry, but grudgingly climbed down from their perch without incident.

"We could see them from up there," one of them moaned. "It doesn't look like there are as many of them as when they went away."

The boy's mother cuffed him hard round the head. "Shut your mouth!" she snapped. People looked away. The boy's words had been heard by many. Fear gnawed at them all. Tension rose in the waiting throng the way boiling milk expands until it runs over its pot.

Sunniva strained to see the first glimpse of the returning warhost. The weather had changed with the thunderstorm and now the sky hung low and grey over the land. A strong wind rushed in from the sea, pulling her hair about her face.

Through the thin afternoon light she peered over the dunes. She pushed her hair from her eyes.

Then, first came the wooden cross standard of Oswald, quickly followed by the king himself, resplendent in purple cloak and polished helm. Around him were gathered his mounted thegns, the richest and most valued of his comitatus. She could not make them out from this distance. Perhaps Scand would ride with the king's retinue, but she could not see him.

At seeing the host moving northward on the road, the watching folk let out a cheer. The tension eased somewhat. But they would need to wait some more to find which men were returning whole and which broken. And which would not feast with their lord again on this earth.

With a start, Sunniva let out a small sound that was lost in the commotion all around her. Her hand flew to her mouth. Tears welled in her eyes. But these were not tears of sadness or worry. They were tears of joy. For, riding on a huge black steed at the head of the column of men, she saw her man.

She recognised the cloak that draped the flanks of the mount. The battered shield that hung from his back was attached with straps that she herself had fashioned for him. The boar helm, his fine sword. All of this she took in, but even without these details she would have known it was him. The way he held his head. The shape of his shoulders. The jut of his jaw.

She felt a warm glow in the pit of her stomach.

Her man had returned as he had vowed to do. The omen had not been bad.

Beobrand had come back to her riding a fine horse. He was riding. Close to the king.

He had returned victorious and with good favour.

She watched Beobrand for a long while as he grew closer. Her fine man.

Other women let out cries and squeals as they too recognised loved ones. Some women were silent. No familiar faces smiled back at them from the ranks of warriors. Yet they did not lose all hope just yet. Perhaps they had just missed them in the crowd. Or they were wounded and being carried on a litter. Sunniva glanced around her at the anxious faces. There would be wails and tears from some that night. That was as certain as ravens spoke to Woden.

She was sorry for them. She knew how much such grief hurt.

She turned and made her way down the ladder quickly. She had to get away. Gloating would be mean, yet she could not keep her smile in check much longer.

Beobrand had come back to her and all was well in the world again.

"He hates me," Beobrand said.

Sunniva stroked his chest, her fingers soothing him. "Nonsense. He is angry at what happened. He needs someone to shout at. He chose you. You need to give him time. Talk to him."

"But he refuses to talk to me," said Beobrand. He sighed. He was conflicted. Content in the warmth of Sunniva's embrace, yet dejected at Acennan's ire. "I tried to speak with him, but he spurns me." Beobrand stared up at the rafters above where they lay. He was still warm and languid from their lovemaking.

"Don't fret, my love. He is your true friend. I have seen it. He sat with you as the wound-fever pulled you towards death. Does he not risk all to defend you in the shieldwall? Give him time."

"I just want him to forgive me," said Beobrand.

"There is nothing to forgive. You listened to the gods and they showed the way to victory. Scand's death is not on your head."

Beobrand was not so sure. He had been reckless. He was not wrong for pushing Oswald to attack at night. Leaving his lord's side was a different matter. Would Scand be alive had he remained at his side with Acennan? Only the gods could tell. Acennan certainly believed it. Beobrand shook his head. Who was he to disagree with his friend?

"I should not have strayed from Scand's side. It was our place to protect him. Or to die alongside him."

Sunniva raised herself on one elbow and leaned over him. Her sweet-smelling hair veiled his face as she kissed him deeply.

"Do not speak so. I want a man who is alive. There is too much death in the world to be wishing for it."

She slid her hand down. Softly caressed him. He closed his eyes and moaned quietly. He could feel himself stir at her touch.

"Oh, and you are alive, aren't you?" There was laughter in her voice. She squeezed gently. He gasped.

"Put worries from your mind, my love," Sunniva said, all the while fondling and stroking his growing shaft. "You have returned to me as you vowed. Soon we will need to prepare for the feast. You will be in a place of honour. Your actions have seen to that, my brave man."

He snorted with derision. He was not brave. Foolhardy perhaps. But her attentions were making it difficult to focus on such things as recriminations. The battle seemed far away and long ago.

He slid his hand down the soft curve of her belly. His fingers brushed through the short hair there and then found the slick warmth of her. Still moist and ready for him, following their recent coupling.

Sunniva made a sound deep in her throat and moved on top of Beobrand.

"We'll be heard…" Beobrand whispered, then drew in a sharp breath as Sunniva guided him inside her.

Through the thin partition made of cloaks and blankets they could hear others moving and talking. Preparing themselves for the upcoming feast. A woman laughed too loudly. The desperate cackle tried to push the fear of the last few days away.

Sunniva began to move her hips. She kissed his mouth long and deep.

"Again, you mean? Let them hear." He could hear the smile in her words. She continued moving. His hands roved up her thighs and gripped her arse. By the gods this felt so good.

"Remember what else you vowed to me?" Sunniva asked, her breath hot against his face.

He tried to think, but his mind was full of her. He pushed more deeply into her and she moaned.

"I can barely remember my name at this moment," he panted.

"You said I would give you a fine son. And I know of only one way that can happen." She silenced any more words with her mouth on his.

Sunniva's rhythm increased. Beobrand matched her, thrusting with urgency.

All concerns of others overhearing them were forgotten.

The warmth of the great hall washed over Beobrand. A great fire burnt on the hearth, its flames giving a ruddy light to smiling faces. But Beobrand also felt the warmth of satisfaction. The pleasure of lying with Sunniva was still fresh. His body remembered the joy of it. He grinned at the memory.

Men looked up from the benches and grinned back. Some waved or called his name, raising their mead horns.

Beobrand was uncomfortable with the attention, but he allowed himself a sliver of pride. He had merely done what any of the warriors would have done in his stead. And yet it had been his wyrd to mount the steed and bring Cadwallon back to Oswald.

"Beobrand, isn't it?" A heavy-jowled man with grey hair staggered into Beobrand's path. He was familiar to Beobrand, but he could not place him. He had seen so many new faces over the last months. Some for an instant over an enemy shield, others at the mead benches of different kings. Many were now dead. It was hard to remember them all.

"I thought I recognised you," said the man loudly, swaying

slightly, like a ship moored in a swelling sea. Beobrand was still unsure of the man's identity, but a needle of doubt pricked the back of his neck.

"You have come a long way since you visited my hall with Hengist," the man said, and Beobrand remembered at once. He was Ecgric, son of Eacgric, lord of a small shire to the south. Beobrand had seen him briefly when he travelled with Hengist. Hengist had taken offence at implications made about his honour. Ecgric had thrown them out of his hall.

Beobrand swallowed. He knew not what to say to this man. When last he had seen him, he had been in the thrall of Hengist.

"I heard the tale of how you killed Hengist. A fine kill indeed. The man was an animal." Ecgric looked Beobrand up and down. His clothes were not those of a famous warrior. Sunniva had cleaned his kirtle and brushed his cloak as best she could. But he had no fine cloak pin at his shoulder. No warrior rings on his arms.

Beobrand said nothing. He wished for nothing more than to sit at a bench and revel in the joy of being alive after so much death-giving.

"And I hear you are once again the hero. Killing Cadwallon, no less!"

"I did not kill Cadwallon," said Beobrand.

"No? But you brought him to our good king Oswald, did you not? So you did for him, right enough. And a great deed that was too. Now perhaps we can have peace."

"I hope so," said Beobrand, trying to edge past Ecgric's bulk. He cast a glance to Sunniva, where she was already helping the other women to serve the men with food and drink. She seemed to sense his gaze and looked back with a radiant smile. "I would like to settle down. Raise a family."

"You are a wise man, for one so young," said Ecgric.

He lifted his horn to his lips to drain the liquid there and was disappointed to find it empty. "Your name is on everyone's lips. Some even whisper that it was you who told the king to attack at night. A daring move. Brave." He cast about for some more mead.

"The king had a vision in a dream. His god led us to victory." Beobrand pushed past the old man, heading deeper into the hall.

Few knew that he had given Oswald the idea for the night raid. Beobrand wished it had never occurred to him. Perhaps the omen of the snuffed out light had been bad. Maybe the gods were laughing at him even now. His lord, Scand, was dead. And Acennan blamed him.

Beobrand stood still for a moment. He watched the mass of merry-making men. A few days before they had stood in the lightning-rent night, blood-letting with fury. They had all lost friends. The beasts and birds would be bloated from the slaughter-meat. Yet here they now sat. Laughing. Eating. Drinking. Later they would swive their women.

It all seemed like a dream. If he thought too hard on these things, he would drown in the misery of his own thoughts. Scand had told him not to dwell on the past. They were wise words. He missed the old lord.

Beobrand shook his head to free it of darkness the way a dog shakes water from its fur.

He looked for the bench where Scand's retinue had chosen to sit.

He hoped Acennan could also heed Scand's advice.

"Hail, Beobrand!" Derian waved him over and Scand's gesithas shuffled along the bench to allow Beobrand to sit.

Acennan sat at the far end of the bench. Their eyes met briefly as Beobrand sat, but conversation would be impossible. Beobrand was saddened. He wished to be done with the bad feeling between them. But not having the chance to talk with his friend did bring its own relief. He could relax; bask in the warmth of the hall and the men who had taken him in as one of their own.

"It is good to see you, Beobrand," Derian's teeth flashed from his dark, grey-flecked beard.

Sunniva leaned between the two men before Beobrand could answer. He caught the scent of her hair. She handed Beobrand a horn filled with amber liquid. With her other hand she placed a trencher of choice cuts of meat on the board before him. She touched his shoulder softly and gave him a smile that dispelled thoughts of sadness from him. She moved away, serving others. Beobrand watched her go. The sway of her hips reminded him of that afternoon. He sighed. He was blessed in many ways.

As if he could hear his thoughts, Derian said, "You are a lucky one. A woman like that to warm your bed and you have sword-skill to match your strength. I can see why Scand liked you so much."

The mention of Scand made Beobrand scowl. "I am sorry he died," he said.

"We all die, Beobrand. Even the great. Even mighty swordsmen like you."

"Acennan blames me," said Beobrand. He took a long draught from the horn. The sweet mead moistened his throat. He had not realised how thirsty he was.

"Acennan blames himself. But it is easier to cast the blame at you. His anger will not last long. His ire burns bright and hot, like a fir cone tossed onto a fire. And it is as quick to burn out. I have known him for a long time. His anger will be gone soon."

Beobrand was heartened by Derian's words. He took a mouthful of meat skewered on his small eating knife. It was boar. His favourite. Sunniva was a woman to treasure right enough.

"What will we do now?" asked Beobrand. "Now that our lord is gone?"

Derian's face clouded. His brows jutted and he leaned forward. He quaffed some mead and scuffed the back of his hand over his bearded mouth.

"You think we should have died with him? Is that it?"

Beobrand was dismayed. He knew many believed that a lord's gesithas should fall with their master, that anything less was a dishonour. But this seemed madness to him. How could throwing away the lives of warriors be a good thing?

"No... I..." Beobrand stammered, "I meant no offence. I too am alive. Throwing lives away is senseless."

Derian sat in silence for a long moment. He cuffed at his eyes.

"I am sorry, young Beobrand. Scand was the best of lords. I sometimes wish I had fallen that night with him. I feel ashamed to yet live."

Beobrand understood this. Death had often beckoned to him; a release from the woes of this world.

"You knew Scand better than I," said Beobrand. "But I knew him well enough to know that he would not wish your death. He would be proud of the way you led the men after he fell. Your actions turned the tide of the battle. Had it not been for the horses' rout, I believe we may have lost."

Derian nodded, but did not speak for a time. He took another swig of mead before turning to Beobrand.

"My thanks to you. I have said those words to myself, but to hear them from another voice gives them more worth."

Beobrand patted him on the shoulder. He felt clumsy. He was unsure how he had come to this. To be comforting a man old enough to be his father. It seemed wrong somehow, as if he was telling a lie. And yet he could see in Derian's eyes that he had needed to hear the words.

"As to what we do now," said the older man, "I am sure there will be a home for all of us. Many fine men have fed the land with their battle-sweat. Lords will not wish to have empty places at their benches. It is never hard to find a home for a good sword-hand."

They ate in companionable silence for some time.

Beobrand noticed Athelstan, sitting at the board on the other side of the hall. The huge thegn was staring at him. His eyes glittered in the firelight, like torches flickering from dark caverns.

Beobrand held his gaze. He hoped he would not need to fight the older thegn again. If Athelstan kept out of his path, he would not seek him out. He was not so sure that Athelstan would be as careful.

Beobrand looked away. It seemed the numbers of men who loathed him grew by the day. Collecting enemies was a talent he was not proud of.

The hall was rowdy. Loud ale-chatter and mead-laughter crashed off the walls like waves washing down a shingle beach. The living toasted the dead. Boasts and tales were proclaimed. The warriors beat the boards with their knives and fists in approbation.

A slim scop stood at the high table and sang of the great battle. He plucked a lyre. His voice was strong and clear, at odds with his slight form. The audience fell still, listening to the rousing tale of how King Oswald was told by the spirit of Colm Cille to attack at night. The bard left nothing out. He had clearly spoken to the men who had fought. Perhaps he had even been there himself. Apart from the language he used – the flourishes and the kennings – he could well have stood in the shieldwall, though Beobrand did not recall him and he looked as if a strong wind would topple him. Beobrand doubted he would withstand the clash of shield and spear.

Beobrand closed his eyes. Allowed the images conjured by the tale-teller's words to form in his mind. He was talented, of that there was no doubt. More nuanced in his delivery than Leofwine had been, but lacking in the raw power Leofwine was able to conjure.

Leofwine. The thought of him brought anew feelings of guilt. How many deaths could be laid at Beobrand's feet? He had failed to protect Leofwine and now Scand was also dead.

Think of the present. And the future. Do not dwell on the past.

He heard the scop mention his name. He had reached the part of the story where he rode back into the camp with Cadwallon tied to his steed. The men around him cheered at his name. They brought thunder to the hall with their fists on the board. Beobrand was embarrassed, but smiled. The approval of his shield-brothers was balm to his sorrows.

His heart lurched in his chest when he saw that Acennan joined in the cheering.

After the scop had finished his tale and the applause and board-thunder had subsided, King Oswald stood. He held out his arms for silence. The great hall quietened. Talk was hushed. Somewhere at the rear of the hall a man laughed uproariously. His friends, less drunk than him, urged him to keep his voice down.

Oswald stood with his arms outstretched in the now familiar pose until he had the attention of all those gathered. The fire still crackled, the smoke wafting about the rafters like murky seas around the wooden ribs of sunken ships. Dogs gnawed at bones. Benches scraped against the rushes as men shifted to gain a better view. The women ceased their incessant refilling of horns and platters.

Silence was impossible in the great hall during a victory feast, but everyone there wished to hear the words of their king. Now was the time they had all been waiting for and yet could not mention for fear they would curse their own chances. Now was the time of gift-giving, when the king would reward those who had served in the battle. Men's lives would change now. Some would be singled out for great riches. Others would feel slighted by a poor gift.

Oswald was a new king to them. He had proven himself in combat. Now was his time to prove that he was a generous lord. That he was gōd cyning, a good king.

They all listened intently as Oswald began to speak. He spoke in his low tone that forced those listening to quieten even more. As he announced the different gifts, assisted by a scribe at his side who held several sheets of vellum, there were frequent whispers throughout the hall when people misheard and needed to ask others for the words he had spoken.

Beobrand noticed with a start that the scribe who stood by the king was his friend, Coenred. The young monk was sombre and pale. The enormity of his role clearly daunted him. Beobrand tried to catch his eye, but Coenred was too focused to notice. Coenred would read from the vellum quietly to Oswald, who would then speak to the gathering with the names of those he was favouring.

The king was a good speaker. He knew he had the room entranced. The listeners snatched his words away and devoured them like starving gulls catching fish guts thrown into the sea. Each man there was eager to hear his name spoken. Anyone not mentioned by name would receive an agreed share of the spoils of war, but a named gift could bring fame and fortune. With each name, Oswald had the knack of finding the face in the crowd and talking directly to the man.

Many names were called and the night wore on. As each warrior was called, he would stand to riotous acclaim from the hall. He would then approach the high table and the gift-stool, and Oswald would hand him the gift, if it was something that could be proffered directly – a sword, a ring, armour. The warrior would then kneel and renew his oath to the king.

The mead horns were long empty. The fire had burnt down to rippling embers. Many were the smiling faces of those who had received recognition for their efforts. But there were still several men, as yet with no gift, who were finding it increasingly difficult to celebrate their comrades' success.

None of the survivors of Scand's gesithas had been recognised. They fidgeted and grumbled. Beobrand sat silent, brooding. He cared little for the gift-giving. He was nobody. A ceorl who had learnt to wield a sword. An outsider from Cantware. He looked over at Sunniva, who stood in the shadows with the other women. She smiled and he grinned back. He was already rich. All he hoped was that he would be able to find a lord to serve and somewhere where he could settle with Sunniva. He should have no difficulty. His prowess was known and there would be many empty benches as Derian had said.

Hearing the name of the bearded warrior snapped Beobrand back to the present. Oswald had called Derian.

The men around Beobrand erupted in cheers as their temporary leader stood. He walked stiffly through the hall until he stood before Oswald.

The king paused for quiet and then spoke.

"Derian, son of Isen, you served your lord, Scand, son of Scaend, with honour and valour until the end. Even at the sad moment of his passing you did not allow your grief to overcome you. It was you who released the Waelisc horses. That action set in motion the end of the battle and the eventual death of Cadwallon, enemy of God and enemy of Bernicia. We are all in your debt."

Beobrand and those around him thumped the board, making horns, cups, knives and trenchers clatter.

When the noise had died down, Oswald continued.

"For your service I give you this fine blade, which was Scand's. It is a great sword, worthy of a lord, and it will serve you well. Take also these silver warrior rings and wear them with pride."

The sword was in its fine scabbard, but all there knew the quality of the weapon that Oswald had previously given to Scand. The warrior rings glinted in the firelight as Derian pulled them onto his left arm, his chest swelling with pride at the kingly gifts and the recognition of his battle-play.

Oswald again waited for the noise to abate before continuing.

"And I would ask something of you, Derian."

"Anything, my king," said Derian, his voice cracking in his throat.

"I would ask that you join my own comitatus. My closest retinue of warriors must be made up of the most loyal and strongest warriors. You are such a man and I would have you join them. What say you?"

"I am honoured, lord king." Derian knelt and held out the sword Oswald had given him, hilt first. "I offer you my thanks, and my sword. I am your man now and forever."

Cheers from the benches. Beobrand shouted as loudly as the others. Derian was a good man. He deserved his reward.

Derian's eyes glistened with emotion when he returned to the bench. He walked as one in a daze. The men clapped him on the back. They wished to see the treasures he had been given. He smiled sheepishly. He was sure of his own position, but what of the rest of them?

"Beobrand, son of Grimgundi," said the voice of the king.

Beobrand had thought he cared naught for the gifts, yet his stomach lurched at the sound of his name on Oswald's lips. He stood. His hands shook. His legs were weak. He felt as if he was approaching an enemy shieldwall. His heart thundered. He could hear the thump of it.

He walked forward, past the cheering men of Scand's retinue. He flicked a glance at Sunniva. By Frige, she was beautiful! He saw the shadowed features of Athelstan, jaw set and brow furrowed.

Oswald stood patiently waiting before his gift-stool. Behind the king, Coenred was staring straight at Beobrand. The monk gave a small nod. A hint of a smile. So he still had some friends.

Beobrand halted before the king and knelt.

"Beobrand, son of Grimgundi, you were a stranger to me. You are come to us from Cantware. Your past is dark and I have heard tell many tales of your deeds. Many great deeds, worthy of song. Yet others of which I can read the truth behind the tales. You stood with my enemy, Edwin, and they say you travelled with the worst kind of man for a time."

There were murmurs throughout the hall. Much of this was known to many of them. Some could be guessed. Had the king heard all of this from someone? Beobrand felt his bowels clench. It was true. He was an outsider. He had done terrible things. For a moment his mind was clouded with black memories. The bitter, tree-crack winter cold of the forest. Cathryn's pleading eyes. Her blood, frozen into the hoar frost. The smoke billowing from his house in Hithe, his father's weak screams reaching him, as he walked away forever. The thole-creak of a rope swinging from an old yew, as Tondberct's tongue swelled and blackened.

Beobrand looked up at the king. Oswald seemed to glow with an inner light. He was proud and certain when he spoke. Perhaps he was truly blessed by the Christ god. Beobrand lowered his gaze. He was not worthy to look at this fine king.

"Do you deny that which I say, Beobrand?" asked Oswald.

Beobrand could not bring himself to look Oswald in the eye. "I do not." The evil thoughts from his past beat at him like the wings of a great raven. "I have done things of which I am not proud."

Oswald looked wistful.

"We have all sinned, Beobrand. The good Lord died to wash away our sins."

Coenred had told Beobrand of the stories of the Christ and his ultimate sacrifice. Beobrand didn't understand it. He kept his head bowed. Unsure what to say.

"To you, Beobrand, son of Grimgundi, I give you the black stallion you rode and on which you brought Cadwallon to me."

There were cheers from the benches. The stallion was a fine creature, worth many scyllings.

Beobrand sighed in relief. He had begun to expect he would receive no gift. Even that he might be punished in some way for some past crime. The gift of the horse showed that Oswald valued him.

"I thank you, Oswald King," Beobrand said. "It is a noble horse. Black as night and brave as Tiw. I will call it Sceadugenga, for it came to me in the night and brought me through shadows and danger."

"A worthy name for a worthy mount. And there is more." The crowd stilled.

"You are not from this land. I know what it is not to belong. For many long years I was exiled. But I have returned. And you have helped me reclaim that which has always been my right. When you brought Cadwallon to me, you brought me what was most precious. Vengeance and peace for my kingdom and my people."

A riot of noise. Oswald held out his hands for quiet.

"It seems to me that in Bernicia you have found your rightful home. From this day forth, you will be considered a thegn of Bernicia. I bestow upon you the estate of Ubbanford. Ubba and both his sons fell against Cadwallon. Ubbanford is fertile land. Good fishing. But it needs a strong man to govern it. It is yours, but you will see that Ubba's widow and daughter receive their fair share of the spoils of battle. They have lost their men for me, they will not want for comfort in this life."

The men hoomed in their throats and hammered on tables at these words. Oswald was truly a good king.

At last Beobrand looked at Oswald's face. The king smiled. He leaned towards Beobrand and spoke close to him. No other would hear the words over the cacophony of the hall.

"You brought me victory, Beobrand. Victory and Cadwallon's head. You gave me both and I thank you. Now give me your oath and take your prize."

Beobrand recited the oath. He could barely hear the words over the raucous cheering from the throng.

Twice before he had said the oath. Both those lords were dead. Could he have done more to protect them? To keep them from harm? He knew not. But he knew that this new king of Bernicia, a servant of the Christ, had given him more than he could ever have hoped for.

For too long he had yearned to find his place. Now that place had a name.

Ubbanford. His mind swam with possibilities.

He stood and bowed to Oswald.

Turning, he saw Sunniva's wide-eyed look of amazement. He allowed himself to believe what he had heard.

He would wed the most beautiful woman in the land of Bernicia. His land.

And he would wed her at a place called Ubbanford. He had no idea where it was or what it was like, but he knew the most important thing about Ubbanford.

It was his.

And he would make it their home.

8

The sand squelched under Coenred's bare feet. His weight made the water ooze out between his toes. Around his footprints the brine bubbled. He looked back and saw his dried-sand steps leading back to the beach. The mighty crag of Bebbanburg rose in the distance, its presence looming like a sentinel.

He turned to face the direction they were heading. The wind whipped across the wet sand. His eyes watered. All around them wader birds pecked and chirruped as they probed and prodded the ground for morsels of food.

Before them lay the island of Lindisfarena. It was a low, grassy expanse above pale sand. Beyond it lay the dark distances of the North Sea. The Whale Road.

Lindisfarena was windswept. Exposed to the crashing tides. It would be a cold haven in winter.

It was home to birds and seals. There was a small settlement there; ceorls who eked out a life from the sandy soil.

And now it would be home to Coenred.

"Watch where you walk, lad," said the man who led them. He was hunched and bent, like a tree that had grown under the strong winds of Lindisfarena. "Follow my steps. If you stray from the safe path, you can be swallowed up by the sands like a fish gobbles up a maggot." The man's voice was thick. His accent so heavy that Coenred could barely make out his meaning. The man looked at the confused expression on the monk's face and chortled to himself.

"You'll be safe with me," he said. He walked on.

"Wait," said Coenred. "The abbot cannot walk so fast." Fearghas was already some way behind them. Surrounded by the other monks, the elderly abbot shuffled along with the aid of a staff and a hand on the shoulder of Dalston, a pimply youth.

Since they had left Engelmynster to the Waelisc, the abbot had seemed to lose his grip on life. He was old, his hair wispy white, yet he had always seemed hale. The destruction of all he had built in Deira had weakened him. He had begun to look frail. The hard march northward had left him exhausted. Coenred had started to fear the worst.

How would he live without the old abbot? The man had taken him in. Taught him. Cared for him. Given his life purpose. Shown him the way of Christ.

Coenred had been gladdened to see the change in Fearghas when they had met King Oswald on the road and then later at Bebbanburg. The king had been exiled at Hii and Fearghas had known him as a youth.

"Christ is coming to Bernicia, Coenred," Fearghas had said, as Oswald had marched south to confront Cadwallon. "Oswald will be victorious by the grace of God and he will see that the one true faith is followed. He is a believer."

That Fearghas was liked by Oswald was clear. On his triumphant return the king had sought out the old abbot. They had prayed together. Then they had conversed for some time in hushed tones.

"He wishes us to build a monastery," Fearghas had said once Oswald had left. "Just like on Hii. A holy place of solitude from where we can pray and follow the Regula. He has given the island of Lindisfarena to God."

Coenred watched Fearghas now as he tottered across the sand. They could have been taken over by boat at high tide, or ridden over the sands. Oswald would have supplied horses. But Fearghas would not hear of it.

"I wish to walk across the sands that are washed clean every day by the waters of the sea, as the soul is washed in the blood of Christ. It is fitting that the island is baptised each day by the ocean. Lindisfarena is a marvel of the Lord."

Coenred looked at the sea in the distance and recalled the view from Bebbanburg earlier that morning. Then, the sea had covered the sand where now they walked. How could they know that the waves would not come rolling back around and fill the sand-flat between Lindisfarena and the mainland of Albion? They would surely perish. They were a long way from either the beach behind or the island before them.

"Are you sure it is safe?" he asked the islander, who acted as their guide.

The man laughed again. "As safe as safe can be," he said. "The waters won't return for a long while yet. Never you fear. You will come to know the ways of the sea and the sand, like a man knows his goodwife's rump." He cackled at his own wit.

Coenred blushed. The mention of a woman's body reminded him of the devil-sent dream. He had awoken that morning with his rod swollen and throbbing with desire. He had dreamt of the fair-haired beauty from the hall. She was Beobrand's woman. In the dream she had been kissing him. Caressing him. Coaxing his body to a feverish state of arousal. Now, though the dream was long gone, he could not get her face, or the curves of her body, out of his mind. He was certain the other monks could guess what he was thinking.

It was wrong to think of her. He had vowed to abstain from temptations of the flesh. How that would be possible with the dreams the devil sent him, he knew not. Much of the time, his body seemed to rule him. He would see a girl, or brush past a woman, only to find himself becoming aroused. The image of Sunniva, with her cascade of golden hair and lithesome body, had lodged in his thoughts like a tick burrows into soft flesh.

He pushed Sunniva from his thoughts with difficulty. Fearghas and the others had almost caught up. He pressed on, not wishing to talk with them.

He cast his mind back to the previous evening.

It had been good to see Beobrand. He truly was blessed. Or lucky. He was successful in battle. Had the love of the fairest woman and had found favour with the king.

It had come as a surprise when Fearghas had asked Coenred to read the gift-list. Gothfraidh, who had scribed the list, had been taken ill with a fever, and Oswald had asked Fearghas to step in. The elderly abbot had decided he would not be strong enough to stand for so long. So Coenred was appointed to the task.

"It is an opportunity to see a great king at work," Fearghas had said. "Do your job well and heed what is said in the hall. Many great men will be there."

Coenred had been nervous. It was a daunting prospect to stand by the gift-stool. The focus of every eye in the great hall had been on him and the king.

Oswald, sensing his nerves, had spoken to him before the gift-giving began. "You have nothing to fear, young Coenred. Wise old Fearghas has faith in your abilities. I trust in his judgement. And so should you."

Coenred had nodded, flushed with pride. But was unable to reply, so dry was his mouth.

Oswald had passed him a decorated horn filled with mead.

"Wet your lips, boy. You will be talking for some time."

He'd taken a sip, feeling the sweet drink soften his throat. And blunt his nerves.

"Come on, boy," croaked the islander, bringing him back to the present. "When the sea decides to come back and drown these sands, it comes as fast as a galloping horse, so it does."

Coenred ran towards the man with a start. He darted a look over his shoulder to where Fearghas and the others still walked at a sedate pace.

The guide guffawed and slapped him on the back. "It is true that the sea rolls in quick. But not yet." He turned and walked the last stretch of sand up onto the dry beach of Lindisfarena. He giggled to himself all the way.

Coenred frowned. He looked forward to the day that he knew the safe path himself. He did not relish the idea of walking this way again with the crooked islander man. Despite knowing that the man was jesting at his expense, he quickly followed him onto the island. You could never be too safe.

He breathed a sigh of relief. He hadn't realised how tense he had been to be walking on the seafloor.

The wind whipped the hair that hung round the back of his head, as he watched the other monks approach. The wide open space was very different from the monastery in the forest that had been his home for the last few years.

Abbot Fearghas and the others joined them on the shore. Fearghas held out his hands.

"My brothers in Christ. We have all suffered trials in the last weeks. God has tested us. But with His grace we have prevailed over adversities. King Oswald is a good king. A Christ-loving king. And he has gifted Lindisfarena to God and to His work. Engelmynster is no more. We must pray each day for the souls of those who fell protecting us."

Coenred thought of Alric and the other men who had stood in a puny shieldwall against the Waelisc warriors.

Fearghas continued: "But God has provided us with a new sanctuary. We are no strangers to hard work. Saint Benedict taught that 'idleness is the enemy of the soul'. Now we must work harder than ever. Let us go forth and build a monastery before the winter is upon us. Let us turn this island of Lindisfarena into a Holy Island. Now, we shall recite the Pater Noster to bless this place."

The holy men lowered their heads to pray. As they chanted the familiar words of the prayer, Coenred looked about him.

"Pater noster, qui es in caelis: sanctificetur Nomen Tuum…"

The scrub and grassland stretched over a low rise. Gulls cavorted in the strong winds above the monks' bowed heads.

"Panem nostrum cotidianum da nobis hodie; et dimitte nobis debita nostra…"

The islander looked perplexed. Scared of the dark-robed, chanting clerics.

He would come to understand that the Christ is a god of love. As would the other islanders.

"Sicut et nos dimittimus debitoribus nostris…"

Coenred did not welcome the idea of hard work. But standing there, surrounded by men and boys who were his only family now, he was suddenly struck by a strange feeling.

"Et ne nos inducas in tentationem; sed libera nos a Malo."

With the last familiar words of the Lord's prayer still warm on his lips, Coenred realised how this island made him feel.

He had never been to this place before. And yet he felt like he belonged.

Like he was coming home.

Beobrand roused himself from the blankets and cloaks where he lay with Sunniva. His head was tender. His mouth dry. It had been the best of feasts. Woden's hall, crowded with mighty fallen warriors and gods, could be little better.

He rose and pulled on his kirtle and britches, careful not to waken Sunniva. Pale light filtered from small windows. A dim dusty ray illuminated the curve of her breast.

His mind returned to the events of the previous day. Reunited with Sunniva, they had coupled ferociously. His mouth curled in a private smile as he recalled the feel of her. The scent of her hair. The weight of her body pressing on his. Being held firmly inside her. He could imagine no greater feeling.

And then the feast and the gift-giving. He had never believed he would receive such honours from King Oswald. Land. A horse. Riches. It was the stuff of dreams.

He pulled aside the partition and made his way stealthily out of the building. He was not the only one awake, but many still slept. It had been a long night. And the mead had flowed.

Outside in the cool morning air, he sat on a barrel to pull on his shoes. He fumbled with the straps of his leg bindings, cursing quietly under his breath. He still could not get used to the missing fingers on his left hand. He concentrated. After a couple more failed attempts, he managed to get the bindings tied. He missed those fingers. But it could be much worse, he knew. Screams came from a building on the other side of the courtyard. There were many men who had returned from

Hefenfelth with dire wounds. Many more had not returned at all.

He did not wish to allow these dark thoughts to spoil the feeling of happiness that he had woken to. The screams ceased mercifully and he pushed thoughts of death from his mind.

There was only one thing that tainted the otherwise fine morning. Acennan still refused to talk to him. Not being able to share his success with his closest friend weighed heavily on Beobrand. He hoped Derian was right and Acennan would forgive him soon.

He stood and threw his cloak around his shoulders. He was again silently cursing his missing fingers as he attempted to fasten his cloak pin when a shadow fell over him.

Looking up, Beobrand gave a start. It was Acennan, as if summoned by his thoughts.

"Here, let me help you," said Acennan, reaching for the clasp. His fingers were thick and strong, but nimble. The clasp was affixed to the cloak in a matter of a heartbeat.

"Thank you," said Beobrand. "I always seem to need your help." He gave a weak smile.

Acennan snorted.

"I am sorry about Scand," said Beobrand. "We should not have left his side."

Acennan did not reply for some time. Then he said, "I have been giving it much thought. You're right. We should not have left our lord's side. But we did. You had no hold on me. I did not need to follow you. I had no right to blame you for Scand's death. I too am sorry. I did not mean what I said."

Beobrand felt as if sacks filled with rocks had been removed from his shoulders, such was his relief.

"No you didn't need to follow me. But I didn't need to lead you either. I was foolish."

"Well, perhaps I should not have followed. You were not my lord... then."

"Then?" asked Beobrand, his heart quickening.

"Well, you'll need a warband if you are to be a mighty thegn, will you not? Some of the lads and I wish to swear our oath to you. We can think of no better lord to serve." Acennan grinned.

Beobrand returned the smile.

"If you are sure. You cannot have looked far if you can find no better lord than I."

Beobrand grabbed his friend's forearm in the warrior's grip. Gratitude flowed through his body like strong mead.

He had woken with land and riches. Had hoped for nothing more. Yet now his faithful friend had returned to him.

And he had brought a warband with him.

Sunniva was breathless. Everything was happening so fast. The morning after the gift-giving, many of the inhabitants of Bebbanburg had slumbered long after sunrise. But now, as the sun reached its zenith, the place was frantic with activity. The courtyard was full of people and animals, all preparing to leave.

Some had already left the confines of the fortress to return to their halls. Taking with them spoils of war and tidings of victory.

Leaving.

She could hardly believe it was true. It seemed an age since she had known the freedom of walking under the open sky, birds and the rustle of trees her only companions. Instead she had suffered the smells and noises of the overcrowded fortress. As often as she could, to escape the noisome hall where she slept, she would stand on the palisade and look out at the land rolling away to the west and the wide expanse of iron-grey sea to the east. Now, she had come up for one final look before they left.

She looked towards Lindisfarena. Earlier she had watched as the small figures of the dark-clad monks had trudged into the distance, heading for the island. One of them was Coenred, a friend of Beobrand's. She had met the boy the day before and liked him instinctively. When she realised he had saved Beobrand's life and the bond of shared experience they had, she liked him all the more. He was light-hearted and quick to smile. Yet there was a sorrow pulling at the edges of his eyes that she recognised all too well. He had suffered much. She hoped he would find happiness on the holy island where the monks planned to build their home.

A commotion in the courtyard below pulled her attention away. A large black horse was rearing, kicking its hooves out and whinnying. The crowds scattered. An hostler clung to the horse's bridle with his left hand. In his right he held a hazel switch with which he beat the animal about the neck and head. The man was furious and screamed abuse at the beast, all the while laying about it with the whip.

A man stepped quickly from the onlookers behind the hostler. From his ungainly limp she recognised the man as Anhaga, the wall-ward. Anhaga stepped in close and caught the man's wrist before he could continue to torment the creature. Then, snatching the switch from his hand, he whipped it across the face of the hostler.

"Hurts, doesn't it?" he said, his words dripping with anger.

The hostler stood open-mouthed. Shocked at what had transpired. Anhaga thrust the switch into his chest. The hostler took it, still speechless. A red welt was beginning to form on his cheek.

"Now be about your business," said Anhaga. "And do not let me catch you beating another fine horse with no good reason."

The man looked around him. He saw no support from the watching faces. Glowering at Anhaga, he turned and stalked away.

Anhaga took the bridle of the stallion and smoothed its neck with his palm. He whispered soothing words in its ear. The crowds realised there would be no further excitement and carried on with their own preparations for leaving.

Sunniva hurried down the ladder and made her way to Anhaga and the horse. She threaded her way through the people, bales, carts and other horses. By the time she arrived, Beobrand was standing by Anhaga's side and they were deep in conversation.

Sunniva's words of thanks dried in her throat. She had hoped to be able to thank Anhaga for his intervention with Beobrand's steed and then to send him on his way. Much in the same way as he had dismissed the hostler. Not with a switch to the face, but just as quickly. The crippled man unnerved her. She was no stranger to men eyeing her with hunger. But Anhaga's gaze roved over her whenever their paths crossed in a way that made her skin creep.

Upon her arrival, Beobrand and Anhaga turned to her.

"Sunniva," said Beobrand, "by all the gods, I swear you are more beautiful each time I see you." Since the gift-giving, Beobrand's spirits were high. He was energetic and happy. She couldn't remember him happier.

"Thank you, my lord," Sunniva replied, demurely bowing her head with a smile. Beobrand laughed at her use of the title.

"Do you not think she is beautiful, Anhaga?" Beobrand asked.

Sunniva kept her eyes downcast, but could feel the cripple's gaze sliding over her like slimy scrofulous slugs. She suppressed a shudder. Not to worry. They would be gone from this place soon enough. To their new home. Her smile returned and she looked up at Anhaga.

Anhaga's grin was broad. "Indeed, lord. She is as beautiful as Frige herself!"

"I am blessed," said Beobrand.

This talk of gods and goddesses made Sunniva uneasy.

"Thank you both," she said. "Now, we have much yet to do if we are to leave this day, Beobrand. Thank you for the help with Sceadugenga, Anhaga. Now we must be getting on." Sunniva turned away from Anhaga. The implicit dismissal was clear. Beobrand didn't seem to notice, but Anhaga frowned.

"You are right, as always," said Beobrand, with a wink to Anhaga. "There is much to do. Perhaps Anhaga could help you."

"I don't think I need his help," said Sunniva.

"He is a useful man. He knows everyone here, and has a way with horses. And unruly hostlers."

"Yes, but…"

"It will be good for the two of you to get to know each other." Seeing the bemused look on Sunniva's face, Beobrand raised his hand to his forehead. "Of course, you do not know. I have asked Anhaga to join us at Ubbanford. He cannot stand as a warrior. His twisted leg makes it impossible." Behind Beobrand, Anhaga frowned again. "But he is a good man. Honest and hard-working and we'll need a steward to help you run the house."

Beobrand misread the look of anguish on her face as confusion.

"Do not fear. It is all agreed. We spoke last night at the

feast and I petitioned the king to give Anhaga leave to come with us."

Beobrand slapped Anhaga on the back.

"You do as she says, Anhaga. She speaks with my voice. Now I must find Acennan." He strode away.

Anhaga said, "Well, my lady, what would you have me do?"

She watched Beobrand's broad back as he walked away. Sunniva's stomach churned. Of all the news she could have heard this morning, this was the most unexpected and disquieting.

She forced herself to look into Anhaga's eyes. His smile did not seem to reach them. He cocked an eyebrow expectantly.

She could think of nothing to say.

Eventually, all she could muster was, "Do my lord's bidding." With that she turned around with a swirl of her cloak and hurried inside the hall where Beobrand and she had slept.

She had to check one last time that all of their belongings had been packed away.

It was important that she check, she told herself.

She was not fleeing. That would be ridiculous.

By the time they had organised their belongings, the sun was falling into the clouds that loomed over the hills in the west.

"They say that Ubbanford is a couple of days away," Acennan said. "Three if we run into bad weather." He nodded in the direction of the clouds. "Perhaps we should stay here one more night."

Beobrand looked at Sunniva. She was as radiant as ever, but there was a slight pinched look about her eyes. Her lips were pressed thin. She hated it here, he knew. She felt caged; longing to be free of the constant noise and chaos of the fortress.

"No, we leave now and put some distance between us and Bebbanburg before nightfall." He turned to the men who had joined him. With Acennan and Anhaga, they numbered nine. Not an army, but more than a band of thieves. He knew them all. Strong men. Good men.

The oldest of them was Tobrytan. Grey-haired and dependable as a rock. And maybe as slow.

Elmer was tall and broad-shouldered. A solid warrior in a shieldwall, slow to anger, but deadly as an angry aurochs if goaded. When he looked on his wife, Maida, or either of his children, his eyes told of a softness of heart that appealed to Beobrand.

Aethelwulf and Ceawlin were both quiet, taciturn men. Dour and drab of face, they were inseparable friends who rarely smiled. But give them a bellyful of mead and they became as boisterous as puppies; laughing and jesting until falling into drunken oblivion. As their lord, Beobrand would need to take care they did not drink him into poverty.

Garr was tall and slim. He moved with a grace that belied his speed. He was a master in the use of the spear, both held in his hands and thrown. It was said he could throw a javelin further than any other man. Having seen him throwing in practice, Beobrand could not dispute the claim.

Lastly there was Attor. He was fleet of foot and rode as well as the best Waelisc horseman, making him a perfect scout; a role he had often fulfilled for Scand. He shunned garbing himself in iron, instead wearing only cloth and leather in battle. Yet many were the ravens he had fed with the corpses of men who had judged him on his slight form and lack of armour. His lust for blood in battle was the subject of many a mead hall tale.

All of these warriors had served Scand. Beobrand felt

humbled by their trust in him. He hoped he would live up to that trust. He held their lives in his hands now. He was their hlaford. The lord who would provide them with food and gifts, in exchange for their loyal service.

He flushed with pride as he recalled the scene earlier that day when the men had sworn their oaths to him. He had spoken the familiar words before, but had never thought to hear them uttered to him.

Each warrior had vowed his allegiance to Beobrand before the king himself. Oswald sat on his gift-stool in the great hall. He was happy to preside over the oath-taking. Many other unions were sworn that day as thegns and ealdormen heard the oaths of warriors.

The scene had embarrassed Beobrand somewhat. It seemed wrong that these men should kneel before him. And yet it was a solemn moment. It could not be ignored or rushed. The last to swear was Acennan.

"I will to Beobrand, son of Grimgundi," he had said, "be true and faithful, and love all which he loves and shun all which he shuns, according to the laws of God and the order of the world. Nor will I ever with will or action, through word or deed, do anything which is unpleasing to him, on condition that he will hold to me as I shall deserve it."

Beobrand had raised Acennan up from his knees and embraced him.

"I accept your oath, Acennan, son of Bron." He had swept his gaze over his new warband. "I accept all of you with a glad heart." He had looked at the faces staring at him. Hard men. Some bearded. All older than he. His mouth had grown dry. What could he offer them?

"I have been blessed. Our king has seen fit in his generosity to give me land and I am honoured." Beobrand inclined his head to Oswald, who looked on with an amused expression. "And I have been blessed with the bravest and most noble of hearth warriors." Acennan and the others grinned. "I am young, but we have fought side by side and you know me, as I know you. I will not forsake you, as I know you will not let me down."

The men had cheered. Beobrand had blushed, but when he looked at Oswald, the king had nodded in approbation.

Now his warband stood in the courtyard, ready to leave Bebbanburg. Elmer, Garr, Aethelwulf and Ceawlin all brought women with them. Along with those women, there were seven children of varying ages. The youngest was Elmer's boy, still a babe, carried in Maida's arms. The oldest was Garr's willowy daughter, a girl of about ten years.

All of them looked at Beobrand, waiting for him. A score of people looking to him to lead. His throat was thick. It was hard to swallow. Sunniva smiled at him.

Well, if he was going to lead, he would need to start.

"Come, my gesithas. My comitatus. We have fought and returned victorious. Now is the time to reap the rewards. Let us travel to our new home. We have earned the rest."

The sun had disappeared behind the hills in the west when they made camp. The horizon was a dim line of gold, the underside of the clouds aflame with the last rays of sunlight.

They were all exhausted. Beobrand had soon realised that travelling with a lame man, women and children would prove difficult. He was used to a faster pace, but soon after leaving Bebbanburg the tears had started amongst the younger children. In the end, three of the children had ridden on Sceadugenga, while the others were carried, either by their mothers or their fathers.

Anhaga had managed to acquire a mule from the stables

of the fortress too, with the promise that it would be returned at the earliest opportunity. It was fully laden with all of the provisions and equipment they thought it could bear. The morose beast rolled its eyes balefully at them, but walked fast enough without them having to resort to beating it.

"Anhaga is already proving useful," said Beobrand to Sunniva. She did not reply. They looked on as the men and women prepared the camp. "He found us this cave. We'll be glad of it tonight when the rain comes."

Sunniva nodded. There was no denying Anhaga's resourcefulness in obtaining the mule. And finding them shelter from the elements on what looked likely to be a wet night could not be a bad thing. And yet, Beobrand knew that Sunniva was not happy about Anhaga's presence. He was not sure why, but was too tired to pry now. Perhaps it was because he was a cripple. Many believed such men were cursed. He would ask her once they were at Ubbanford.

A couple of the men were lighting a fire under the overhanging slab of rock he had referred to as a cave. Huge rocks made up a deep recess in a hillside. It was not really a cave, being open to the elements at the sides, but it would provide protection from rain. And the heat from the fire would be reflected from the rocks. It was a good place to camp.

Anhaga removed the burdens from the mule and tethered it. Beobrand saw to Sceadugenga himself. Once the animals were tended to and the fire was lit, it was full dark. The younger children were already asleep. The women began to cook a pottage over the fire, using a large clay pot.

Beobrand beckoned to Acennan and the men. They walked some way from the fire and the protection of the cave. Around them was utter blackness. The wind-rustle of trees sounded like cowardly whispers of treachery in the dark. The men's eyes glinted with reflected light from the fire. The scent of damp loam was heavy in the air. It would be raining soon.

"Cadwallon is no more, but we must remain vigilant," said Beobrand. "The land is Oswald's, but it is not tame. Each of us will take a watch tonight."

The men grunted and groaned, but they did not complain. They knew he was right.

After they had gone back to the camp, Acennan placed a hand on Beobrand's shoulder. Beobrand started. He was nervous.

Acennan chuckled quietly. "No need to worry, Beobrand. I know you. You think too much. All will be well. You have me to help you." The stocky warrior walked to the fire.

Beobrand remained at the edge of the camp for some time. Staring into the darkness. The wind was picking up. A chill shivered his spine.

All will be well.

His mother used to say that. He had never truly believed it as a boy. Now, with the weight of new leadership pressing upon him, it seemed a vain hope.

Rain fell noisily in the night. It kept many of them awake. The lip of the cave was veiled in a sheet of water. It was as if they stood behind a waterfall. The small flames of the fire glimmered in the wall of water. A child cried, scared by the constant crash of the storm.

Beobrand was glad that Anhaga had led them to this cave. They were dry and warm enough in the shelter. And yet he could not sleep. What would await them at Ubbanford? He could stand in shieldwalls. Stand toe to toe against a warrior bedecked in war harness. Yet to impart the dire news of the deaths of Ubba and his sons to the lady of the hall was a prospect that filled him with dread.

He reached over to Sunniva's warm form in the darkness. He was gentle, not wishing to awaken her should she be asleep. But he wanted to feel her touch. His hand brushed her back and she stiffened. He withdrew his hand.

"What is wrong, my love?" he whispered, close to her ear. He breathed deeply of the scent of her hair.

For a long while she did not reply. Perhaps he'd imagined her reaction. Maybe she slept still. Then she rolled over. Her face was wet. Slick with tears. His stomach lurched. It pained him to see her thus. But he was no stranger to grief. Sometimes you needed to weep. He reached up and wiped her tears from her cheek. His rough, sword-callused hand felt clumsy against the smooth perfection of Sunniva's face.

"I miss my father and my mother," she said in a small voice.

"I miss my family too," he said. He could not bring himself to speak of his father.

"I have no brýdgifu." Beobrand started at the mention of the bride gift, the dowry paid by a bride's family that would belong to her and her alone.

Sunniva continued: "You need not speak to my family to agree the handgeld. I understand why you do not marry me. There is no need. And I am happy to be yours. I love you. But I had always dreamt of my handfasting to be before my friends and family. Now, I have no family, and my friends are left behind or gone."

Beobrand's heart clenched. He had been blinded by the turn in his own fortunes. He had not seen Sunniva's desires.

"Do not think that I do not wish to marry you," he said, urgency lending a sharpness to his words. "I love you and I must be favoured by the gods themselves to have received so much." Sunniva flinched. He knew she disliked referring to the gods. She believed it tempted them to pay heed to the lives of mortals. Better to be left alone.

"Do not fear for your brýdgifu or the handgeld. I cannot bring back our families." He cursed inwardly at his clumsy words. The handgeld was a price he should have paid to Sunniva's family. To his own ears he sounded more concerned for the cost of their marriage than their love. "But I will see to it that you are provisioned for. Your morgengifu will be fine. I have it all planned," he lied. He would have to think of something to offer her as her morning-gift – the present he would give her on the day after celebrating their marriage. Still, perhaps he could delay the decision for a few days.

"Let us plight our troth tomorrow, here, before these good people. Then we will seal our handfasting with a feast at our new home."

Her tears had ceased. He held her close to him; stroked her hair.

The noise of the rain lessened.

He sensed that the worst of the storm had passed.

The storm blew over them in the night and the day dawned chill and misty. Some of the wood they had stored for the morning had got damp and now the fire smoked and spat like an angry wyrm. There had been no incident in the night and the group seemed in good spirits.

The children ran around the clearing outside the cave. The womenfolk prepared food. The men packed gear into sacks. Anhaga piled provisions onto the mule. It stood, sullen and stolid. Somehow it managed to convey its disgust at being so laden, with a flick of its ears and a snort. Anhaga whispered soothing words to it. The mule seemed unimpressed.

When they had broken their fast and were ready to leave, Beobrand summoned them all.

"There is something, or rather someone, I have neglected over the past few days." The men looked on with interest. The women stood thin-lipped and disapproving. It seemed they knew what and who he had neglected. The thought came to him then that it was these very women who had prompted Sunniva's distress the night before.

He held out his hand to Sunniva. She stepped close and placed her small hand in his.

Her hair shone in the hazy morning light. She wore the blue dress she had worn that summer day back in Gefrin where they had lain together for the first time. Beobrand felt himself stirring at the memory. Gods, now was not the time for that! He looked away from her with a sheepish grin.

He caught Acennan's eye. His friend smiled and winked. It seemed he had a good idea what Beobrand was about to say too. Perhaps they all did.

"I have received many gifts these last few days. Treasure and land from our lord king. Your oaths. But the treasure I value most is here." Beobrand turned back to gaze at Sunniva. She smiled back at him. Her eyes glittering.

"I wish for all of you good people to witness now as I, Beobrand, son of Grimgundi, stand before you with Sunniva, daughter of Strang. I hereby take her hand and with this handfasting I solemnly plight my troth to her until death parts us. Do you, Sunniva, daughter of Strang, plight your troth to me?"

"I do, and gladly," Sunniva said, her voice quiet but steady.

"Then so be it. Let all who have witnessed this know that

we are now wed. I will seal the promise with the morgengifu when we are settled at our new home. At Ubbanford we will also celebrate the handfasting with a feast."

The assembled folk let out a ragged cheer. The women looked less fierce now. They seemed to approve of his actions. Acennan flashed his teeth in a grin.

"Now, let us be on the move," Beobrand said in a loud voice. "The day is free of rain and we still have far to travel."

Everyone moved to ready themselves for the journey. Beobrand noticed with surprise that Anhaga was already limping out of the clearing, the mule plodding along behind him. The man was not the fastest of travellers, but he was eager to please.

Sunniva pulled him close and placed a kiss upon his lips.

"Thank you," she said.

He held her at arms' length and drank in her beauty.

He shook his head. "I should be thanking you," he said.

Part Two
Secrets And Shadows

"Grendles modor,
ides aglæcwif yrmþe gemunde"

"She had brooded on her loss, desolation had brewed
In her heart, that female horror, Grendel's Mother"

—BEOWULF

9

It took them the best part of two more days to reach Ubbanford. It would have taken longer had Anhaga not known the land so well. He led them along paths that could barely be discerned. Tracks overgrown with thick vegetation took them down to infrequently used fords across streams swollen with the recent rain.

The first day they made good progress, though they all grew tired of the children's moaning. More than once a grizzling child would be made to wail when its father became weary of the whimpering. Each time a child was cuffed Beobrand had to strive hard to suppress a shudder. He supposed the shadow of his father would always be with him. But none of these children were treated harshly. Their tired parents would follow a command with a slap, not with a fist.

Beobrand watched Sunniva as they travelled. She loved the little ones, and would often carry the smaller children. What would their children be like? Would he be a good father? Did he carry his father's rage within him? Could he turn into a figure of fear to a child?

His mother had told him he was not his father's son.

He was still unsure about what she had meant, but he vowed he would never allow himself to treat a child or a woman the way his father had.

Beobrand looked forward to reaching their destination. If nothing else it would bring some respite from the noise of women and children. He still dreaded having to bring the news he bore for Lady Rowena. But he was a thegn now, and such was his duty. He could kill easily enough. Now he must learn to lead. Part of that was to be able to give bad tidings as well as good. As with a battle, the waiting before is almost as bad as the fight itself. He wished to have this task over with. The closer they got to Ubbanford, the more withdrawn he became. He knew he had to deliver the news, but he didn't have to like it.

They camped that night on the edge of a copse of blackthorn. As the sun set, they could see in the distance a ring of huge standing stones, black shadows against the glare in the west. They clawed their way out of the earth like the tips of a giant's fingers.

"Is it safe to sleep so close to those stones? Who knows what evil creeps abroad near such ancient cairns?" Acennan asked, though who he addressed was unclear.

Anhaga replied, "I have camped here before and nothing bad befell me." Then, as if an afterthought, "Except for this leg, of course. I went to sleep that night hale. I awoke a cripple." He continued to unbridle the mule. His face betrayed no emotion, though Beobrand was sure he saw a twinkle of humour in his eye.

Acennan spat. "Truly? Then this is a place of evil. We should not rest here."

Beobrand laughed. "Can you not see that he jests? Isn't that so, Anhaga?"

"Of course, my lord," Anhaga answered. Then, after a pause, "If you say so."

"Enough of this," said Beobrand. "The joke wears thin. I do not wish one of the bairns to hear you and be weeping half the night." Anhaga frowned and stomped off to fetch firewood.

"Now Acennan," Beobrand said, "organise the men to keep watch all night. Not for creatures of the otherworld, but for any rogues who would seek to take that which is ours."

A light drizzle fell throughout the night. In the morning they awoke stiff and cold. The scant shelter of the trees did nothing in the face of the soft rain. The damp had seeped into every item of clothing. The moisture seemed to rise as much from the loam beneath them as fell from the leaden sky.

The mood of the travellers was dour. There was little conversation as they packed up the camp and headed north.

"How far now?" Beobrand asked Anhaga.

"Not too far. About half a day at this pace once we pass the stones."

"Good. A dry hall and a warm hearth is what we all need now."

"Aye, and some mead," said Acennan. "Let's not forget mead."

But the mead and hospitality of the hall of Ubbanford would have to wait.

They continued north and a little to the east, crossing several small streams with little difficulty. The hills they traversed now were much smaller than those further south. Yet some were still steep and the drizzle made slopes treacherous. Around midday, they topped a large hill which fell away down to a broad river. At that moment, the murmuring rain ceased and the clouds parted. The sun, unfettered from the clouds, shone brightly, licking the waters of the river as it coiled off into the distance.

Beneath their vantage point, on the southern side of the river, nestled a few buildings. There was a hall, some smaller dwellings, and animal enclosures. Smoke hazed the air above the settlement.

"That is Ubbanford, my lord," said Anhaga.

It seemed a fine place. Cradled in a loop of the mighty river Tuidi and shielded from both north and south by hills, it was all he had imagined and more. He could barely believe it was truly his. He turned to beckon to Sunniva who was making her way up the hill behind him, leading Sceadugenga, who patiently carried four children on his back.

Not his, he corrected himself. Theirs. He would share it all with her.

"Look, my love," he pointed to the cluster of buildings below. "Our new home. Ubbanford."

He looked down again. Eager to take in all the details.

He frowned. Was that a scream he had heard? He scoured the valley for the source of the noise. Movement in the corner of his vision gripped his attention like a hand grasps a throat. There were mounted men outside one of the enclosures. He counted six horses. As he watched, one man dismounted and approached a figure standing at the gate of the enclosure. Then, in the sunlight, the gleam of metal. A vicious blow. Again a scream reaching them on the wind. Thin and distant.

Ubbanford was under attack.

Beobrand turned to Sunniva. "Help me get these children down." He reached for a small boy, whose nose was caked with dry snot. He lifted him from the saddle and placed him on the wet grass. He moved on to the next child, a slightly older girl, who had the sense to hold her hands out to him, making it easier to pick her up. Sunniva sensed his urgency and lifted a third child. Anhaga lifted the fourth.

"What is it?" asked Sunniva, who had not seen what Beobrand had spotted.

Beobrand's face was stern. Hard, blue eyes glaring from deep sockets with the battle fury that had come upon him. He swung up onto Sceadugenga's saddle.

"Acennan, my shield," he said. Acennan did not question him. He had seen the look on Beobrand's face and knew not to argue. He pulled his lord's shield from the pack mule and ran to the black stallion. He helped Beobrand on with the shield straps.

"What is afoot, Beobrand? If we are to fight, you should wear your byrnie."

"There is no time for that."

Beobrand struggled to control Sceadugenga, who had become skittish, sensing the mood of his rider. The horse stepped to the side and threatened to rear. Beobrand tugged savagely on the reins.

"Arm yourselves. Leave the women here with Anhaga. The rest of you follow me. It seems someone is intent on stealing cattle from Ubbanford. And if they steal from Ubbanford, they steal from me."

With that he dragged his heels into the sides of Sceadugenga and the mount leapt forward, galloping down the slope.

The first thing that Aengus mac Nathair knew of the attack from the south was the thrumming of heavy hooves pounding down the hill towards him. He turned to see what was approaching, half expecting it to be one of his own men showing off his horsemanship. Instead he saw a stranger on a huge black steed. The stranger's face was hidden under a metal helm. His dark cloak billowed behind him like the wings of a huge raven. On his left arm he carried a round shield. The central boss gleamed dully. In his right hand he held the longest, wickedest sword Aengus had ever seen.

The hoof-falls drummed like distant thunder. The sheen of the horse's coat gave it the appearance of oiled metal.

The rider was almost upon him. He showed no sign of slowing. Where had he come from?

A moment ago, Aengus had been congratulating himself for silencing the old fool who had sought to stop them taking the livestock from Ubbanford. He had never been allowed to lead a raid before, but his father had given him command this time. After all, word had reached them that Ubba and his sons had died. Ubbanford was ripe for the taking. Women, children and longbeards too old to fight were all that lived there now. But they were rich. Kine, sheep and pigs could all be taken easily.

And Aengus had been itching for a fight. To be able to prove himself to his brothers and his father. He was as strong as Broden and as clever as Torran. He would show them all. His short sword dripped with the blood of the old man he had hacked down. But where he had felt strong and brave a moment before, now his bowels had turned to water.

He stood transfixed in the face of the rider. Where were the others? The men who rode with Aengus? Why did they not move to protect him?

At the last instant, Aengus made a feeble effort to defend himself. He raised his blade and aimed a jab at the chest of the black horse. He mistimed his attack. The full weight of steed and rider hit him with enough force to lift him from his feet and send him reeling to the ground. His sword skittered from his hand.

His breath was forced from his lungs. He could not breathe. He opened and closed his mouth, trying to pull in air.

Beobrand gritted his teeth against the impact with the young man, but when it came, he barely felt it. Sceadugenga crashed into the boy without flinching. The boy careened backwards and fell to the ground, where he lay gawping like a beached fish.

Beobrand pulled on the reins, spinning Sceadugenga towards the mounted riders. They all looked on in disbelief at what had just transpired. But they were armed and posed a threat. He fought to control Sceadugenga, who turned a quick circle. Beobrand could not fight from the saddle. He swung his right leg over the horse's back and jumped from the steed.

He gave a quick glance over at the boy sprawled on the muddy ground near the entrance to the fenced enclosure. He had rolled over and was attempting to rise. But he would be no threat for a moment more.

Seeing Beobrand dismounted, one of the horsemen, a bearded man of middling years, with long dark hair streaked with grey, decided it was time to attack. He spurred his mount forward with a shout of defiance.

Beobrand stepped to the right quickly and smashed his shield boss into the horse's long snout. He delivered the blow with crunching force. The horse whinnied and reared. The bearded man yelped and clung to his reins. The horse bucked and then reared again, pawing the air with its hooves. The man lost the battle to stay seated and fell into the mud. The horse instantly galloped away.

The other four horsemen seemed undecided on a course of action. They sat slack-jawed, holding their mounts steady.

The bearded man sat up roaring, furious at his ignominious fall. Beobrand took three quick paces forward and kicked him in the face with all his strength. Teeth shattered. The man's head snapped back and he collapsed into the mud, senseless.

Beobrand grunted. It felt as though he had broken a toe.

He chanced a quick look up the hill. Acennan and the others were running down the wet grass. They bore shields and spears. The sun glinted from their battle-harness. He bared his teeth in a savage grin. These were his gesithas. His hearth warriors. And they were fearsome to behold.

"Hold!" he shouted at the horsemen. "I do not know who you are, but know this. I am Beobrand, son of Grimgundi, thegn of Lord Oswald, king of Bernicia, and I am the new lord of Ubbanford. You have struck down one of my people and for that I demand payment."

"What payment?" asked one of the men. His accent was thick, the words were not natural for his mouth.

"This one," Beobrand pointed Hrunting at the boy he had charged down with Sceadugenga, "seems brave enough to slay an unarmed old man. I am armed. And I am not old. I demand he fights me." Beobrand walked over to where the boy's short sword lay in the mud. With the tip of Hrunting, he flicked the sword towards the youth. The blade spun in the air and landed close to him. He stood shakily and picked up his weapon.

The horseman who had spoken said, "That is Aengus, the youngest son of Nathair. You cannot fight him."

"I don't care if he is the Christ who some say is the son of a god. He is on my land and has killed one of my own."

At that moment, Acennan arrived with the rest of his warband. They were all panting from the run. But they were not spent. They stood tall and menacing, brandishing their weapons with the assurance of men used to battle-play.

Beobrand noticed other onlookers peering from behind houses. Staring from darkened doorways. The good folk of

Ubbanford were watching. He would show them that their new lord would protect them and exact vengeance from those who crossed them.

He addressed the riders. "The rest of you can go back to this Nathair and tell him that if he seeks to steal from me again he had best be prepared to die." Then, turning to Acennan, "If any of these men interferes with me and young Aengus here, kill them all."

Acennan gave a curt nod.

Beobrand turned his full attention to Aengus. The young man's face was pallid. His eyes were as those of a startled animal. He looked from side to side. But there was no escape.

"It is not fair," Aengus said in a whining voice. "I have no shield or helm." His accent was as heavy as the other man's. They spoke the tongue of the Angelfolc, but Beobrand would wager it was not what their mothers spoke to them.

"Fair? Fair, you say?" Beobrand forced the words past teeth clenched in anger.

Beobrand pulled his war-helm from his head. Dropped it on the turf by the enclosure fence. Then, clumsily, he shook his arm free of the shield straps. He propped the linden board against the wooden gate post, next to the corpse of the old man. The greybeard's shoulder had been hewn deeply. The grass around was stained red. It saddened him to think that he would never know this man who had stood bravely before six armed men.

"Now we are evenly matched, you and I," Beobrand said to Aengus. "We are both young, and we each have a sword. Now use yours. You have my word that should you prevail, my men will allow you all to leave in peace. Do not let it be said that Beobrand, son of Grimgundi, is not fair."

Aengus did not move. His bottom lip quivered. Beobrand

did not want to see him cry. The boy reminded him of Tondberct. He had been happy to kill and rape, but had faced his end with tears and jabbering. A coward's death. Beobrand could almost hear the creak of the rope over the yew branch from where they had hanged Tondberct.

"You had no qualms with using your blade a few moments ago. Now use it to fight me, or I will cut you down where you stand." Still Aengus made no move. So Beobrand closed the distance quickly, raising Hrunting high to give the boy a clear view of his unprotected midriff.

Aengus seized the opportunity. He leapt forward with great speed, sending a darting lunge at Beobrand's stomach. Beobrand dropped the tip of his blade and parried the blow. He took two steps back. The boy was fast.

The spell of inaction now broken, Aengus pressed his attack. He aimed a furious flurry of blows at Beobrand. Beobrand parried and dodged, slowly edging backward. His opponent pushed forward, hope shining in his eyes. Another swinging strike aimed at Beobrand's head. Another parry. The smithy sound of metal on metal was accompanied with sparks as the blades clashed. This had gone on long enough. Beobrand was loath to allow Hrunting's edge to be damaged.

Taking a step back, Beobrand swung his sword wide, leaving himself open. To the onlooking warriors it was clear what would occur next. But Aengus was blinded by his own desperate hope; by the belief that he could best this huge warrior who claimed lordship over Ubbanford.

Aengus lunged at Beobrand's chest. Beobrand spun on his left foot, shifting his body to the right, allowing Aengus' blade to slide harmlessly past. At the same instant he brought down the heavy blade of Hrunting into the young man's outstretched arm. Such was the force of the blow that the arm was severed just below the elbow. Sword and hand fell to the earth. Aengus let out a shivering squeal the like of which none of those watching would ever forget. Blood spouted. The slaughter-dew gushed onto the churned earth.

Aengus fell to his knees. He gripped the stump of his arm to his chest. He mewled and choked. All who watched were silent. They knew the sword-sleep would be upon him soon. Aengus looked around him one last time, his eyes wide. Afraid. Then he slumped to the earth. Still clutching his ruined arm, he moved no more.

The bearded man who Beobrand had felled with a kick stirred and sat up. He groaned groggily.

Beobrand turned to the man who had spoken before. "Get him back on his horse and get off of my land."

The man did not argue. Nobody said a word as they lifted their injured comrade onto his horse. Acennan and two of Beobrand's gesithas lifted Aengus' corpse and placed him on his horse. They used strips of his cloak to tie him to the animal. Acennan handed the reins to one of the horsemen.

The horsemen left Ubbanford in stunned silence. They trotted down to the Tuidi and splashed through the shallow water of the ford. On the other side of the river the path disappeared into dense wood. The riders were quickly swallowed by the darkness under the trees.

Beobrand looked down at his mutilated left hand. It was shaking. The heft of Hrunting in his right hand kept it steady. But the sword weighed heavily now. He examined the blade closely. It was gore-slick. It would need cleaning. And sharpening.

Beobrand snorted without humour. So much for protecting Hrunting from more parries.

Aengus had strong bones.

Where it had sliced through the young man's limb, Hrunting's blade bore a large notch to the steel cutting edge.

Sunniva watched Beobrand with concern. He sat on a bench at one end of the hall of Ubbanford. After the fight he had been withdrawn. His hands shook as he washed them in a basin. The water was the colour of rust when a thrall threw it out into the afternoon sunlight.

She had never seen Beobrand kill before. She knew what he was capable of; had heard the stories. She'd seen him fighting with his fists. But she had never seen him weave the sword-spell that made him so formidable. She had looked on from the hilltop and marvelled at his movements. He seemed to flow like water. The bright blade of his sword flickered. Ripples on a stream.

The suddenness of the violence had shocked her. As had the ease with which he took the young man's life. The spray of blood was clear even from the distance where she waited with the women, children and Anhaga. She had known Beobrand was a warrior. A killer. But she wished she had never seen him fight. His presence had always calmed her. He was her protector. Now she had seen what his protection meant, she could not forget what she had witnessed.

He looked up at her. His eyes were shadowed, his stare vacant. She started. A small tremor snaked up her back.

He was still Beobrand. Her Beobrand. Her man.

"Let me serve you some mead," she said, reaching for a pitcher.

"No, let me," a stern-faced woman said. The older woman lifted the ewer, and filled an earthenware cup that rested on the board before Beobrand.

"Thank you, Lady Rowena," Beobrand said. He shook his head slightly, then drank deeply. He forced a smile. "It is good mead. Thank you for your hospitality. I wish we could have met under better circumstances." Beobrand swept his eyes around the room, as if expecting an enemy to leap from the shadows. The hall was warmly furnished with wall hangings. A small fire crackled merrily on the hearth, the smoke wafting up to hang in the rafters before seeping into the blackened thatch. The hall was not large, but it was well appointed and comfortable.

Rowena and her daughter, Edlyn, a gangly girl with dark tresses and huge, limpid eyes, had approached them after the horsemen had crossed the ford. The lady of Ubbanford had introduced herself and her daughter and welcomed them into her husband's hall. Beobrand had told Acennan and the rest of the men to stay outside. To keep watch in case the raiders returned. And so that he could talk to Rowena without an audience.

"Nonsense," Rowena had said. "Those bastard Picts won't return today. Leave a couple of men. The rest, and the women and children must come inside and eat. My husband may be… away, but let it not be said that Ubbanford is a mean hall."

She set the thralls and village women scurrying about to prepare food for her guests. Cheese, ale, mead and bread were soon on the board.

"Later we can eat meat," she said. "But for now, slake your thirst and fend off your hunger with simple fare."

The men and their families set-to and the sound of contented eating and drinking filled the hall.

At last, her duties as hostess seen to, Rowena came and sat at the high table with Beobrand and Sunniva. Edlyn came and sat at her mother's side.

For some time, none of them spoke. Then Rowena said, "Killing Aengus was not wise. His father, Nathair, and his other sons will seek blood payment for his death. We are few here. They are savages. They will return and we will pay the price for your quick anger."

Beobrand bridled.

"They had killed one of your men. I sought to avenge him."

"Yes. Poor, brave, Ahebban. I do not feel sorry that you killed that turd Aengus. I give thanks to Woden for his death. Yet weregild for Ahebban's murder would have been more use to me than a bloodfeud."

Beobrand frowned. She was right. He'd been a fool to allow himself to give in to his battle lust. "I am sorry, my lady. You speak words of wisdom. But I could not stand by and allow the slaying of one of my people go unpunished."

"Your people?" She raised an eyebrow, inquisitively. "I thought I heard you say before that you are the new lord of Ubbanford. There can be only one reason for this. Tell me what tidings you bring."

Beobrand flushed. How could he be so clumsy? The mead churned in his stomach. He had stumbled to this moment he had hoped to approach with caution. Now there was no turning back from the course.

He stood and called out in a voice that carried over the conversations and eating, "Acennan, fetch the items we are to present to the Lady Rowena."

Without replying, Acennan rose and left the hall.

Beobrand looked down at the Lady Rowena. Her dark hair was streaked with silver. It was braided and tied back. She was no beauty, but she was striking. She reminded him of his mother. He stood solemnly awaiting Acennan's return.

The hall fell quiet as Acennan strode up to the high table carrying a small chest and a cloth-wrapped bundle. He placed them on the board and retreated.

Beobrand unwrapped the bundle to reveal a scabbarded sword. He held it out to Rowena hilt first and knelt before her. Beside her, Edlyn let out a small sob.

"My lady, here is your husband's sword. It is with a sad heart I must tell you that Ubba, son of Ubben, fell defending Bernicia and King Oswald in the battle south of the Wall."

The hall was still. Even the smallest children seemed to sense the solemnity of the moment.

"And my sons?" Rowena almost whispered, yet all there heard her words. "What of Almund? And Ealdian?"

"I am sorry, my lady. They fell with honour. They died where the fighting was fiercest. They stood bravely and fought well. You should be proud."

She was silent. Beobrand did not know what else to say.

Rowena's lips pressed together tightly. Her forehead wrinkled. Her eyes glistened. But she did not cry. Edlyn let out a ragged gasping sob and crumpled into her mother's arms. Rowena stroked her daughter's hair, but kept her eyes fixed on Beobrand.

"What is in the chest?" she asked.

Beobrand lifted the lid. Silver glinted inside.

"King Oswald bade me convey his thanks for the faithful service of Ubba, Almund and Ealdian. Many others did not heed his call to arms. This portion of the spoils of the battle is for you and your daughter. You should not want. Your men made the greatest sacrifice and they will not be forgotten."

Rowena brushed her fingers over the contents of the coffer. The cold chink of metal reminded Beobrand of the rattle of a byrnie.

"And you are my new lord?" Rowena asked, fixing him with a cool stare.

He swallowed. "King Oswald has gifted me Ubbanford. I would be honoured if you would stay and offer me your counsel."

"What counsel could I offer you?" Her voice was desolate. Barren. "You are like all men. You believe every problem can be solved with metal. Iron or silver do not bring happiness." Rowena's eyes flicked to Sunniva, who stood to one side, where she nervously shuffled from one foot to the other.

A ghost of a smile played on Rowena's lips for a moment. "Though perhaps you know that already, young Beobrand."

She stood abruptly. "For now, eat, drink and rest, my lord," she emphasised the last two words, "while my daughter and I retire to grieve in peace. We will see what counsel I can give you later."

With that she swept from the room, behind the partition at the rear of the hall, ushering Edlyn before her.

10

Dead.

Coenred could scarcely believe it.

Yet there he lay. His skin sallow and waxy. Never to move again in this world.

Abbot Fearghas had left them peacefully enough. After the violence and savagery of the last year, it was a blessing that the old man had been allowed to slip away into the arms of Christ surrounded by those who loved him.

He had been unwell for many days. The brief improvement Coenred had seen in him after they had met with King Oswald was quick to fade. His new vigour was short-lived, like the flame-flare of fat dripping onto a fire. Fearghas had directed the monks in the construction of their new home, but before they had even completed digging the vallum, he had begun to cough, a dry, hacking bark that reminded Coenred of the voice of the seals that thronged the beaches and waters around Lindisfarena.

They had taken the old abbot to the house of Ecglaf, the villager who had guided them from Bebbanburg. He was a man of some standing amongst the island folk. Ecglaf's wife, a woman who looked enough like Ecglaf to have been his sister, cared for Fearghas, brewing herbal infusions and rubbing foul-smelling unguents on his chest. But his cough grew ever worse.

The brethren had prayed for their abbot, but he'd urged them to continue digging the perimeter for their new monastery. They were to construct simple round huts within the confines of the trench.

"You will need the cells to be complete when the new abbot arrives," Fearghas had said when some of the monks advocated concentrating on their prayers for the sick abbot. A sudden bout of coughing had racked him. He'd spat into a bowl and then fallen back onto the mean bed where he lay.

"But you are our master," Coenred had said.

Fearghas had lain silent for a long while. His rheumy eyes had played over the gathered faces of the monks who surrounded him.

"I was never your master," he'd said. His voice had rasped like flint scraping flint. "I was your abbot. Your father in Christ. And I will go to sit with him soon." His eyes had seemed to focus on the soot-streaked thatch above him. Perhaps he could see through the roof. To heaven itself.

The monks had leaned in close. Fearghas was so still. Deathly pale and unmoving. They believed he had spoken his last when he coughed again, making them start.

He had laughed then, until the coughing seized him.

"How I love you all," he had said, when he was able to speak once more.

Coenred had stepped close. Lifted a cup of water to his lips. The stench of decay lay upon Fearghas. Oozed from him. Wafted from his mouth as if his very insides were rotten.

"We love you too, father," Coenred had said. And in that

moment he had known it was true. He felt tears well. His eyes burnt. His throat grew tight.

Fearghas' hand gripped his with a strength that belied his frailty. He fixed Coenred with one of his infamous looks.

"Coenred, my son. You must take news of my passing to King Oswald. Remind him of his promise to God. This island is to be Christ's forever."

The tears had fallen then. Droplets pattered on Fearghas' robe, darkening the wool. "Yes, father," said Coenred. "But do not speak so. You will not die."

"We all die, Coenred. As you well know. Take the tidings of my end to the king. And tell him to send for a bishop. This land needs a shepherd. A shepherd from the blessed isle of Hii. You must bring a bishop back. You and that Cantware warrior friend of yours. You'll need company on the journey, for it is long."

Tears had blurred Coenred's vision. Fearghas' white hair wreathed his face, as if it rested on a cloud.

Coenred felt the old man's bony dry fingers squeeze his hand one final time. "Bury me on this Holy Island. Overlooking the sands which are washed clean each day."

Fearghas had spoken no more. His hand had fallen from Coenred's grasp, to lie limply upon the abbot's chest.

The monks wailed. They would pray for Fearghas' immortal soul all the long night, keeping vigil over his earthly remains.

Coenred did not pray. Nor did he wail. He looked down at the body of the man who had saved him and wept quietly.

The lilting sound of the Latin of the monks' prayers washed over him like the sea washing over the sands, cutting it off from the mainland.

After some time, Coenred couldn't help but smile at the old man. Even in death Fearghas had seen fit to give him a difficult task to perform. Take news of the abbot's death to the king. And then bring a bishop from the island of Hii.

Coenred had no idea how to get to Hii. All he knew was it was further than he had ever travelled. It was so far away that it was in a different sea to Lindisfarena.

Was this one last punishment for being a poor student?

"You are sure of this?" Acennan asked. The dappled mare he rode was smaller than Sceadugenga, but as only Beobrand and he were riding, they could talk without fear of being overheard. The rest of the warband trudged behind them. They wore what armour they had. They each carried spear, seax and shield. Their gait was easy enough, but their faces were grim. There was every chance they were walking into a fight.

"I am sure," replied Beobrand. "The Lady Rowena's first words to me were that I had been unwise to kill the boy. She was probably right."

"It is what we love about you," Acennan said, smiling. "You do not think too much before acting. No warrior wishes to follow a lord who treads as careful as a barefoot man in a forest filled with thorns."

Beobrand snorted. "I must talk to this Nathair before he sends his men back to Ubbanford. A bloodfeud must be avoided. Winter will be tough enough, without worrying about our neighbours."

They turned a bend in the path. Beobrand straightened his back and peered into the distance. The land was all new to him. They travelled a well-worn track, through dense forest. Perfect land for an ambush. It was unlikely, but he was well aware that he had already ensured they had enemies north of the Tuidi.

Two days had passed since they had arrived at Ubbanford. It was very possible that Nathair had already decided to retaliate for his son's death. Beobrand hoped Rowena was right when she said the old Pict would not act rashly.

Following the announcement of her husband and sons' deaths Rowena had taken some time to compose herself, but from that moment on, she had been a perfect hostess. It was clearly a difficult situation. Beobrand had brought more mouths to feed into the small settlement. And there was only so long they could all dwell under the same roof, in the hall that Rowena had called her home since her marriage to Ubba many years before.

The men who had women began building new houses the day after they arrived. The river valley rang with the sounds of axe on wood and the thud of wedges being driven into logs to split planks. Smoke drifted from firepits where wet wood was buried to enable it to be bent and fashioned for walls and fences. The people of Ubbanford joined the newcomers. The sooner the new families had homes, the less chance they would need to accommodate them in their own huts.

Seeing the activity gave Sunniva the idea for how to solve the problem of Rowena and the hall.

"You must tell her that you will build a new hall for us, Beobrand," she had said to him that night as they lay together in the dark warmth near the hall hearth embers.

Beobrand had been almost asleep. His mind was wandering into the forests of his dreams. Her voice pulled him awake. He thought for a moment. Knew she was right. As usual. Were women ever wrong? He grinned in the darkness. He pulled her close and kissed her. She returned the kiss and let out a small sigh of pleasure.

"I thought you were asleep," she said.

"I would be, if you'd stop your prattling!" he replied, receiving a playful slap for his cheek.

"You are right about the hall. Rowena must keep her home. And anyway, when retainers flock to me, I'll need a larger hall than this." He spoke only half in jest. Just days before he would never have believed he would have had his own warband. Now he dreamt of a great hall filled with a throng of gesithas.

"I will talk to her tomorrow," he said, kissing her again. "And I will say we should plan a feast to celebrate our handfasting."

A fox burst from the cover of the undergrowth, spooking the horses and bringing Beobrand back to the present. Sceadugenga skittered to the side, colliding with Acennan's mount. Beobrand tugged on the reins until the stallion was once more under control. The fox seemed as surprised as they were. It blinked at them for a moment, still, as if frozen. It then disappeared into the brush at the other side of the path. A streak of red fur in the forest gloaming.

Acennan's mare, a solid, docile animal, seemed hardly to notice that anything untoward had occurred.

"Your horse is as dull as you," Beobrand said.

"And Sceadugenga acts first before thinking of the consequences, just like his rider," replied Acennan instantly.

Beobrand laughed. He was glad he could count on Acennan's friendship and humour once more.

Up ahead the forest thinned. The grey light of the overcast day washed onto the path. They had been walking for a long while. Beobrand reined in and turned in the saddle to address the men. His men. He was uneasy sitting astride the steed while they walked.

As they didn't have enough horses for them all to ride, Beobrand had wanted to walk along with his gesithas. Acennan would not hear of it. "You must ride," he had said. "The men need to look up to you. You are young, but they respect who you are in battle. But you are not their friend any longer. You cannot seek to be liked by them. Or to be one of them. They must respect you. Love you. Fear you even. You must be a lord. You must ride."

In the end, Beobrand had agreed. He saw the sense in what Acennan said, but he had made Acennan ride with him. If he was to be apart from the men, he needed at least one ally.

Now he surveyed the warriors' expectant faces and he saw Acennan was right. They looked up to him. He could feel the weight of their expectation. He would not let them down.

"We are getting close to Nathair's hall," he said. "Lady Rowena said it lay not far beyond the forest edge. You will keep your blades sheathed. I do not wish for more bloodshed. I will talk to this Nathair. We will not fight. Any man who starts a fight will answer to me." He cast his gaze across all of the men. He saw only earnest concentration and belief in him gazing back.

"Come, my gesithas, let us show this Pict who his new neighbour is." He swung Sceadugenga's head round and touched heels to his flank.

The hall and the surrounding buildings were as Rowena had described to him the day before. A dour longhall hunched in the middle of a group of smaller buildings. The hall's roof was moss-strewn and ragged. White smoke trailed from several of the squat huts to be lost in the low cloud that brooded over the village. The smell of woodsmoke and cooking reached them. A stream ran across the path. Several lichened planks spanned the brook.

Beobrand hesitated for a heartbeat, before urging Sceadu-genga to cross the boards. He prayed a silent prayer to Woden that the bridge was stronger than it appeared. His horse's hooves clattered over the wood, which seemed sound enough. He heard Acennan's mount crossing behind him.

A scream rent the tranquillity of the scene. Sceadugenga's ears lay flat on his head. He tossed his mane. Beobrand held the reins in his left, half-hand and patted the stallion's neck with his right.

A woman, who had evidently been washing clothes by the stream, ran as fast as she was able towards the buildings. She screamed all the while in a tongue that Beobrand did not comprehend. She was a plump, comely young woman. Her hair streamed behind her as she ran. Her breasts and buttocks bounced and jiggled fetchingly beneath her dress.

"By Frige, I think I'm in love," said Acennan.

Beobrand shot him a cold look. Now was no time for jests.

Figures began to congregate before the hall. Some carried farm tools. Some bore spears. All were armed.

Beobrand continued to ride slowly forward. To halt now would be to show fear. He sat tall in his saddle. Expression stern. Back straight. He kept his eyes fixed on the hall. At the edges of his vision he detected movement. Women and children ran for cover. Heading for sanctuary in some secret part of the forest. Perhaps some would even hide inside a hollow tree, just as he and Coenred had hidden from marauding Waelisc warriors all those months ago. To be the bringer of fear to the inhabitants of this place saddened him. Yet he knew it must be so. He meant no harm to those who fled, but should the men stand against him, he would give them no quarter.

He reined in Sceadugenga in the open area before the hall. The crowd of people shuffled nervously. Their loathing for him came off them like a stench, yet nobody had the courage to speak out.

Beobrand waited until Acennan, seated on his mare, was positioned to his right. He heard his gesithas come to a halt behind them. The villagers' eyes darted from the mounted thegns to the grim-faced shield-bearers arrayed in a wall of wood and metal.

"Nathair!" Beobrand shouted. There was no response. The villagers fidgeted. Some threw glances over their shoulders, looking for their lord.

"Nathair!" he repeated. "I would talk with you. We do not come to fight."

There was a long pause.

"Perhaps this Nathair is too frightened to show himself," said Acennan.

Beobrand ignored his friend. His gaze was fixed on the door of the hall. A swarthy man with bald pate and straggly grey hair stood there. Either side of him were two young men. One was broad and burly, like the old man. He held a large axe in his massive fists. The other was slimmer and carried no weapon. And yet he was somehow more forbidding. Weasel-quick eyes seemed to miss nothing.

Several other men followed them out of the hall-gloom. They blinked at the hazy light. Beobrand recognised the men who had ridden with Aengus. The black-bearded warrior he had felled with a kick glowered through bruised and puffed eyes. He would not hesitate to kill Beobrand if given the chance.

The crowd parted. Allowing their leader and his retainers to step from the hall and approach Beobrand. Though Nathair did not come too close.

"I am Nathair mac Gaven, lord here," the balding man said, his voice clear, yet thickly accented. He stared directly at Acennan and said, "And I am not too frightened to show myself."

Acennan flashed his teeth in a grin.

"You must be the new lord of Ubbanford," Nathair said, turning back to Beobrand. "It was you who killed my son, I am told."

"I am Beobrand, son of Grimgundi, thegn of King Oswald and the lord of Ubbanford. And I did kill your son."

Nathair looked down at the ground. Sighed deeply. "A lord must protect his own," he said after some time. "Why have you ridden here today? We are still mourning our loss."

"I come to tell you that I slew your son as payment for the murder of one of my people. I do not seek to quarrel with you. I do not wish for a bloodfeud between us. I look for peace."

"I understand," said the old Pict. "A feud would be costly. Many would die. These lands are tough enough, without fighting your neighbours."

The axe-wielding man stepped forward. "You dare come here? You talk of peace, yet you murdered my brother. You are right to fear the bloodfeud. I will not rest until you are food for the fox and the crow. I will drink my mead from your skull before I am done."

Beobrand placed his hand on Hrunting's hilt. His eyes were the colour of a cloudless winter sky.

"If you force me to draw my blade, it will not be sheathed until it has drunk its fill. I warn you once more. Do not seek revenge for your brother's death. Do not come to Ubbanford to steal livestock. Do not raise a hand or weapon against my people, or I will descend upon this place with Thunor's fury."

Beobrand encompassed his warband with a wave of his hand. "We all stood in the darkness at the Wall, as Cadwallon's force crashed against our shieldwall. We held back the king of Gwynedd at the ford of Gefrin. I do not recall seeing your faces there."

Nathair stared at Beobrand with defiance. The son with the axe cast his eyes down. Perhaps in shame.

"Ubba and his sons answered their king's call. They paid with their lives, and their names are spoken with reverence. They have glory in death. They answered Oswald's call, while you Picts cowered north of the Tuidi." He thought of Scand and the countless others who had stained the earth red at Hefenfelth. "You were quick to ride on Ubbanford when it had no lord." Beobrand felt the battle fury surging within him. He gritted his teeth. Held back the ire.

"I will not warn you again. If you cross me or mine, I will slay you all. Leave us be, and you can live in peace. A peace bought for you with the blood of others braver than you."

Nathair's face was thunder. "You would speak to me thus? Here? Before my people? My son's corpse lies in the hall. Talk not of bravery and sacrifice. Where was Oswald last winter when Cadwallon's wolves stalked the land? Where was his brother, Eanfrith? We defended ourselves then."

"Enough!" shouted Beobrand. Sceadugenga started and shook his mane. "Is this not the land of Bernicia? Then your king now is Oswald. He is returned from exile and he has defeated Cadwallon. Go to Bebbanburg and swear your oath to Oswald. He is your lord, or this is not your land." He let the threat hang in the air.

Nathair opened his mouth as if to speak and then thought better of it. He was pale. With fear or anger, Beobrand could not tell. His son did not meet Beobrand's gaze. His knuckles were white on the axe-haft. The dark eyes of the thin man on the other side of Nathair did not flinch. There was a cunning there. And a malice. But above all, there was hate. By Woden, he hoped that they would listen to his words.

"I have said that which I came to say," said Beobrand. "Heed my words. Do not provoke me."

Beobrand pulled hard on his reins, swinging Sceadugenga's head to the left. Acennan followed him.

His gesithas parted to allow them to pass, then turned and followed Beobrand and Acennan out of the settlement.

When they had clumped across the boards over the stream, Acennan turned to Beobrand. "That went well," he said with a broad smile on his lips.

In Ubbanford the building of new homes continued. The weather remained dry, but a chill seeped into the valley, reminding them all that winter was on its way. Each day the people of Ubbanford, both newly arrived and old inhabitants alike, set to the work needed to provide shelter and food over the coming months. Lumber was brought from the forest, while the children and women foraged for mushrooms and acorns. Fish and eels from the river were smoked over wooden frames. The high field was ploughed and winter barley sown. New friendships were forged with the sweat of hard labour as men and women pushed themselves to have all the preparations ready by the first frosts and snows they knew would come.

The mornings were dank and misty. The wide river that ran to the north of the settlement was often fog-cloaked. The weak winter sun struggled to burn away the mists, but by the afternoons, the sky was clear. They knew the still weather would not hold for long. Blotmonath approached, with the slaughter of livestock. And as sure as salmon swim up the Tuidi, winter storms would come.

The sound of hammer on anvil rang out. More piercing than the dull thuds of wooden mallets being used in the construction of buildings. Beobrand smiled at the sound. Sunniva had been overjoyed to find that there was a working forge in Ubbanford. But the realisation had been tainted when Rowena had told them that Ahebban, the man killed by Aengus, had been Ubbanford's smith. Rowena was shocked when Sunniva offered to work the forge.

"Surely you do not have the skill or the strength," she had blurted out. Then, seeing the look on Sunniva's face, she had quickly changed course. "I mean no offence, but I have never heard of a lady who can work metal."

Sunniva had smiled. "I do not have my father's skill, or strength, but I assure you I can wield the hammer and work iron as well as most smiths. It will be good to be useful."

To her credit, Rowena had recovered her poise quickly. Turning to her daughter, she asked, "Edlyn dearest, would you like Lady Sunniva to teach you?" Edlyn had remained shy and solemn since their arrival, but she was clearly entranced by Sunniva and was never far from her. Finding out that the beautiful lady she admired could also perform work traditionally carried out by men, only made her more admirable in Edlyn's eyes.

"Oh yes, please, mother," she had replied, her eyes aglow with the promise of spending time with Sunniva and learning something special.

And so it was that Beobrand found Sunniva and Edlyn at the forge. He stood for a while, watching their progress. Both had their hair tied back safely away from the sparks and fire. Sunniva lifted a piece of metal from the anvil and doused it in a bucket. The water hissed and steamed angrily. Edlyn said something that he couldn't make out. Sunniva laughed. It was the best of sounds. To see Sunniva happy brought him great joy.

Anxiety at his new responsibility gnawed at him. Had it

been wise to go to Nathair? He felt it was the right thing to do, but he was worried that perhaps he had stirred more air into the coals of the Pict's hatred for his son's slayer. Acennan had said he thought Beobrand could not have done differently. After all, Beobrand was a sworn thegn of Oswald now. And the Picts must also swear their oath to the new king.

"They will not want more bloodshed," he had said. "They'll leave us alone now. Like a beaten dog."

Beobrand hoped his friend had the truth of it. Some beaten dogs turn mean. And bite.

But so far they had seen no more of Nathair or his sons. Ubbanford was peaceful apart from the constant noise of activity.

Sunniva saw him standing lost in his thoughts.

"Well, my lord, to what do we owe the honour of your visit to our lowly smithy?" she said. She went to him and kissed him lightly on the cheek. Edlyn giggled.

Beobrand grinned. He could not be anxious in the face of such cheery beauty.

"The two of you shine brighter than the sparks that fly from the iron you work," he said. Edlyn blushed. Sunniva raised an eyebrow and stepped in close. She whispered in his ear, her breath hot against his cheek, "And do I stoke your fire too?"

Beobrand flushed. By all the gods, Sunniva was as alluring as Frige herself! He knew not how to respond with young Edlyn looking on.

"We shall see later," he answered at last. Sunniva winked at him impudently. He felt himself stirring. He forced himself to focus on the reason for coming to the forge. "I came with a message from Lady Rowena. We have decided that there will be a feast two days hence. We will make the Blotmonath sacrifice and then celebrate."

"A feast," said Edlyn, her voice flat. "To celebrate what?"

All the joy and humour was gone in an instant, like spit on the forge fire. The girl had just lost her father and brothers. He could understand why she felt little inclination to be festive. Beobrand frowned, angry at himself. What could he say?

Sunniva came to his rescue. She turned to Edlyn and placed a hand upon her shoulder.

"It has been a year of much sadness for us all, Edlyn. We have all lost loved ones." Sunniva's eyes brimmed with tears, a reflection of Edlyn's own tear-filled gaze. "But there is much to celebrate. We celebrate that we still live. Beobrand and I wish to celebrate our handfasting with all of you. And we also wish to give thanks that we have found such good friends as you. Will you not join us in the feast? We would not be able to find joy without you there."

Edlyn rubbed her eyes with the back of her hands.

"Of course I will join the feast, Sunniva," Edlyn said at last. She sniffed.

"Good. Your mother, you and I will spend this evening planning and preparing what we shall wear. It will be a welcome diversion." Sunniva met Beobrand's gaze again. He nodded his thanks.

She had such an easy way with Edlyn. And with the smaller children of Ubbanford.

In two days they would celebrate the harvest of the land, make sacrifice for Blotmonath and celebrate their handfasting.

Sunniva loved children. Perhaps Frige would bless them with a child soon. They certainly ploughed that furrow often enough. Would their wyrd bring them a child? A strong boy as Sunniva had promised him?

Now that would be something worthy of a feast.

11

The smoke from the pile of wood billowed. The damp wood spat and guttered angrily. Sunniva blinked as the acrid clouds wafted into her eyes. She would have thought that she would no longer cry when standing near a fire, having worked at the forge all her life. Yet still the slightest hint of smoke and her eyes streamed. And this was not even a fire worth speaking of. There was wood aplenty, but it was wet and refused to take. She should have been asked to stack the woodpile. She would not have allowed this to happen. To allow the fire not to light. To do so would be to show that the gods had turned their faces from Ubbanford.

This was the Blotmonath sacrifice. There was always a fire, the flames taking the sacrifice to the gods. The sacrificial oxen's blood lifted to Woden's corpse hall as a smoke-gift.

The sun had set, an afterglow in the west showing where it had fallen beyond the horizon. The fire should have been ablaze by now.

Sunniva shivered. All around her stood the residents of Ubbanford. They awaited the sacrifice. And the fire. More smoke churned out of the wet fuel. A sudden downpour had soaked the wood shortly before they had gathered here. Everything else was ready for the feast. They all wore their finest clothes. The men had combed their moustaches, and polished their warrior rings, those that had them. The women wore such jewels as they possessed. Some had woven dried flowers into their hair.

Now here they all stood, unable to complete the ritual of Blotmonath.

It was a bad omen.

The gloaming grew closer in the valley. The ox that was tethered to a post lowed pitifully, as if it knew its fate.

Yet still the wood smoked and spluttered. A mere splash of the ox's lifeblood would snuff out what sparks there were.

The people fidgeted nervously. They looked at Beobrand and his gesithas. Cast glances at Sunniva. These outsiders had brought ill fortune to their hamlet, those faces said.

The wind came as sudden as a bad dream. The trees on the other side of the Tuidi whispered in the distance and then small tongues of flame licked the logs, fanned by the breeze. For a few heartbeats they were all silent, raptly watching the fingers of fire. Then, with a sound partway between a sigh and a cough, the wood erupted into flame.

Sunniva breathed again. She had not been aware that she was holding her breath.

Beobrand turned to her. His face was drawn. He too must have been worried. He smiled briefly, with relief, it seemed to her, then stepped forward to address the small crowd.

The brilliance of the firelight threw the rest of the valley into darkness. It was as if they alone existed on middle earth. The land beyond the fire-glow was hidden in shadows. The sky was a smothering cloak. The flickering light from the flames lit Beobrand's face. His blond hair, reddened by the firelight, blew back from his face. To Sunniva's eyes, he seemed wreathed in fire.

All around, the eyes of the Ubbanford folk glimmered.

"Old and new friends alike, we are gathered here to shed blood. The cold of winter is breathing at our gate. Soon frost and snow will cover the land. As every year, it is custom to slaughter the cattle that will feed us through those long cold months. With this first slaying we pay tribute to the gods. The gods of the earth and of the sky, that they may watch over us in the long dark times until the new year is born."

Sunniva was pleased to see some of the villagers nodding in approbation of Beobrand's words. His youth worried him, she knew. He feared his elders would not respect him. But he spoke well. Men listened. He would be a good hlaford to them. Of that she had no doubt. The ceorls just needed to see it too. They had seen him wield his sword in their defence. Now they would see him in a different light. That of provider and leader of the feast.

Beobrand continued, raising his voice above the crackle of the fire and the rustling trees on the river bank. "I pray to Woden, father of the gods, to watch over us with his one eye and to bring me wisdom. I ask the goddess, Frige, to accept the offering we make here to enrich the soil so that our seeds will grow next year. And I ask Thunor to cast his hammer on others this winter and to leave us be."

One of the older men hoomed deep in his throat.

Beobrand pulled his seax from his belt sheath and stepped towards the ox. The beast rolled its eyes.

Acennan and Anhaga gripped the animal's horns, holding its head steady. As befitted her rank, Lady Rowena approached with a large earthenware bowl. The world beyond the firelight was black now. There was nothing else. Just the folk, the fire and the sacrifice.

"May the spirits of the valley also smile upon us and take their share of this blood offering," Beobrand said. He plunged his knife deep into the throat of the ox. The beast and the crowd moaned in unison. Hot blood gushed. It splashed and steamed into the bowl. Rowena's hands were soon slick with the stuff.

The bowl was quickly full and Rowena stepped back, allowing others to catch the precious liquid in their own pots and bowls. That blood would be used for puddings, or simply cooked and eaten. One bowl of life was enough for the gods. The people needed its sustenance more.

The ox bent its knees and lowered itself down onto the ground, while the villagers bustled around it. There was laughter and good-natured pushing from some of the children. The blood-flow slowed and the beast's life poured from it into the people's vessels. The animal slumped, tongue lolling.

Beobrand and Rowena carried the blood-bowl carefully to the bonfire.

"From the people of Ubbanford to the gods and spirits of the land, water and sky. Accept our sacrifice," Beobrand said in a clear voice. With those words, they tossed the contents of the bowl onto the hottest flames of the fire. Steam and smoke hissed and raged. The stench of burnt meat surrounded them.

They were plunged into almost total darkness as the flames were partially doused. Some of the children screamed out in fear.

Edlyn's hand found Sunniva's. She gripped it tightly. The blaze had looked strong enough. What if the flames did not come back? But she need not have worried. As she looked, the flames returned, burning away the bloody offering.

The gods would receive the tribute.

The people cheered. They were not many, but their voices were strong. Loud enough for the gods themselves to heed their call.

The menfolk moved to the animal and began to butcher it. They worked quickly with seaxes and axes, hacking the carcass into manageable hunks of meat and bone. Acennan used a large axe to sever the head of the beast. The horns were fine. They would make good drinking cups. They were removed from the skull before Acennan lifted the huge bovine head and carried it to the deep hole that had been dug near the fire.

Beobrand placed a hand on his friend's shoulder. Blood dripped black from the neck and nose of the beast. The tongue flopped and drooled.

"We offer this ox head to the ground," said Beobrand, "that it may please the Cofgodas who guard our soil from spirits of evil. May it feed them this winter."

Acennan placed the brawny head into the hole. He then used a shovel to push some of the embers from the bonfire on top of the offering. Sparks flickered into the night. Bright specks that could have been the very eyes of the Cofgodas spirits looking on from the dark. Acennan shovelled the freshly turned earth into the hole then, burying head and embers alike.

Beobrand came to Sunniva and took her right hand in his. She caressed gently the stump of his fingers. It was somehow reassuring to feel the evidence of his past battles. This was her man. He spoke well. He loved her and would kill for her. And he was a good lord.

"It is well done," said Beobrand. "Now, let us go to Ubba's hall and feast."

They cheered again.

The air of tension had fled as quickly as the sparks vanished into the cold night air.

Beobrand sat at the head of the hall and smiled. The gift-stool was comfortable, worn smooth by years of use by Ubba and his father before him. Rowena had offered him the seat as was his due as her new hlaford. She was gracious indeed. She had been pleased when he had told her that she could keep Ubba's hall and that he would build a new hall. From that moment on, she had done her utmost to make the people accept Beobrand and his retainers. He could not have asked for a better ally.

The smell of cooking meat pervaded the hall. Cuts of the ox sizzled on spits that children turned near the fire.

All the inhabitants of Ubbanford were in the hall, except for two night wardens posted outside the doors. Acennan had insisted.

"You wouldn't want that Pict bastard to come in the night and burn the hall with us all inside, would you?" Beobrand thought for a moment of his father. The flames had taken his life and their home. It was not a death to sing of.

Later, the children and womenfolk would leave, and the men would have a symbel. Oaths would be sworn. Boasts would be made. The memory horn would be passed. And it would be a surprise to all if any mead or ale remained come morning.

But for now, everyone from the settlement was packed into the hall. It was as loud as the clash of shieldwalls. Yet this was the happy cacophony of community. Laughter. Chatter. Shouting. Bawdy jokes.

Not the battle clamour of death and pain. Beobrand closed his eyes for a moment, forcing himself not to think such black thoughts.

"Are you well, my lord?" Sunniva was at his side. She offered him ale. He held out his drinking horn.

"I am all the better for having you at my side," he said. He stroked her leg as she leaned forward to pour him drink. She bent and kissed his cheek.

"I can scarce believe that I am lord of these people."

"And my lord too," she said. "You spoke well tonight. The people are content."

"As am I. It is pleasing to see the people happy. Soon we will build a home for ourselves. Until then, I hope you are content too."

"I am." Sunniva pushed a loose strand of hair behind her ear. "Lady Rowena is very kind." She paused. Looked towards the hearth fire.

"What is it? Does something ail you, Sunniva?"

She bit her lower lip. "It is nothing. You will think me silly."

"Nonsense. What is it? I would know what upsets my wife."

For a long while she did not respond. Just when Beobrand thought she would not speak, she said, "It is him."

Beobrand didn't understand. "Who?"

"Him," she said, signalling with her chin.

He followed her gaze.

"Anhaga?" he asked, a tinge of vexation entering his tone. "We have spoken of this."

"I know. I said you would think me silly. But he looks at me... with a hunger." She shuddered.

"Anhaga is a good man. I am certain of it. He is oath-bound to me. He wishes no harm to you."

"I know what he wants," she snapped. Lady Rowena looked

at them quizzically for a moment before turning her attention back to Edlyn, who was speaking incessantly at her side.

"Sunniva, my love." Beobrand took her hand in his; touched her cheek so that she looked directly at him. "You are the most beautiful woman most men will ever see. Men will always look at you. But they will not touch you, for you are mine. And I would kill any man who did you wrong. Anhaga is a faithful man, I am sure, but if the cripple makes you uneasy, I will speak to him."

"No. I know you speak the way of it. Do not talk with Anhaga of this. It will make things more difficult for me. I will need to work with him if I am to run your hall."

Beobrand let out a sigh. Why was everything so complicated with women? He quashed his frustration and allowed himself to relax once more. "Good. He will be of use to you in many ways. He is quick-witted and honest. All who knew him in Bebbanburg vouched for his good character."

Sunniva nodded, but her lips were pressed into a thin line and her brow was furrowed. She was not convinced. He decided to move the conversation away and on to happier things.

He looked over at where Rowena was listening to her daughter, who was gesticulating wildly as she recounted a tale.

"How is the forge? Is there anything you need?"

"It is wonderful to be able to work metal again. There was a moment yesterday when I half expected him to be there. Just behind me where I could not see. I could feel his presence."

Beobrand squeezed her hand. It seemed more difficult than he'd thought to move her mind from sad thoughts.

"I am sure his spirit looks on with pride," he said. "And your young apprentice? How does she fare?"

"Edlyn is a sweet girl. And good company. She is a treasure."

Beobrand seized the opportunity. "Talking of treasure," he said quickly, "that reminds me. There is something I need to do. Please take your seat and I will address the folk."

Sunniva sat, smoothing her dress over her thighs nervously.

Beobrand stood. He held out his arms as if in supplication to the gods, as he had seen Oswald do. In battle, men turned to him naturally. He was taller than most. Hale and strong with great sword-skill. But here, in the mead hall, he was unsure of himself. He felt clumsy as he ever did speaking before others. He looked to Acennan. His friend saw him standing there and nodded. He turned to those around him on the benches and bade them be silent.

The fire burnt hot on the hearth. The faces of the feasters were made ruddy by ale, mead and heat. The chaos of dozens of voices washed over Beobrand as he stood there. For a moment he wondered if they would cease talking. Perhaps he would be left to sit back down. Ignored like a chastised child who sought attention from his elders.

Then, unnervingly rapidly, the hall grew quiet. One heartbeat the room was a confusion of noise, the next it was hushed.

Beobrand looked over them all. They were all his people now. From homeless to lord in a year. His wyrd was woven with bold threads, of that there could be no doubt. Amongst the upturned faces he saw his gesithas and their women. They wore expressions of expectation. Pride. They were keen to hear his words. In his dreams as a boy back in Hithe he had sometimes pictured himself as a thegn in a great hall. But he had never imagined this scene. To be standing before a throng who called him hlaford.

Lowering his arms to his side, Beobrand spoke in a clear voice. "Folk of Ubbanford. Good folk. My folk. We are reaching the end of a harsh year. We have lost loved ones."

He glanced to either side. Sunniva, Rowena and Edlyn looked back at him, their eyes glistening.

"We have fought battles."

Acennan and the other warriors nodded.

He remembered Tata, her body broken on the altar of Engelmynster. Recalled the vision of Cathryn's corpse, cold and mutilated on the forest floor. His face clouded. "Innocents have been killed."

"Let us raise the horns to our fallen. Fill your cups and drink deeply. Let their names never be forgotten." He took his drinking horn and lifted it high. Around the hall, the action was repeated.

"To the fallen!" Beobrand said. He took a long draught from the horn, the cool liquid bitter on his tongue.

"To the fallen!" His folk echoed him. Silence fell on the room as they all drank. Then the clatter of horns and cups being slammed onto boards. People began to talk. Perhaps tales of those they had lost.

Beobrand held out his arms again. Silence returned quickly.

"We must never forget those we have lost, or the hardships we've faced. But I do not wish to dwell on these things tonight. Tonight must be a celebration. We celebrate the simple things. That we have food on the table. A roof above us. The gods have accepted our sacrifice. Yet there is more I wish us to celebrate."

He reached out to Sunniva. She stood and took his hand.

"It has been a hard year for Sunniva and I too. We have no living family." Her small hand was cool in his. "But we found each other. We are handfasted. Wed together as man and wife." She squeezed his hand. "Having no family means that there was nobody to agree the brýdgifu or the handgeld."

The women's faces in the gathering stared back at him, eager to hear what he would say.

"But in losing our families, we have found you. You, the folk of Ubbanford. And we would celebrate our handfasting with you."

His gesithas and some of the drunker ceorls cheered. Fists thumped the boards. Plates and cups rattled.

"I see you are hungry and wish to slake thirsts already dampened with more mead and ale, so I will not speak for much longer."

Acennan, red-faced and smiling, cheered and raised his horn in salute. Laughter rippled around the hall.

"Stop your crowing, Acennan." Beobrand raised an eyebrow in Acennan's direction. "If you are so keen for me to finish, perhaps the night wards would like to be relieved of their duty and allowed to join the feast." Beobrand's smile took the sting from the rebuke.

Acennan returned the smile, lifting a hand in apology. "Sorry, lord. Please continue."

"We have been wed for some time now, and yet Sunniva is still without her morgengifu. So here, before you all, I wish to give her that which is hers by right. A morgengifu that is fit for a lord's lady."

He turned from the throng and lifted a small wooden box from under the gift-stool.

He faced Sunniva and said, "In this cask I give you half of the treasure handed to me by Oswald King. This gold and silver is yours from this day forth. You may use it as you see fit."

Sunniva's smile was wide. Her face seemed to glow in the light of the hearth-flame.

"There is more I would give you. Silver and gold is not enough. It can be stolen or misspent. And it cannot fill an empty belly. So I gift to you also my lord's right to the fish from the river Tuidi that is within the hides of my land. This I will see is proclaimed to the king when next I go to Bebbanburg. Oswald King will know of our handfasting and the value of your morning-gift so that no man may refute these words."

"Thank you, Beobrand Lord," Sunniva replied, her voice slight, but carrying throughout the hall. "To be your wife is enough for me, but I accept this morgengifu from you gladly."

She kissed him softly on the lips. He breathed deep of the scent of her.

Then addressing the hall in his loudest tone he declaimed, "Now I truly have talked too long. My throat is dry and my stomach grumbles at the smell of the meat on the spit. Drink, eat and celebrate. Tonight is a good night."

The throng erupted in cheers and shouts. They all returned to conversations at their boards, and the sound was again like the waves washing over stones on a beach. Rowena nodded to him, as he sat. He watched Sunniva as she moved towards the hearth. She spoke to one of the thralls there who sliced meat from a joint and laid it on a trencher for her. What grace and beauty. To think he had believed himself cursed not six months ago.

Sunniva made her way back towards him. Beobrand watched her, entranced. Beyond her, his gaze was drawn to another's stare. Anhaga's eyes followed Sunniva's swaying hips as she walked. Beobrand and Anhaga's gazes met. For a brief moment a darkness seemed to fall over Anhaga's face, then he looked away. Could there be some substance to Sunniva's fears? No, it was madness. Whatever the man thought, surely he would not risk death.

Sunniva handed him the trencher of meat. The smell of the oozing beef made his mouth fill with liquid.

But he had barely taken a single bite when a commotion at

the end of the hall drew his attention. The doors swung open. The door wards entered with a third man between them. A hush fell on the gathering again, as everyone turned to see who had come.

Beobrand stood quickly. Upsetting his drinking horn and spilling its contents. Were Nathair and his sons seeking vengeance?

"Who comes to my hall in the dark of night?" Beobrand asked, his face and voice stern.

The man bowed and pushed back his cloak to show he was unarmed.

"I bring a message from Oswald King for Beobrand of Ubbanford."

"I am Beobrand."

"You are to come to Bebbanburg with all haste."

12

Beobrand and Acennan rode into the courtyard of Bebbanburg through a driving rain. The sea below the fortress was a turmoil of white and grey. There were no ships abroad on the foam-flecked waves. The clouds were low above them. The gloom and the rain made the place seem somehow smaller. None of the islands were visible and the land to the west was veiled.

Bebbanburg was less crowded than when they had left, and those who still resided there would not venture out on such a day unless they had no choice. The messenger who rode with them announced Beobrand and Acennan at the lower gate. He was clearly well-known to the gate-wardens who waved the three bedraggled riders past with scarcely a glance.

Once inside they dismounted and led their mounts to the stables. There they found the hostler and stable boys playing tafl. They jumped up as Beobrand and the others clattered into the building.

"Hope we're not disturbing you," said Acennan.

"No, lord," replied the hostler. His eyes darted, his gaze never seeming to find what he was looking for.

"Do not fear. Anhaga is not here," said Beobrand. "But I will beat you myself, if you raise your hand to Sceadugenga."

The black stallion showed the hostler the whites of his eyes and snorted.

"Yes, lord. Sorry, lord." The man rushed to take the reins from Beobrand. "I'll have this fine steed rubbed down and fed soon enough. He'll be well cared for."

"Make sure he is." Beobrand fixed him with an unflinching stare. The hostler averted his eyes quickly and turned to the stable hands.

"Look lively now, you lazy good for nothing whoresons," he screeched. The horses flinched.

"Charming man," Acennan said as they walked to the king's hall. "Reminds me of my father," he chuckled.

Beobrand gave Acennan a sour look. "Reminds me of mine too. If he is not careful, he will end up like him."

They gave up their weapons at the door of the hall. Their cloaks were sodden and dripping, so they removed those too and handed them to the door wards who seemed unsure of what to do with them.

Inside was the familiar scene of a lord's gesithas at their rest. Small groups of men talked and played games in different parts of the hall. They looked up as Beobrand and Acennan stepped into the smoky darkness. Little light oozed through the small windows. Embers glowed dimly on the hearthstone.

They made their way to the central hearth, eager to warm themselves after the cold wet journey from Ubbanford. Beobrand picked up a couple of sizable logs from the pile near the hearth. He tossed them onto the embers with a spray of sparks and a sudden flare of light.

"Always one to make a grand entrance," said a familiar voice behind him.

Beobrand spun around to see Wybert lounging on a bench. His legs were outstretched to the fire. A cup nestled in his hand. He was changed somehow from when Beobrand had seen him last. More confident, perhaps even more belligerent. Maybe ale made him bold.

"Well met, Wybert," Beobrand said. "I trust you are well."

Wybert frowned. "I would be better if I did not have to see your face again." Wybert stood unsteadily and lurched towards Beobrand.

Beobrand readied himself for an assault, but it did not come. Wybert tottered to a halt and hawked phlegm into the fire. Mead sloshed from the cup he still held.

"It is not by choice that I am here, Wybert. The king has called me hither."

Wybert spat again. "Of course. The great Beobrand has been called by the king. What makes you of such import? Why do the gods smile upon you when they piss on the rest of us?" Wybert staggered towards Beobrand. "You should have died back in Engelmynster. Then none of this would have come to pass." Beobrand held out his hands to stop Wybert from falling into the fire. "Don't you touch me!" screamed Wybert. "I will kill you!"

All talk and play in the hall had stopped. Men stood. Some moved closer.

Beobrand shoved Wybert away. "Do not make such threats, Wybert. I did not kill Leofwine. I loved him and I loved your father too. I do not wish to have your blood on my hands. Do not force my hand. You are no warrior to stand against me."

"No warrior? My arms are strong. My spear sharp. I can kill you as easily as any man." Spittle flew from Wybert's lips.

"Wybert, sit down!" Another voice. Beobrand looked into

the gloom of the hall and saw the formidable bulk of Athelstan striding between the benches and watching men. "Be seated, Wybert. You are not yourself."

Wybert seemed to shrink. He glanced at Athelstan and mumbled something. He turned from Beobrand and found a bench.

"I would thank you not to pay heed to Wybert." Athelstan picked up a drinking horn and tossed out the contents onto the hearth. A hissing cloud of mead made Acennan cough. "He can fight well enough," Athelstan continued, filling the horn with fresh mead and offering it to Beobrand, "in fact, he shows some skill in training. But he cannot hold his mead and keep his mouth shut."

Beobrand accepted the horn and took a swig. The sweet liquid warmed his throat.

"Not holding his drink, eh?" said Beobrand, with a twisted mirthless smile. "Seems to be a common complaint."

Athelstan frowned, but chose not to react to the jibe.

"So, you have seen Wybert train?" Beobrand continued.

"Aye, he is one of my gesithas now. He will make a fine spear-man."

"Yes, he has seen me practise with shield, spear and seax," Wybert slurred. "Athelstan knows my worth."

Athelstan rounded on the young man. "Speak no more, Wybert! If you say one more word, I will beat you into stillness myself. Leave us now."

Wybert rose abruptly to his feet. For a moment, Beobrand thought he would attack Athelstan. But then Wybert said, "Sorry, my lord," and turned to leave.

"What have we here? The good thegns of Bernicia bickering and squabbling like puppies fighting over scraps." All eyes turned to the new speaker. Beobrand recognised the soft voice that carried so well even before he saw Oswald stepping down from the raised platform at the end of the hall.

"I would not have you fight each other," Oswald said. "We have enemies enough as it is."

Beobrand thought it best not to speak, so he merely bowed his head. Athelstan did the same.

"Now, both of you, join me at the high table. I would speak with you of things that are afoot. Errands you must perform."

"Of course, Oswald King," Beobrand managed. Ignoring Wybert, he walked with Athelstan to the king's table.

Beobrand recognised all those seated at the table. The bearded Derian flashed his teeth at him. "Good to see you, boy," he said.

Next to Derian sat the king's brother, Oswiu. He was grave and sombre. Unsmiling. He did not acknowledge Beobrand, but gave Athelstan a slight nod. On the other side of the board sat the person Beobrand least expected to see. Coenred looked out of place surrounded by such strong, powerful men. His forehead had been recently shaved, and his hair at the back had grown. The style was that worn by the other Christ monks. The result was that he looked older, somehow more serious. Coenred gave Beobrand a small, nervous smile.

At Coenred's side sat an older monk, Gothfraidh, who Beobrand remembered from Cadwallon's execution.

Oswald sat at the head of the table. Beobrand and Athelstan seated themselves opposite each other. Athelstan next to Oswiu, Beobrand squeezed on the bench next to Coenred. Beobrand's clothes steamed gently in the warmth of the hall.

"I see the elements did not treat you well on the journey, Beobrand. Soon you can dry your clothes and fill your belly. First I would talk to you. I am glad you are both here,"

Oswald said. He fixed them with a withering look. "I have missions for you."

Beobrand wondered what mission the king could have for him. But he said nothing.

Oswald spoke in a soft voice that would not be heard by the other men lounging in the hall. Beobrand glanced over his shoulder and saw that Acennan had sat at a bench and appeared to have joined in a game of knucklebones. Beobrand had seen him play before and knew his large hands and cat-like speed made him a formidable opponent.

"Cadwallon's death has brought us peace, but other wolves are drawing closer. They know we are weakened. We cannot field a fyrd strong enough to defend the land from the likes of Penda of Mercia. We must strengthen our position.

"I plan to ride south, into Deira. There I will make clear my claim to the throne of that land by virtue of my mother's blood. Freeing Deira from the yoke of Cadwallon will give my claim added weight. A unified Northumbria brings power. Strength together."

Beobrand had never been party to the schemes of kings before. He was filled with awe. The man's self-belief and vision were inspiring.

Oswald continued, his eyes ablaze with the plans he was laying out before them.

"But that will not be enough. Not if I am to be Bretwalda. High King of Albion. I will be the Christian king that Edwin never was. But for that, I will need more allies. Athelstan, you will ride south, taking messages first to Penda, and then to Cynegils of Wessex."

"The roads will be difficult. The rivers swollen," Athelstan said. "Snow will be on us soon. Such a trip would be best undertaken after the winter snows have thawed."

"You are right. The journey will be difficult and spring would make for easier travelling, but I cannot wait for spring. Penda will not sit idle. You can be sure of that. No, I must move now and both you and Beobrand will travel in winter, difficult as that may be."

Beobrand took a sip of mead from the drinking horn to wet his lips and spoke for the first time. "Am I not to travel with Athelstan, lord king?"

"No, young Beobrand. Athelstan rides south. Your journey will be into the north. Through the lands of the Picts and into Dál Riata."

Beobrand's mouth went dry. He had heard tell of the northern lands beyond Bernicia. Wild expanses of mountains and lakes, filled with native savages who painted themselves with woad and fought naked. What could Oswald want from that northern wilderness?

"You," Oswald said, with a smile, "will follow my brother, Oswiu, into the north, to the sacred isle of Hii. And you will bring me back a bishop."

13

As if to remind them of the folly of their decision to travel as the year grew old, the rain continued to beat down following the meeting with the king in Bebbanburg. Preparations for the trip were made quickly and after only a day of warmth and dry they were ready to set off north.

Beobrand avoided Wybert. The man had never liked him and no good would come of their meeting. Instead, while thralls packed food and clothes for Oswiu and his retinue, Beobrand and Acennan spent most of their time playing knucklebones with the men they would soon travel with. Acennan knew all of Oswiu's gesithas. They had spent time together in exile with the sons of Æthelfrith. He had fought alongside most of them in Hibernia. He was well-liked amongst them. Beobrand was known to them. His battle-fame was already the thing of tales. They accepted him as one of them. A killer, despite his youth.

At first Beobrand had been unclear why he, of all the thegns who served Oswald, had been chosen to accompany those travelling to Hii. That was until he found a moment to talk to Coenred. They shared a loaf and some cheese in a secluded corner of the hall.

"It is good to see you, Coenred," Beobrand said, wiping ale from his lips with the back of his hand. "I swear on Thunor's hammer you have grown since last we met. But I do not comprehend why Oswald King sends me north in search of a bishop, whatever that is."

Coenred look into his ale cup for a time. When he looked up, his eyes glimmered, wet with tears.

"Abbot Fearghas died," he said.

"Oh. I am sorry. He was a good man." Fearghas had been there for Beobrand when he most needed help. He had allowed Beobrand time to recover in his monastery, despite his presence there putting his brethren at risk. Beobrand sighed. Another good man dead. "But I still do not understand. Why send me north? And what is a bishop?"

"It is a leader of the Christ church," answered Coenred. "A kind of priest."

Beobrand shook his head. "You followers of the Christ have too many names for priests."

"As to your other question, Fearghas tasked me to fetch the bishop from Hii. And he asked me to tell the king that you should accompany me." Coenred must have read Beobrand's expression, for he continued, "I do not know why or to what end. But Oswald loved Fearghas and would not deny him this dying request."

Beobrand frowned. This made no sense. The old man had no good reason for this. He clenched his jaw. He had only just found a place to call his home, and now he must leave? Surely these were the ravings of a dying man. Meaningless babblings. But he knew this was a battle he could not win. The king had decided and thegns did not win arguments with kings.

"Well, the sooner we leave," Beobrand said, his voice gruff

with annoyance, "the sooner I will be back at Ubbanford. It is where I should be. With my folk."

And with Sunniva.

"Yes, and I have work to be done on Lindisfarena. I am sure the other monks will not be able to build cells without my help." Coenred smirked. It was the first time Beobrand had seen him smile for a long time. "I do not know how I will cope without the brothers' guidance. I may even forget some of my prayers."

"That would be unlike you. You were always so hard-working," Beobrand said. Coenred's shift in mood was infectious. "Let us hope that the trip does not take too long, or you may forget all of the teachings of the Christ you have learnt."

"And the longer we travel, the more chance I will need to rescue you from some danger or injury." Coenred's smile broadened.

Beobrand slapped the young monk playfully on the shoulder. It felt good to spend time with Coenred again. Beobrand had forgotten how much he enjoyed his company.

"As I recall it, Coenred, it is I who usually ends up saving you."

"I believe we are neither of us in the debt of the other when it comes to life-saving." Coenred laughed. "But it is true that your rescues tend to make better songs. I'll give you that!"

The rain showed no sign of letting up when they left the next morning.

Oswiu, astride a dappled grey gelding, grumbled that the rivers would already be impassable. Beobrand overheard the atheling and called over the noise of the horses and rainfall.

"We can cross the Tuidi at Ubbanford. And we can over-night in my hall."

Oswiu glanced at Beobrand, as if surprised he had spoken. "And you can rut with your pretty woman one more time before we head into the lands of the Picts." Oswiu's retainers laughed. Beobrand felt his face grow hot.

"To Ubbanford then," Oswiu said. "Lead on, Beobrand."

It was long after dark when at last they rode down the hill into the valley Beobrand had begun to think of as home. Smoke hung low over the houses. Rain still fell, though with less virulence, as if the gods themselves had grown weary of the constant pounding of the earth with water. With the easing of the rain, the temperature had begun to fall. So by the time they arrived at Ubba's hall, the riders were wet, cold and miserable.

Acennan had ridden on ahead, giving Sunniva and Rowena a little warning of Beobrand's return.

One would never have known that the ladies had not had days in which to prepare for the lord of the hall and the king's brother. The women stood in the doorway of the hall as the horses plodded through the mud. Both were radiant. They wore their finest clothes and jewellery. And they were in full control.

At their command men and boys ran to take the mounts. The women ushered the warriors into the welcome warmth of the hall.

As the guest of honour, Oswiu was offered mead from the Waes Hael bowl by Sunniva.

"You are well come to Ubba's hall. May you have good health," said Sunniva, her voice low and timid in the presence of the atheling.

Oswiu, usually taciturn and dour, smiled broadly. Beobrand felt a prickle of distaste at the prince's lingering gaze at Sunniva.

But he could not blame Oswiu for looking. She was indeed a feast for a man's eyes.

After Oswiu had drunk deeply, smacking his lips with pleasure, Sunniva passed the bowl to Beobrand. Her gaze was open and full of love for her husband. Thoughts of jealousy fled from Beobrand. She was his alone.

He drained the remainder of the contents of the bowl. The mead trickled down inside him. The drink and Sunniva's presence warmed him. By Woden, he would miss her on the trek north. He was not looking forward to having to tell her of their mission.

"You keep the name of Ubba's hall, then?" Oswiu enquired. His eyes stayed on Sunniva, but Beobrand chose to answer.

"Yes, my lord. We plan to build a new hall. Ubba's lady, Rowena, and their daughter, Edlyn, will remain here." Beobrand indicated Rowena, and Edlyn, who stood in her mother's shadow.

"Very noble of you," Oswiu raised an eyebrow.

"I thought to follow the will of your brother. The king did not wish Ubba's kin's sacrifice to be forgotten."

Oswiu frowned. "Of course. Lady Rowena, we are sorry for your loss. Ubba and your sons helped to bring peace to Bernicia."

Rowena seemed pleased with the atheling's attention. "Thank you, my lord Oswiu." She bowed.

"Now," said Oswiu, "what is that wonderful scent of food I smell? Travelling in this weather makes one hungry."

It was some time before they were all seated and food was being served. The hall was crowded with Oswiu's retinue. The heat and smoke from the hearth mingled with the steam coming from the damp clothes of the travellers, making the hall hazy, as if with fog.

Beobrand was unsure how the ladies of Ubbanford had managed to organise a feast for so many in such a short space of time. When he asked Rowena, she merely smiled and said, "It is always good for womenfolk to have some secrets from men. Just enjoy the food."

And enjoy it he did. There was salted beef, smoked fish, a warming pottage, and fresh bread. All washed down with copious amounts of ale and mead.

Beobrand was on his third horn of ale when Sunniva leaned in close and whispered, "You will not wish to drink too much. I have heard tales that drink can dampen a lover's fire."

Beobrand spluttered, coughing ale onto the rushes.

"If you are to leave me alone for many days or weeks," she continued, "I will need you to be at your best this night. I wish to have a fresh memory of you for the long dark nights of winter ahead." She winked.

"So you know what we are to do? Where we are going?" Beobrand had been worrying how to broach the subject with her unduly it seemed.

"Of course, I do. I asked Acennan."

Beobrand glanced over at his friend. He was not sure if he was pleased or angry at Acennan's indiscretion. Acennan was engaged in a drinking contest with some of Oswiu's gesithas. They pounded the boards with their fists as the stocky warrior drained the contents of a drinking horn without pause.

"Do not blame Acennan. If I was to wait for you to tell me, my hair would be grey." She kissed him lightly. "I am not happy that you are leaving so soon, and to travel so far. But I know you are the king's man. You must do as you are bidden. And I will not spend the time we have together crying over your leaving." She reached under the table and stroked his thigh gently. "I can think of much more pleasurable ways to pass the time."

Beobrand swallowed. He decided he was not angry with Acennan.

The warmth of Beobrand's embrace was still with Sunniva as she watched him ride away. The rain had ceased in the night, but the iron-grey sky brooded and threatened. The Tuidi was cloaked in thick mist. The riders were hidden before they were a spear's throw distant. Sounds of their travel carried in the still morning, and she heard the splash of hooves in the ford. The jangle of harness. Murmured voices.

She had sent Beobrand off with a kiss and a smile. He had waved to her and she had returned the salutation with a cheerful expression. Now though, she let the smile fall from her lips. When would she see him again? Winter was coming. To travel north was madness. Yet she knew she could not change the king's decision. She had not spoken of her anxiety to Beobrand. It would have served no purpose, save to unsettle him.

He was concerned enough. He had not said as much, but in the dark secrecy of their bed furs he had spoken of the journey. Of leaving her at Ubbanford. And she had heard the worry in his voice. They had smothered their fears with passion. At last, panting and sweat-slick, they had slept a short while in each other's arms.

The noise of many men preparing to travel had woken them while the sun still slept.

"I will leave the men here," Beobrand had said, as he cinched his sword belt. "I do not wish to leave you unprotected. I don't believe that bastard Nathair will do anything, but perhaps an unguarded hall would prove too much temptation."

"You will take Acennan with you at least," she had replied. "I need to know you have someone looking out for you."

"Very well," Beobrand had replied. "I'll leave Tobrytan in charge. He is a good man."

Now, staring into the mist for any last fleeting glimpse of Beobrand, Sunniva wished she had tried to convince him to stay behind. She knew it would have been pointless, but she could not help feeling that something awful would befall him.

She had felt these things before. Cried tears of self-pity and fear when he had left for battle. And he had returned to her. She must put these thoughts from her mind. There was much to do. There was a hall to build.

She turned to head to the hall. With a start she almost collided with Anhaga who must have crept up behind her.

"Is there anything you would have me do?" he asked.

Her skin prickled. A chill ran through her. "Get out of my way!" she said, her voice shrill.

He stepped to one side to let her pass, clumsy and halting on his twisted leg.

She paused. If she was to survive the winter without Beobrand, she should try to put aside her dislike for the cripple. He would be useful in helping her run the household.

"I am sorry," she said. "You startled me."

Anhaga looked as pleased as if she had presented him with a cartload of silver. "No need to apologise, my lady." His tone was subservient. But could she detect something else? Something darker? Sinister?

She suppressed a shudder.

She swept passed Anhaga and strode back to the hall.

Without turning, she knew that his gaze followed her until she was out of sight.

Closing the hall door behind her, she sighed.

It would be a long winter.

The weeks of travel into the north seemed endless to Beobrand. The days were filled with rain and sleet. Wind screamed in the bones of trees that skirted the paths they walked. A few days after leaving Ubbanford, the first snow fell in the night. They had been lucky that evening to find a hall to shelter in. Most nights they were able to sleep under a roof. The Pictish lords were, on the whole, hospitable. Many remembered Oswiu from his previous visit when travelling south with his brothers and they now craved news of Eanfrith and Oswald. On hearing of the death of Eanfrith and the victory of Oswald over Cadwallon, their reaction was usually similar. They understood it was best to keep on the good side of a king as powerful as Oswald now was. Putting up his brother and retinue for a night was a reasonable price to pay for the potential of later favours. Beobrand wondered whether the fact that Finola, sister of Gartnait, king of the Picts, still resided at Bebbanburg with her son was ever mentioned. The threat to her seemed clear to him, but he did not wish to speak of it with Oswiu.

On these evenings in strange halls Beobrand would talk to Coenred. Glad of whatever warmth they could glean from the smoky peat fires, they would let the lilting tongue of the Picts wash over them. They understood none of the language. All the others had lived for many years in exile, or even been born in the northern kingdom of Dál Riata. There they had also apparently picked up some of the words of the Picts. None could converse better with the natives of Gartnait's kingdom than Oswiu himself.

As they moved further into the north, the snow fell more heavily and more frequently. The hills grew steeper. The rivers more swollen and treacherous to cross. Beobrand could not count the times he had been soaked to the skin. Some of the paths they trod were so steep and ice-clad that they needed to dismount, for fear of a horse slipping and sending them tumbling to their doom. The cold reminded him of the time he had spent in the forest with Hengist. But then they had hunkered down in the shelter of trees and the river bank. Now there was no place to hide from the elements.

Of the company, Coenred fared the worst. He was thin and unsuited to the rigours of travel. The gesithas took pity on him, lending him cloaks and furs. In the end he was so wrapped up, with nothing more than his eyes showing between tufts of fur, that he resembled some kind of stunted bear. The men laughed at him. Coenred was too cold to take offence. Despite all the borrowed gear, he still spent most of each day shivering. Teeth chattering. Numb fingers shaking on the reins of the small horse he rode.

On one particularly bitter day, when the wind bit into their faces and the rain that pelted them was mixed with ice, they had travelled along the coastline of a great firth. A storm blew down across the estuary, hurling frigid water at them with a savage glee. Such was the fury of the storm that Beobrand closed his stinging eyes, relying on Sceadugenga to follow the other horses. They longed for a sanctuary from the cold that night and rejoiced when they saw a cluster of buildings arrayed near a low shingle beach. Some way back from the churning water squatted a building that was larger than the rest.

They rode up to the entrance unhindered, their cloaks whipping about them. Oswiu dismounted and approached the two door wards who stood in the wind-shadow of a porch. He flashed them his best smile and spoke in the tongue of the Picts. One of the guards entered the hall, while the other eyed up the group of mounted men who waited impatiently to be invited in to share the warmth and hospitality of the lord's table.

After a long while the hall doors had been flung open and a large, bearded man was silhouetted there. He spoke to Oswiu. His tone was not friendly. Oswiu raised his voice, gesticulating wildly. The large man shouted a long stream of words and then spat at Oswiu's feet. Oswiu flushed with fury. He spouted abuse at the man, as he turned and walked back into his hall. The doors slammed. The door wards returned to their posts. They would not meet the gaze of any of Oswiu's retinue.

Oswiu stood still for a time. Then he mounted and told the men to prepare for a long night.

Eventually they spent the night shivering in the lee of a hill, with no fire for warmth.

After they had chewed on some stale bread, washed down with water so cold it burnt the throat, Beobrand turned to Acennan.

"What did the Pict say to Oswiu?" he asked.

"He said a lot of things," Acennan replied, keeping his voice low. "None of them nice."

"I do not need an interpreter to understand as much," said Beobrand.

Acennan shrugged. "He said he would bow the knee to no Seaxon. He said that neither Oswald nor his brother were welcome in his hall."

"And he will regret it." Both Beobrand and Acennan started at the sound of Oswiu's voice. He was wrapped in a fur cloak and they'd thought him asleep. Now he glowered from the darkness and his voice was flint and iron.

"I will not forget the man's insolence. I will return here one day. And he will pay dearly for this night."

Beobrand did not know the name of the lord who had refused entry to Oswiu. He may have been sitting in the warmth of his hall while they sat hunched around a spitting fire of damp twigs. Yet Beobrand did not envy him. For the Pictish lord had made an enemy of Oswiu, son of Æthelfrith, atheling of Bernicia.

Beobrand remembered Cadwallon. The blood running into the earth. The Waelisc king's sightless eyes staring into his own.

The sons of Æthelfrith did not make good enemies.

Coenred shivered uncontrollably. He could barely hold his horse's reins. All sensation had left his fingers long ago. He leaned into the horse's neck, trying to take some of the warmth from the beast. But it did no good.

The horse slipped on an icy stone, hidden beneath the snow. Coenred grabbed hold of the mane. He did not want to fall. It was a long way down from the animal's back, and a lot further into the valley. His bones would shatter if he fell. Of that he was certain. They had been chilled for so long they would splinter like icicles.

At least it was not raining anymore. He had thought it would never end. Images of one of the stories Fearghas used to tell had come to him in those long, dreary, sodden days. A tale of a man and his ship built to withstand a great God-sent flood. Filled with all the animals of the world, so the story went.

Coenred shook his head. How was that possible? He had seen some large ships since moving to the coast, but none that could house more than a handful of animals. None would be large enough even to host the horses of the company he rode with.

He looked along the line of horsemen. Oswiu led the way. Beobrand and Acennan brought up the rear. Coenred gripped the reins tightly and glanced back at them. Beobrand raised a hand in greeting. Acennan, round face shining and ruddy, grinned. Neither of them seemed to feel the cold as he did. He knew all these warriors scoffed at him. He was weak. Thin. Of no use in a battle. And yet the king trusted him to carry the message to the abbot of Hii. And Fearghas had entrusted this mission to him. The brilliance of the sun on the snow brought tears to his eyes. Why had Fearghas sent him on this journey? He missed the other monks and, despite his jokes with Beobrand, he would have enjoyed helping to build their cells on Lindisfarena. The work would be hard but the island had felt like home from the moment he had stepped onto its beach. It seemed right to construct the shelter he would inhabit.

Well, no good would come of weeping after the whey was spilt. He knew he should not complain. But by the holy rood it was so cold. As soon as the words had formed in his mind, Coenred regretted them. Fearghas had told him once, "Pray to the Lord with words of hope and love. He will listen to your woes and miseries if that is all you can give, but think of all the people he must hear."

Trying to be thankful, Coenred offered up a silent prayer of gratitude that his horse had not thrown him into the valley. Still, it was hard to be grateful for feeling as if your toes would snap off at the slightest knock. The wind cut his cheeks and his eyes streamed.

And then, as he crested the brow of the rise and joined the others who had congregated there, all thoughts of discomfort fled. Gone was his desire to be anywhere else. For below them was the ocean. It was a deep blue at the edges of his vision, with the sun shining white from its surface like burnished rippling silver. Across the expanse of water lay several islands, nestled green gems on the shimmering blue. To the north, separated by a stretch of sea, lay a huge isle, the end of which could not be seen.

Never had he seen such a sight. The ocean rolled on endlessly into the horizon-haze of the distance. The isles scattered off of the mainland made him think of God throwing rocks into the ocean, the way a child would place stones in a stream for stepping. Coenred could not stop himself from smiling with the joy of it. His complaints about the journey and the elements now seemed shallow. Stupid. He was suddenly glad Fearghas had sent him. The cold in his body seemed unimportant when the power of the Lord was displayed so clearly before him.

"Behold, the western isles of Dál Riata," said Oswiu. "This is the edge of Domnall Brecc's kingdom in Albion. We have endured the worst of the journey." Oswiu shaded his eyes with his hand and stared out at the largest island to the northwest. "It seems we are further south than I had thought. We will head for the coast and find a ship to take us on to Hii. If God smiles on us with the weather, we should be in Ségéne mac Fiachnaí's hall by Geola."

14

In the end Geola was many days in the past when they finally crossed over to the holy island of Hii. They had spent the shortest day of the year in the hall of Lord Tavin. He was an affable, if gruff, man, well-known to Oswiu, who had stayed with him many times during his exile in these parts.

They had found a ship to take them to Hii, but their plans for the crossing had been dashed as clouds rolled in and a new storm battered the coast.

"The weather here changes as suddenly as a woman changes her mind," Tavin had said, when they had reached his hall on the coast of Muile, the largest of the western islands. Hii lay beyond it, off its most south-westerly point and they had been hoping to reach the holy island before the weather broke. A bedraggled company they were, and Tavin had laughed to see them so. Many days later, the drain on his winter supplies had made him less prone to jests. He had been as pleased as they were to see them move on.

None was more pleased than Beobrand. He had never liked winter. Hated being cooped up in the dark and smoke.

Bad enough in a place you called home. To be an uninvited and unwelcome guest, surrounded by the sounds of words you could not understand saw Beobrand become increasingly short-tempered. He longed to be done with this mission. It made no sense to him that he had been sent.

But here he was. In another smoky hall, while the atheling and the learned holy men of Hii debated who to send as a bishop back to Lindisfarena.

The winds had abated somewhat, and they had been able to make their way along the coast of Muile, and then the short crossing to the isle of Hii. It was as remote a place as he could have imagined. Each night the sun plunged into the ocean far away. There was no sound but for the wind, the waves and the birds.

On the first night on the island, Coenred had found Beobrand looking out into the west as the sun dropped towards the end of the earth.

"Is it not a wondrous vision?" Coenred had said. "This place is truly holy. I understand now why it is so important."

"Why is that?" Beobrand had asked.

"Here we can know God. There are no distractions from prayer and learning."

Beobrand had snorted. "Distraction is not a bad thing." He longed for the distraction of Sunniva's warm limbs intertwined with his.

"Maybe not for you. But for men of Christ, peace and silence are to be treasured."

"It is possible to have too much quiet," Beobrand had said, his face clouding. "It leaves too much time for thinking. And remembering."

That was three days before and since then, Beobrand and the other warriors had played their fill of tafl and knucklebones.

There was little food to be had. Not enough mead or ale. And no women.

"How can it take so long to decide who to send back with us?" Acennan suddenly blurted out. He stood and spat into the small hearth fire that struggled to keep the cold at bay. "We must leave before Solmonath, if we are to be back to our homes for the Hreðmonath sacrifices."

Several of the men nodded, grunting in agreement.

Coenred stood and said, "Wise men think long before making decisions. Though you would not understand that, it seems to me."

Some of the men laughed. "Be careful, Acennan," said Beobrand, "the boy would not beat you with a sword, but his tongue is sharp!"

"As for Hreðmonath," continued Coenred, "you have no need of these sacrifices. Christ died on the tree for you. It was the ultimate sacrifice." Coenred's words had the weight of strong belief behind them, lending them heft. And the talk of sacrifice gave the men pause. Death was the strongest of magic. Everyone knew this.

The door swung open. All eyes turned to the figure framed there. Fresh air breathed new life into the fire. Smoke wafted around the room, as thick as morning fog.

Oswiu stood in the doorway. "The bishop of Lindisfarena is chosen. We can return to Bernicia."

The mood of despondency in the smoke-choked hall lifted.

"There is only one thing we must do first," said Oswiu.

"We are to do what?" Beobrand asked. His tone was incredulous, but he was careful to keep the irritation from his voice.

He had seen little in Oswiu to imagine the atheling had an abundance of patience.

"It is a small thing. This woman—"

"This witch," interjected Acennan. Beobrand shot him a warning glance. It would do them no good to anger Oswiu.

"Well, she holds some sway over the locals. Attends births. Provides salves," Oswiu continued. "You know the way peasants are."

Beobrand looked at Acennan. His friend's face reflected his own thoughts. If she was harmless, why had the monks not solved their problem themselves? It did not escape his notice that Acennan and he were the only two warriors present who were not part of Oswiu's comitatus. Did that make them expendable?

Still, there seemed no way out of this. Oswiu ordered. They obeyed. And the sooner they faced what was ahead, the sooner they could return to Bernicia. To Ubbanford. To Sunniva.

"What is it that this woman is said to have stolen from the monks?" Beobrand asked. His mouth was dry all of a sudden. Picking up a wooden cup from the board before him, he took a long swig.

"It is a thing of great value. A silver platter. It was brought here by my mother. Oswald asked that we bring it back to Bebbanburg, its rightful home."

"Why only send the two of us?" Acennan asked. "If it is so important, we could all go."

"Are you afeared? Acennan, the great warrior, scared of a woman?"

Acennan bridled. He straightened his back. Placed both his broad hands on the table. Beobrand willed him to hold in check his ire at the affront.

Oswiu and Acennan held each other's gaze across the board.

Unspoken threats were loud in the silence. After some time, Oswiu said, "I meant no harm, Acennan. I merely jest." It seemed Oswiu did not wish to push Acennan too far. He was wise not to anger him. Even athelings and kings bleed and die. Perhaps Oswiu was thinking the same thoughts. Perhaps he remembered his brother Eanfrith here on this isle, alive and well just the year before. Greatness is no defence against a strong sword.

"The brethren here do not wish to raise this hag any further in the eyes of the people. To send many warriors, or an atheling of Bernicia, could elevate her. You are to bring an end to this problem quickly and quietly."

Beobrand chose to ignore the implication in Oswiu's words. He did not wage war on women. "And once we retrieve this plate, we leave?"

"Yes. We are all eager to return. This winter has been long. I too have left a woman behind, Beobrand. I know you feel the absence keenly."

Beobrand nodded. Acennan had relaxed, but his eyes glittered with a silent anger.

"It will be good to get back," Beobrand drained the rest of the ale from his cup. "We have been too long away. Where does this woman abide?"

"In a cave on the coast of Muile. It is not far. The monks will take you tomorrow."

Beobrand stood. Acennan pushed himself up, keeping his eyes fixed on Oswiu all the while.

Beobrand touched his shoulder.

"Well, if we are to face a woman who has the ear of the elder gods tomorrow, we should get some sleep."

Together they walked away leaving Oswiu staring after them, an unreadable expression on his face.

"I have a bad feeling about this," said Acennan.

Beobrand opened his eyes from where he lay near to his friend. The embers on the hearthstone cast a dim red glow into the room. Beobrand could just make out Acennan's shape. They were both wrapped in their cloaks against the night chill that seeped into the hall. Acennan's eyes glinted like distant torches on a dark hillside. Beobrand had hoped for some sleep. They had already talked long into the night and he'd thought they were done with this conversation, but clearly Acennan had other ideas.

"We will get the plate and then we can all go home. There is nothing to fear." An edge of frustration crept into his voice. He was tired, and the mention of home brought images of Sunniva to his mind. He wanted to sleep, for in his slumber he sometimes dreamt of her. Though in his experience the more he yearned to see her in his dreams, the less likely Sunniva was to come to him at night. The gods toyed with him, he supposed.

"But why send us?" Acennan continued. "And how could this cunning woman have taken the platter in the first place? There are no women on the island. Did she swim here and back?"

"We have talked of this already. We do not know the answers, nor will we."

Acennan snorted in the gloom. "Well, Oswiu won't tell us, that's for certain. He knows more than he was telling us, mark my words."

"Perchance so," said Beobrand, sighing wearily, "but if he chooses not to tell us, we will never know what he has, or hasn't hidden from us. We both agree that this is unusual, but unless you have devised some way to change the situation, I say we should sleep."

One of the other warriors, closer to the fire, farted loudly, breaking the stillness of the hall.

"I say you should sleep too," said a gruff voice from the darkness. "Stop blathering like goodwives and sleep. Tomorrow you can talk to this woman all you like. You can even ask her how she got her hands on the plate."

Another voice joined the discussion: "Aye, and who knows. She may be a beauty. Here we are, cramped up on an island of Christ monks with not a single cunny between us and you are bleating about having to see a woman. I wonder about you two, I really do."

Laughter rippled through the warriors who were still awake and sober enough to understand.

"He's got a point," said Acennan, a smile in his voice, "we'd better get our rest then. We may need our strength."

And in that way it seemed Acennan had set his mind at ease, for in a matter of moments his snores reverberated around the darkened hall.

Beobrand, who had been so close to slumber a few moments before, now lay in silence. He listened to the sound of the hall. An ember popped. One of the men coughed. Several were snoring. Outside, wind beat against the frame of the building, making it creak and groan, like an old man who complains of his joints when bending. Beyond the wind, he could hear the distant murmur of waves breaking on the beach.

Tomorrow they would cross those waves and seek this mysterious woman. Only a woman, nothing more. But Acennan was right, there was something wrong about this whole thing.

They were to face a woman. Two grown men with swords and shirts of metal. They had no need to be afraid.

But as he lay there, unable to bring Sunniva's face to his mind or to find the sleep that had so recently promised its sanctuary, Beobrand trembled.

He would never admit it to Acennan, but he was frightened.

15

The dawn brought with it a foul wind which blew down the strait between Hii and Muile. Seeing the white tops of the waves, Beobrand and Acennan decided not to don their armour. To be thrown into the sea weighed down with ring shirt would see them pulled to the depths with no chance of rescue. They cinched their belts tightly, drew their cloaks about them, and slung their byrnies over their shoulders.

At the water's edge, on the beach of white sand, waited three monks. On the sand rested a currach, a boat made of little more than skin stretched over twigs. Beobrand, used to the more substantial overlapping planks of the ships that plied the oceans to the east and south of Albion, could not see how this leather contraption could carry them safely over the wind-blown water. He touched the hammer amulet at his neck and spat. Gods protect them. They would drown before having to confront this witch.

The oldest of the monks stepped forward with a smile. In his hand he held a long wooden paddle. "Do not fear. This little breeze is nothing. We'll get you over to Muile in no time." The monk's name was Biorach. He spoke the tongue of the Angelfolc with a lilting accent, but his words were easily understood. They had met him before when they first arrived on the island and Beobrand liked him instinctively. He was as broad-shouldered as any warrior, with great shovel-like hands. His face was open, a smirk never far from his lips.

Beobrand looked sceptically at the currach. "We will not sink that thing?"

"Heavens, no," Biorach laughed. "She would take many more of us if needed. With just the few of us, she'll positively fly over the waves. Skimming like a stone."

Beobrand looked eastward at the beach across the stretch of water. Salt spray lifted from the waves. It felt like drizzle. He hoped it was not his wyrd to die this day.

"What do you think, Acennan?" Beobrand asked.

"I'm thinking we've been talking too long." Acennan pushed past Biorach and threw his byrnie into the currach.

"Careful," said Biorach. "If you rip the skin, you will be finding out just how cold that water is at this time of year."

Acennan looked abashed.

Before Beobrand could say any more, he saw a small group of people walking down towards them from the huddled monastery buildings. As they grew closer, he recognised Oswiu and Coenred. The rest wore the dark robes of the Christ follower brethren.

Oswiu raised a hand as they approached.

"I have brought the new bishop of Lindisfarena." He indicated the man to his right. He was tall and thin. His nose narrow and his chin weak. Like all the Christ monks, his forehead was shaved all the way to the top of his head. The hair that grew at the back of his head was tawny and luxuriant. It would better suit a woman, in Beobrand's opinion. The wind flicked his long locks about his face.

"This is Cormán," said Oswiu. "He is come to bless your short journey."

Beobrand looked at Cormán, then at the currach and the rough sea beyond it. He knew not whether this Christ god had power, but he supposed it could do no harm to have his blessing. He nodded at the bishop. "Thank you," he said. Coenred caught his eye. He was grinning behind Cormán. Perhaps at hearing Beobrand giving thanks for his god's blessing.

Cormán raised his hands to the sky and intoned in a sonorous voice that did not match his slim frame. He spoke words in the language all the Christ followers learnt. Beobrand did not understand any of it, but he kept a sombre expression until the priest had finished.

For a moment then they all stood still on the beach. Nobody seemed to want to move, so after a time, Beobrand said, "Well, we should leave before the weather gets any worse." He turned to help carry the fragile boat into the water, when Coenred stepped forward.

"I will go with you," he said. His voice shook. With cold or fear, Beobrand could not tell. "Fearghas sent me here for a reason. I feel God's presence here. He speaks to me." Coenred's voice grew stronger, the more he spoke. Cormán was wide-eyed, surprised perhaps that the young monk would speak out so. Oswiu seemed pleased.

"If you are to face evil," Coenred continued, "you should not face it alone. I will come, with my bishop's blessing. Evil magic should not be confronted with only force and iron. I will bring the word of our Lord to protect and guide us."

"You go with my blessing," Cormán said at last. "Go forth and bring back that which has been stolen from us." He made the sign of the cross over them with his hand outstretched. A ripple of fear trickled down Beobrand's spine. There was magic in the wind. In the words and the symbols. He could sense it.

He hoped it would be stronger magic than that of the witch they were to face.

He was suddenly thankful that he had remembered to leave some red cloths hanging from the lintel of the stable where they had left their horses. Sceadugenga was not close. All their steeds had been left under the protection of a lord on the mainland. But if there were witches abroad at night, the red cloths should keep them from riding his mount.

He would rather be riding Sceadugenga now. He had grown fond of the horse, used to its gait. But the stallion was far away. Beyond the sea and Muile. He prayed to Woden that he would see the horse again, and ride it safely back to Ubbanford.

They moved to the currach and helped lift it. It was heavier than it looked. They carried it swiftly down into the water and then climbed on board, while Biorach, standing up to his thighs in the surf, held it steady.

When they were aboard, Biorach climbed in with a practised movement and began to paddle.

Beobrand grasped Coenred's shoulder. "I am glad you are joining us. Perhaps we will have need of your God's power before the day is over."

"I told you I would need to rescue you on this journey," Coenred replied, though the smile on his lips did not reach his eyes. There was nothing but fear there.

"Rescue us?" snorted Acennan, who gripped the edge of the currach with white-knuckled strength, as they were bobbed and jostled by the waves. "If we run into trouble, the only way you'll rescue us is if we throw you to the hag so that we can flee while she is feasting on your skinny carcass."

All colour drained from Coenred's face. The skin of the

boat flexed and writhed beneath them like a living thing. They were making good progress, as Biorach propelled them forward with an easy action of the paddle.

The currach swayed and sagged on the swell.

They reached the midpoint of the crossing, for it was not far. The waves here were larger. They tossed the currach from side to side. Beobrand's stomach lurched. He had never been a good seaman. When travelling from Cantware to Bernicia, he had made up for his lack of seamanship with his willingness to learn and his strength. But here, there was nothing for him to do except look to their destination and will the pottage he had eaten to stay in his guts.

They were nearly there when Coenred turned and vomited noisily over the edge of the boat.

Acennan laughed, but looked as if he might soon follow Coenred's example. "Don't worry, boy," Acennan said, "I was only jesting of leaving you behind. I am sure you can run faster than either of us with your lanky legs." Beobrand forced a smile. Coenred let out a groan and retched again and again, until nothing more came out.

And then they had arrived. One of the monks leapt into the water and pulled the bark into the shallows. They helped Coenred out and up onto the beach. He walked on wobbly legs, like a newborn foal.

Wet and shivering, Beobrand waded up out of the sea. The sensation of the currach's motion clung to him like a half-forgotten dream, making the beach seem to move under his feet.

Coenred was pale. Sickly and shaken. He would be of little use to them as he was. Acennan was also pallid, but seemed to be recovering quickly from the crossing.

"Let us get our byrnies on," said Beobrand. Hopefully, this would give Coenred a little time to compose himself.

They helped each other to slide and wriggle into their iron shirts. The weight of the armour comforted Beobrand. It was solid and it had already saved his life. And yet it also unnerved him. It reminded him of shieldwalls. Fallen friends. The stench of bowels and blood in the mud.

The monks had pulled the currach up the beach, well beyond the high-tide line. Coenred sat with them. There seemed a little more colour in his cheeks.

"I am sorry," he said, eyes downcast as he ran his hands through his hair.

Beobrand reached out and pulled him to his feet. "Do not speak thus," said Beobrand. "You have nothing to be ashamed of. You have shown to me many times that you are brave. It took great courage to enter that boat and join us. Do you see any others here to help us?" He clapped Coenred on the shoulder.

"Now, how far is this witch's lair?"

"Not far," said Biorach. "I will lead you there."

And so they left the beach. The white sand made way to scrubby grass and stunted trees. Biorach searched for a moment and then found what he was looking for. A path of flattened earth led between the trees. They stepped onto the track between the denuded bones of gnarly, bent boles.

Above them, against the tumble of heavy clouds that broiled in the sky, gulls and other sea birds wheeled and cavorted. Their shrieks echoed in Beobrand's mind like the death-screams of warriors.

They followed the path inland in silence. They saw no living thing but birds. The track led a winding route through foliage that in summer must have been dense and heavy. Now the trees shook their gnarled bones at them as they passed. The brown bracken quivered and rustled.

Biorach led the way with a purposeful stride. Beobrand followed close behind, his half-hand rested on Hrunting's hilt. His right frequently touched the amulet at his neck. Acennan brought up the rear, keeping an eye on Coenred, who looked as if he might puke again.

The further they travelled from the sea, the calmer the air grew. A stillness fell on the woods as they made their way down into a hollow. The land here looked as if a giant hand had scooped out the earth, leaving a massive bowl-like depression. The sun was hidden by clouds, but Beobrand judged it to be close to midday.

Before them ran a stream. It flowed across the floor of the bowl.

They slipped and slid down the path into the hollow. All sound of the sea vanished.

The brook was loud in the quietude of the glade.

Biorach held up his hand. "I will go no closer. The woman you seek lives in the cave from whence that stream flows. Follow the burn and you will come to the hag's lair." He seemed embarrassed not to accompany them further. "I will wait here for you. But I will not stay until darkness falls. If I am no longer here, make your way back to the beach."

Beobrand nodded. "Coenred," he said, "you should stay here with Biorach. We do not know what we are to face."

Coenred, his face pallid in the gloom of the glade, raised himself up to his full height. Set his jaw. "I will not stay here. I will go with you. After all, you may need rescuing," he said. His attempt to smile merely served to make him look sick.

Beobrand fixed him with a long stare. The boy had been

a true friend since the first time they had met. And he was as brave as any warrior. Braver than many. Beobrand nodded.

"Very well," he said.

An explosion of sound made them all start. Coenred let out a cry of alarm.

It was a jackdaw, black and grey feathers a blur as it launched itself from a branch. With a high-pitched call, it flew overhead, following the course of the brook upstream.

Beobrand spat. He forced his fingers to unclench from his Thunor's hammer amulet.

"Come. It is just a bird." He touched Hrunting's pommel for luck. "Let us retrieve what we have come for and be gone from this place."

The jackdaw had flown beyond their line of sight, but they could still hear its squealing call. Tchack, tchack, tchack.

They walked toward the sound. Could it be beckoning to them? Beobrand looked to Acennan, but there was no comfort for him there. Acennan was as pale as Coenred. His eyes were wide and wild.

Cold fingers of dread ran down Beobrand's spine.

They followed the stream out of the glade.

"It is just a bird," repeated Beobrand. But the words rang hollow to his own ears.

That was no forest creature. It was a malignant spirit.

It had been watching them. And now it was calling them to their doom.

The brook led them along the floor of a valley. On either side the trees loomed and leered. Overhanging, moss-covered limbs reached for them as they walked. No breeze reached this place. The only sounds were the echoes of their own movements and the trickling of the water. The quiet was unsettling. Beobrand glanced at his companions. Each had fear etched into his features, but they were close behind him.

"Biorach said it was not far," Beobrand whispered. It seemed wrong to disturb the silence. "We should be there soon."

They continued on. Their feet slipped on the slick stones of the path that followed the stream. Everywhere was moss and lichen. The very air seemed to be green. Its earthy redolence was cloying. Behind Beobrand, Coenred gagged.

They rounded a bend, passing a huge alder that extended over the path and brook, forming a branch archway. They ducked their heads and stepped beneath it.

The jackdaw, which had been sitting on a branch of the tree, let out its cry again. With a flurry of wings it blasted from its perch. Startled, Beobrand gasped and stepped back abruptly, knocking into Coenred, who in turn lost his footing on the moss-clad rocks and tumbled over into the stream. Acennan reached out and hauled the monk from the water.

"Are you hurt?" Beobrand asked.

Coenred shook his head, but did not speak. He was looking beyond Beobrand's shoulder. Turning, Beobrand peered into the gloom of the overgrown stream bed. The stream ran from a cleft in the hillside before them. The cave entrance was a gash in the rock. It was around the height of a man, though Beobrand could see he would need to stoop to enter. From the cave there issued a thin trail of smoke. It was as if a mighty wyrm lay within the darkness, exhaling its sulphurous breath.

Before the cave mouth there stood a stout pole, upon which rested the massive skull of a horse. The skull was stained brown. On twigs and branches all around the totem were small ribbons. Strips of cloth of all colours dangled from the trees. Some of the branches sported other items, which had been tied with twine. Beobrand saw small figures carved in wood or bone. Offerings. Gifts for the gods. Presents for the inhabitant of the cave.

The jackdaw sat on the brow of the skull. It eyed them with an uncanny intelligence. Its eyes were almost white in the gloaming of the vale. It cocked its head, twitching erratically.

Beobrand could not break its gaze. It held him in its thrall. This evil spirit would devour them all. His stomach churned. They should leave now, while they yet lived. This place would be their undoing.

A sudden movement behind him broke the spell. Acennan stepped forward and threw a pebble at the bird. It missed, but the jackdaw leapt from the skull, circled in the air and flapped into the black mouth of the cave.

Could it be that the bird was in fact the witch in animal form? He had heard of such things.

Coenred mumbled words of the Christ tongue under his breath.

Acennan shrugged. "It is only a bird," he said.

Beobrand nodded his thanks to Acennan. Despite the chill he felt a trickle of sweat down his back.

The cave mouth, all angles of cracked and mould-green rock, loomed before them. Beobrand looked at the others. They were on edge, but their faces were set now. Determined. There was no other way but forward. They must face their wyrd. He suddenly felt foolish for not bringing any means of making light. They would need to enter the tomb-like darkness with no torch light to guide them.

"If we journey too far into the cavern to see, we will return here to make a torch." His voice cracked. His throat was dry. He sounded fearful to his own ears. Acennan and Coenred did not seem to notice. They merely nodded. They were ready to follow him.

Taking a deep breath of the stagnant air, Beobrand stepped into the rocky maw.

He crouched slightly, so as not to dent his helm. The smoke that wafted over his head carried the scent of cooking meat. He sensed the others crowding in behind him. Their bodies smothered much of the weak, watery light that came in through the cave's entrance.

The way was narrow. A damp stone path led alongside the stream. The water gurgled words in the darkness that only the rocks could comprehend.

Beobrand drew Hrunting from its scabbard, the weight of it a comfort. He shuffled forward. One foot before the other. His shoes slid on the stone. His breath was loud in the confined space.

He moved further into the blackness. Acennan and Coenred's steps echoed in the dark. He could see nothing ahead. It was madness to go onward. Death could be lurking ready to strike and he would not see its coming. He remembered when his eyes had been bandaged after the battle of Elmet. The fear he had of being blind for the rest of his life. As good as blind now, his head began to ache, perhaps with the memory of the blow to his eye all those months ago.

He was on the verge of halting to return to the light outside when he noticed something ahead of them. A small glimmer, as of moonlight reflecting on a pool at night. He peered into the darkness. Yes, there was light ahead. He moved slowly forward. One step. Two. The light grew stronger, as did the smell of food.

Beobrand's eyes now made sense of what they saw. The cramped pathway into the hillside turned to the right. There was light coming from that turning. It shone on the wall before them, which was slick with running water.

"Well, do you plan to stand there all day?" spoke a female voice. "Or are you going to join me and Muninn for something to eat?"

The sudden sound of the voice, loud and echoing in the stillness and gloom, made Beobrand start. He stood upright, banging his helmeted head into the rock roof of the tunnel. He heard Acennan curse.

There was nothing for it now. Their wyrd had led them to this place. Now they must face this witch, and pray to all the gods that she would not weave her foul magics upon them.

Raising Hrunting before him, he touched Thunor's hammer with his left hand. He stepped over the stream and walked around the bend in the tunnel.

The sudden brightness of rush lights and flame-glow made him blink. He was in a large cavern, many times the height of a man. It was dry and as warm as any hall. A fire burnt. A pot hung over it. The roof of the cavern was jagged. Huge teeth of rock hung down like the giant fangs of a dragon. The shadows from the fire made the teeth rove and shift. As if the great dragon was breathing.

All around the edges of the cavern, in the darkened recesses, where the light barely reached, hung clumps of twigs and leaves. Wyrts for spells. Pots and jars were stacked in every nook. From the far side of the cave, the sightless dark eye sockets of a human skull stared. This was the domain of a witch, of that there was no doubt. The very air reeked of magic. And power.

Beobrand took a step into the cavern, to allow the others to enter. He might need their assistance against the crone.

But the woman who sat beside the fire was no crone.

She was no hag such as people said rode horses into a fever at night, or caused a mother's milk to dry up. On a stool in the middle of the cavern sat a comely woman. She was older than Beobrand, but slim of waist and shapely. She was looking straight at him and he felt his face flush. Her eyes flashed. She was as beautiful as a thunderstorm. All darkness, with flickers of brilliance. If Sunniva, with her golden locks and radiance was day, this woman was night. Her hair was black, yet streaked with the grey of moonlight filtered through clouds. Her colouring was just like that of a jackdaw. For an instant Beobrand's heart thundered. The bird had been the witch!

Then he noticed the movement beside her face. The jackdaw, all black and grey like its mistress, sat upon her shoulder. It cocked its head and twitched. Its white eyes glared at Beobrand.

She reached up and stroked the head of the creature. It nuzzled her ear.

"Muninn told me you were coming, Beobrand Half-hand," she said. "Though why the mighty murderer of Hengist would seek me out, I cannot say."

Beobrand's skin grew cold. Damp with sudden sweat. The witch knew his name. What evil could she do with such knowledge? Everyone knew that names have power to those with the ear of the elder gods. How did she know him? And she knew of Hengist also. And his part in his death.

His knuckles whitened on Hrunting's hilt. Hengist's killing was as clear to him as the moment it had happened.

"I killed Hengist, it is true." He was pleased that his voice sounded strong and assured. "But it was no murder. He was a coward. He deserved death. I took the weregild for many with his killing. Nobody grieves for him."

She leapt up. Her stool clattered over. The jackdaw flapped

into the air, its call ringing around the cave. Her rage was as sudden as lightning strikes from a cloud-dark sky.

"You speak with the voice of a man but the words of a boy! What do you know of grief?" Her anger filled the cavern.

Beobrand felt his own ire rise to meet hers. "I have lost many loved ones. You may know my name, witch, but you do not know me!"

The fire of her rage dissipated as quickly as a summer storm. She smoothed her skirts. Her hands white as doves against the dark cloth.

"I hear that you cursed Hengist before he died. Denied him his chance to be chosen for the hall of Woden." Beobrand realised with a start that she spoke the tongue of the Angelfolc with no accent. No lilt of the Waelisc. Where was she from, this dark woman of anger and magic?

"He deserved no less. He killed my kin. I saw him murder innocents. He was an animal."

Her face clouded. "And you are so different, are you, Beobrand?"

He shuddered again at the sound of his name on her lips.

"I did not come here to talk of Hengist. Or of me."

She glared at him for a moment, before righting the stool and sitting again.

"Indeed," she said. "And what is it you came for, Beobrand?"

"We have come for the silver platter you stole from the Christ followers of Hii."

"Stole? Stole?" Her tone was incredulous. "Is that what they have told you?"

"They say you took the plate from them. It belongs to the sons of Æthelfrith. Oswald is now king in Bernicia. It must be returned to him."

"The Christ lovers speak in riddles and lies. They come to

me. They pay me with silver. And then they send warriors to retrieve the evidence of their deeds."

A sliver of doubt needled its way into Beobrand's mind. "Why would they come to you?" he asked. "Why would they pay you?" He was not sure he wished to hear the answer she would give.

She laughed then, the sound like breaking ice.

"There are two things men seek from Nelda," she said. "And the Christ men do not look for magic of the old ways. They think their nailed man-god is a match for Woden."

"Why do they come to you, if not for your witch skills?" asked Beobrand.

"What else is it that all men seek from a warm woman?" Nelda looked directly at Coenred as she spoke. "There are no women on the isle of Hii. The Christ does not allow it. Yet some of the brethren do not only enjoy the flesh of other men and boys. Some need something more." She winked and licked her lips lasciviously.

"Lies!" shouted Coenred. "You are a devil."

"Perhaps I am a devil. But in this I speak the truth. They come here and lie with me. And like any man, they will do anything for a fuck."

Coenred made the sign of the rood before him and began speaking in the tongue of the priests. He raised his voice, perhaps hoping to drown out her words with his prayers. Beobrand placed his left hand on Coenred's shoulder.

"Perhaps you'd like a fuck too, boy?" She lifted her dark skirts, revealing a lithe ankle, a well-formed calf, pale and shapely in the darkness.

Coenred panted, breathless, almost sobbing.

"Stop this!" snapped Beobrand. "Enough of your games, witch. Give us what we have come for and be done."

"I see so much of him in you," Nelda said, ignoring him.

"Who?" asked Beobrand.

"Hengist," she looked wistful at the name. "You are so like him. You deny it to yourself, but others can see it in you. I see him in you."

Beobrand shook his head. He was nothing like that monster. But he remembered the freezing forest. Cathryn lying on the ground. He had felt himself become aroused. And in battle. In the shieldwall, did he not revel in the killing?

He had killed Hengist for what he had done. Would he never be free of him?

"Hengist is a corpse," he said, his voice as savage as a sword thrust. "I am alive. And we are nothing alike." He took a step toward her. "Now give us the plate."

Nelda reached behind her and lifted an object from a sack where it had lain hidden. The light of the fire and the candles glinted from its burnished surface. It was a circular plate of solid silver. Around its rim was intricate scroll-work. It was an object of true beauty. And immense value.

"I asked Cormán for this plate especially. He refused at first, but I told you, men will do anything for a fuck."

Why this plate especially? Had she orchestrated this whole series of events? To bring them here? Beobrand could not tell her motives, but there was more to this woman than they had been led to believe. And there was something about her. Something familiar. Though he was certain he had never seen her before.

"Give it to me," said Beobrand. He took another step forward.

She stood. Held the plate high. It shone in the darkness like a full moon. "It is not yours to take."

"It is my king's and I will have it." He strode toward her.

The jackdaw screeched from the shadows. Coenred whispered his prayers.

Nelda did not flinch as he got close. The scent of her was strong in his nostrils. Sweet and musky. She raised the plate high above her head and somewhat behind her. He would need to reach over her to get it. But he was taller and stronger. It would not be difficult. Then they could leave this place. And be free of this woman.

And her words.

"Take it then," she whispered. He reached over her with his left hand. Their bodies were close. Like lovers. But he did not wish to touch her. Who knew what spell she could weave if they touched?

He made a lunge for the platter, as she moved it further from his grasp.

He spied the movement at the same moment that Acennan cried out. "Beobrand, no!"

A flash of light on metal. There was a knife in her hand! Nelda's face distorted into a mask of utter evil. Lips pulled back from sharp teeth. She hissed like an animal. "Now you will die, murderer!" she screamed, as she stabbed at Beobrand's throat.

He flung his head back. Her blade raked sparks from his byrnie. Without thinking he punched forward with his right hand at the same time. In his fist he held Hrunting and its pommel crashed into Nelda's face. Her lip split, blood splattering black in the gloom. She fell to the cavern floor. The silver plate clattered and rang out in the hollow of the stone vault.

The knife had fallen from her hand and Beobrand kicked it away into the depths of the cave. With an almost human shriek, the jackdaw flew from the shadows, all wings, talons and sharp beak aimed at Beobrand's face. But the battle lust was upon Beobrand now. The movements of others seemed slow and predictable. He effortlessly swung Hrunting in a backhanded arc. The bird fell twitching by its mistress's head. There its wings fluttered and its beak twitched. But it was broken. Dying.

Nelda let out a sobbing cry. She stared up at Beobrand, ire and blood making her features ugly. He stepped above her. Now she would pay. All they had wanted was the plate, but now she would die.

He lifted Hrunting, readying himself for the downward blow that would rid the world of this witch.

She sneered. "And you still say you are nothing like Hengist?" She laughed, a gurgling sound through blood and broken teeth. "Do you also believe you are not your father's son, Beobrand Half-hand?"

He stopped his hand then. Heard the echo of his mother's last words to him in Nelda's voice. He remembered her fearful face when Grimgundi, his father, had taken his fists to her.

Beobrand stood over Nelda, sword in hand, shirt of metal heavy on his shoulders. Had he come to this? Was this the way of the warrior he had sought? To strike down women. And for what?

Acennan stood beside him. His sword was drawn. "Let me finish the whore," he said. His face was pale, but set hard as granite.

"No." Beobrand sheathed Hrunting.

"But she would have killed you," Acennan said.

"Yes, she would." He took a deep breath, stepped over the prostrate form of Nelda. He lifted the plate from the ground. It was heavy and cold in his grasp. Perhaps she was right. Was he really so like Hengist? Did his blood rule him?

"But she did not," he said. "And now we will leave this place. We have what we came for."

Acennan looked doubtful, but Beobrand led him away. Back to the tunnel and the stream. Back towards the light.

Acennan took one of the rush lights from a ledge near the exit of the cavern to guide their way. They left the cave and made their way rapidly back towards the daylight.

They still had some way to go when they heard a scream of animal rage echo in the tunnel. The hair on the back of Beobrand's neck bristled. Words they could not comprehend reverberated in the darkness. Then a screech, as of someone in terrible pain.

"I curse you, Beobrand Half-hand," Nelda's words dripped venom. "I curse you, as you cursed my son! You will never know happiness. You will die alone. You will not be chosen for the hall of Woden. I curse you!"

They burst forth into the grey light of the winter afternoon. Despite the shade in the valley and the dimness of the cloud-veiled sun, they blinked at the brightness.

They did not speak as they hurried back along the stream. They were all keen to be as far away from that dark place as possible. As they moved closer to the glade where Biorach awaited them, the memory of Nelda seemed to fade. Like a nightmare fades on waking.

Yet, for Beobrand, like the worst nightmares, her words did not fade. They rang in his mind.

Nelda was Hengist's mother! And she had cursed him. A curse for her slain kin. He knew the power of oaths made for vengeance. He could only imagine the strength of a curse made by the mother of a killed son.

As if he knew what Beobrand was thinking, Acennan said, "You should have let me kill her."

Beobrand did not answer. He could not. It was too late for recriminations or regrets. He had spared her life to avoid becoming like the men he despised. But in saving her, he had brought down her curse on him.

It was too late now, but deep down, he feared that Acennan was right.

16

Sunniva hit the glowing metal hard. Sparks flew. She turned it using the tongs in her left hand and beat it again. It was a simple piece. A large nail for the new hall. She had made several over the last few days. It was an extravagance, but she wanted the door of the new hall to be iron-studded and grand. She gave it one final tap to straighten the point then, judging it to be complete, plunged it into the bucket of water. It hissed briefly, like an angry cat. She set the finished nail alongside the others.

She wiped sweat from her forehead. The heat from the forge and the exertion from the ceaseless effort kept her warm despite the bitter chill of the day. She looked up the hill. The frame of the new hall stood there, stark and bare against the drear sky. She could see movement there. Progress was good. Beobrand would be pleased. Proud of her.

She bit her lower lip. Felt the tears threaten.

"What is it, Sunniva?" Edlyn asked. The girl spent most of each day with her. She worked the bellows for her, and Sunniva was showing her the art of the smith. She was a hard worker. Sunniva enjoyed her chatter. It helped her to keep her mind away from the dark places it threatened to travel. Now, Edlyn's eyes were full of compassion. The girl worried for her. Sunniva knew it. Edlyn had sensed the change in her mood in the last few days, and sought to buoy her spirits whenever she could.

"It is nothing, dear one," Sunniva said. But she knew the girl would not rest without an explanation, so she added, "I was thinking of Beobrand."

"He has been gone a long time." Edlyn paused, then seemed to hear the words she had spoken and how they would sound to Sunniva. "But the snows have been very bad this winter," she continued in a hurry. "Mother says they would be even worse further north in Dál Riata."

Sunniva forced a smile. She missed Beobrand terribly. Every day without him was a trial. She found herself constantly looking to the ford. Hoping to see him returning on the huge steed, Sceadugenga. But Geola passed and snow had covered the land. Rowena had told her not to worry. The men would return. But the winter nights were long and cold. And Sunniva was lonely. Edlyn and Rowena were good company in their way, and she felt welcome in Ubba's hall. The wives of Beobrand's gesithas were friendly enough. But they did not invite her to dine with them. Or cook with them. Or weave with them. She was their lord's wife now, and not for the likes of them.

Sunniva had no family here. Edlyn was but a girl. A girl who had recently lost her father and brothers. Sunniva could not burden her with her worries.

Her secrets.

Absently, her fingers brushed the leather apron she wore, flattening it over her stomach.

She watched as in the distance, two of Beobrand's warband

lifted a plank. They moved it into place and held it firm while a third man hammered in pegs to secure it. The hall was taking shape. Bored and lonely she had decided to start work on the new home they had agreed on. Winter was not the best time for the work. They often needed to put away their tools, sometimes for days on end when the rain beat down as if it would never stop. But they cut wood. Shaped planks. Made nails.

And the hall grew.

The men seemed to enjoy the work too, despite their moaning. It gave them purpose. Kept them busy. And tired.

One of the women had said to her just the day before, "You're keeping my man so busy, he is too tired to trouble me at night. Thank you for the rest, lady." She had winked at her. Sunniva had blushed.

"You only miss what you no longer have," Sunniva's mother had always said. Sunniva wondered now whether the woman would be as pleased of the rest if her man had been away in the north for months.

"Lady Sunniva," a voice brought her from her reverie with a start. Sunniva tensed.

Anhaga.

She took a deep breath.

She turned and there stood the crippled man. How could he move so quietly with that twisted foot? He seemed always to be creeping up on her. She shuddered, remembering the last time he had come upon her unannounced and unbidden. His face was still not healed. His lip had returned to its normal size, but the scab remained. His eyes were no longer swollen, but they were mottled with the storm-cloud shades of old bruises. Dark circles underlined his eyes. His nose had been broken and was now as crooked as his leg.

"Anhaga," her voice was flat, "what do you want?"

He sighed, perhaps at the coldness of her tone. "I have come for nails."

Edlyn, eager to please and wishing to dispel the uncomfortable atmosphere that always fell when Sunniva and Anhaga conversed, fetched a small basket filled with nails. She handed it to Anhaga.

"Your face looks like it is getting better," she said, colour coming to her cheeks.

"Thank you," Anhaga replied. "It was stupid of me to fall on the ice." He flicked a glance back at Sunniva. Their eyes met and she turned away.

"Still, I suppose I am lucky," he said.

"Lucky?"

"I could have hurt my other leg in the fall," he said with a grin made hideous by the bruises.

With a last lingering look at Sunniva, he turned and limped towards the waiting men on the hill.

They had been away for so long that Beobrand had almost forgotten what Ubbanford looked like. Yet now, after all the months of travel, cold and battered by the elements, he had returned home.

Home.

It seemed strange to think of the place in that way. Strange, but right.

Sunlight finally forced its way through the heavy clouds that had threatened rain all day, to shine on the buildings that nestled by the river Tuidi. It was cold, but the sun warmed their spirits as much as their bodies.

They rode through the ford. The high water, swollen with

rain and snow-melt, nearly reached the feet of the riders. The horses slowed, picking their way across the slippery rocks beneath the surface.

Sceadugenga tossed his mane, as if he too was pleased to return to familiar territory. Beobrand had been surprised by the depth of his own emotions when he was reunited with the stallion after the weeks on Hii and Muille. The horses had been well treated, and the red rags seemed to have worked their magic. No night hag had come to ride Sceadugenga into a lather of sweat. His steed was safe from any night terrors. It was Beobrand who found his nights tormented by a witch.

He often awoke to half-remembered dreams of darkness and evil. With Nelda's words echoing in his mind. Her scent still in his nostrils, as if she had been lying close to him while he slept.

He talked little of his nightmares. Of his fears. Of Nelda's curse.

Coenred had tried to console him. "The witch has no power," he'd said. "Only Christ has power over life and death." This was ridiculous, of course. Beobrand knew Coenred meant well, but when he looked at the boy's face he wondered if he even believed the words himself. He had been pallid and shaken when they had left Nelda's cave. If the Christ alone had power over death, why fear a witch? Or a sword?

Acennan had only talked of the encounter once.

"I should have killed her," he'd said.

Beobrand had shaken his head.

"Killing women is not my wyrd."

Acennan had snorted.

"Well, you killed her bird alright. Only a bird, like I said. And she was just a woman. A grieving mother. Do not dwell on her words, Beobrand. They are as hollow as an empty horn."

Just a woman? With no power? Beobrand wished he could believe that. But how had she known so much? She had drawn him to her lair for vengeance. She had failed to slay him there, but would her curse follow him? Had she pronounced his doom?

His fears had lessened somewhat with the passing of time and distance. But she was always there. On the edge of his mind as they travelled south.

The journey had been long and arduous. The return had been less eventful, and with less rain and snow. But it was the same distance. The same mountains needed to be traversed. The same rivers crossed. The Tuidi was the last great river. To pass it meant they were once more in the heartland of Bernicia.

"It looks like your new hall is already built," Acennan pointed to the hill that dominated the settlement.

Beobrand looked and saw men working on the frame of a large building. It was not close to being complete, but the scale and shape of it were clear. It would be a great hall. Something to be proud of. A hall fit for a warlord and his lady.

"Sunniva seems to have got the men working," Beobrand said. He scanned the village, but there was no sign of her. He yearned to see her. It had been so long since he had held her in his arms.

He looked to the forge, half expecting her to be coming from the smith's hut. But there was no smoke emanating from there. No sound of hammer on iron. A tendril of fear wormed its way into his mind. Nelda's curse hung over him the way a cloud of flies buzzes over a pool of blood. "You will never know happiness. You will die alone."

Where was Sunniva?

As he looked, he saw the men on the hill leave their work

and head down towards them at a run. Beobrand spurred Sceadugenga up the pebbled beach onto dry ground. Suddenly fearful for his wife, he cantered towards Ubba's hall.

Before he reached the hall, two armed men stepped from the doorway. They carried shields and spears. Wore helms. They were prepared for attack.

He reined in before them. Sceadugenga snorted, his breath clouding the air before the door wards. Beobrand recognised the men. They were his men. His gesithas.

"Your lord has returned," said Acennan, pulling his own steed to a halt.

One of the men stepped forward and removed his helm. It was Tobrytan.

"You are well come home, my lord," he said.

"Is all well here?" asked Beobrand. "Does the Lady Sunniva fare well?" Fear gripped his throat. His voice was strained.

Could Nelda's curse reach here? Had something happened to his love?

"Aye," said Tobrytan. "Never fear. We have protected her." He seemed affronted at Beobrand's obvious fear for Sunniva's safety. "She is safe enough inside the old hall."

Such a feeling of relief flooded through Beobrand, that he almost fell to his knees as he dropped from Sceadugenga's back. He threw the reins to Tobrytan.

"My thanks," he said, and without pause, ran past the bemused warrior and into the hall.

Sunniva sat by the hearth fire. The gloom of the hall was a blessing. Bright light and loud sounds were as painful as knives in her skull. She needed solitude. She had sent Edlyn away. The girl had not disguised her disappointment. Sunniva regretted speaking harshly to her, but her head was fit to burst. She could not listen to Edlyn's prattling. Not today.

Lady Rowena was her only company. She understood, and was content to sit in silence. After some time, Rowena had picked up a comb and started brushing Sunniva's long hair. Sunniva had flinched, thinking it would cause her aching head more anguish. Yet, after a few moments, the motion began to soothe her. Rowena was good to her. Sunniva did not know what she would have done without her in the last weeks. She confided in Rowena. Trusted her. Having Edlyn to keep her mind occupied and Rowena to offer a friendly ear, to listen and not judge, had made the winter bearable.

She feared what would have become of her without Rowena in the last days. Her mind had grown dark. Her torment ever more difficult to push away.

She closed her eyes, trying to forget. She focused on the strokes of the comb running through her long tresses. Recently, these headaches had become more frequent. Nothing seemed to keep them at bay. She had tried different wyrts and poultices that old Odelyna concocted for her, but to no avail. Only darkness and rest gave any respite.

With a crash and a gust of cold air the door to the hall was flung open. The flames flared up with the draught. She opened her eyes and sighed. Surely Anhaga could not need her again? She had told him to leave her be. She thought he, of all people, would understand her need for peace.

But it was not Anhaga who loomed in the doorway. Dark against the brilliance of the afternoon sun, stood a huge figure. She squinted. The light shot shards of agony into her head. Was this Nathair? Or one of his sons? She had secretly thought that the day would come when they would attack. And, although the gesithas would defend them with their lives if necessary, she was under no illusions of the possibility they would not be saved.

Sunniva and Rowena both stood. Rowena took her hand. Squeezed. They would face whatever danger befell them together. But what of Edlyn, and the other women? And the children? Sunniva felt the weight of the lives of the folk of Ubbanford then.

"Who goes there?" she said, her voice shrill. "What do you mean by entering Ubba's hall?"

"It is I, your lord and husband," said the figure. The sound of the voice brought tears to her eyes. She had longed to hear it so many times in the dark days.

Sunniva let out a sobbing cry.

Beobrand, hale, strong, reassuring, strode across the hall.

"My love," he said, his arms outstretched.

All strength left her. She collapsed into Beobrand's embrace. He crushed her to his chest.

Her head throbbed and the iron rings of the byrnie pinched her. But she did not care. She allowed the tears she had held in check for so long to flow now. Great sobs racked her. She cried tears of sorrow. Bitter and hot anguish at all that had befallen her. All she had lost.

Yet her weeping was not all of sadness.

Beobrand's large hands caressed her head gently. Smoothed her already shining hair.

"My love," he whispered over and again in her ear.

Elation made her smile through the pain and the crying.

For her man had returned to her.

"Well, what did you think of Cormán?" Beobrand asked. He cared little for Sunniva's opinion on the Christ priest from

Hii, but she seemed reticent to come to bed. He was tired, having ridden all day, and then drinking vast quantities of ale and mead well into the night. He watched Sunniva with bleary eyes as she brushed her hair by the light of a rush light. The shape of her body beneath the shift she wore was obvious. The swell of her breast. The curve of her hips. He swallowed. Gods, he had missed her so. He could feel his body awakening at the sight of her and the promise of what lay beneath her undergarments.

Despite his growing passion, his tiredness tugged at his eyes. He would not allow sleep to consume him yet. He shifted in the bed, propping himself up on one elbow. He must keep awake.

Sunniva had not answered him. Perhaps she had not heard. Or maybe she listened to the sound of the others still carousing in the hall beyond the partition. They had retired early. Sunniva had looked pinched and tired all night. She had not complained, but she was not herself. After some time, when he thought it would not be seen as an insult to their guests, Beobrand had announced that he felt unwell and would go to his bed.

Acennan had caught his eye as he left with Sunniva. He had smiled and winked. It seemed he did not believe Beobrand's pretence of illness. Beobrand did not care. All he could think of was to be alone with Sunniva. Throughout the night he could scarcely pay attention to anything else.

"Well, what did you think?" he repeated.

Sunniva looked at him, her eyes dim, unfocused. "Hmmm? The priest?"

"Yes, Cormán."

Sunniva thought for a moment before replying. At last she said, "He seems arrogant. For one who comes to this land as a stranger, he would do well to learn the tongue of the Angelfolc."

"I have thought similar things," said Beobrand. The priest's face seemed permanently fixed in a scowl of disdain. He clearly believed himself above those whom he was sent to teach in the ways of the Christ god.

"Now, come to bed, my love," said Beobrand, lifting the furs and blankets enticingly.

Sunniva drew in a long, deep breath. She then put down her brush and slid beneath the covers.

Her thigh brushed against him. Their feet touched. A thrill ran though his body. He suppressed a shiver. They had barely touched, yet he could feel himself harden and grow. He burnt for her. So many weeks, so many dark nights alone. The other men had bedded thralls or servants in the halls where they had stayed. Beobrand had kept his desires in check. Sunniva had given herself to him absolutely. She was his anchor, keeping him steady in the tumultuous seas he had found himself in. War, blood, honour and oaths. The affairs of kings and athelings. He was afraid that should he allow himself to give in to his lust with another woman, he might lose Sunniva. And he needed her. Of that he was certain.

He reached for her, his whole right hand pulling her towards him. He could already imagine the taste of her mouth. The softness of her lips.

She tensed beneath his hand. Resisted moving.

"What is it, Sunniva?" he asked in an urgent whisper. He strove, but failed to keep the frustration from his voice. The warmth of her body engulfed him beneath the furs. His hand rested on her arm with his wrist brushing her breast. His whole body thrummed like a lyre string.

"I... I am sorry, my husband." Sunniva's voice was brittle and small.

A coolness entered Beobrand then. The wings of jealousy and doubt began to flap at his mind. Had he been wrong to hold himself faithful to her all these months?

"Sorry for what, Sunniva?"

She tensed once more under his hand. Perhaps at the harshness of his voice.

"I would give you that which you seek. I want it too, believe me," she said. "My bed has been cold these many weeks. But I am not well."

All at once his anger snuffed out, before the spark of jealousy had fully kindled.

"Are you sick?" he asked. He thought of her pallor throughout the evening. He cursed his stupidity and selfishness.

"It is nothing," she answered. "I just need to sleep. Tomorrow, I will feel restored, I am sure." She offered him a thin smile. "I think I will need all my strength to cope with your passion. I fear my head would split in two should we lay together tonight. I am sorry."

"Do not be sorry, my love." He leaned over her and placed a gentle kiss on her lips. "I have waited through the snows of winter to feel your fire again. I can wait one more night."

Her small hand caressed his chest, and she murmured something in the dark that he could not make out.

"Sleep now, Sunniva," he whispered. Her hand ceased moving, and her breathing deepened.

He lay there, his body still inflamed at her touch and proximity and listened to the revellers in the hall.

For a time his mind battled against sleep. Questions and fears assailed him. What ailed Sunniva? Could it be that Nelda's curse was working its evil on her?

But soon the warmth of Sunniva's body next to his, the talk and laughter of the folk in the hall, and the drink he had consumed, all served to lull him to sleep. His last thought before he succumbed was that he was sure to dream again of the cave. Of Nelda and the curse. And yet, perhaps the presence of Sunniva kept the night hag at bay, for he fell into a deep and dreamless sleep and did not awake until late the next morning.

Whispers awoke him.

Beobrand thought at first they were words spoken in a dream. He strained to make out what was being said, but he could not. The hall was not silent. There was talking and the sound of furniture being scraped on the floor. The whispers, while nearby, were as unfathomable as the sibilant wave-wash of shingle on a beach.

Eyes still closed, he reached out a hand to touch Sunniva. It was warm under the furs, but his nose was cold. Perhaps Sunniva felt better this morning. But his left hand did not come into contact with the pliant flesh he had been anticipating. Sunniva had left their bed. The covers were still warm where she had lain until recently.

He opened his eyes. Pale daylight filtered into the hall through small windows. It seemed he had slept late. He felt refreshed, his head clear, in spite of the mead from the night before.

The sounds in the main hall grew louder, presumably as more of the guests roused themselves. The whispers also rose in volume. He recognised Sunniva's voice in those hushed tones now, yet the words still eluded him. There was an urgency in her tone.

Who was she talking to? Perhaps Rowena or Edlyn.

Then the other whispered voice was raised loud enough for him to make out the words. "You should tell him." With surprise, Beobrand realised the voice was that of Anhaga. What could the cripple and his wife be talking about with such vehemence? He recalled Sunniva's concerns about Anhaga. How he had dismissed her fears. His heart clenched. Had she been right? He had left her with this man against her judgement. The previous night he had been shocked to see Anhaga's face. It was a mass of old bruises. He had told the story of a fall on the ice several days before. What if he had lied? Could there be another reason for his injuries?

Beobrand rose from the bed quickly. He pulled on his kirtle, all the while listening for more clues in the whispered conversation.

Sunniva said something, but her words were masked by a sudden guffaw of laughter from the hall.

Anhaga's reply was clear: "You must tell him. He is your husband. Your hlaford."

Beobrand stepped from his sleeping area. He stood tall. His chin jutted in defiance. He bristled with concern. Anger was not far behind.

Anhaga and Sunniva both turned toward him, their mouths open in surprise. Sunniva was wan. Anhaga could not hold Beobrand's gaze.

"Tell me what?" Beobrand's voice was as sharp as Hrunting's blade.

Anhaga looked at his feet.

"Tell me what?" Beobrand repeated. "You seemed sure of yourself a moment ago, Anhaga. Why not tell me yourself?"

Anhaga shook his head. "I am sorry. It is not my place."

"Sorry for what, man?" Beobrand's brow furrowed. He

clenched his fists at this side. He would crush this cripple if he had laid a hand on Sunniva.

Sunniva stepped between them; placed her palm on Beobrand's chest.

"Do not be angered with Anhaga." She looked up at Beobrand. Her eyes glowed, brimming with tears.

"Why are you upset?" he asked.

She ignored the question and turned to Anhaga. "Go now, Anhaga. Leave my husband and I to talk."

Anhaga needed no encouragement. He limped away as quickly as his deformity would permit.

Taking Beobrand's hand Sunniva led him back into their sleeping quarters.

"Sit, my husband, and I will tell you my tidings."

Intrigued and still unnerved, Beobrand sat on a small stool. "What tidings, Sunniva?"

Sunniva smoothed her dress over her stomach then stepped close to Beobrand.

"Do you remember the oath you made? Before you went to Hefenfelth?"

Beobrand nodded, unable to speak now. For he well remembered the words he had spoken. He remembered the makeshift bed. The cramped sleeping area. The rush light blowing out. He was suddenly certain of what she would say next.

"You promised to return. To marry me. Both of these things you have done." She took his hands in hers, knelt before him. "But you vowed one more thing. I do not know if I will bear you a son, but I am with child. You are to be a father."

The world seemed to swim before Beobrand for a heartbeat. He felt lightheaded. Weak. He was glad he was seated. Otherwise he feared he would have fallen to the ground.

"When?" he managed after some time.

"I do not know exactly, but when we were in Bebbanburg, of that I am certain. Our baby will be born sometime around Eostremonath."

"You are sure...?" Doubt prickled like a fish bone scratches a throat. He had been away for months.

"Of course I am sure." Her voice turned brittle as winter twigs. "Your seed was planted before you left for the north. I just did not know it." The tears fell then. Her lip quivered. "Do not doubt me, Beobrand. I could not bear it. The babe is yours. You are to be a father."

A father! He swallowed. He did not wish to doubt her, but questions assailed him. There were at once too many thoughts in his head to latch on to any single one. Then he settled on a dark thought. A question that must be answered. He could make no sense of it.

"Why were you speaking to Anhaga of this? How is it that he knows of my child before me?"

"Hush, my love. Remember that you have been far away." Beobrand frowned at the reproach he imagined in her words. "I did not feel well last night. I wished to wait till the right moment." He felt a pang of guilt at his clumsy advances of the night before. Yet even now, the sight of her intoxicated him.

"You were right about Anhaga," she continued. "He has been a true friend. I was... taken ill some days back. Anhaga helped me then. I had to tell him what ailed me. He frets over me now like a woman. He is worse than Rowena and Edlyn."

"They know also? Am I the last to know of my own child?" Beobrand made an attempt at outrage, but he could not keep the smile from his voice. He was to be a father!

"I have told nobody else, my husband. I am so very pleased you have returned to me. I have missed you more than you will ever know."

"And I you. Eostremonath, you say?"

Sunniva nodded, wiping away her tears.

A spring birth. He counted back the months. They had been at Bebbanburg, as Sunniva said. How could he have doubted her?

He stood and raised her up from her knees. He kissed her, his lips firm and hot on hers. He laughed to himself as he felt his body respond to her touch.

"You are pleased then?" she asked.

"Pleased? Of course I am pleased. The gods have blessed us." He kissed her again, long and deep.

Then, in a loud voice, he said, "I am to be a father!"

From the other side of the partition there rose a roar of approval from his gesithas and the gathered guests.

He blushed, and kissed Sunniva again, tenderly. He whispered for her ears alone, "I love you, Sunniva, Strang's daughter."

17

"You are well come, brother." Oswald smiled and opened his arms expansively. Oswiu stepped into his embrace stiffly. He seemed embarrassed by this show of fraternal affection, but Oswald appeared genuinely pleased to see him.

Not for the first time, Coenred felt small and alone watching these great men. He did not fit in amongst them. And there was nobody to welcome him home with love. He should not dwell so on his own feelings. Fearghas had always said he needed to think more of Christ and less of himself. He would miss the abbot's advice. He was invariably right.

"And this must surely be our bishop. Cormán, is it not?" The king stepped forward and took the priest's hands in his. He spoke then to Cormán in the tongue of the Dál Riatan's. The words were fluid, like water cascading over pebbles. Cormán replied and spoke at some length. Oswald frowned.

Coenred had picked up a smattering of the language of the Hibernian monks, but not enough to follow the conversation. One thing was clear though, the new bishop was unhappy about something.

Oswald clapped his hands and called for a servant.

"Show our guest to his sleeping quarters. We will send for him when we are to eat." The servant nodded. Oswald spoke again to Cormán, who responded with a sour face and a tilt of the head.

Once both men had left the hall, the atmosphere changed. Oswiu and his retainers openly relaxed. Coenred was not surprised. Cormán made him uneasy too. He had not mentioned what the witch had said about the man. Neither had Acennan or Beobrand as far as he knew. It was not their place. Yet it cast doubt in his mind as to the bishop's holiness.

Nelda had spoken with the voice of the devil. Lies, to turn them against Cormán. But she did have the plate... Stolen, as the bishop had said, surely. Coenred had thought much on these matters. And watching the man over the last weeks, he could not dispel the niggling doubt that the witch spoke true. It felt wrong, petty, to question the will of the brethren of Hii. Yet he could not see how this man, with his imperious air and disdain for the warriors of the Angelfolc, could replace Fearghas.

"Cormán seems tired from the journey," said Oswald.

Oswiu snorted. "Tired? If it is tiredness that makes him so, then he must always be tired." A couple of his gesithas chortled.

Oswald ran his fingers through his hair. "I have to say I am somewhat surprised at Ségéne's choice of abbot and bishop for Lindisfarena. I do not remember Cormán being a man who would relish such a challenge. Bringing Christ to the heathen savages of Bernicia. Still, who am I to question their choice? I am sure, with God's blessing, he will do well."

"We shall see," said Oswiu, though his face did not hide his scepticism. After all, he had endured weeks of the bishop's company, so was less inclined to give him the benefit of God's blessing. "Now, do you greet your brother with nothing more than an embrace? We have much to talk of, and talking is thirsty work."

Oswald led the way to the high table. Thralls brought drink. Coenred again felt out of place. He was unsure of what to do. He seemed to have been forgotten. But he had not been dismissed, so he sat at the far end of the table and took a cup of mead.

When they had all been served, Oswald said, "I do not see young Beobrand here. I pray that nothing befell him on the journey."

"He is hale," replied Oswiu. "He sought my leave to remain on his estate. His woman is with child and he has had problems with a Pictish neighbour."

"Problems?" Oswald raised an eyebrow.

"It seems when they heard Ubba and his sons were dead, this Nathair decided he could take Ubba's livestock." Oswiu took a long draught of mead. "Beobrand showed him he was mistaken."

"Indeed? I believe Beobrand to be an extremely persuasive neighbour."

Some of the men laughed. They all knew Beobrand.

"Well, he certainly persuaded Nathair's son. He sliced off his arm. Mark my words, there will be trouble there. But Beobrand needs to protect what is his."

"I have not seen this Nathair or his sons."

"The Picts north of the Tuidi do not seem keen to pledge their oath to you, brother. They will need to bend their knee soon. Or we will have to make them."

Oswald contemplated his younger brother for some time. His face was inscrutable.

"We are beset by enemies on many sides, it is true," he said at last. "But the Picts are not the largest threat. That remains Penda. The messages to him have been received, but it is still unclear how and where we should meet. Neither of us wishes to end up like Eanfrith. We must find neutral ground, and each bring a warband of considerable strength. Our spies tell us he does not seek war at this time, but we must face each other. Parley and agree terms of peace. Failure to do this will leave him believing we are weak."

Oswiu was solemn. "What of Deira?"

Oswald brightened. "I am recently returned and bring glad tidings. They have accepted me as their rightful king. Northumbria is united once more. By the grace of God."

"This is fine news indeed." Oswiu clapped his brother on the shoulder. "You will be Bretwalda yet."

Oswald's eyes glittered. "If the Lord wills it, it could be so. Athelstan returned some weeks ago. Cynegils of Wessex has accepted my offer."

"Truce and allegiance?"

"Both. Our bloodlines will be joined. I am to marry his daughter."

Mist curled over the winding course of the river Tuidi below Beobrand. He leaned on one of the beams of the frame of his new hall. Despite it being early, the sun had already warmed the wood. He took in the valley below. The cluster of buildings of Ubbanford huddled under a thin veil of hearth smoke and mist. On the hill to the south were the shapes of sheep. He could make out the movement of a shepherd and his scraggy dog. The man's calls and whistles, thin with distance, reached Beobrand's ears.

He breathed deep of the clear morning air. Here, on the hill overlooking the settlement, the scent of woodsmoke was almost imperceptible. Turning, he walked the length of the hall, counting the paces as he went. He tried to imagine it complete with walls of wood and roof of thatch.

"It is ambitious," he said to Sunniva. "I'd wager it is as large as the hall at Gefrin was. Perhaps even as big as the hall at Bebbanburg."

Sunniva flashed him a grin. The sun caught her hair. It was as fine as spun gold. Her cheeks were flushed with the bloom of happiness. She seemed to have fully recovered from the ailment of the previous day. Now that he knew of her condition, he could detect the slight bulge of her belly. Her breasts were perhaps a little larger.

By Woden and all the gods, she was a treasure to behold.

"Are we talking about the hall, or are you just going to disrobe me with your eyes?" she said, raising an eyebrow archly.

Beobrand blushed. "I had almost forgotten how lucky I am." It was true that his wyrd had brought him much misery. But here, with his beautiful wife before him, in the shadow of his own hall and his lands laid out below him, he felt blessed.

At the edge of his mind were thoughts of darkness. Caverns. A curse.

But the day was bright enough to burn away his worries and fears as easily as it would melt the mist from the valley.

Sunniva came to him. Placed her arm in his and kissed his cheek. "I had not forgotten you, my strong man."

"Did you miss me then?" he asked.

She frowned, serious all of a sudden. The levity of moments before gone.

"I missed you more than I can say." She gazed into the

distance, lost in her own thoughts. After a time, she spoke again. "So, you are pleased with the hall?"

"I am. I had not imagined building on this hill."

Sunniva nodded. "Rowena warned against it. She said in winter it will be hard to get up and down from the rest of Ubbanford." She pursed her lips. "And she is right. It was difficult on the worst days, when it rained or snowed. But it commands the valley. From here you can see all of Ubbanford and also the ford itself."

Beobrand looked down at the river. The mist was thinning as he watched. The sky's reflection gave the water a light sheen.

"You chose well. It reminds me of Bebbanburg on its crag."

Sunniva beamed. "I thought the same. I am glad you approve."

"I do." He thought of Gefrin then. How easily it had been conquered and put to the torch. With height came strength. Ubbanford, with its new hall, would not so easily be taken. "It is a good defensive position. And with the neighbours we have, that may be important. What of Nathair and his sons? Any sign?"

"Garr saw the sons riding someway to the south when the snow was thickest. He followed them for a time, but they rode away when they saw him. He thought they were perhaps out hunting."

"Hunting? In mid-winter?"

"The winter was bitter and long. Wolves came down to Ubbanford from the hills. They took one of the ewes. The men went on a hunt. They were gone for three days. We were worried for them," she smoothed her dress over her belly and pulled her cloak about her, as if suddenly cold, "but they brought back some fine pelts. It could be that Nathair's folk were about the same business."

"Are you well?" Beobrand asked. Sunniva had grown pale. "Perhaps we should not have walked up here."

"It is nothing."

Beobrand looked at her sidelong, not fully convinced.

"It is good that Nathair has heeded your warning," she said.

Beobrand nodded.

"I hope the summer sun does not rekindle his sons' desire for vengeance." He remembered the hatred in their eyes, recalled his own anguish at the loss of his brother, Octa. "Their brother's life was mine to take, but I do not believe they will rest until they are paid for it with blood."

18

Coenred wished Fearghas had never sent him on the mission to Hii. The journey had been tortuous, but had led to visiting that most holy of isles. He had met great men there; brothers in Christ who had known Fearghas. They had treated him well, almost as if he had been Fearghas' kin. He had enjoyed the serenity and beauty of the western isles, Hii in particular with its white sands and endless vistas of the vast ocean.

But travelling into Dál Riata had also brought him into contact with Nelda. He cursed himself for offering to join Beobrand and Acennan. It had been foolhardy.

Or perhaps brave.

One thing was for certain, the encounter in the dank cave had unsettled him terribly.

And then there was Cormán.

The man seemed to lack all of the qualities that the other monks had. He was impatient, and was always complaining. Travelling south had been taxing for many reasons. It had been cold and arduous. Even dangerous at times with the threat of bandits or Pictish warbands. But chief amongst the things that made the journey difficult to bear was that Cormán seemed to view Coenred as his personal servant. He treated him little better than a thrall.

He expected Coenred to see to his every need and was quick to find fault. Coenred did not understand the priest's native tongue, and Cormán seemed resolutely to refuse to attempt to converse in the language of the Angelfolc, so they communicated in Latin. Coenred was not one of Fearghas' best pupils, yet his Latin was passable. But the slightest mistake caused Cormán to fly into a rage, screaming at Coenred.

It was intolerable. It could not be that Nelda spoke true about the bishop, but Coenred could not bring himself to love the man as he should love a heavenly brother.

He watched him now as he basked in the attention of the amassed congregation of Oswald's hearth warriors.

Cormán sat with head bowed and hands clasped together. He gave the appearance of a man deep in thought. A spiritual man. A man to be trusted. A man to be listened to.

Oswald had called upon Cormán to address his thegns before the new bishop went to Lindisfarena. The king wished to show off his new Christian leader to his men.

Coenred stood to one side of Cormán. He looked out at the men as they made their way into the hall.

Many of them were followers of Christ, having been baptised in Hibernia or Dál Riata, though to watch them in the mead hall at night, one would find it hard to believe. Others who had more recently joined Oswald's retinue were reluctant to be here. They were wary of the magic of the Christ god, but they could not deny his power, having granted them victory at Hefenfelth. Still, they were unsure. Most of these shuffled to the rear of the hall, near the doors, which had been left open to let in the light and fresh air of the clear spring morning.

The shutters had been flung open and the floor swept clean. There was no fire on the hearth.

Oswald sat at the high table next to Cormán. He smiled to see his men gathered to hear the words of Christ. He had given orders for a church building to be constructed within the confines of the walls of Bebbanburg. It was not yet complete, so for now, the great hall would serve.

Oswald stood and held out his hands as if in welcome. He stood thus until the talk and fidgeting abated.

"My comitatus. My most trusted thegns. I present to you, Cormán, Abbot of Lindisfarena and Bishop of Bernicia. As you know, he has come from the most holy isle of Hii. We are blessed to have his presence amongst us and I am sure we will learn much from him." Coenred bent close to Cormán's ear and whispered a translation of the king's words. Cormán beamed at the praise.

"I have asked him to lead us in the Eucharist and to give us Christ's blessing before he retires to Lindisfarena to do God's work with the brethren there." He swept the hall with his gaze. "I pray that those of you who have yet to be washed in the spirit of the Lord, will soon learn to love the one true God."

Oswald beckoned to Cormán to rise.

"As Cormán has yet to learn the words of the Angelfolc, I will act as interpreter."

Cormán stood, swallowed deeply and began to speak. His words came quickly, with no pause for Oswald to translate. After a time, Oswald touched him on the shoulder and whispered something to him. Cormán flushed. In the silence, Oswald spoke.

"Cormán says he is pleased to have been sent to bring the people of Bernicia the truth of the Lord Jesu Christ."

The king turned to Cormán and raised an eyebrow. The bishop took the hint and continued speaking. However, his nerves seemed to have made his voice even less audible, his words more garbled and with even less pause for Oswald to convey their meaning.

Again, Oswald was forced to place his hand on the priest's shoulder. From his vantage point, Coenred could see the king frowning slightly.

Some of the men in the hall, those who had travelled to Hii to bring back the cleric, smirked.

Oswald took a deep breath before continuing. "The bishop will now perform the rite of the Holy Eucharist, where those who are baptised partake of the body and the blood of Christ."

A voice from the far end of the hall: "Blood, you say?" A murmur of unease ran through the gathered men. It seemed the king had misjudged some of his audience. Coenred bit his lip. It must have been difficult for Oswald to put himself in the minds of those who had not lived for years with the brethren on Hii.

Oswald, clearly flustered now, but still in control, said, "It is bread and wine. It is to remember the sacrifice of our Lord on the rood. It is not meat and blood. Christ was sacrificed so that we would no longer need to spill blood in sacrifices to satisfy the hungry old gods." He spoke briefly to Cormán. The abbot nodded.

"I will show you that this thing holds no evil." Oswald fixed the speaker by the door with his stare. "I will be the first to partake of the Eucharist."

He turned his attention to Cormán. The bishop drew himself up straight, aware that this moment was his. All eyes were upon him.

Before him on the table lay a loaf, resting on the silver

platter retrieved from Nelda's cave. Coenred was aghast. His skin prickled at the wrongness of what he saw. To have the holiest of sacraments touching an object made unclean by witchcraft! This was a thing of evil.

Or stupidity.

He was certain that Oswald could not know of the plate's history. The king was a pious man. Coenred's doubts over Cormán resurged.

The bishop flicked his luxuriant hair with his left hand. The unconscious gesture both nervous and somehow effeminate.

He cleared his throat, lifted the platter before him. He raised it up high. Its polished surface gleamed in the ray of light from one of the windows. Speaking words which he must have heard hundreds of times before, his voice was much more firm. Sonorous, it carried over all those gathered. For some, the words were familiar. For the non-Christians, they were the secret sounds of magic. The tongue of a god from a distant land.

"Suscipe sancte Pater omnipotens aeterne Deus, hanc immaculatam hostiam, quam ego indignus famulus tuus offero tibi Deo meo vivo et vero, pro innumerabilibus peccatis et offensionibus et negligentiis meis…"

The onlookers were silent. A stillness had fallen on them as the priest spoke. Coenred understood the words of the offering of the host. As did Gothfraidh, who stood at the other side of the hall. But he doubted any of the warriors there comprehended the liturgy. Perhaps they had heard it before, but for many, Cormán could have been pronouncing their doom just as easily as offering the bread to the Lord with entreaties of salvation.

Many were the wide eyes of the thegns. The unknown was a thing to be feared. The talk of blood and the otherworldly nature of the prayer made the colour drain from several faces. Yet their king had told them there was no evil in this. That it was a good thing.

And he was a good king. So they watched and waited, their curiosity outweighing their disquiet.

"… et illis proficiat ad salutem in vitam aeternam. Amen." Cormán finished and, pleased at the attentive listeners, permitted himself a self-congratulatory smile.

With a flourish, he proffered the platter to Oswald.

Perhaps he was still not in control of his nerves, or his newfound confidence made him careless, but in turning to the king he caught the edge of the wine-filled chalice that stood on the table. With a gasp, Cormán made a lunging grab at the cup, but merely succeeded in splashing its contents over Oswald's tunic. At the same moment, he lost his grip on the platter. The loaf slipped from the burnished surface and fell to the floor. There it caught the last drops of wine as they dripped from the table.

Oswald stood unmoving for a moment. For an instant his face was consumed with rage. Cormán took a step back.

"Blood! The king is splashed in blood!" A voice called out from the rear of the hall. Many voices joined in the clamour.

Oswald gained control of his ire and the situation rapidly. He held out his hands.

"It is not blood. It is merely wine, as I have told you."

"But you said it signified the blood of the Christ god," one thegn said.

"I did," replied Oswald. "If you wish to see any omen in this, see that I have once more been anointed by the one true God. As I was baptised in water, now I am baptised in the wine of the Eucharist."

There were murmurs, but no more cries or shouts.

"I think we have had enough excitement for now." He cast Cormán a dark glance. "We will leave this blessing for another moment."

With that, he swept from the hall, through the partition and into his sleeping chambers.

The hall was instantly abuzz with the voices of the throng as they filed out into the daylight.

Cormán, as pale as lamb's wool, sat heavily.

Coenred felt sorry for him. He knelt and retrieved the bread. Then he righted the chalice.

"Thank you, Coenred," Cormán said, in a small voice. Coenred was still reeling from what had just occurred, but this startled him further.

Cormán had never before offered him his thanks. And it was the first time the bishop had seen fit to use Coenred's native tongue.

Beobrand walked beside the wide expanse of the Tuidi. The day was still, the sky clear. A light breeze rustled the new leaves of the trees on top of the slope on the north side of the valley. But no wind reached him. The rushes and grasses that grew thick on the bank of the river did not move.

On the hill above Ubbanford his men were working on the new hall. The sounds of their labour were too muted by distance to impinge on his restful mood. He was alone. He welcomed these moments of peace when he could walk by himself. It seemed that as lord and husband he had precious little time for his own company. His own thoughts.

A movement on the river brought him to a halt. Unmoving, he watched. He had seen something, but now all was still again. The river's waters flowed lazily past. He scanned the dark undergrowth that overhung the opposite bank. Then he saw it and smiled.

Standing on a branch of a fallen tree that jutted over the river was the ghostlike form of a heron. As he watched it shifted its head slowly, searching the water for fish, and also seeming to survey Beobrand. It was a huge bird. Its snakelike neck topped with tufted head and deadly beak.

"Good to see you, my friend," Beobrand said, keeping his tone calm and quiet.

He often saw the bird. It was always in this area of the river. Once he had startled it on the bank where he walked, and it had lifted languidly into the air with a creak of wings that appeared large enough to carry a man. Ever since that day, when he had spotted the heron, it was in the shadows of the northern bank.

He marvelled now at how still it could stand. It seemed content to allow the river to flow, sure in the knowledge that fish would swim below its vantage point.

As if it had heard Beobrand's thoughts, its beak, savage as a seax, speared into the water. It made barely a ripple. It came up with a flicker of silver flapping in its maw. The fish disappeared quickly. The heron's explosive speed was replaced by stillness once more, as it resumed its vigil.

Beobrand had only spied the bird catching prey once before and just as he had then, he was awed at how effortless the kill had been. He wondered how it was that animals had such skills. Were they taught by their parents? Or did they learn from other birds? Did the gods speak to them, guiding them? Or was it just their way, with no training?

His own father had taught him many things. He grudgingly acknowledged to himself that he knew about livestock and crops from listening to his father's words. Grimgundi had also taught him about fear. Beobrand unwittingly clenched his fists. Yes, fear was a lesson he had taught well. The power of the man had been terrifying for his children. And their mother.

Beobrand stared into the eddying waters of the Tuidi, but his mind was far away.

Muscles in his forearms knotted and bunched. He did not wish to think of his father. The man was dead. He could hurt nobody now. But it seemed to Beobrand that his spirit was unquiet. Distance and time did little to dim the memories of the beatings. Beobrand flinched, as if expecting a blow. Yet the movement that had startled him was merely the heron taking flight. He shook his head to clear it of the fog of a past that was best forgotten. Would death itself not keep his father from his thoughts?

Soon he would be a father himself. Would Sunniva bear him a son, as he had said back in Bebbanburg? Or a maiden child? Would the child resemble one of his siblings? Strong, brave, dependable like Octa perhaps? Or, if a girl, would she have the impish features and giggling personality of Edita? Or caring, quiet and always eager to please, like his beloved Rheda?

Whether son or daughter, Beobrand vowed silently to all the gods that he would never treat his own offspring as his father had treated them. But was it possible that he too would find it easier to talk with his fists than words? Violence came easily to him, it was true. A natural killer.

Beobrand shuddered. He recalled then his mother's dying words. "You are not your father's son." He had never fully understood her meaning. Had she meant that he did not need to become like Grimgundi? Or did her words reveal something else? Something more profoundly unsettling?

He would never know her true meaning. And yet her words drove him. He was not his father's son. He would not become that which brought terror to his childhood. He was strong and gifted at sword-play. And strength should be used to defend children. He cursed himself that he had not had the strength to stop his father years before.

He closed his eyes. Breathed deep of the cool air.

Grimgundi was gone. He could not torment him now.

He took another breath. The stillness washed over him.

Silence.

His eyes flicked open. What had startled the heron? His presence had never been enough to set the bird to flight in the past. Where were the sounds of other birds? The river flowed stealthily between the banks. Beobrand scoured the far bank. He saw nothing to provoke alarm.

Was that a movement? A flash of pale skin between the trees?

He peered into the gloom of the woods across the river. Uneasy now, he began to move back towards the houses of Ubbanford. He was all too aware that he was alone and unarmoured. The trees were separated by close to fifty paces of deep water. Surely he was safe. But a sudden movement caught his eye and he realised in a heartbeat that the distance of the far bank did not provide him with sanctuary.

A flicker of motion blurred his vision. Without fully knowing why, he threw himself to the ground. He heard the thrum of the bowstring at the same instant as an arrow thudded into the turf behind him. A second arrow followed.

It flew true, but skittered off a branch near his head. It whipped up and away.

The archer was skilled. Beobrand could not stay where he lay. The next arrow would find its mark.

He leapt to his feet and sprinted along the riverbank. His supple leather shoes slipped on the moist grass. He felt something tug at his cloak. He kept running.

The archer would be impeded by the heavy foliage on the north side of the river. He would be unable to match Beobrand's pace. Each shot would be more difficult. Especially with a fast-moving target. Yet it was possible there was more than one bowman.

Reaching the first houses, Beobrand decided it was safe to revert to a walk. His lungs burnt. He drew in great gulps of air.

Acennan sat before the hall. A comely young woman carried buckets of milk past him. She walked slowly to avoid spilling the precious liquid. Acennan seemed content to watch the sway of her hips.

He spotted Beobrand and said, "You have returned sooner than I thought."

Beobrand's breathing was still ragged. "I tired of my own company."

Acennan raised an eyebrow. "I am not surprised. It can be tedious to spend time alone with you." He snorted. Acennan then reached behind Beobrand and plucked something from his cloak. "Though judging by your new jewellery," he held up a goose-feather fletched arrow with a vicious iron head, "I would imagine you were not as alone as you would have liked."

Sunniva felt the quickening in her belly. It frightened her. But the strange bubbling sensation of her child moving within her brought a smile to her lips, despite her fears. She often thought of her mother. She missed her advice. Her tender affection. She even missed her scoldings. Yet now, as her time approached, she missed her more than ever.

Rowena was kind and supportive, but she was not her mother. There was a distance, an aloofness, to her that left Sunniva feeling lonely.

Odelyna had come to see her the day before. The woman was grey-haired and wizened, her manner terse, abrupt. But she had assisted the women of Ubbanford to bring their babies into the light for decades.

"The woman knows more about giving birth than the goddess Frige," Rowena had said. She wished to lighten Sunniva's mood, but her words made the mother-to-be frown. The pain in Sunniva's head had been constant for some time and she felt giddy if she attempted walking more than a few steps. The last thing she wished for now was for the goddess of fertility to take offence at Rowena's words.

Odelyna had prodded Sunniva and asked her many questions. At last, she had declared that Sunniva's child was well, and would be born in Eostremonath. The mother, she said, had headaches caused by the baby's warrior-like nature. "He'll be a great thegn, just like his father," she'd said. "But you know what happens with strong men, they always give their women headaches." The old woman prescribed an unctuous concoction of mandrake, mugwort, betony and honey and said she would return daily to check on Sunniva.

From where she lay in the dark, Sunniva heard the arrival of men into the hall. Footsteps approached. The partition to the bedchamber opened. Beobrand entered. She smiled to see him. She worried what might happen, now that the weather was improved. The village seemed tranquil. Safe. But it was an illusion.

"How do you fare, my love?" he said, kneeling beside the

bed. The sombre aspect of his face told her all she needed to know about her own appearance. His fear for her was etched in his features.

"My head is a little better." She pushed herself into a sitting position, being careful not to show her discomfort. "I believe the rest, and Odelyna's ointments are working. What did you find?"

Beobrand shook his head. "We made our way quickly to the place where the bowman hid, but whoever it was had not waited for us. From the look of the place it was only one man. Two at most."

"Nathair's sons?"

"The men from these parts say that his eldest son, Torran, is a skilled hunter. By all accounts he has a keen eye with a bow."

"What will you do?" She could see no escape from the threat of attack that loomed over Beobrand now. He would not be safe while Aengus' brothers sought vengeance.

Beobrand sat still for a long while. His eyes were shadowed.

"I will talk with Nathair once more."

"Will that work?"

"I do not know. I would avert more blood. And I believe Nathair would not seek open feud with me. But I fear the old wolf cannot control his pups."

Sunniva's face suddenly lit up, as if a ray of light had fallen upon her from an open shutter.

"You talk of pups. Give me your hand and feel your own move inside me."

She took his hand and placed it on her swollen belly. Beobrand kept his palm lightly touching the linen garment there, but she pushed it more firmly onto her.

"You will not break me. You should see the way Odelyna prods and pushes!"

Beobrand grimaced at the thought.

"What you womenfolk do when your husbands are not present is best left a secret," he said.

"Hush now, and wait."

After a moment, it came again. A burbling sensation of movement inside her and she saw Beobrand's face change. Gone was the concern and worry. Replacing it was joy and awe. And love.

"Our son is strong," he said.

She was too tired to play the game and ask him how he knew it would be a boy child. The throbbing in her temples increased. She did not have the strength to worry any further about anything. Her man was with her. Their child kicked. Her headache was sure to abate after she took some rest.

"Yes," she said, closing her eyes. "Our son is strong. Like his father."

"And his mother's father," said Beobrand.

"Yes," her voice was blurring, sleep tugging at the sounds, "with such forebears how could he not be as strong as a boar?"

She felt Beobrand's strong fingers brush her hair from her forehead. He placed a soft kiss upon her brow. The rasp of his beard brought to her mind the ghost sensation of her father.

Now was not the time for concerns and fears. There would be time enough for problems another day, when this damn headache had gone away. She allowed the calm of slumber to drift over her.

19

Following the calamitous display before the king's retinue that morning, Cormán retired to his room.

Coenred was pleased to find himself with no chores. He knew though, that he was still the youngest monk in Bebbanburg, and should Gothfraidh see him, he would be called on to perform some task or other. He would certainly have to spend time in prayer. For so long, he had been around others. From smoky halls to windswept trails through the mountains of the north, but always surrounded by others. Never a moment to himself.

He looked about him for sign of Gothfraidh, but he was nowhere to be seen.

Coenred would spend the day alone with his thoughts. Able to think. And to pray.

The day was dry and bright. He left the fortress and walked the dunes. Finding a secluded spot, he lay down, out of the breeze. The sand was sun-warm and dry. He pushed his fingers into it. Beneath the surface it was cool and moist.

He lay there for a long while. Feathery clouds formed and scudded across the pale heaven.

The marram grass whispered. Sea birds wheeled and spun in the air, their voices like those of children squealing with delight. The muffled crump of waves breaking on the beach.

There was no other person in Coenred's world. His mind tried to pull him towards dark thoughts. Dank thoughts of caves and curses. The bloody images of his worst dreams threatened his peace. But he pushed them all away. He watched the clouds. Listened to the birds. White as doves they were. He whispered the Paternoster over and over until the words held no more meaning to him than the screeches of the birds or the wind through the grass.

His mind found solace in the sounds. He closed his eyes. Gone were the images of blood and darkness. Softly and slowly, sleep embraced him.

When he awoke the sun was low in the sky. The air had turned chill.

He hurried back to Bebbanburg. He began to question the wisdom of leaving the fortress on his own. Given the events of the morning, the bishop's mood would surely be sour. Coenred did not wish to find out how being embarrassed before the king and his thegns had affected the bishop's temperament.

He hurried on, the sound of the birds now like laughter at his stupidity, the crash of the waves ominous. The breeze that had been soothing now cut at his skin.

Preparations for the evening's feast were well under way when Coenred ran into the yard beyond the gate of the fortress. Thralls and servants bustled about their business. A glimpse through the open doors of the hall showed the fire burning bright on the hearth stone. The boards set. Benches in place.

"Where have you been?" The voice was indignant.

Coenred turned his attention from the great hall, to see

Gothfraidh standing before him. The old monk's face was blotchy. With colour high on his cheeks.

"Well?" Gothfraidh said.

Coenred stammered for a moment. Several retorts bubbled up in his mind, but he pushed them all away. Nothing he said would mollify Gothfraidh. Old Fearghas had taught him well not to always say the words that came to him. Sometimes it is best to bear anger and punishment in silence. Words seldom change the outcome for the better.

"We will talk more of this later," Gothfraidh continued, clearly frustrated at Coenred's silence. He probably took it for insolence, which is exactly what Coenred wished to avoid. "Bishop Cormán has been asking for you. Though why he would wish to see you, is beyond my ken. Go now. The feast is soon to begin."

Coenred did not wait for a second chance. He scurried off. He wondered whether he was escaping one punishment to receive another. Cormán's temper was terrible. But there was nothing for it. He would go to the bishop and pray that he had not spent the day plotting a terrible penance for him.

Reaching the door to the bishop's quarters, Coenred drew in a shuddering breath and knocked.

There was a mumbled response from behind the partition door. He could not make out the words, but recognised the voice as Cormán's and guessed the meaning from the tone.

It was dark in the small chamber that Oswald had provided for Cormán. The cloying scent of burning tallow from the candle was heavy in the darkness. After the clear air of the beach, the thick atmosphere stuck in Coenred's throat like phlegm.

Cormán sat hunched on a stool beside the wooden cot bed. His features were in shadow. He did not look up.

Coenred coughed gently, and said, "You asked for me?"

Cormán turned to him now, as if only just realising he was no longer alone. The flickering light from the candle fell on his face. His mouth was open, slack-jawed. His eyes seemed to focus on something far behind Coenred. For a long while Cormán remained thus, staring silently. Coenred squirmed.

"The feast will commence soon, my bishop," Coenred said at last, unable to bear the silence.

"Feast?" Cormán started as if slapped awake. "Oh yes. It must be late."

Silence fell on the room again.

"Do you need something from me?" Coenred asked.

"Come sit on the cot, Coenred, I would talk to you." Cormán patted the bed. Coenred noted that Cormán had used his name for the second time that day.

He took a step towards the bed.

"Do not be afraid," Cormán said. The very words brought fear into Coenred's heart where before there was mere unease. What was that other smell he could detect? He scanned the room quickly. Took in the shape of a jug and cup on the small table. Was that the aroma of mead?

"Sit," Cormán repeated, again indicating the bed. His voice was blurred from drink, Coenred was sure of it. He did not wish to be here, but could see no way out.

He sat.

"Bless you, child," said Cormán, "you have been good to me. I know I am not always easy…"

Coenred could feel his cheeks grow hot. He did not know how to address this Cormán. This was a man he had not spoken to before. The dark of the room bore down on him. Like the stone-vaulted roof of a cave.

"I have seen the way you look at me, Coenred." Again,

Cormán used his name. He was more uncomfortable by the moment. "You are oft afraid. But you need not fear me. I see the goodness in you. The way you sought to help me before the king today. I thank you." Cormán shifted his weight. The stool creaked. Outside a dog barked.

Cormán placed his hand on Coenred's shoulder. Coenred tensed at the touch.

"You have no need to thank me. Shall we go to the feast now?" He made to stand, but Cormán held him where he was.

"There will be time enough for the feast later."

Everything was wrong here. Coenred knew it. Could sense it as surely as he had known that Nelda was evil. She had said terrible things about Cormán.

Could they be true?

Cormán's hand dropped to Coenred's lap. For an instant it lay there on his thigh, pale and limp. "You have been very kind to me, Coenred." Cormán's hand slid from just above Coenred's knee up towards his groin. The fingers caressed and probed his flesh through the rough wool of his robe.

Coenred was appalled. He sat transfixed watching the pallid, fleshy hand spider-creep towards his crotch. This could not be happening. This was sin most foul. This man was his abbot.

His bishop.

The shepherd.

Protector.

Cormán's fingers reached their goal. Coenred shuddered as Cormán fondled and groped.

Coenred found his voice at the same instant that he broke from the stillness that had held him motionless.

"Stop!" he shouted and pushed Cormán's hand away.

The bishop, panting loomed over him. Pushed him back onto the cot. "You have wanted this for a long while," he slurred, mead-sickly breath dribbling over Coenred, "show me some more kindness."

The man was evil. He would take his pleasure with Coenred, just as the men had sated their lust with his sister Tata. They had taken everything from him. All that remained was Christ and his brothers in the faith. Now Fearghas had left him. Was this pitiful excuse for a bishop going to deprive him of the one remaining certainty in his life?

Unbidden he thought of Beobrand. Would that his friend were here now. He would put a stop to this as quickly as one snuffs out a candle flame. But Beobrand would not save him. Not this time. Coenred had told him many times that he did not understand Beobrand's desire for vengeance. But in that instant, with Cormán's hand groping at him, his weight overbearing, his putrid breath making him gag, he could think of nothing more than being rid of the man. He owed it to Tata, who had not been able to defend herself.

Summoning strength from deep within him, like air being blown into the heart of a forge's fire, Coenred screamed.

"Get off of me, you devil!"

He raised his knee with brutal force into Cormán's groin. The bishop grunted and tried to roll away. He was not fast enough. Coenred's rage, unleashed now, ripped through him; a rabid beast in search of blood. He snarled like a cornered dog and lashed out at Cormán's face. He made contact with his fist, a glancing blow, but he felt cartilage crunch as Cormán's nose broke.

The bishop retreated from the incensed novice, fending off Coenred's blows with his raised hands.

Coenred leapt to his feet and fled the room.

*

What have I done? What have I done? The words ran through Coenred's mind over and over as he ran across the courtyard. He had no idea where he was running. He just knew that he had to flee. He had struck the bishop. There had been blood. He thought he had broken his nose. How had it happened? What had possessed him to hit Cormán?

He skidded on some horse dung, unnoticed in the gathering gloom. He lost his footing. Hit the ground hard.

Winded, he gulped, trying to suck in air. He couldn't breathe! He had hit the bishop and now he was going to die, unable to breathe. Was this God's punishment?

He panicked. His lungs were empty, but he could not draw breath. Was this how he would die? He should not have lashed out.

Then, all of a sudden, cool air whistled into his chest. The panic eased. He would not die. He was not being punished by God.

He could still feel the lingering touch on his thigh. See the lecherous leer. It was the bishop who should be punished. Not him.

As if in answer to his thoughts he heard a scream of rage behind him. He was innocent and the bishop was guilty of a terrible sin. But Coenred was no fool. He knew that the world did not work in that way. Often the innocent pays for the crimes of the evil. He leapt to his feet. He must get away from this place. It was his only hope. He ran towards the main gate, but saw it had been barred for the night.

Where to go? He cast about for an escape. He saw none.

"Stop, boy!" Cormán's voice cut through the general hubbub that emanated from the great hall, where the feasting had already begun. He spoke in the words of the Angelfolc. His accent was strong and the words sounded like the voice of one who attempts to sing, but has no ear for music. "Stop, boy!" He screamed again, then added in Latin, which none save Coenred and any other monk within earshot would understand, "He must face justice!" His voice was thick with drink and indignant anger.

Cormán did not speak well, but his ire was clear. His words and gesturing towards the young monk merely emphasised his meaning. Coenred watched as two wardens left their post outside the doors of the hall and made their way towards him.

His heart sank. There was no escape now. He resigned himself.

Cormán continued to scream as the guards, almost apologetically, took hold of his arms. They marched him to the hall entrance, where the bishop stood in the pool of light cast from within. He was all bloodied nose and wild gesticulation. He seemed close to taking leave of his senses, such was his rage.

He reached for Coenred, who flinched, trying to avoid Cormán's touch. But the wardens held Coenred firm, apparently the sight of the bishop's bloody face enough to prove the boy's guilt in their eyes. They allowed Cormán to grab Coenred by the ear. They appeared eager to relinquish their hold on him, for they let the bishop lead Coenred into the warmth and light of the hall.

Cormán twisted the ear in his grasp and dragged Coenred forward. It hurt badly. Coenred recalled not so long before when one of Hengist's men had pulled him into driving rain using his ear in just the same savage way. Beobrand had saved him then. He felt the heat of the hall fire against his cheeks now. The ruddy faces of those gathered in the hall turned to stare. There would be no rescue for him this time.

The hall gradually fell silent.

Oswald was looking forward to the feast. The smell of meat and mead bringing the anticipation of a full belly, the promise of convivial conversation. Tales, boasts, riddles, laughter. He longed for the respite from the trials of leadership.

It had been a wearing day. The catastrophic events of the morning's aborted attempt at sharing the Holy Eucharist an all too recent memory, vivid in Oswald's mind. He had hoped to show the men the solemnity and power of the Christian teachings, and introduce them to Cormán. But instead of convincing any doubters and stilling any concerns people may have in the appointment of the new abbot and bishop, the very man who was so key to his plans turned a simple ceremony into what many of the more traditional thegns saw as an omen of blood. Oswald had been careful not to show his full displeasure in the bishop, but he was furious. Why had Ségéne sent Cormán? The men who had travelled with the bishop disliked him. Oswald was not surprised. Cormán had always been a prickly man, prone to peevishness. Oswald was willing to bow to the decision of Ségéne and the brethren of Hii, but this morning's debacle had served to make him further question the appointment. He needed a man who could lead Bernicia to righteousness. To do that, he would have to be someone who could interact well with all manner of people in the kingdom. From the haughtiest thegns to the lowliest ceorls; Angelfolc, Waelisc and Picts alike. Oswald dreamt of leading a nation united under one ruler and one god. He was the man to rule on earth. He could wield the sword and defeat the foes of Bernicia with his brother at his side. But he needed a man to shepherd the people into the light of Christ's love.

If only Fearghas yet lived. He would have been the perfect man to stand at his side. He was humble, yet full of wisdom. Kind and loving, yet strong and disciplined. And he could speak the tongue of the Angelfolc. His mission into Deira had given him much experience in teaching. As a child Oswald had known the old abbot before Fearghas had set out south to carry the word of the Lord to the Northumbrians.

But Fearghas had gone to be with the almighty Father. It saddened Oswald. But life was full of sadness. You can only move forward and tackle the events as they unfold. He did not have Fearghas' wisdom, but he knew that no plans played out as intended in their conception. So it was that he had sent north for a new bishop. It had pleased him when Fearghas had sent the boy, Coenred, with the tidings of his passing and instructions to send to Hii for a bishop. The old abbot understood what was needed. Lindisfarena would become the sister of Hii. The east a reflection of the west.

Why the brethren had seen fit to send Cormán was still a mystery, but he would have to suffice. There were other things to concern Oswald. He must arrange a meeting with Penda soon. And also marriage to Cynegils' daughter. So many pieces in this game of tafl. A wrong move could spell disaster. Death. Or perhaps worse, a return to exile. Loss of the newly reconquered kingdom. Better to die in defence of what was his rather than to lose it all and flee like a whipped cur. Eanfrith had got that much right at least. Failure now was not an option. But success was a tenuous thing to hold on to. He could feel his doom lurking at every turn. He prayed and planned, but any mistake could see it all come crashing down.

The sudden flicker of firelight gleaming on red hair drew his eye. Finola, Eanfrith's widowed queen, sat at the far end of the high table, with the boy, Talorcan. She saw Oswald looking and smiled. She was a clever one. She was unhappy, he knew, but she never complained. He wondered sometimes at her lot. Although he was sure she would rather return to her people, she was treated well. Perhaps she was happier than when Eanfrith lived. He knew his brother. Had seen how he was with her. It brought sorrow to his heart to see one of such poise and beauty reduced to a peace-weaver. Another piece in the great game he played. But such was her part. He needed the support of her brother, Gartnait. So she and the boy remained at Bebbanburg.

A thrall stepped to his right and filled his fine glass beaker with pale mead. The beakers were a thing of wonder. Glass moulded and fashioned by some skill that no craftsman Oswald knew of could master. They had been brought on a ship from afar and had cost him dearly. Part of a set of four, he used them infrequently, for fear that they would be damaged. There were only three left, now, one having toppled from the board when it was upset by a thegn made unsteady on mead. The beaker had fallen and smashed into tiny shards. They were sharp as bone needles, and there was no way to repair the cup. Today he had chosen to use one of the beakers. Seeing it gave him pleasure. It reminded him that the abilities of man knew no limits. There were always new skills to discover. Crafts to master.

He nodded his thanks to the old Waelisc woman who poured the drink. She kept her eyes averted, but he noticed her hands were steady. She did not tremble in the presence of the king. For a moment he contemplated whether this was a good thing.

A commotion distracted him. Perhaps the food was ready to be served. He hoped so.

Looking down the long hall, he could see the doors that

had been left open to the clement night air. The hearth fire raged. The movement beyond it rippled and danced. Who was that there? The room grew hushed. Oswald could not see clearly through the heat-flicker of the flames. He stood. In the entrance to the hall stood Cormán. But he was not garbed in clean robes ready to partake of the king's table. The man swayed unsteadily. His blood-splashed face was contorted by anger. His long locks, usually as well-groomed as any lady's, stuck out like the denuded branches of a leafless winter tree. In his right hand, the bishop held the ear of the young monk, Coenred. The boy, face pale, eyes wide, looked terrified.

Oswald felt the flash of his own anger. Was Cormán avowed to spoil everything? Would he never have peace while the man resided in Bebbanburg? The sooner he was gone to Lindisfarena, the better.

"What is the meaning of this, bishop?" Oswald kept his voice in check, did not allow it to rise. Despite this, the words were heard by all. "Why do you interrupt our feast?" The bishop did not respond immediately and Oswald realised he had addressed the man in the tongue of his people, not the musical words of the Hibernians. He repeated his questions for Cormán.

"My lord," Cormán said, his voice slurred and whiny, "this boy struck my face. Has drawn blood from Christ's bishop! I demand justice!"

Oswald looked from the bishop to the boy. He could think of no reason why Coenred would strike his superior. He thought well of the young monk. He had been recommended by Fearghas and in all his dealings with him, Oswald had been impressed by the boy's intelligence and eagerness to please. The bishop had done little to endear himself to the king or those who escorted him from Dál Riata.

"Demand, you say? In my own hall you would make demands of me, bishop?" Many of his retinue would not understand the words Oswald now spoke, but the ice in them was clear.

Cormán swallowed, as if attempting to hold himself back. "The boy must be accountable for his sins!"

"His sins are God's affair, not mine. But if you seek justice for a crime, you must come before me at the proper time."

"But my king…" Cormán's tone was pleading.

Oswald cut him off. "Yes, I am your king and you would do well to remember it." He fixed Cormán with a cool stare until the priest closed his mouth. "You can come before me tomorrow, bringing witnesses to speak on your behalf. Until then, unhand the boy." Cormán held the king's gaze for longer than was proper. Oswald wondered again at the choice of this man to lead his people into the fold of Christ's followers.

Eventually, Cormán released Coenred's ear. The novice rubbed at it.

Weariness engulfed Oswald. All he had wanted was to eat and drink in peace and now the accursed bishop had made that impossible.

"Bishop, you are bleeding. Attend to your wounds. Begone."

Cormán stood for a long while, his brow furrowed. Eyes burning with an impassioned hate. Oswald could not tell if his loathing was aimed at him or the boy.

"Very well, Oswald King. I will return on the morrow and I expect justice to be done."

With that, the furious bishop spun on his heel. Flicking his hair away from his face with his hand, he stalked out of the hall.

20

"Nathair!" Beobrand shouted. "Come out. I would speak with you."

Beobrand removed his helm and rested it on the saddle before him. He ran his half-hand through his sweat-drenched hair. It was a warm day. The winter had truly retreated back into the northern mountains of Dál Riata. The Tuidi valley was as balmy as a summer afternoon.

"Do you suppose the old goat is deaf?" said Acennan. He sat astride his dappled mare beside Beobrand. Against his wishes, they had come to Nathair's hall without more of Beobrand's gesithas. Beobrand didn't want to start a fight. Yet it seemed to Acennan it was too late for that. Blood had been spilt. And those arrows had flown from a bow held in the hands of a man. Most likely a Pictish man. Not an elf of the forest.

But Beobrand had been adamant. "If we ride in force, we show fear. And we will anger Nathair. We have ridden onto his land once with my warband. Perhaps this time we can talk more calmly."

Acennan had not liked it one bit. He had made Beobrand wear his battle gear. He, too, was sweating under his heavy byrnie, his head soaked beneath his iron helm. He cuffed away beads of moisture from his forehead and looked around the village. The throngs of people they had seen on their first visit were absent. They must all be busy in the fields ploughing and harrowing.

They had seen some as they had left the forest and ridden over the small wooden bridge. They could see more with wooden hoes and rakes on the hill beyond the settlement.

A movement behind them made Sceadugenga snort, and take a quick step, circling on the muddied ground before the great hall.

Nathair stepped from between two squat huts. He was flanked by a pair of warriors. They were dour and broad-shouldered, armed with spear and shield. Beobrand recognised their kind. They had the air of men at their ease with violence.

The grizzled Pictish lord grinned. "No, this old goat isn't deaf, but perhaps you are." He looked at his men, who guffawed obediently. "We could have walked right up behind you and pulled you from your saddles."

Beobrand felt his cheeks redden. The man was making a fool of them. "You could have tried, old man. But it would not have ended well for you." His ire was threatening to run free. He could feel it pulling at its bit. It was all he could do to rein it back. He took a long breath. He had not come here to fight. He swung from the saddle and indicated for Acennan to do the same.

"So, what brings you here?" Nathair asked, a smile still playing at his lips.

"I have come to speak with you. And to return some-thing that I believe belongs to your son, Torran." Beobrand reached up to his saddle bag and pulled out the goose-feather fletched arrows.

Nathair eyed the arrows soberly, all humour gone.

"Come then, Beobrand, son of Grimgundi. You'd best come inside."

"I hear you, southerner," Nathair picked up the earthenware jug and refilled the wooden cup before Beobrand. Beobrand nodded his thanks. "And I have thought on your words," continued the old Pict, "since last we met." He scowled, and spat onto the rush-strewn floor.

Beobrand looked around the hall. It was dark and drear. A small fire crackled on the hearth. Smoke drifted and swirled around the pillars and rafters. Weapons and war gear adorned the walls. A great sword hung behind the lord's chair. It was sheathed, but gold glinted from its pommel. A couple of wiry hounds worried at a bone in the shadows. They growled softly, setting Beobrand on edge. The room reeked of stale food and sour ale. It smelt old. Decayed.

Here in the gloom it was easy to forget that outside was bright spring sunshine. From within these walls, it would not be difficult to believe the world was always winter. Beobrand took a draught of mead, watching the grey-haired lord over the rim of his cup.

The man looked wan. Tired. His skin had the jaundiced pallor of age. Both the hall and its lord were decrepit. Shades of their former glory.

"I still grieve for Aengus. But I have no quarrel with you. He was ever headstrong. Foolhardy." His hand shook as he lifted his drinking horn to his cracked lips. "I have spoken with the men who were there at his end. They say you warned him."

Beobrand glanced at Acennan. It was uncomfortable to

listen to these words from the father of the boy he had slain. Acennan raised his eyebrows. He gave a slight shrug and concentrated on his own drink.

"He died well," said Beobrand. He did not know how to offer condolences to this man. He knew what it was to suffer loss, but he could feel no remorse at Aengus' death. "It was a warrior's death."

The old man fixed him with a dark stare. His eyes glinted in the shadows. It was the predatory glare of a wolf. He may be old, but he still had teeth. There was no softness in those eyes. Nathair had not become leader of his people with tenderness. Beobrand would do well to remember that.

Beobrand held the man's gaze. He would not back down. The challenge was there. It could not be ignored. Nathair knew that he could not hope to stand in combat against the young warrior thegn from Cantware, so he attempted an exertion of his will. For a moment, all was still in the hall. It was as if the very air itself held its breath. Then Nathair broke the stare. He seemed to crumple.

"Aengus never knew what it was to be a warrior. His mother spoilt him." He rubbed a hand over his face. "She was a wonderful woman, his mother."

For a time nobody spoke. Nathair's warriors sat sullenly at the far end of the table. They appeared embarrassed by their lord's show of weakness. Eventually, Nathair let out a trembling sigh. He scrubbed at his face with the heels of his hands.

"I do not seek vengeance for my boy's death," he said, his voice once more strong.

Beobrand picked up one of the arrows that lay on the board before them. The white feathers stood out in the shadows like snow on a midnight mountainside.

"So what of this then? It was not my wyrd to die pierced

by these arrows, but your sons wish to exact the price for their brother's death."

Nathair glowered, his brow furrowed.

"I will speak with them."

"Make sure you do. There need be no more bloodshed between us."

"I will speak with them," the old man repeated, his voice cracking with emotion. "I am yet lord here!"

His warriors shifted uncomfortably on the bench.

Beobrand drained his mead and stood. He had had his fill of this place. Wished no longer to remain here in the dark with this old wolf.

"If your sons attack me or my people, I will kill them. I will not allow another attack to go unanswered." His words were clear and sharp as ice. "If you would have peace between our people, you must keep them in check."

Nathair surged to his feet. He hammered a fist into the board, making cups clatter and jump. The dogs started and sprang up, alert.

"Do not talk to me thus. I am yet lord here!"

Beobrand looked about them. The grimy hall. The dusty sword hanging forlornly from a beam. The redolence of age was sharp in his nostrils. Nathair, diminished and grey, quivered unsteadily, one hand resting on the board before him.

He may yet be the lord. But death had its hand upon him. And upon Nathair's death, his sons would vie for the right to lead. The pale fletchings of Torran's arrows caught his eye as he turned towards the door. Towards the welcome warmth of daylight beyond.

He did not seek more bloodshed. He did not wish to feud with the sons of Nathair. And yet those arrows and Nathair's frailty told him the truth of it.

He bid the old Pictish lord farewell. Outside, the warmth of the sun dispelled some of the gloom that had settled upon him. He swung up into Sceadugenga's saddle. Acennan mounted his own steed beside him.

They rode away in silence. The sun warmed them, but deep inside, Beobrand felt a chill.

Death stalked the old man, and once it had taken him, it would seek out more victims. Vengeance and blood awaited the sons of Nathair.

Beobrand's face was grim as they crossed the stream and entered the cool shade of the forest.

Nathair's sons would come for revenge. They would come and he would be waiting.

They would not find the vengeance they craved. Beobrand touched the hilt of Hrunting. They would find only death.

21

Coenred mumbled the paternoster under his breath. Tears prickled behind his eyes. His throat was thick with pent up emotion. He did not know what his punishment would be, but he knew he would be found guilty. The word of an abbot and bishop against that of an orphan novice monk. There was only one outcome to the trial before the king. All eyes were upon him. He shivered, but it was not cold. A trickle of sweat caressed his back.

He had slept fitfully. Gothfraidh had agreed to watch over him, and the dour monk had sat awake most of the night. He must have been exhausted but his face gave away nothing of his feelings. His expression was sombre. Disapproving.

In the middle of the night, when the feasting had ended and the fortress was as silent as it ever was, Gothfraidh had seen that Coenred was awake. "Why did you do it, boy? What were you thinking?"

For a time, Coenred had lain on the hard floor and stared into the darkness silently. What good would it do to tell the tale of what had happened? Gothfraidh would not believe him. Perhaps it was his fault anyway. Was it possible that he had somehow encouraged Cormán? He had thought of the dreams in which he saw Sunniva. In them he touched her, and she would kiss him. Stroke his body. He would wake erect and throbbing. Sticky with his spilt seed. It was wrong to have such dreams. The devil must be in him. Perhaps the devil tempted Cormán through him.

"I know you are awake, Coenred," Gothfraidh had said, his quiet voice loud in the stillness. "Why did you do it?"

If it was the devil within him, perhaps Gothfraidh could cast it out. He hadn't held out much hope of that. Gothfraidh seemed weak and ineffectual. Yet in the darkness he had been so alone. It was very likely that telling of the events would not help him, but he could see no way in which it would harm his cause. He was sure to be flogged. Perhaps even killed.

Coenred had sniffed in the dark.

"I did not want him to touch me," he'd said, his voice meek.

A long silence.

"Touch you? Touch you where?"

"I don't want to say."

"Are you saying the abbot tried to touch you... there... er... between your legs?" Gothfraidh's voice had taken on an edge. Coenred knew he should not have talked. Gothfraidh would beat him now. Nobody would believe him.

"I don't want to say."

"It is very important that you tell the truth. You know that, don't you?"

"Yes. I am not lying."

"Do you swear on the holy book and your immortal soul that bishop Cormán attempted to touch you?" In the darkness, Coenred had heard Gothfraidh draw in a ragged breath.

"He did not attempt it," said Coenred. He remembered the man's breath. The weight of him. His groping fingers.

Coenred's self-pity had changed to anger in a flash, the way fat dripping onto a fire throws up vicious spitting flames. "He did it. He put his hands on me. There. And squeezed. He asked me to show him some kindness." He'd let out a sob. "There will be no kindness for me now."

Gothfraidh had not answered for a long while. Then he'd said, "Coenred, do you swear what you say is true on all that is holy?"

"I do."

"Very well. Let us pray together for guidance and we shall see what tomorrow brings."

And so it was that Coenred now stood before the king and his thegns. Cormán, eyes blackened from his broken nose and dark with sullen fury, was standing to one side. Gothfraidh, face stern, was positioned off to the left of the hall. Coenred cast about for a friendly face, but there was none. Gothfraidh hardly acknowledged him when he glanced his way. The old man had prayed earnestly with Coenred in the darkest marches of the night. It had comforted him and he would not forget the man's kindness. He had spoken no harsh words; offered no judgement on Coenred's actions. Instead, he had knelt beside the boy and led him in the prayers that were so familiar to them both. The mumbled words in the night had calmed Coenred.

Coenred's attention snapped back to the present as Oswald rose and addressed those assembled.

"Cormán, abbot of Lindisfarena, bishop of Bernicia by the grace of God and the will of the lord abbot Ségéne mac Fiachnaí of the holy island of Hii, you stand before us as accuser of Coenred, brother monk of the brethren of Lindisfarena." The king's brother, Oswiu, translated the words into the tongue of Hibernia. It seemed they meant for all those gathered to understand the proceedings.

The king continued. "Of what crime do you accuse the boy?" The king's face was impassive.

"Oswald King, I accuse Coenred of striking me." Oswiu held up his hand for Cormán to pause while he translated.

"The evidence of his crime is there for all to see," Cormán continued, gesturing at his bruised face. His nose was clearly canted at an angle where it had been straight before.

When Oswiu had translated, Oswald asked, "You have a witness of this crime?"

Cormán frowned when he heard the words translated. "I do not. We were in my chamber. There was nobody else present."

"So you have no witness?" The king's tone was imperious.

Cormán's poise slipped slightly. His voice took on a whining tone. He had expected this moot to be a formality. "God is my witness. I am a man of God, I would not deceive in this."

"Is Coenred not a follower of Christ?"

"He is a young fool. He sought to attack me when no one could see. Long has he disliked me."

"Why do you believe that?" Oswald raised an eyebrow.

"I have seen how he looks at me. When I ask him to perform some task or other."

"And what task did you wish him to perform when you called him to your chamber?"

Coenred fidgeted. He had not expected the king to talk for so long to the bishop. And with Oswiu atheling interpreting, the exchange dragged on in a faltering fashion. Yet he was eager to hear how Cormán would answer.

Cormán shot an evil glance at Coenred. "I had misplaced something of value. I believed he may have taken it."

Once Oswiu had spoken the words, Coenred blurted out, "That's a lie. I took nothing. And he had lost nothing."

Oswald raised his hand for silence. "Hush, Coenred. You will have your chance to speak." He turned back to Cormán.

Coenred bit back the angry words that burnt in his throat. What good would they do? His fate was sealed.

Oswald spoke once more. "So, Cormán, you accuse Coenred of striking you without provocation. Does anyone here vouch for you?"

Oswiu translated. Everyone looked around the hall at all those who stood witness at this trial. Nobody stepped forward.

Cormán looked to Gothfraidh, who seemed to have found something of great interest amongst the rushes on the floor of the hall.

Cormán stuttered, "I am recently arrived here. I know nobody here."

"Nobody speaks on your behalf," the king said. "Nobody vouches for you." His tone was as final as death.

Colour rose in Cormán's cheeks. He opened his mouth to speak, then closed it again. He looked around the room once more, desperate for aid. None came.

Resigned at last, he nodded. His shoulders slumped.

Oswald turned to Coenred.

"Now, Coenred, what have you to say in your defence?"

Coenred swallowed. His throat was as dry as if he had swallowed a spoonful of ground barley. He did not wish to speak of the events of the night before in front of all these men.

He looked at Gothfraidh, seeking guidance. The old monk was looking him in the eye. He nodded and then surprised Coenred by speaking. "Just tell them the truth, boy. You have done nothing wrong."

Coenred swallowed again. "I…" his voice cracked. It

reminded him of the screech of Nelda's jackdaw. He shook his head, dispelling the memory of that foul creature. "I did strike Cormán."

"That is a grievous sin, Coenred," Oswald said, his voice hard.

"But why did you strike him, Coenred?" asked Gothfraidh. "Speak up for all to hear."

Coenred looked at the staring faces. Hard faces. Bearded warriors. Many of them had been his companions on the journey to Hii. They were tough men. But honest. Fair. Honourable. They would expect the truth from him. It shamed him to speak of it. Yet he had done nothing wrong. He had merely defended himself. Any man would do the same.

"I..." again his voice broke in his throat. "Christ teaches that we should turn the other cheek when struck. I have failed in that."

"So you say that Cormán struck you first?" Oswald frowned. "You are a servant of the monastery. It is your lord's right to beat you, if you have done wrong."

Coenred fixed his eyes on Oswald's. "No, lord king. Cormán did not strike me... he..." His words dried up.

"Then why did you strike him?" Oswald's expression softened. "If you do not speak, I will be forced to find you guilty as accused."

Gothfraidh spoke once more. "Tell the truth, Coenred."

Oswald turned to the old monk and snapped, "Enough, man. You have spoken your piece when not bidden to do so. Now be silent. It is on Coenred to unburden himself." Then back to Coenred, "This is a serious matter, but know this. I am losing patience with you. Speak now or suffer the consequences for the actions you have already confessed to."

Coenred looked around the room once more. He saw no

animosity on any face save for that of Cormán. Gothfraidh nodded encouragement, urging Coenred to speak.

"It shames me to speak before so many of what happened," Coenred said, his voice small, yet audible. The onlookers stilled all movements. Their breathing shallowed. They leaned forward to better hear the novice's words.

"Your words must be witnessed, Coenred," Oswald said. "It is the way of our people. Now, grasp the nettle and speak."

Coenred drew in a deep breath. He detected stale mead and ale in the air of the hall. Cold ash, sweat, the tangy bite of tanned leather.

"I struck the abbot," the word, meaning father, lodged in his throat. Cormán was no father to him. He coughed. "I struck him to defend myself. He was crazed with drink. He sought to… touch me."

A murmur of unease ran through the room.

As throughout the moot, Oswiu acted as interpreter. At hearing the words in his own tongue, Cormán exploded into a fit of rage.

Coenred could not comprehend the words, but the invective was clear. Cormán denounced Coenred for a liar.

"Silence!" Oswald's face was dark. He fixed Cormán with his stare. The bishop quietened.

"Touch you?" the king asked Coenred.

"As no man should touch another." Coenred cast his gaze to the ground. He sighed. He could still feel the touch on his thigh. On his groin. It was a shameful thing and now it was known to all.

There was a commotion in the hall as some of the thegns surged to their feet. A bench was overturned. One man, a broad bearded warrior who had travelled to Hii in the winter, cried out, "For shame! This bishop is no man! He should be gelded."

Other men hammered their fists into the board in approbation of the sentiment.

Oswald held out his hands for calm. Silence came after
some time.

"There will be no gelding here. It is a boy's word against
that of a respected priest of the island of Hii. There are no
witnesses to this crime."

Oswiu translated. Cormán allowed himself a small, smug
smile.

Oswald ignored him.

"Will any here vouch for Coenred?"

The bearded thegn said, "I, Godric, son of Godric, will
vouch for the boy's good nature. He travelled the hard road to
Hii with scant a complaint. He is brave and honest. Defence of
one's person is not a crime. It is the priest who should be tried."

Many of the men nodded and muttered their support for
his words.

Another of the men who had ridden with him stood.

"I also vouch for the boy."

"As do I." Another of Oswiu's thegns rose.

Soon, all of the men who had been sent into the lands of
Dál Riata stood. Each pledged his oath that Coenred was
honest and honourable.

"It is good to see this support for Coenred," said Oswald.
"I too believe he is innocent in this. However, I would have
more than the word of a boy in a matter of such gravity."

Gothfraidh took a step forward. "I was not present in
Cormán's chamber last night, so I did not witness what
occurred there. No man did, save for Cormán and Coenred.
But I believe Coenred's story. It is not the first such story I
have heard."

The gathering gasped as one.

Oswiu translated. Cormán slumped. His face pallid behind the bruises.

"Some years ago, when both Cormán and I resided on the island of Hii, a young novice came to me with a story so similar to Coenred's that it could have been told by the same mouth. But that is not possible. For that boy who came to me is dead." Gothfraidh took a shaky breath. The onlookers were silent now. Rapt and horrified at the tale Gothfraidh told.

"He came to me and spoke of how Cormán had touched him. Forced him to do terrible, sinful things. I was weak then. I did not wish to believe him. I spoke to Cormán of the accusations and he said the boy was deluded. There was no evidence and no witnesses, so I chose to believe Cormán. The boy died of the bloody flux the following winter. I have not thought of him in years." Gothfraidh's eyes were focused on a place far away in the past. "But when Coenred spoke to me last night. Told me what Cormán had done. What he had said. I heard the echoes of that boy's voice from beyond the tomb." He crossed himself. "I did not believe him then. But I will not allow Cormán to prey more on boys while I still draw breath." He drew himself up straight. Raised his head and squared his shoulders.

"I say that Coenred is innocent and Cormán is guilty of sins of the flesh."

Cormán blustered for a time on hearing the words from Gothfraidh. He raised his voice, exhorted the name of God. He screeched in Latin, hate and anger splashing from him the way blood flows from a mortally wounded beast. A speared boar will make much noise, and blood will gush forth readily, yet its end is already sealed.

Oswald, his face pale, his jaw set, held out his hands for the final time.

"Cormán, you are condemned by the words of those from your own brethren. I will not sentence you for your crimes and sins. That is for a higher authority than mine. Yet I will not allow you to reside within my realm. You will return from whence you came. I will send a letter to Ségéne of Hii asking for a new bishop. One who is more suited to the tasks in hand. There you will face whatever punishment he sees fit for you."

Oswald did not wait for Oswiu to translate his words this time. He stared at Cormán and spoke the words himself in the lilting sounds of the Hibernians. Cormán wilted in the face of that stare. His shoulders slumped. His downcast eyes glistened.

The king then addressed all those gathered.

"You know that it is my will that Christ will be worshipped by all the people of Northumbria. For that, we need a leader who is holy. A man who is godly in all he does. Cormán is not such a man. Hii will send a new bishop, and we will pray that he is holy." He raked them all with his stare. "You are all oath-sworn to me. And I would have no word of what was spoken today leave this hall. The people need not know why the bishop returns to Hii." The king cast a contemptuous glance as Cormán, who now seemed on the verge of collapse. "Cormán will be a name forgotten. Hidden from history. Unsung and unremembered. Let none of you speak of him again or of what transpired here today."

Coenred looked at all the men who had stood in his defence. Coenred had thought he would be punished. He had not hoped that he would be able to remain at Lindisfarena. But Oswiu's thegns and Gothfraidh, even the king himself, had stood behind him. Vouched for him. It was almost like having a family.

Gothfraidh came to his side and placed a hand on his shoulder.

Coenred could maintain his composure no longer. Tears welled up and streamed freely down his cheeks. He was not to be punished.

He had friends. Family.

And a home.

22

The next weeks passed in a peaceful haze of warm sunshine. The days grew ever longer and each day the land soaked up the warmth of the sun. There were days of clouds and rain, but the showers fell softly with no vehemence. The roots of barley and peas drank thirstily of the moisture. The plants flourished, bursting with verdant life. As the plants welcomed the rain, so did the people of Ubbanford. It gave them respite from their work. Everybody was busy. Planting, lambing, repairing the damage to fences and houses caused by the winter storms. Beobrand and his gesithas spent every dry day working on the new hall. Its wooden bones were completed and work commenced on the walls. It was a great hall. A symbol of strength overlooking the village. None could approach Ubbanford without spying the hall on its hill.

Beobrand wondered whether the hall would be finished by the time Nathair's sons decided to strike. They heard rumours of Nathair's health declining. But for the moment at least, his sons had not decided to test their strength against their neighbour on the south of the Tuidi.

Beobrand was glad of it. He did not seek more battles.

More blood. He would be content to spend the summer building and farming. But Acennan convinced him that they should not allow their skills to wane. He reminded him how Scand would drive his men to train. And so, every few days, Beobrand would lead the men through the drills of battle-play he had learnt from the old lord. They strained, shield against shield, and practised the use of spear and blade. The training was exhausting after the work on the hall, but the men knew that to ignore their battle-skill would be as bad as allowing a sword to rust.

The days when they were not practising with their weapons were long and full of hard toil. Beobrand enjoyed the physical labour, pitching in with the men. Lifting, carrying, sawing, nailing. The dark memories from the last year retreated with the winter cold. Nelda's words, shrieked into the gloom of her dank fastness in the earth, sometimes played in his mind. Was it possible that she was really Hengist's mother? It seemed inconceivable, and yet, he recalled her face. The set of her jaw. Her eyes, dark and probing. And he knew it to be true. How she had found herself so far north and west, he could not tell. He shuddered despite the warmth when he thought of these things. What power had she exerted to draw him to her? Surely her curse must carry that same potency. He pushed these thoughts aside.

It was easier to dispel these anxieties in the smiling sun-shine of the day. At night, in the dark and stillness, Nelda's presence felt close. He recalled the scent of her breath. He had not confided in Sunniva about the meeting with the witch. The warmth and sunlight, coupled with Odelyna's skills as a healer seemed to have worked their own magic on her. She was less pale. The headaches less frequent, less severe. But she was still weak. She could no longer work the forge.

Her belly swelled as quickly as the fast-growing peas in the southern field. She was nearing her time and was restless. On days when she felt well, Beobrand had a comfortable chair carried up to the hill for her to oversee the construction of the hall. Their hall.

She liked to sit in the shade of a shelter the men had made for her and preside over the work. The men too, Beobrand noticed, worked harder when she was there. There was less banter and fewer rests. They looked upon her with loving eyes, working hard to impress her. That these warriors had taken to him as their hlaford still surprised Beobrand. When he looked at Sunniva, her golden hair glowing in the spring light, a rose petal blush on her cheeks, her demure smile, it was easy to see why the men admired her. She may not have been born of noble rank, but she carried herself with grace. Underlying all her beauty and elegance, lay an iron will that the gesithas recognised as necessary for any in a position of power.

Beobrand saw it in her too. Each day he discovered something new about her. Some hidden knowledge from her past. Some insight into her character. She was tired by the end of each day, and they would often retire early to their bed. They would lie close together in the darkness and talk. She would caress his chest absently, driving him mad with a desire he was unable to satisfy for fear of hurting their unborn child. He would listen to her, stroking her hair. The winter had been long and cold for both of them and they now filled the void that had grown between them with words.

On this day, Sunniva was not present on the hill in her usual spot. She had felt unwell that morning, complaining of pangs of pain. Beobrand had sent for Odelyna. He had loitered nervously beside the bed as the old woman had begun to examine Sunniva, but the healer had promptly tired of him and shooed him from the room.

Beobrand and the men worked sullenly for a time. Little work of substance was completed. They were all concerned for Sunniva. Often they would stop and look down the hill to the settlement. At mid-morning there was a flurry of movement from the houses nestled in the valley.

All work ceased as the men saw their lord shading his eyes for a better view of the activity. A horseman was coming towards them. He was riding hard.

"That's Anhaga," Acennan said.

"Aye, and he is on Sceadugenga," Beobrand replied, his voice clipped and tight with nerves.

He began to stride down the hill to meet the mounted man.

Anhaga was not a good rider, but Sceadugenga liked him and carried him well. The stallion pulled to a halt a few paces before Beobrand. It snorted and pawed the earth. It longed to be given its head, to gallop far over the hills. But this was not the day for a long ride.

"Lord," Anhaga panted, "you must come." He dismounted clumsily onto his twisted leg. He stumbled and handed the reins to Beobrand, and said, "The Lady Sunniva's time is here. You must hurry."

Beobrand grabbed the black mane of the stallion and swung himself into the saddle. Without a word he kicked his heels into Sceadugenga's flanks and they sped off down the hill.

Beobrand squeezed his eyes shut as another scream reverberated around the hall. He hammered his fist into the board before him in frustration. He knew there was nothing he could do to help. This was women's work. But the feeling of impotence filled him with rage.

He sensed movement and looked up. Anhaga had stepped from the shadows where he had been lurking. He righted the drinking horn that Beobrand had upset. The cripple did not look Beobrand in the eye. He merely picked up the pitcher and refilled the horn. Then, with a bow, he stepped back away from the benches. His face was pinched. His movements awkward. The tension in the room was palpable.

The hall was empty save for Beobrand, Acennan and Anhaga. Beobrand found some solace in the company of his friend. Anhaga had limped in some time ago and Beobrand could not bring himself to turn the man away. He had been a faithful servant to Sunniva throughout the long winter. The man doted on her, and she seemed to tolerate him now. Several times Beobrand had found them talking quietly together. Their hushed conversations never continued when he was present. Absently he wondered what they talked about. There was something they were not telling him, but Sunniva brushed away his concerns when he questioned her. He did not press the matter, but he would seek a better answer once the babe was born. He did not like secrets being kept from him.

As if in response to his thoughts of childbirth, another shrill anguished wail emanated from the sleeping quarters of the hall. The womenfolk were all there attending Sunniva. When he had arrived at a gallop earlier in the day, Odelyna had let him in briefly to see his wife. Sunniva's skin was blotchy, her colour high. A sheen of sweat covered her, her hair plastered to her forehead. To see her thus had unnerved him. His mother and sister Rheda had the same panicked glazed look when he had nursed them in their final moments. He had felt his knees grow weak at the sight of Sunniva. He'd fallen beside the cot where she lay and taken her hand in both of his. He'd kissed her brow. The heat from her skin was shocking. He could not let her see the fear in his face. It would do her no good. He must be strong for her.

"Sunniva, my love," he'd said, forcing a thin smile, "they say the time has come to bring our child into the world."

She'd returned his gaze. "I am scared," she'd said. "It hurts so."

He'd looked to Odelyna and Rowena.

Odelyna had stepped forward. "I've never known a woman who said she enjoyed childbirth. The pain is normal. It will pass soon enough."

"You hear that, Sunniva? The pain will be over soon," he'd smiled again, this time more broadly, "and we'll have our son. Remember?"

But Sunniva had closed her eyes and dug her nails into his hands. She had let out a groan deep in the back of her throat. The groan had built into a shriek that must have ripped her throat, such was the force of it.

"Now, lord," Odelyna had said, with a tenderness to her voice that Beobrand had not heard before, "you must leave us women to our work. There is nothing for you to do here but fret, and you can do that outside just as well, but without getting under our feet. We'll call for you when the child is born."

That had been long before, when the sun was still high in the sky. Now, the sun had set and the last light was fading on the western horizon. Anhaga busied himself lighting tapers and torches around the hall. He coaxed new flames from the embers on the hearth. But he did not ask if he should send for food to be served. He read his master's mood well enough. Beobrand would not eat while Sunniva suffered so.

"It is always the waiting that is the worst," said Acennan, breaking the heavy silence that had fallen upon them as they awaited the next scream of pain. "Be it before a battle, or before a birth, the waiting's the hardest to bear."

Sunniva let out another guttural groaning cry.

"Well," continued Acennan, "hardest to bear for us men, anyway. I am sure the womenfolk would have something to say about the waiting being tougher than the work of pushing out a baby." He smiled ruefully.

Beobrand did not smile. He drained the mead from his horn. Standing abruptly, he paced from one end of the hall to the other.

"Is it normal?" he asked.

"Is what normal?" said Acennan.

"The screams? The pain? And does it always take this long?"

"I am no expert, but I believe a first child is often the worst."

"Perhaps it is so," said Beobrand. "I remember my mother when birthing Edita. It was all over before we knew she had started the pains. Edita was her sixth child. Two babes had died the same days they were born. Or were already dead. I never knew which. Father and Mother would not speak of them." Beobrand ran his hands through his hair. The uneven sensation of the missing fingers on his left hand was now natural to him. "I was only a boy. I asked so many questions. I just wanted to know what had happened. All I got was a beating in the end. And they never spoke of them."

Why did his mind insist on thinking of these things? Unbidden, his every thought came back to death. They were all gone now. All of them. He had often wondered whether he was cursed. But those were just the thoughts of a child. A man makes his own wyrd. His wyrd was interlocked with that of Sunniva. He was strong, and they would have strong offspring. Theirs would be a family to be reckoned with in years to come.

Without warning, he remembered the words of Nelda. They echoed in his thought-cave as if she was speaking them still: "I curse you, as you cursed my son! You will never know happiness. You will die alone."

He shuddered. He wished to be free of these thoughts. But he could no more control them than a man could hold back the tides.

A scream, ululating and full of exhaustion and woe, came from the living quarters.

Then a new sound, smaller, though no less urgent. The thin wailing of a newborn child pierced the partition at the rear of the hall.

In the silence that followed, Beobrand caught Acennan's eye. The squat warrior nodded.

The babe's crying grew louder, more demanding. A rush of relief washed over Beobrand. He felt he would fall, such was the strength of emotion that coursed through him. He placed a hand on the board to steady himself.

A moment later, the door at the rear of the hall opened. Lady Rowena stepped into the dim flame-light. Her face was a pallid smear in the darkened doorway.

"Lord Beobrand," she said, her voice thick, hoarse, "you have a son."

The room was dark and warm. Rush tapers gave off a fretful light. The tang of sweat hung in the air, mingled with other scents.

Blood.

And shit.

Beobrand had smelt the like before. It was the stench of the battlefield. Visions of the shieldwalls' clash, the screams of the wounded and dying tumbled into his tired mind.

Was it like battle, this women's work of childbirth? There had been screams here too. Terrible wails of anguish and agony. He looked about the noisome room. A baby even now was squealing with a noise it was hard to believe could come from one so small.

Rowena took the swaddled parcel from Odelyna and lifted it up to Beobrand. The baby did not cease its crying.

"Your son," Rowena said.

Beobrand made no attempt to touch the child. He looked at it with incredulity that it had come into this world from within Sunniva's belly. It was so tiny. Its features were screwed up into a wrinkled mask of utter fury. Its lips quivered as it screamed lustily.

"What is wrong with it?" he asked.

"Nothing is wrong with him," Rowena said, shaking her head. "He is hungry and angry at being pulled from the dark warmth into the world. With your leave, I will take him to Maida. She will feed him. The Lady Sunniva is too tired at present."

Beobrand nodded. Elmer's wife was good with her own children; she would care for the baby well. He was as one who has drunk too much mead. Slow. Clumsy. Odelyna was fussing over Sunniva and now turned to Beobrand.

"Lord," she said, with that same tenderness in her voice he had noticed earlier, "your lady has had a difficult time of it. Speak briefly with her, for she must rest."

Beobrand nodded and dropped to his knees beside the cot.

Sunniva looked asleep. Her face was still, her eyes closed. He took her hand and kissed it.

"My love, we have our fine son," he whispered.

Her eyes fluttered open.

"Beobrand," a smile touched her lips, then her brow furrowed. Her hand clasped his with a sudden ferocity. "Is he well? Where is he? I do not hear him."

"Hush, my dearest. Our son is well. Rowena has taken him to Maida. She will feed him while you rest. All is well."

She relaxed, allowed her head to fall back onto her pillow. Odelyna moved about the room efficiently tidying things away.

Beobrand was still shocked at the strain and suffering etched on Sunniva's face. He stroked her hand. "You have done well, my love. You need to rest, and then you can see our son again."

She made a satisfied noise at the back of her throat. Seemed to drift into sleep again.

"We need to think of a name for him," she said quietly, eyes still closed. "Would you like to name him after your brother perhaps? In his memory and honour?"

Beobrand had given no thought to a name. The idea of having a child had seemed so distant. But now he played with the idea in his mind. Octa. It was a strong name. His brother had been a warrior of renown. It would do his son proud to bear the name.

"Yes," he kissed her hand again, "Octa would be a good name for our fine boy."

"Octa," she whispered. She opened her eyes. They were dazed with exhaustion. And something more. Glazed with pain. Her hand gripped his tightly. Grimacing, she let out a groan.

"Sunniva?"

Beads of sweat sprung up on her brow. Her eyes roved around. It was as if she did not see him.

"Sunniva, my love. Rest now." Her grip tightened. She began to pant, thrashing her head against the pillow in torment.

Terror scratched its talons down Beobrand's neck. Somewhere in the back of his mind he thought he could hear the echo of a witch's curse.

"Father…? Why are you angry?" Sunniva's voice was that of a child. Tentative and tearful.

"I am not angry," answered Beobrand. Father? What did she mean? Panicking now, he looked to Odelyna.

"What ails her?"

"Step aside. Let me look at her." Odelyna's tone was curt. Was there an edge of fear in her voice?

Beobrand looked down helplessly as the old woman touched Sunniva's head. She recoiled as if stung by a bee.

"Step back, man," she said. She flustered around the bed while Sunniva began to cry. Long wailing sobs racked her frame.

"Father, please don't shout so. I'm sorry," Sunniva wept.

Beobrand took a hesitant step back, allowing Odelyna room to work whatever magic she had at her disposal.

He did not ask why Sunniva spoke thus. He had seen it before when his sister's spirit was close to flight, she had begun to speak of things that were not there. Did they see the spirits of those who had gone before them? Despite the warmth in the room, Beobrand's skin prickled with a sudden chill. The hairs on his arms rose.

Sunniva would not die. Odelyna was here. He had let Rheda and his mother slip away, but he had no magic. No knowledge to save them. No wyrts or potions. Odelyna was old and wise. She may be a cantankerous old crone, but she would save his wife from the clutches of death.

Sunniva could not die.

The old woman had taken some leaves from a pouch. She touched them to the taper flame. Pungent smoke wafted into the room. Odelyna murmured words under her breath. Words of power. Words of the old gods.

All the while, Sunniva raved.

"You can save her, can't you?" Beobrand asked.

Odelyna continued with her chanting.

"You can, can't you?" Beobrand could hear the fear in his own voice. This was not the fear of battle, when you believe that an enemy may strike you down. There, your strength and guile could save you from the sword blow. Your skill at sword-play could turn death to your will.

Here, in this fear-filled, smoky womb of a chamber, Beobrand faced that most terrifying of things: the fear of losing a loved one with no way to fend off the inevitable. He had faced this before. Seen it too often for one of his years. But never had he believed Sunniva was so fragile.

He must be mistaken. This was not as bad as it looked to him. One look as Odelyna's drawn features told him otherwise. Her chanting was frantic now.

Sunniva let out a shriek and then fell still.

Beobrand rushed to her side, barging past Odelyna, who let out a cry and stumbled out of his way. Wraiths of smoke eddied around him. His throat was thick with the sickly scent.

Sunniva lay still, her eyes closed. Oh no! Woden, All-Father, do not take her from me. Do not take her. Do not take her.

He clutched her hand. It was as hot as the edge of the forge where she could so often be found. There was some evil fire in her. Had she been elf shot? Was this Nelda's curse at work?

She was unmoving. Was she gone? Beobrand choked back a sob. It could not be so.

Sunniva's eyes flickered open then. Beobrand released a

ragged breath. She lived! Everything would be well again. He felt foolish to have allowed himself to become so upset.

"Sunniva, I was afeared. Thought I'd lost you."

"I am here, my love," she said. "I will always be here." She offered him a small smile. Her voice was tired, her eyelids drooped. Her eyes closed. Her hand felt hot enough to burn.

"You need to rest now," said Beobrand.

Her eyes opened once more. There was an urgency in them now. Sunniva fixed him with a piercing stare. "Wait! Do not leave me. Send for my son. I must see him."

"You can see him later, when you have rested."

"No. Send for him now. I will have time to rest soon."

A chill ran over Beobrand. Sunniva's voice had changed. When he made no move, Sunniva turned to Odelyna.

"Please, Odelyna," she implored. Something in her tone, or perhaps some secret communication between the women made Odelyna nod, turn and leave the chamber.

Alone together for the first time in days, Sunniva and Beobrand gazed into each other's eyes for a long while.

In that moment, Beobrand knew that which he had most feared would come to pass. Sunniva said nothing, but he knew.

"But you are well now..." his voice faltered.

She shook her head on the pillow. Tears welled in her eyes, trickled down her flushed cheeks.

"I am sorry, my love," she said.

Beobrand felt tears burn his own eyes. His sight blurred.

"Don't speak so... you are well." His tears scored wet trails down his cheeks. This could not be happening. Yet he knew the truth of it. The light in Sunniva's eyes was dimming.

"Don't leave me!" he said, sudden anger flashing. "Don't leave me alone, Sunniva."

She squeezed his hand tightly.

"You will never be alone," she said, a ferocity in her tone. "I will always be with you and our son."

Her hand relaxed its grip on his.

"Our son, Octa," she said, her voice almost too hushed to make out the words. A smile played on her lips for the briefest of moments. Then her life-breath left her with a whisper. Sunniva's head slumped to one side on the pillow as if she had fallen into a deep sleep.

That night, the people of Ubbanford heard many screams coming from the old hall. First the pained cries of childbirth had punctuated the villagers' conversations. Womenfolk had looked at each other knowingly. They shared the pain Sunniva suffered. It was the common bond of all mothers. The men did their best to ignore the screams, drinking more deeply than usual from their cups and horns.

There had followed the welcome wailing of a hale child breathing its first breaths. The women looked at their own sleeping children with a remembered fondness that was often forgotten in the daily strife and struggle of life. They felt blessed to have healthy children. Those who had lost children were moved at the sounds of new life. It was a warming sound and many silent prayers were offered up to the gods for the child's health and long life.

Shortly after, the night was shattered by the loudest and worst cry of all. This was a sound none of them welcomed. It was an inchoate scream of loss. Grief, ire and utter anguish all added their voice to this one animal sound. Children awoke, sure that a night-stalker had come into the settlement. Parents hushed them, sent them back to sleep with soft words. Men and women embraced. Many made love in the dark that night. They still had someone to hold. Someone to keep them warm. To keep the darkness of solitude at bay.

There was no mistaking the meaning of that last scream in the stillness of the night.

Their lord had lost his lady.

The gods had given life with one hand and taken payment in death with the other. Such was the way of gods.

Most men accepted their wyrd. Took what the gods chose for them. Be it good or bad.

Beobrand screamed his rage into the night so that even the gods would hear.

Beobrand was not like most men. He had fed the ravens and wolves more than warlords twice his age. He had defeated champions and kings. To hear his scream in the darkness was to hear the voice of death and vengeance.

Beobrand was not one to accept his wyrd without a struggle.

The longbeards, sitting by their hearths shook their heads. Death could not be conquered. It was the end of all things.

They knew this, but their new lord was young and strong. His battle-skill was already legendary. He would no more be able to change that which had happened this night than he could stop the sun from rising in the morning. But they were afraid of what he might do in his grief. Young men were not wise. The gods alone knew what mischief Beobrand could be responsible for.

That night the old men slept fitfully and their sleep was tinged with nightmares.

PART THREE
THE CURSE

23

Acennan found Beobrand slumped by the river. It was cold in the shadow of the valley. Mist curled over the water. On the far bank, as still and brooding as Beobrand, stood a heron. As Acennan disrupted the silence with his arrival, the great bird shifted its head slightly. To catch a better glimpse of him perhaps. The bird appeared to decide he was no threat, for it resumed its stance of silent vigil on the water, ignoring the men on the other riverbank.

Beobrand sat with his back to the grey bole of a birch. He did not acknowledge Acennan's approach.

Dew lay thick on the long grass and foliage at the river's edge. Acennan's shoes and leg bindings were soaked through. If Beobrand had sat there all night, he must be drenched.

"I was worried for you," said Acennan. "You should come back to the hall."

Beobrand drew in a deep breath, let out a sigh.

"Leave me, Acennan," Beobrand croaked, his voice hoarse. "I do not wish to talk."

The memories of the night were hazy in Beobrand's mind. He knew what had happened, but it was as if he glimpsed the events through a fog. He had screamed his anger at Woden. Spat his contempt for Thunor. Bellowed with fury at Frige. Coenred's Christ god had felt the lash of Beobrand's sorrow and hatred that night. The gods forsook him at every turn. His life was awash with death and blood.

His wyrd had brought him happiness for a fleeting time, before snatching it away once more.

Nelda's word's whispered in his thoughts. She had said he would die alone. She had cursed him. Hengist's mother's magic would bring about his doom. Mete out the suffering and vengeance that her son could not.

Clumsily, Beobrand lifted the flask of mead, but it was empty. A single drop of the sweet liquid touched his lips, its honey flavour reminding him how much he had drunk. His stomach lurched. His head ached. Water filled his mouth as bile bubbled up in his gullet. He rolled to one side and vomited noisily.

When he had voided the worst of the contents of his guts, his stomach heaved again, in an attempt to bring up the poison within him. But no matter how long he puked, he would never be rid of this pain.

The retches turned to sobs.

Acennan took a few steps down the riverbank. The heron looked sadly over at the noisy men. Slowly, it spread its massive wings and flapped away downriver. Over the water it went, disappearing into the mist.

For a time the only sounds were Beobrand's coughing sobs and the creak of the heron's wings.

Beobrand wiped his mouth on his sleeve; rubbed his eyes with the heels of his hands. He stood shakily, leaving a steaming puddle behind him.

"Leave me," he repeated, "there are no words. Not for this."

"I understand your pain."

Beobrand felt the ire kindle in an instant. The taste of his bile was acid in his mouth.

"You understand? How can you? She is gone! Taken from me. I am cursed…" His anger dissipated as quickly as it had come. He was too tired, too spent.

"Perhaps we are all cursed," Acennan said. Beobrand looked at his friend. There was a shadow over his features.

"Yet," Acennan ran his hands through his hair, "we do not need to be cursed to lose the ones we love." He stared into the mist for a time. A fish broke the smooth surface of the river with a muted splash. Ripples rolled out. Beobrand was silent. His mouth was foul-tasting, but his stomach seemed more settled now. He stepped to the water's edge, knelt and cupped cool water into his hands. He rinsed his mouth and spat. He splashed some onto his face.

"I had a wife once," Acennan said into the silence. "And a boy."

Beobrand straightened.

"You never mentioned them before," he said.

"I do not like to talk of them." Acennan sighed. "I think of them often, but to speak of them… hurts still. It hurts less than it did, but it still hurts."

Beobrand swallowed the lump in his throat. "What happened to them?"

"They died." Acennan sighed.

Beobrand did not answer for a long while. He knew very little of Acennan's life before they had met. He had asked him about his travels. About battles he had fought in. Warriors he had seen in the shieldwalls in Hibernia. He vaguely recalled asking him once if he had a woman. Acennan had answered, "No, not any more." Beobrand had sought no more details.

Sunniva would have been so angry with him. She always asked Beobrand after the health of his gesithas' children and wives. He never knew the answers to her questions, which annoyed her. The wellbeing of his men's brats and women had never seemed important.

His eyes filled with tears.

"I am sorry, Acennan," he said, his voice cracking with emotion. "In the darkest part of the night, I thought of Sunniva and my brother. And my sisters. I could see them. They beckoned to me. It would be so easy. To take my seax and cut my throat. Like an animal at Blotmonath."

Beobrand stared into the grey waters of the Tuidi.

"I meant to do it. I could join them." He snorted a mirthless chuckle. "But when I went to pull out my seax, I couldn't find it. I'd left it back at the hall."

"I am glad of that then," Acennan said. "For to take your life would be the death of a craven, and I know you to be no such thing. Besides, you have a son now. Would you want him to never know his father? Who only heard tell of him as a man who took his own life through grief?"

Beobrand glowered, but did not answer.

"You are no coward, lord. There are great tales to tell of your exploits. There will be more. A son deserves to hear such tales from the mouth of his father."

Beobrand thought of his own father. Was he also looking on from the afterlife, waiting for his son to join him? He would be laughing to see Beobrand's anguish.

"I am no craven," Beobrand said. He squared his shoulders, took in a deep breath of the cool morning air.

"Let us return to the hall. I would meet my son."

★

When they returned to the hall Anhaga was waiting at the door. His face was pale, drawn and gaunt. He wrung his hands in distress and as he followed them into the hall, Beobrand noticed that his limp seemed more pronounced. His eyes were bloodshot and swollen. He had grown close to Sunniva these past few weeks. He was taking her death hard.

The cripple bowed his head, but seemed incapable of speech.

Rowena, hearing them arrive, rose from a chair at the rear of the hall.

"My lord, I am pleased to see no harm has come to you. We were worried."

No harm? His heart had been ripped from his chest. His bowels torn from his guts. His skin flayed from his bones.

"I wished for peace. To think," he said. "Where is my son? I would see him."

Rowena cast a quick glance at Acennan. He nodded.

"The babe is well. He is with Maida. He is sleeping." She took a step forward, gently placed her hand on his arm. Her eyes were full of pity. "Which is what you should be doing."

She was right. The weight of the last day and night pressed down on him. His eyes were heavy. He could barely place one foot before the other.

"Yes. I will sleep." Perhaps he would dream of better things. But he doubted that. The gods brought dreams to men, and they had turned their back on him. He made to move past Rowena, but her hand held him still. Would she not let him rest?

"What?" Exhaustion and sorrow made his tone sharp. As brittle as ice.

For a moment, Rowena seemed unable to utter a sound. Then she composed herself and said, "You cannot sleep in your chamber, lord."

"Come, I would sleep now. Enough of this." He brushed

her aside. Another hand gripped him. This time it was strong. Unyielding.

Beobrand spun round. He had no time for this. His wife was dead, and he merely wished to fall into a slumber where he could forget.

Acennan's jaw was set. But he did not release his hold on Beobrand.

"Come with me and we'll find somewhere for you to sleep," Acennan said.

Beobrand stared at him for several heartbeats. His mind was still addled by drink, tiredness and the trials of the night. Slowly, he understood why they held him back. He blinked away tears. He would not cry again. Certainly not before Rowena and Anhaga.

He shook off Acennan's hand.

"Is… Is she…" Beobrand bit his lip, then continued. "Is she being tended to?"

"Yes, my lord," Rowena replied. "The womenfolk are with her. I awaited your return, but I will go back to help with Sunniva's preparations now."

Beobrand turned away from them then. The sound of her name too much for him. He strode towards the doors.

"I will rest now," he said, but did not look back. "Awaken me when I can see Octa."

"Octa, lord?"

Beobrand halted in the doorway for a moment.

"My son," he said, and stepped into the early morning sunlight.

It felt to Beobrand that he had scarcely closed his eyes when a strong hand shook him awake. He groaned. His head throbbed. The scar beneath his left eye ached. The old wound to his ribs pained him as it had not done since last he had stood in battle. He should never have drunk so much mead. The puking had strained his muscles and the drink had not chased his pain away.

He sat up gingerly. He had been deep in a dreamless sleep, but now the memories flooded back like the seas reclaiming the sands of Lindisfarena.

"What do you want, Acennan?" he croaked.

His stocky friend handed him a cup full of fresh water. He drank greedily. His mouth was dry and felt unclean.

The light had changed. When he had lain down, shafts of bright sunshine had dappled the room. The sun's fingers had found their way to poke behind the shutters. Now, there was no light save for the rush taper Acennan held.

He had slept the whole day.

"Is Octa awake now? Can I see my son?"

"Octa is well, but there is someone else you need to talk with first."

"Who?"

"It is strange," said Acennan. "In the mid-afternoon, a visitor arrived. He has been awaiting you for a long while."

"Who?" Beobrand repeated.

Acennan looked as if he would not reply, then thought better of it.

"You won't want to see him, but he says it is a matter of import. He brings riches. Cattle. Hack silver. It is most strange."

"Who?" Beobrand said for the third time, in an exasperated tone.

"Athelstan," answered Acennan.

Beobrand was speechless for a moment. Athelstan here? What could the old bastard want with him?

"And he brings treasure?" Beobrand asked. "What for?"

"That is the strangest thing of all. Perhaps he should tell you himself."

Beobrand rose from the cot and began to dress.

"Do not make me wait to hear this from the mouth of that man. Tell me what you know. The past day has been too long to play games now."

Acennan nodded. "Very well. He says he brings you were-gild."

"Weregild? For what? What wrong has he done me that he should bring me the law price? I have not seen the man in months."

"Not for a wrong to you, lord," Acennan took in a deep breath and seemed to steel himself. "He says the weregild is for a wrong done to Lady Sunniva."

Athelstan stood as Beobrand entered the hall. His shoulders were slumped, his eyes downcast. His usual arrogance was not present. The burly thegn motioned with his hand and the men who had been sitting with him also rose. Beobrand saw they were Athelstan's closest hearth warriors. Men of courage. Hard men. Dealers of death, like their lord.

Beobrand's own warband sat alongside Athelstan's men. Many were old friends. Shield-brothers from the time of Oswald's exile. There was a tension in the air, but it seemed to stem from recent events and the tidings Athelstan brought, rather than any conflict between the two groups of warriors.

All of these battle-hard men seemed timid now. Subdued. They fidgeted as Beobrand and Acennan approached.

"Well?" Beobrand said. "What brings you to my hall?" He was in no mood for formalities.

Athelstan could not meet his gaze. He opened his mouth to speak, then closed it without uttering a sound.

"Speak, man," said Beobrand, "you have travelled this far. You had best tell me that which you wish to say."

"I come at a dark time," said Athelstan. "We have heard of your loss. I am truly sorry." The older warrior's bearded face was ashen. "This makes the news I bear even more difficult. I bring tidings of a terrible crime."

"These are the darkest times. I have no stomach for riddles now, Athelstan." Beobrand pulled a bench out from the table and sat. Despite the long sleep, he had no strength. His body ached. All he wanted was to sleep once more. He did not wish to have to listen to Athelstan. Acennan had said he had spoken of weregild for Sunniva. For what, he did not know. Beobrand could not imagine, but at the thought of injury being done to his wife, he felt his ire already building within him, like a stream swelling behind a dam of pebbles.

Athelstan and his men sat. Acennan beckoned to one of Rowena's slaves.

"Bring food and drink," he said.

The young woman, dark hair swishing, scurried away, keen to distance herself from the men. Violence was in the air, its scent as strong as the woodsmoke from the hearth.

"Speak, Athelstan," Beobrand said.

"You know me as a man of honour," Athelstan said.

"I know no such thing. I know you for a bully. A man who would paw another's woman before his men and laugh."

One of Athelstan's gesithas stood abruptly, reaching for his seax.

Athelstan raised his hand. All colour had fled his face. "Sit, Betlic."

Betlic glowered, but sat down.

Athelstan continued. "We have not been friends, it is true, but I would that you believe me when I say I have never meant you harm. I would never have harmed your lady. That I come here now should vouch for my honour, for it is not a pleasant task I have. It would have been easier on me to remain in my hall and hope you would not find out about the events I must tell you of."

Beobrand frowned. "Tell me then, and have done with it."

Anhaga limped up to the table with a platter of cheese, bread and cold meat. The dusky slave girl brought mead and ale.

None of the warriors touched the food or drink.

"You will remember that I had taken the oath of Wybert, son of Alric."

"Of course, but what of Wybert. I do not see him here." He was glad Wybert was not there. The man hated him and Beobrand did not want to be reminded of past failures.

"Indeed. Wybert is not here. He is no longer in Bernicia. Or even in Northumbria, I would wager."

"Again, you speak in riddles. Just tell me what has happened."

"Very well." Athelstan paused. He reached for a cup and beckoned to the slave. She poured ale and he took a long draught. He wiped the froth from his moustache, squared his shoulders as if standing before a strong enemy and set about recounting his dark tale.

"Some months past, after we had returned from the lands of Mercia and Wessex, Wybert set out hunting with another of my gesithas, Synn. The winter was bad and wolves had been spotted. They said they would like to have wolf skins to wear. I did not care for the hunt. The journey south had been long and cold. I preferred to stay in my hall by the fire. Getting old, I suppose." He took another swig of ale. Having started his story, he seemed to find the words easily. Beobrand sat in silence, awaiting the news that concerned Sunniva. Beneath the table his fists were clenched.

"Days passed and when they returned, they did not have pelts to show for the hunt. I laughed at them then. I was pleased to have stayed home, in the warm. Well, winter gave way to Solmonath and we forgot about the failed hunt. Until a few days ago." Athelstan paused again. Drank. Took a slow breath. "Wybert had been drinking. He was loud, boasting and telling tales with the other men in the hall. The boasts got bigger, the tales more outrageous until Wybert made a boast that brought silence to the room."

Athelstan's men looked down at their hands. They had been there in that hall. They knew what had been said.

The muscles in Beobrand's jaw bunched. His teeth ached from the pressure, but he did not pay heed.

Athelstan scratched his beard.

"What was the boast?" asked Beobrand.

Athelstan could not meet his eye.

"You have walked the path of this tale to this door, Athelstan," Beobrand said. "Now you must open it."

Athelstan hesitated, then gave the slightest of nods. "He told how he had ploughed Beobrand half-hand's woman."

There was a gasp from Beobrand's gesithas.

Beobrand closed his eyes. Could this be true? His stomach twisted. Bile filled his throat. He swallowed it back with an effort. He would not disgrace himself before those gathered here. Athelstan continued talking into the bleak silence of the hall.

"Wybert laughed, as if he thought we would be proud of what he told us. We were not. He spoke of how they had come north knowing you to still be in the land of the Picts. They came to your hall. I believe when they came here, they found your men away, hunting the very wolves that they had been stalking. I do not know how it happened, or why, but Wybert told us they had forced themselves upon the Lady Sunniva."

Beobrand stood abruptly. He shook his head. He did not wish to hear this. He stepped from the bench. The room was filled with smoke. It stung his eyes. Stole the air from his lungs. He pulled in great breaths through his open mouth.

"Why do you come here? Why do you speak of these things?" Beobrand's voice was clipped, shards of iron thrown from blades clashing in battle. "If Wybert is not with you that I may exact payment from him, why have you come?"

"I would have brought them to face justice. Both men. But Synn fought us and perished. Wybert fled. He broke his oath to me. Stole a horse and rode south. He is no longer my man. But he was. So, I have come that there may be no bloodfeud between us. I was his lord. I bring weregild for his acts."

Beobrand rounded on his gesithas. "How could this happen? You had to protect her. You made your oaths to me and yet you have forsaken my lady. You have failed me." Beobrand shook with the strength of his emotion. His gesithas were aghast. They had known none of these tidings. Their faces were grey in the dim light of the hall. They hung their heads in shame.

Tobrytan, tears in his eyes, went to his lord and threw himself at his feet.

"Lord, have mercy on us. We did not know." He wailed with a grief as real as Beobrand's, for the men had all loved Sunniva. "We failed the Lady Sunniva. We failed you. We did not know. Oh gods, we did not know!" He sobbed into the rushes, undone by his anguish.

Beobrand could not look upon him. "Was there nobody here to protect my wife?" Beobrand asked.

Athelstan spoke. "Wybert talked of beating one of your

servants. He said the man was puny, but fought with all his might to defend his mistress. Wybert and Synn beat him about the face cruelly. Left him senseless."

A slight movement to Beobrand's left drew his attention. Anhaga stood there, trembling and wide-eyed. Those eyes had witnessed the terrible events Athelstan spoke of. In an instant it all made sense to Beobrand.

With his disfigured left hand he lashed out and grabbed Anhaga by the throat of his kirtle. He pulled him savagely close. Spat words into his fearful face.

"You knew! It was you, was it not?"

Anhaga did not answer. His eyes shone with terror at his lord's wrath.

"Why did you not stop them?" Beobrand screamed at the wretch. "Why?" Having taken hold of the cripple, Beobrand suddenly found an object for all of his rage. This man, this cripple, who Sunniva had never trusted, had been present at the moment she was defiled and he had failed to stop the men.

Without a thought, Beobrand's right fist crashed into Anhaga's cheek. It was Anhaga's fault. He pulled back his fist and pummelled it into Anhaga's face again. The man let out a cry of pain, but did not seek to protect himself. Why would he? He was a coward. A pathetic creature that allowed women to be raped.

Beobrand punched him again. And again. Blood streaked Anhaga's face. Beobrand's knuckles split. Slick with blood, his own and that of Anhaga, his right fist became a smith's hammer. His left hand, gripping the kirtle tightly, became the anvil that held Anhaga in place.

The man became limp, insensate, yet Beobrand continued to strike him, the head lolling this way and that as he struck.

Hands gripped his arms.

Slowly the uproar of the hall filtered through the haze of fury. He pulled his gaze with difficulty from Anhaga's bloodied face. Turned to see who dared to lay their hand upon him.

Acennan. His friend's canted nose a reminder of another such violent assault. Another time, and another place.

Slowly, the room came back into focus. Aethelwulf and Garr were beside Anhaga. They were uncertain. They looked on their lord with fear. Their fate had not yet been decided. They too had failed Beobrand. They looked at the blood-streaked limp form of the hall steward and saw their own future there. Beobrand shook his head. He slowly relinquished his grip on Anhaga. Garr and Aethelwulf caught him and carried him away. They looked glad to be gone from their lord's presence.

Acennan gripped Beobrand's shoulder. Whispered, "Come, my friend. Sit. You must eat and drink."

Beobrand's hands began to shake. He clenched his fists in an effort to stop the trembling. He walked stiffly to the gift-stool at the end of the hall. He sat heavily. The hall was silent. He looked at the blood dripping from his right fist. He always shook so after combat. It would pass soon. But this had been no combat. He had beaten the man senseless. Anhaga had not defended himself. And if what Athelstan said was true, the cripple was the only man who had stood up to Sunniva's attackers. He had worn the results of the beating upon his face when they had returned from Dál Riata.

Acennan called for water for Beobrand to wash his hand. The slave girl brought a wooden bowl and a cloth. Beobrand nodded his thanks to Acennan. He sighed as he rinsed away the blood. His knuckles were already bruising, the split skin smarting at the touch of the cloth. The water was pink when the thrall took it away. Beobrand noticed that her hands also shook as she lifted the bowl.

At the lower tables the men had started to converse in hushed tones. Acennan remained by Beobrand's side, but did not speak. There was nothing for him to say. No counsel to give. This day had been one of nightmare. His wyrd had led him into a darkness greater than that of the winter of his arrival in Bernicia. His wyrd brought him loss, followed by gain, then greater loss. It was the gain that made the loss the more acute. Perhaps this was what the gods enjoyed. He felt like a plaything of the gods then. Cursed, despite having his own hall, a warband and treasure. These things were as nothing now.

Cursed.

He could almost hear Nelda's screech in the darkness outside of the hall. Was she still plotting and weaving her magic from her cave on Muile? Or perhaps she travelled south to wreak her revenge for her son's death. Perhaps she was even now in Ubbanford, lying in wait for him with her dagger and her hate.

He shivered.

Shaking his head to clear it, he called for mead. He drank deeply.

The furnace of his rage was a banked fire now, the flames dampened down by his sorrow and shame. He had not been here to protect Sunniva. He had allowed this to happen. Once again he had been unable to defend those he loved most.

Vengeance may not bring peace, but it was all he had left.

He held up his hand for silence. The knuckles throbbed. All the men turned their attention to him.

"Athelstan, we have not been friends, it is true. But you have come here with good faith. You are a man of honour, as you say. I thank you for that. There will be no feud between us. And you may take your treasures back to your own hall."

Athelstan made to reply, but Beobrand silenced him with a gesture. "If I accept the weregild, I accept payment for the crime, and I do not. I will have blood for what was done. No treasure can recompense me. There will be no feud between your household and mine. But Wybert is no longer your man. Here, before you all, I pledge vengeance on Wybert. Let it be known that I will not rest until he is dead. I swear an oath before you and all the gods that I will take Wybert's life. He is as one dead even now. His life is mine."

The men gathered there looked upon Beobrand, lord of Ubbanford, thegn of Oswald of Bernicia and they saw the truth in his words. This was the slayer of Hengist. They saw the steel in his eyes and the flint in his heart.

They saw death. And they pitied Wybert.

24

Athelstan left the morning after the revelations in the hall. Ubbanford was no place for him. The day was barely begun, the shadows long and the air still crisp when he gathered his men, bade a formal farewell to Rowena, for Beobrand had not yet risen, and headed south towards his own lands.

After Athelstan's departure, Beobrand rose and left the hall where he had lain in a mead-hazed stupor. He saddled Sceadugenga and mounted. Acennan hurried after him.

"Wait, Beobrand. I will fetch my mount and ride with you." Acennan's concern was clear.

"No. Stay here," Beobrand said. His eyes were distant and cold, like sea ice.

"You should not ride alone," said Acennan. "I will ready my horse."

"No, Acennan. Stay here and protect my son."

Acennan nodded slowly. He could not refuse such a request, but he feared for his friend. After the eruption of fury in the hall that saw Anhaga now confined to his bed, Beobrand had shown no more emotion. It was as if in death, Sunniva had taken something of him with her.

Beobrand moved as one in a daze. As someone who is in great need of sleep, or one who has slept for too long and too soundly, to awaken in the mid-afternoon after a feast, unsure of what day it is.

Acennan watched with worry etched on his face as Beobrand, sitting high on his black steed's back, galloped out of Ubbanford.

The day dragged on slowly. The men busied themselves as best they could, but they were acutely aware of their failure to their lord. There was no light-hearted banter that day.

Beobrand returned late in the afternoon, Sceadugenga lathered in sweat, and he stalked into Ubba's hall.

His people were gathered there, and they all looked to him as he entered. Rowena and Edlyn's eyes were red-rimmed. Maida rose with Octa in her arms, but Beobrand ignored them.

"Tobrytan," Beobrand said. The grizzled warrior looked up, his face set. Ready to face his punishment, be it death or exile.

"My lord."

"Organise the men tomorrow and fetch wood."

Tobrytan looked confused.

Beobrand continued, "You will build a pyre such as would be fit for a king of old. Build it atop the hill. We will send Sunniva's spirit to the gods tomorrow at the setting of the sun."

Tobrytan bowed his head. This was not what he had expected.

"Was Sunniva not a worshipper of Christ?" asked Rowena in a timid voice. The events of the last days had taken their toll on her too, and her face was pinched, her movements and tone cautious, as if she was afraid her actions might cause a disaster.

"She was not," replied Beobrand. "She sent her father on in the old way and she would have wanted the same."

Rowena did not reply, but dipped her gaze. None could meet that barren stare for long.

Beobrand turned back to his men. Maida looked up expectantly, but he paid her no heed. She frowned and looked to her husband, Elmer, but he did not notice. He was enthralled with his lord. Guilt lay heavily on him.

"See to it that there is enough wood," Beobrand said, taking in all his gesithas with his gaze. "I trust you will not fail me in this."

The men bowed their heads. None replied as Beobrand left the hall.

Sunniva was clothed in her favourite blue dress. He remembered she had worn it the first time they had lain together, on the sunny hillside above Gefrin. Her head had been bound in linen, over the top and below her chin, leaving her face exposed, eyes closed and peaceful. It would almost be possible to think she slept.

There was little light in the chamber where she lay, but Beobrand could not pretend she was merely sleeping. Her pallor belied that. Her stillness was not that of one who is deep in rest. It was the absolute lack of movement of the dead.

Beobrand had seen many corpses before, but he had never seen one so beautiful. Her hair had been brushed until it shone, dully lambent in the taper's flame-glow. Her skin was as smooth and perfect as the finest polished stone.

And as cold.

His breath caught in his throat. A sob escaped him. He fell to his knees before the bed where his wife lay.

"I'm so sorry," he said. "So sorry. I should have been here. I didn't know. Why didn't you tell me? Oh, my love…"

He allowed the tears to flow then. He had been holding them in check all the day as he rode the hills. He had pushed Sceadugenga hard. The stallion seemed to understand his master's need. The horse galloped with a furious power. The wind whistled and his hooves thundered. Beobrand revelled in the raw energy of the beast. The speed and danger of falling. He rode with abandon, half hoping to be thrown. But Sceadugenga was a good steed and Beobrand was not unhorsed. He rode as if he could outpace the grief that threatened to consume him.

But in the end, he had not been surprised to find that the horse had led them back to Ubbanford. The sun was low in the sky then and Rowena had met him at the door of the hall.

"Lord," she had said, "the pyre is ready. You should take some time to bid Sunniva farewell before we take her up the hill."

He had looked at her blankly then, but allowed her to lead him through the hall to the sleeping chamber where his dead wife awaited him. Rowena had left him alone with Sunniva in the gloom-laden room. Beobrand was glad of that now.

He had not faced Sunniva since her death, and the sight of her lying there had all but unmanned him. It would not do for his men to see him thus. He roughly wiped the tears from his face. He stood and kissed Sunniva's blue lips.

They were soft, yet cold. Unmoving. He closed his eyes for a moment. The touch of her mouth on his was familiar, and yet strangely cool and different. Like looking at a well-loved landscape that is disguised under a blanket of fresh snow.

He shuddered. Stood.

"Fare you well, my love," he whispered.

★

Nobody could recall a larger funeral fire.

It could be seen from far beyond the extent of Beobrand's hides of land. The sun dipped below the western horizon and Beobrand touched a torch into the dried tinder and twigs at the base of the wood pile. The wood was dry. His men had done well. The flames licked hungrily up the kindling, crackling and spitting sparks as a light breeze fanned the fire. Smoke spewed forth from some of the larger logs as the heat reached them.

Sunniva lay peacefully on top of the pyre. Smoke began to billow around her. Wisps of her golden hair rose and wafted around her face, lifted by the wind and heat.

The onlookers were silent. Awestruck, they watched as their lady's form was consumed. Her spirit would fly free in the smoke. The gods would surely take her into their hall.

Beobrand had not spoken since coming to this place. He was aware of the presence of his people around him. Every one of the inhabitants of Ubbanford was atop the hill that night. He had nodded to Acennan as, together, they had undertaken the grim task of lifting Sunniva onto the heap of wood. Acennan's eyes were dark and full of sorrow.

Sunniva's father, Strang, had been much heavier when they had lifted his body less than a year before. When they had found Strang, neither would have imagined they would be lifting his daughter's body mere months later. She was so light. Beobrand's mind brought back to him unbidden the image of Rheda. She too had been light, fragile. One moment so full of life and energy, the next no more than meat.

His vision blurred. He bit his lip. He would not cry. Tears would do no good. They never had.

Gently they had lain Sunniva down and descended the ladders they had used to raise her to the height of the top of the funeral pyre.

She was so lovely. He swallowed against the harsh lump in his throat. He watched as the smoke began to engulf her. He would never see her again. He blinked back tears. She was leaving middle earth. Leaving him alone.

Without warning Beobrand spun towards Maida, who stood a few paces back from the pyre. She held Octa in her arms. He was swaddled in a blanket. Elmer stood beside her, one broad hand placed protectively on her shoulder.

Reminding all the warriors present of why he was such a fearsome opponent in battle, Beobrand took a bounding leap towards Maida, instantly closing the gap between them. Instinctively she recoiled, holding Octa away from him, towards her husband.

"Give me my son," Beobrand said.

"Lord," Elmer answered for her in a hesitant voice.

Beobrand cast a glance back to the fire. The flames were moving higher. There was no time to explain or to argue.

"Give him to me," he shouted and snatched Octa from the woman's clutches.

She shrieked. Others screamed out too.

Beobrand ignored them and stepped back towards the fire. Acennan blocked his path. Their eyes met.

"Step aside, I mean him no harm," Beobrand said.

Acennan hesitated for a heartbeat, then allowed him to pass.

Heat was rolling off of the fire now, making it difficult to get close. Sunniva was all but hidden by the conflagration of smoke and flames. But her form was still visible. The shape of her face darkly silhouetted within the blaze.

Octa began to wail. It was the first time that Beobrand had held his son.

Their son.

He held him aloft, high above his head.

More screams from the women. Did they believe he would toss his child onto the fire? Did they truly believe he was capable of such a thing? Perhaps.

He supported Octa's tiny head in his half-hand, the babe's feeble body in his right. He shifted him so that he would be able to see into the high part of the bone fire.

"That is your mother, Sunniva, daughter of Strang," he said. "You will not see her again in this world, so look upon her now and do not forget, my son. Octa."

He held him thus for a long while until his arms began to tremble. Octa stopped his weeping. He seemed entranced by the flames. Or perhaps by the vision of his mother.

The people of Ubbanford fell quiet too. They were silent as their lord said farewell to his wife, and welcomed his son into this world. They watched as Beobrand stood beside the raging fire. He was still and solid. The flames cavorted and danced.

After a long while he lowered the small bundle that was his infant son. He held him close to his chest, his muscular arms wrapped around Octa to protect the baby from the heat.

He took a step backwards, and the women smiled. He meant no harm to the child.

When he was at a distance that was safe for the babe, Beobrand planted his feet and stood, as immobile as rock, gazing into the fiery heart of the pyre.

His gesithas saw a warrior, broad of shoulder, and hale of frame. The womenfolk saw the way he protected his child and they saw the new father. A young man, unsure, and alone, and their hearts melted for him.

Acennan looked sidelong at Beobrand and saw a friend. The firelight moved on his face. The glistening trails of tears were quickly burnt away in the glare of the pyre. It was impossible to take away Beobrand's jagged hurt, but it would soften in time, the way a rough stone will be smoothed by the constant tides of the sea.

His people looked upon Beobrand as he stood vigil over his wife's bone fire and they each saw something different. Yet there was one thing that all of them agreed on.

He was their lord.

The next days were dark in Ubbanford. The sun's orb rose high in the sky each day. There were mere threads of clouds in the warm afternoons and those who worked on the new hall's construction, or in the fields, sweated and squinted against the brightness of the light.

Yet a pall of darkness hung over the village as surely as if a storm cloud had settled above it.

Beobrand's men felt keenly their failure. They awaited their lord's punishment, but none came, which only served to make them feel worse. They knew they had done wrong and wished to feel the brunt of Beobrand's wrath to expiate their guilt in some measure. The lack of ire directed at them made for an excruciating blend of self-loathing and self-pity. Fights broke out. Words of blame were uttered. Friendships soured.

In an effort to keep busy, the warriors resumed work on the hall on the hill. Where before they had accompanied their work with good-natured banter and jests, now they toiled with scarcely a word being spoken. The work did not progress as quickly as it should have with the fine weather. Their hearts were not in it. They would look at where Sunniva used to sit in the last days before her confinement and then their eyes would be drawn to the grey-black stain on the hill. The place of her pyre. More than one of the men needed to wipe tears from their cheeks. There seemed to be more stray dust blowing into eyes than before Sunniva's death. Perhaps it was ash from the remnants of the blaze that had consumed her flesh.

For Beobrand the days were long. He rode far on Sceadugenga. He traversed rivers, passed beneath the thick canopy of brooding forests and climbed the steep hills to the south, from where he could see a great distance all around. He avoided contact with others, preferring his own company. He had no desire to talk, but that left his mind free to wander. And the paths of his memory were treacherous, like an ice-locked marsh. Any misstep could plunge a traveller through a skin of ice into the dark morass of a frigid mere, never to return.

Sceadugenga's hooves picked a sure trail through the land of Bernicia. Beobrand's thoughts were not so sure-footed. When he stumbled into the darkest memories, he was glad of his solitude. What would his men have thought of their lord, a man they looked up to for his battle-skill and strength, with hot tears of shame and regret streaming down his young face?

On the day following the pyre, Beobrand took a clay pot and collected the ash. This he secured on Sceadugenga's saddle and rode south. He passed in the shadow of the standing stones that had been raised by some ancient race. Perhaps they had been erected by the same giants who built the Wall further south, though that seemed unlikely. The circles of stones that dotted the countryside were large and imposing, but more natural somehow than the Great Wall, or the straight roads such as Deira Stræt.

He saw few people. This land was wild and untamed. The windswept hills spoke to him. They cared nothing for the passing of life. Kings were as nothing to them. He touched the earthenware pot where it nestled behind him in a leather saddle bag. The land would not remember Sunniva. Or any of the others he had seen die. Where were the people who had raised the stone circles? Where were the giants who built the Wall? They had gone the way of all things. And yet, remnants of their existence were still to be seen. Perhaps that is all men can hope for. For some small part of their lives to remain visible to others after their death.

And then of course, there were children.

He could still not envisage Octa the wrinkled infant becoming a child. Or a man. It seemed impossible to Beobrand that he was truly a father. His own father's shadow loomed over his thoughts. Would he be a truer father to Octa, than Grimgundi had been to him? Would Octa hate and fear him, as he had loathed his own father?

As he rode, alone with his thoughts, with only the ghosts of family and loved ones for company, he understood why he had fled from Ubbanford. Why he had scarcely acknowledged Octa's existence. He had told himself that babies were for women, and this was true. But there was more than that.

He had imagined that he somehow blamed the child for Sunniva's death. Those black thoughts had come to him, but there was a further reason that he ran from his son.

Beobrand was frightened. He was terrified that he would be the same man his father had been. That he would beat and threaten Octa, hammering the child into a weapon to be used against him, just as he had turned on Grimgundi.

He reined in Sceadugenga by a trickling stream, allowed the horse to drink. Along the banks of the stream grew rushes. Spear-straight they rustled in the breeze. Beobrand gazed at them. They brought back the images of the shieldwall. The thicket of waving spears. He had risen to prominence by dealing in death. Perhaps he owed something to his father after all. All those he hated had made him the man he now was.

A warrior.

A weapon.

A death-bringer.

First Grimgundi, with his beatings. Then Hengist, his brother's slayer, abuser and murderer of innocents, had trained him in the ways of battle.

And was Grimgundi even his father? His mother's dying words still plagued his memory. What had she meant by them?

He ran his deformed left hand over the stubble on his jaw. His beard was growing fuller now, as if by siring a son he had truly become a man. Or perhaps it was when he began to slay men.

There was one thing that he was sure of. As certain as the fact that a tree can be felled by a man with an axe. Whatever his past, and however he had come to this, he was a warrior now. A weapon-wielder who would bring death on his enemies and those of his lord.

Wybert was his enemy now, and Beobrand would go to whatever lengths were needed to find him. And to kill him. Vengeance did not bring peace with it. He knew this now. Yet it was all there was for him.

Revenge. And service to his lord.

With all of these thoughts vying for supremacy in his mind, Beobrand pushed on southward. He did not ride aimlessly. He knew where he was heading.

He crested the last hill and peered down into the valley. The sun was behind the western hills now, the valley in shadow. He could just make out the blackened beams of the great hall. The hollow shell like the jutting ribs of some giant's carcass. The other buildings were mostly burnt-out husks. Cadwallon's

Waelisc host had destroyed the once proud township of Gefrin. The glow of the blaze had been visible in the sky all the way to the coast.

There were a few small buildings that seemed to have avoided the fires, or perhaps had been rebuilt since, as inhabitants of Gefrin returned to their homes. Trails of smoke drifted from the intact buildings. Beobrand spotted a man leading a donkey behind one of the dwellings.

Beobrand looked about him. The day had been warm. Ragged clouds streaked the sky. It would grow cold in the night, but he could not face talking to strangers now. He found the trail he was looking for and followed it some way down the slope of the hill.

The secluded meadow, surrounded by rowan and pine, was as he remembered it. The sweet scent of heather brought back the memory of that warm summer day. Sunniva had been so beautiful. He had been intoxicated by her. The touch of her small hands on his body. The warmth of her pliant flesh beneath him. The taste of her mouth.

Beobrand dismounted. Reaching for the saddle bag, he lifted the urn containing Sunniva's ashes. Placing it reverently on the ground, he prepared a meagre camp. He removed Sceadugenga's saddle and tethered him nearby. He had not come prepared for sleeping outside but he did not wish to light a fire. It would attract attention from Gefrin below. It would be a cold night. But he would not be alone. He clutched the unyielding earthenware pot to him, wrapped both himself and it in his cloak and stretched out on the lush grass.

This was where they had first lain together.

It seemed fitting that it was where they would spend their last night.

The stillness of the hill enveloped him. He had ridden long

and hard. His body was tired. His mind tortured. Yet sleep came rapidly.

He did not recall his dreams when he awoke the next morning, but the dew that fell on his upturned face in the darkness mingled with the salty tears that were already on his cheeks.

25

The sun cast long, stark shadows into the Tuidi valley when Beobrand returned. His body ached from the saddle. He was tired, but his head was clearer than when he had set out. Thoughts threatened to pull him into an abyss of despair. He could feel them tugging at his memories, striving to drag him into a darkness that lurked at his core. He would not despair. Wyrd had set him on this path and he would see it through.

He focused on what he had. A hall. Land. A warband of loyal gesithas. A son. But what good were all these things, if he could not find happiness? He could not prevent himself asking the silent question. The darkness scratched and gnawed at his mind. How could he continue? He had lost all those he loved. At every turn he was surrounded by death. He truly was cursed. Forsaken by the gods.

Beobrand saw a rider off in the distance. He was glad of the distraction from the slavering maw of his black thoughts. He reached to his side and loosened Hrunting in its scabbard. The hilt of the sword at once settled his nerves. Calmed his mind. There was a certainty in the sword's presence. Its purpose was clear. It would not fail him. Beobrand bared his teeth and dug his heels into his steed's flanks. Should the lone rider prove to be a brigand, he would rue the day he chose Beobrand, son of Grimgundi, as a victim. The stallion leapt forward into a gallop, clearly with power in reserve despite the long ride back from Gefrin.

They closed the distance quickly, the other rider also spurring his horse into a run. Sceadugenga whinnied a greeting to the other horse. At the same instant Beobrand recognised the rider. They drew close and Beobrand pulled Sceadugenga to a halt. The horse tossed its head, blowing and snorting. The dappled horse of the other rider moved in close, rubbed its nose on Sceadugenga's flank.

"Well met," said Acennan, struggling to control his mount as it nuzzled the black stallion. "I should not have allowed you to travel alone. You cannot be trusted to look after yourself." He spoke the words with a smile. But Beobrand recognised the strain on his friend's face. He had been worried.

Beobrand shook his head. "I gave you no choice. I needed time to think."

"Still, I will not allow it again. Do not ask me to breach my oath to you. I swore to protect you. I cannot do that when I am not at your side."

Beobrand yanked Sceadugenga's reins. "If these horses have any say in it, we shall always be together. I believe they are smitten with each other."

Acennan grinned, but Beobrand's face clouded at his own mention of affection.

"Come," said Acennan, "let us ride for Ubbanford before darkness falls," steering his horse and the conversation away.

They rode in silence for a short while, then Beobrand asked, "What news?"

"We've begun work on the roof of the hall. The thatch will

be laid soon. Anhaga is no longer abed, but limps about with a face like soured milk."

Beobrand frowned. "I believe I owe the man an apology."

"I think you do." Acennan looked at Beobrand's saddle bags. "I... I didn't think you would return with... that pot."

Beobrand reached behind him and touched the earthenware reassuringly.

"I had planned to bury it..." he hesitated, stumbling over the words. "I had planned to bury her alongside her father and mother. At Gefrin."

"What changed your mind?"

"The men I met there were a dark and twisted sort. I was sure they would dig the urn up as soon as I'd left. Take whatever they could find of value. In the end I chased them away."

"Chased them?"

"Well, I showed them Hrunting's blade and they fled like hares. One fell full on his face in his fear." A grim smile played on his lips as he remembered drawing Hrunting and releasing some of his pent up ire. The dam that held his anger in check had been close to breaking, and it had felt good to scream abuse at the ceorls, threatening death and worse.

Acennan guffawed. "I'd have liked to see that." His face grew serious. "So you brought her back with you?"

"Yes. And I brought Strang and Sunniva's mother too." He patted the other side of his saddle. "I did not like to touch them. They deserve rest. But I decided that they should be together. I will bury them all on the hill in Ubbanford." He touched the amulet at his neck, then brushed his fingers on Hrunting's hilt for luck. "I trust that Strang's shade will know I meant no harm by disturbing his rest."

Acennan suppressed a shudder. "He was a good man."

"He was."

They rode on in silence, each lost in his thoughts. The sun touched the western horizon and golden light kissed the tops of the buildings of Ubbanford as the two riders reached the brow of the hill to the south.

Below, before the old hall, three horsemen were reining in. The glint of the falling sun on metal reached them. Beobrand glanced at Acennan questioningly.

"I do not know who they are," Acennan said, in answer to the look.

"Then let us see who comes to Ubba's hall," said Beobrand, kicking Sceadugenga once more into a gallop.

Acennan shook his head and followed his lord down the hill.

"I cannot go now." Beobrand eyed the man who stood as straight as a spear before him. He was lean, with a full moustache. Beobrand recollected seeing him before at Bebbanburg, but had not known his name. Anhaga clearly knew him well. By the time Beobrand and Acennan had ridden into Ubbanford, the crippled steward had been ushering the man and his two companions into Ubba's hall.

On seeing Beobrand, Anhaga had flushed, the bruises on his face standing out like storm clouds in the darkening early evening light. He had bowed low, flinching as Beobrand jumped from his mount, as if expecting blows to rain down on him.

Beobrand, ashamed at his treatment of the man, took him gently by the arm and raised him up.

He spoke to Anhaga in a soft voice meant only for his ears. "Do not fear me, Anhaga. Forgive me. I would speak with you at length later." He looked Anhaga in the eye. The steward was wary still, but he gave a slight nod. Beobrand squeezed his arm briefly.

"Now, who have we here?" he asked in a louder tone.

"This is Erconberht, son of Erconberht. He is sent here by the king himself."

Now, standing in the hall, surrounded by Beobrand's gesithas, with women, thrall and ceorl alike, bustling around with food, Erconberht looked amazed at Beobrand's answer to his request.

He must have decided that the young thegn had not understood him for, after a moment, he repeated his message.

"Oswald, son of Æthelfrith, King of Bernicia and Deira by the grace of the Lord God, bids you come to Bebbanburg."

Beobrand beckoned to one of the thralls, a dark-haired, slender Waelisc girl, and she came and refilled his cup with mead. He drained it and indicated she pour more. He noticed absently that her hands did not tremble as they had after he had beaten Anhaga. The warmth from the liquid oozed through him, leaking into his limbs and his head. He was aware that he was drinking too fast, but the blurring of the jagged pain inside was welcome. He had been alone with only his thoughts for company on the ride to Gefrin and back, and his thoughts cut and scraped wherever they touched. Mead smoothed the edges.

"I heard you the first time, Erconberht," Beobrand said, his tone harsher than he had intended. "I cannot go now." His mind turned to the urns he had removed from his saddle bags. "I have matters I must attend to."

"But lord," Erconberht said in an outraged tone. "The king himself has summoned you."

"By Thunor," Beobrand slapped the table before him. Mead sloshed out of his cup. "I heard you!"

The hall was suddenly quiet.

Erconberht stood his ground, his brow wrinkled into a dark frown. Acennan stared at Beobrand. Their eyes met. Acennan gave the slightest of nods, confirming what Beobrand already knew. His head was clouded. Fuzzy from the drink. From grief and fatigue. Yet all he had left in this world had been given to him by his king. No matter how much he wished to hide away, to wallow in his sorrow, he could not. He was his lord's, bound by his oath. If he refused his king's summons he would be an oath-breaker. A nithing. His men would leave and he would be left with nothing.

But the thought of losing his men was not what moved him. He could not break his oath. His word was his alone. He would not lose his honour.

"I cannot leave at first light as you would wish," he said at last. His words sounded slurred to his own ears. He sat up straight. "But I will answer my king's summons, as is my duty."

Erconberht inclined his head slightly. His face was impassive, as if nothing untoward had been said.

"You are to bring as many spear bearers as you can."

"Are we to march to war then?"

"That is not for me to say," answered Erconberht. "But bring your warband with you to Bebbanburg."

The men in the room pondered those words. There were glances from some of the women. Surely war could not be upon them again so soon.

"Very well," said Beobrand. He was tired of this. He could face these questions and concerns in the morning. For now, all he wanted was to drink, until he had to think no more.

"In the morning you will ride back to Bebbanburg and tell Oswald King that Beobrand, son of Grimgundi, follows with his warband. But for now, eat and drink. The board is laden with food. Enjoy it."

He beckoned to the thrall again.

She had deep dark eyes, and long lashes. She could almost be thought of as pretty.

Beobrand opened his eyes slowly. Gingerly. His head throbbed. His mouth was sour from mead. The gloom of his chamber was still. Comforting. Absently he reached out and stroked the warm skin of his wife's back.

The shape next to him let out a soft moan and stretched languidly.

His hand recoiled, as if he had touched a forge fire.

That was not Sunniva. Sunniva was dust and crumbled bones. Cold in an urn.

Memories from the previous night tumbled in his mind. The hall, hot and noisy. Smoke from the hearth. The sweet flavour of mead. The thrall girl refilling his cup over and over. His hand reaching out for her. Pinning her small frame to the bed while he thrust angrily into her. The shuddering release.

The tangy scent of their coupling reached his nostrils. His gorge rose.

He grabbed his kirtle and britches and stumbled from the dark room.

How could he have done such a thing? And in the bed he had shared with Sunniva. Self-disgust bubbled up from the depths of him and he barely made it out of the hall and into the daylight before he emptied his guts in a steaming puddle on the earth. He retched again. Dizzily, he leaned against the door frame. Another spasm made him arch over, but nothing more came. He spat and made his way groggily back into the hall.

The dark-haired thrall was leaving the sleeping area at the back of the hall. She spotted him and instantly cast her gaze downward. Beobrand looked away, as if by not seeing her, he could pretend the events of the previous night had never occurred.

"Would you care for something to break your fast?" said a voice close by.

Beobrand started, he had not noticed anyone approaching. Spots danced before his eyes as he spun to see Anhaga. The steward's face bore the reminder of Beobrand's rage. Anhaga's expression was impassive, but did Beobrand detect a certain disapproval in his eyes? He looked back to the slave girl. She left the hall. Beobrand relaxed somewhat.

"Just some bread and ale, Anhaga. Then we must talk."

The food and drink went some way to settling Beobrand's stomach, but his head still pounded as he walked beside Anhaga some time later.

Beobrand had suggested they walk up the hill to the new hall. Anhaga had said nothing, but followed his lord and was now limping determinedly in an effort to keep up with him. Beobrand slowed his stride. He cursed himself silently. Did he think of nobody but himself? To make the man walk when he had meant to show him that he was sorry for his actions. Anhaga must think him cruel.

He supposed he was. That part of himself that made him a deadly foe in battle could quickly make of him a monster. A man who would beat those weaker than himself. A man like his father. Or Hengist.

He would not let that happen. He would apologise, something neither of those brutish men would ever have considered.

The weather had turned and seemed to fit his mood. Clouds had rolled in. The sky was a melancholy grey. His right foot ached, reminding him of the kick that must have broken at least one toe. A thin drizzle fell that had soaked both men to the skin before they were half-way up the hill.

Anhaga slipped on the wet grass, falling forward. Instantly, Beobrand flung out his left hand and caught hold of Anhaga's cloak in an effort to right him. But the sodden wool slipped through the weakened grasp of his injured hand and Anhaga pitched forward onto his hands and knees with a grunt.

Both men cursed at the same moment. Each angry at his own disability.

Beobrand offered his right, whole hand to Anhaga, who, after a hesitation, clasped it and pulled himself up.

"I should not have beaten you," Beobrand said. He felt an acute shame at what he had done to this man. "You are a man of honour. Alone of all my men, you stood between Sunniva and her attackers." Beobrand struggled to find the right words. "I should not have beaten you," he repeated at last.

Anhaga could not meet Beobrand's earnest eyes.

"I am sorry, lord," he said. "I should have done more. I should have stopped them... I..." His words faltered, caught in his throat.

"You are no warrior, Anhaga. You did your best."

Anhaga's face clouded. He looked up at Beobrand.

"I dreamt of being a warrior once. As a boy I was skilled with spear and seax."

"You have not always been... thus...?" Beobrand glanced at Anhaga's twisted foot.

Anhaga smiled, but there was no mirth there. It was the resigned smile of one who has given up dreams. And forsaken hope.

"No, I have not always been crippled."

They walked on in silence. The hilltop was quiet and still. The rest of the men had been kept away by the rain.

Beobrand looked at the half-finished hall. His gaze was drawn to the site of the pyre. The blackened ground was testament to the end of his own dreams. His own hopes. Then he thought of his son, Octa. So tiny. So weak. Yet he would grow and he would need a father.

Anhaga broke the silence and, as he talked, Beobrand understood that he had never really spoken to the man before. He knew nothing of him.

"You and I have both suffered disfigurement. We have that in common, if nothing else." Anhaga stared wistfully at the remains of Sunniva's funeral fire. "I was not always crippled, just as you were not born with missing fingers."

"What happened to you?" asked Beobrand.

"The same thing as you," said Anhaga, with a strange expression on his face. "I fell foul of Hengist."

"Hengist?" asked Beobrand, looking sharply at Anhaga. "You knew him?"

Anhaga wiped rain from his face, wincing as his fingers rubbed the bruised flesh around his mouth. He did not look at Beobrand, instead staring into the murky, rain-blurred distance.

"I knew him." He sighed. "We were friends once. Long ago."

"You grew up together?"

"Yes. We played and hunted. Teased other children. We were like brothers. He was older than me. Stronger, taller, a better fighter and hunter. I wished I were like him." Anhaga shook his head. "I pushed myself to match him in all he did. We trained together and I learnt the way of weapons, but he was a natural.

Like one born to wield sword and spear. It was said that his father had been a great warrior. It could be true. You saw him fight. It was frightening. But I yearned for his skill."

Beobrand rubbed at the stumps of his missing fingers. He remembered the savage glee with which Hengist had fought. The speed. The grace. He too had wished to be like him.

"What happened?" Beobrand asked. He could scarcely believe that the threads of their wyrd had become so tangled.

"King Edwin's Christ priest came to our village. He was a tall, dark man. He spoke with a strange voice. From the lands over the sea to the south they said he came. It was the first we'd heard of the Christ. We had worshipped the old gods before then, and they had served us well. This stranger spoke of eternal life, and no more sacrifice. It had been a hard winter and people were eager to listen."

Beobrand nodded. People were always quick to turn to whichever god offered the most rewards. Everlasting life and an end to sacrifice was an attractive proposition.

"Hengist's mother was the holy woman and well-respected. She had always been treated well by the folk of the village. But when she stood before the Christ priest and cursed him, he was unmoved. He seemed to feel no fear. We had always feared Nelda's wrath."

Beobrand's eyes narrowed at the mention of her name. So it was true. The woman in Muile was Hengist's mother. And it seemed the weft and warp of her life was also woven with theirs. Beobrand remembered her rage. The flashing blade in the dark. Her screaming curse. He prayed their paths would not cross again.

Anhaga continued, oblivious of the effect of his words on Beobrand. "Her temper was as quick and deadly as her son's and nobody would cross her. The tall priest stood there and let her spout her spells and witchcraft. In the end he closed his eyes. Held up his hands and spoke words in a tongue none could understand." He paused, his eyes unfocused. His mind was back at that place all those years ago.

Beobrand did not speak. He waited for Anhaga to continue. This was the most he had heard the cripple talk and he regretted never having taken the time to learn more of him before. Was he so wrapped in his own world that he cared nothing for others? Acennan, his good friend, had told him he had been married. Had once had a child. How was it possible that he had not known these things?

"I can remember that day," continued Anhaga, "as if it was yesterday. The priest spoke his words in a quiet voice and the village became still. Nelda too was silent. As the priest spoke, the sky grew dark. People stood and looked up as black clouds gathered. Then the priest opened his eyes and pointed at Nelda. In his left hand he gripped the symbol that hung around his neck. It was like the hammer of Thunor, but is said to look like the tree on which Christ was nailed. I'll never forget what happened next."

Beobrand's throat was dry.

"Tell me."

"He said in our tongue, 'In the name of our Lord Jesu Christ leave this place that these people may know the truc word of God.' For a moment, nobody moved. And then there was a crash of thunder loud enough to make grown men scream. It was chaos. Terror gripped us all. People threw themselves to the ground. Then we saw that lightning had struck the sacred ash tree where Nelda performed her rites. It was burning."

"So the Christ god destroyed the sacred tree?" Beobrand spoke in awed tones.

"It didn't take the villagers long to act on what they had

seen. Their fear of Nelda changed to hatred and anger. They drove her out. She fled westwards. I never saw her again."

Beobrand did not mention his encounter with the witch on Muile, but he could not prevent a shudder. How had she travelled so far? And to what end? How had she heard of her son's death at his hands?

"But what of Hengist? And your leg?" he asked.

"Hengist did not leave with his mother. I wish that he had. He was almost a man by then and was fond of a girl. Othili was her name. She had skin as pale as milk. Freckles on her nose. Eyes the green of a summer forest."

At the mention of Othili, Anhaga's face lit up, despite the bruises. It was easy to see that Hengist had not been the only one fond of this girl.

"She was beautiful," said Anhaga. "Hengist would have destroyed her beauty. That is all he ever did – destroy."

"Did he hurt her?" asked Beobrand, images of Cathryn, bloodied and broken, flashed in his mind.

"He tried," Anhaga replied, his face grim at his own memories. "I found them in the woods near the village. Othili was screaming. I ran under the trees, fearing that some wild creature might have set upon her." A humourless smile played on his lips. "I suppose in a way, I was right. Hengist was on top of her. Had ripped her clothes. Well, I didn't stop to think, I attacked him with my fists. He was taken by surprise and I have told you I was hale and skilled in the ways of combat. I dragged him off and beat him until he seemed defeated. I paused for breath, not sure what to do. I had not believed before that I could best him. While I stood there panting, he ran off. I chased after him. I should have seen that it was too easy. He was as cunning as Woden's wolf."

Beobrand could picture the scene. Anhaga was a good

storyteller. Perhaps this story had remained secret within him for a long time. The shame and ire he felt were plain to see on his face. Now the rest of it came pouring out in a torrent.

"I rushed after him, leaving Othili behind. I could think of nothing more than catching Hengist and making him pay for what he had done. I know now that he was leading me on. He shouted abuse back at me, in case I lost his trail in my haste. But I was a child and foolish. I had bested him once and believed now that I had the advantage. I realised he had stopped shouting or making any noise the instant before he was on me. He came out of the trees where he had hidden and I knew in a heartbeat that I could not win against him. Not on these terms. Not when he had the surprise and we faced each other with only our guile and strength." Anhaga shook his head, clearly still ashamed of his own foolishness. "In moments he had me on the ground. My face was bloody. I was stunned and unable to move. He held me down with all his weight. I begged him for my life then. What a craven fool I was. I had believed I was a man, but I was a boy and Hengist laughed at me."

"You were no coward, Anhaga. It was a thing of bravery you did. You stood up to him to defend the girl. You did the same for Sunniva. You are no craven." Beobrand meant the words. His respect for this man grew.

"He held me by the throat and punched me again and again. I was helpless... pathetic."

"No. Not weak or pathetic. He was a formidable warrior." Beobrand looked at Anhaga's mottled face and recalled pummelling it in just the way he described. Was he truly a man like Hengist? He would not allow it to be so.

"You beat him," Anhaga said.

"I wore a metal shirt. Carried a fine sword. A helm and

363

shield. And I still lost half my hand. It was my wyrd to kill him, but you are no weakling."

"But I am a cripple," Anhaga said, closing his eyes and rubbing his hands across his face. "I was almost senseless when Hengist told me I would never be able to run after him or anyone else ever again. I watched, dazed and unable to defend myself as he took a large rock and smashed my foot. It still hurts you know. To this day."

Beobrand's toe throbbed as if in sympathy and his hand went unwittingly to his chest. His ribs still ached when the weather changed. He sometimes felt pain in the fingers he no longer had. At times, the ghost of them itched.

"He wanted to make sure," continued Anhaga. "So he took his seax and cut the sinews in my leg too. Then he left me there. Bleeding and weeping." Anhaga paused and let out a ragged breath. He seemed to have gained in confidence as he told his story. It must have weighed heavily upon him all these years. "The next time I saw him was years later. By then he was a thegn. I spoke with him once. He acted as if he could hardly recall what had happened. As if it was just a childish prank."

"What of Othili?"

"She married another. Her father would not allow her to wed a cripple."

They were silent for a long while, each lost in his own thoughts and memories.

At last, Beobrand spoke. "You are right, there is much alike between us. We value the same things. Stand up for what we believe, no matter the outcome."

Anhaga snorted in derision. "Except you kill your enemies. I get myself beaten."

"Do not talk so. You think killing makes me a better man than you? Happier?"

"You are richer." Anhaga cast his hand out, encompassing the hall and all the buildings at the foot of the hill. "You have all this."

Beobrand nodded. "You speak true. The sword has brought me riches, but I would throw it all away to have Sunniva back."

Anhaga said in a small voice, "I am sorry. At least you had her for a time."

Beobrand looked at him. Perhaps Sunniva had been right about Anhaga. Perhaps he had desired her. Maybe even loved her. But Beobrand was sure he had never meant her harm.

Beobrand raised his face to the sky. The cool drizzle washed down his cheeks. His headache had abated somewhat. Soon they would need to leave for Bebbanburg to find what Oswald had in store for them. But first, there was an urgent matter to attend to. He turned to Anhaga.

"It would please me if you would help me bury Sunniva and her parents. I think she would have wanted that. You proved a trusted friend to her. And to me."

Anhaga's eyes brimmed with tears. He swiped them away with the back of his hands.

"Thank you, lord. I would be honoured."

26

The drizzle had stopped by the early afternoon. A watery light filtered through clouds that promised more rain. Beobrand looked over his shoulder at his men. Aethelwulf, Ceawlin, Attor and Garr trudged along in the wake of the mounted men who led the way. All of the warriors carried their shields slung over their backs. They were bedecked for war. Spears, shirts of iron, polished helms. They were strong men. Good men, but they still suffered under the pall of their failure to defend Sunniva.

Beobrand knew that they had not been to blame for the attack she had suffered, nor for her death, and yet he could not bring himself to forgive them. Perhaps that would come, but it was too soon.

He had left Tobrytan and Elmer in Ubbanford. They were solid and dependable. They would watch over the settlement. He had gone to Elmer's hut before he had left. There, as the children played and fought and Maida worked the loom, he had said farewell to his son.

Maida had given him a glowing smile when he'd asked to hold Octa. He supposed she disapproved of his lack of affection. But he knew not how to love this tiny babe. He would learn. And he would not become such a man as his father. He clutched to the words his mother had spoken in death. He was not his father's son. He would love the boy and teach him. But for now, he needed to heed his king's bidding.

"I thank you for caring for Octa. I will not forget your kindness."

"You do us a great honour, lord," Maida had beamed. He would need to give Elmer and Maida suitable gifts when he returned.

Beobrand glanced to his right. Acennan rode there, astride his dappled mare. Some way behind, Anhaga swayed on the back of the donkey he had borrowed from the stables at Bebbanburg several months before.

"Why does he ride with us?" asked Acennan in a lowered voice, though not so quietly that Anhaga would not hear.

"He always wished to be a warrior. I know what that is like."

"But he is a cripple. He'll be of no use in battle," scoffed Acennan.

"Do not speak thus. He has proven his mettle and his worth. I do not say he can stand in the shieldwall should it come to that. But he has earned my respect and gratitude. I have said he can carry my shield. With this damn hand I need help."

Beobrand looked down at his hands. There was thick dirt under his nails. It was the dirt from Sunniva's burial. Anhaga and he had dug grave holes for the three urns. They had placed the pots and the items that each might wish for in the next life gently in the ground. Beobrand put a fine antler-toothed comb for Sunniva. Her hair was one of the things that remained clearest in his mind when he conjured up her image.

They had bowed their heads when the graves were covered

and Beobrand had said in a voice little more than a whisper, "Rest well, my love."

It was as they walked down the hill to prepare for the journey to Bebbanburg that Beobrand had asked Anhaga to join them as his shield-bearer. Beobrand looked back at where he rode on the sway-backed donkey. He hoped he would not regret the decision. It seemed right. He owed the man something for his service and the harsh treatment he had received. To think that he had known Hengist. Was made a cripple at his hand.

They rode on.

"What did you speak of for so long on the hill?" asked Acennan.

Beobrand recounted the story of how Anhaga was crippled.

"By the gods," said Acennan, "Hengist has been dead these many months and yet still we hear his name spoken at every turn. He cast a long shadow that one."

Beobrand rubbed his left hand. "That he did. But we do him too much honour to remember him. Let us talk no more of him. He is dead and gone, a shade now."

"Indeed," Acennan smiled, "we have talked of the dead long enough. What I want to know is what the living have in store for us in Bebbanburg."

The great hall of Bebbanburg thronged with men. Warriors from across Bernicia and Deira gathered to hear their king speak. They had been summoned and they had answered the call of their lord. The hall was hot and noisy. The hearth fire burnt, but the day had warmed. The door wards had thrown open the doors in an effort to lessen the cloying heat, yet it was still overly hot; the air acrid with sweat and smoke.

Coenred carried the bundle of vellum, ink and quills carefully. Beads of sweat prickled his forehead as he threaded his way through the hall. A laughing thegn slapped another huge fellow on the back who staggered into Coenred's path. The young monk took a darting step and avoided the collision. The ink pot, balanced precariously on top of the parcel of vellum, tottered and almost fell. Perhaps he should have left the ink for a second trip. If he dropped it, Gothfraidh would be furious.

"Coenred?" said a familiar voice.

He turned and looked up into the face of his friend, Beobrand.

"I had not expected to see you here," Beobrand said. "I thought you would be with your brethren on the holy island."

"Until yesterday, I was there, but I was summoned, along with another of the monks. We are to write what is decided and agreed."

Beobrand looked blank.

"Agreed about what?"

Embarrassed, Coenred realised that the king had yet to speak to the gathered thegns.

"Err... I'm sure that is best coming from the king." He changed the subject. "I have heard dark tidings from Ubbanford. Are they true?"

Beobrand's face clouded. Coenred could see that despite his youth, Beobrand's eyes had a haunted quality about them. Pinched and sad. His mouth seemed pulled into a permanent scowl.

"You have heard the truth. Sunniva died."

"Oh, Beobrand," Coenred wanted to reach his hand out to his friend, but his arms were full of the writing utensils. "I am so sorry." He recalled the lovely fair-haired girl who had left with Beobrand. How could it be that so many young people died? How did God allow it?

"Let me take these things to Gothfraidh. Then I will come back and we can talk. I would hear all of your news, for I believe there are some good tidings too."

And so it was that a little while later Coenred was seated in a relatively quiet corner of the hall with Beobrand. He noted that, despite the day being young, Beobrand had already begun to drink mead.

"It is good to see you, Coenred," said Beobrand. "You look well. Life on Lindisfarena suits you, it seems."

"It is bleak. Sometime the wind howls and the sea threatens to engulf the island. But I do like it. I enjoy walking on the beach. Watching the birds. There are so many. And the seals. So many wonders of God's creation."

"And what of the bishop? What of Cormán? I have not seen him here. Does he still make your life miserable?"

Coenred stammered for a moment, unsure of what to say. Oswald had forbidden them to speak of what had transpired. Coenred looked at Beobrand's grim features. His broad shoulders. The scar below his left eye. He recalled the burning anger that had coursed through him at the bishop's touch. Beobrand would feel that same anger if he were to tell him what had occurred. But he would be as likely to follow the bishop back to Hii and murder him there. Beobrand's fury burnt long and was deadly.

"Cormán did not stay. Oswald sent to Hii for a different bishop."

"Oh," Beobrand looked surprised, "that is another reason to trust Oswald. He is a good judge of character."

Coenred smiled, glad to be able to move away from the subject of Cormán. "Well, he gave you position and land, so he must be," said Coenred. "And I hear you have a son?"

"Yes. He is called Octa."

"I give you joy, Beobrand. It is a great blessing."

For a moment, Beobrand looked as though he might strike Coenred.

"I do not feel blessed," he said, at last, and drained his cup.

An awkward silence fell between them.

Beobrand signalled to a thrall to bring him more mead.

Coenred fidgeted. What could he say to this man? He had achieved so much, and yet lost what was most important to him.

He was relieved when Gothfraidh approached.

"Come along, boy," the old monk said, his tone acerbic. "You were supposed to be preparing the quills. Do you expect me to do everything? No, don't answer that! Come along."

Coenred raised an eyebrow at Beobrand.

"Let us talk more later. The king will address you all soon, I believe."

Beobrand nodded and took a swig from his cup.

Beobrand belched. His eyes stung from the smoke that drifted around the press of men in the great hall. New logs had been thrown onto the hearth and it spat and grumbled as the flames took.

Reaching for his cup, he found it empty. Blearily, he looked around for someone to fill it for him. He did not immediately spot anyone willing, so he heaved himself up from the bench where he sat and staggered towards a table that groaned under the weight of food and drink. It was early evening and the feast was just beginning. Men had arrived throughout the afternoon until the hall was crowded with warriors.

Beobrand had not stopped drinking mead since he had arrived. Meeting Coenred had reminded him of his failures.

The people he had lost. The mistakes he had made. The mead went a long way towards dulling those memories. Acennan had approached him after some time and told him that it was perhaps not wise to drink so freely before the king had spoken. Beobrand had growled and waved him away.

He had come when Oswald had called, hadn't he? He would do his lord's bidding, but he did not have to be sober to do so.

He picked up a jug and weaved his way back to his place at the bench. Some of the men called his name in greeting. He did not acknowledge them. He did not wish to talk.

In the shadows at the edge of the hall, Beobrand noticed Anhaga. He stood with others who were not important enough to be given a place at the boards. He seemed uncomfortable, whether from having to stand or at being surrounded by so many hale warriors, Beobrand did not know.

With some effort, Beobrand managed to seat himself without losing his balance. He refilled his cup and took a sip. The drink was sour in his mouth now. He had drunk more than his fill. Tomorrow he would regret it. But for now, he was pleased of the mead's veil. Looking up, he saw the immense bulk and gnarly arms of Athelstan. The huge older warrior squeezed himself between two men and took the place opposite Beobrand.

Beobrand scowled. This was the last person he wanted to speak to or even see. He did not want to be reminded of Wybert or of what he had done. How he had failed Sunniva. It was too much.

"What do you want with me?" he slurred at Athelstan.

Athelstan reached over and took the jug from Beobrand. He filled a cup and raised it in toast.

"I would drink with you to the memory of fallen shield-brothers and lost friends. I can think of nobody better to drink with than you, Beobrand, son of Grimgundi. Though," he drained his cup and quickly refilled it, "it seems you have a head start on me, so I will need to drink quickly if I am to catch you up."

Beobrand stared at the man. His mind was fogged with the drink, but something in Athelstan's words touched him. Angrily, he felt tears pricking at his eyes.

"Very well," he said, cuffing at his face. "Let us drink together. As you know I am younger and stronger than you," he bared his teeth in a semblance of a grin, "so it is for the best that I am already drunk. It is just possible that I may fall before you."

Beobrand drank down the contents of his wooden cup and slammed it onto the board. The men around them laughed. They had been tense, fearful of offending the morose Cantware thegn whose anger was legendary. The arrival of Athelstan seemed to have lifted his spirits or at least given him a drinking companion. Someone to occupy him and to take the brunt of any violent outbursts. They knew of Beobrand's loss and it was understood by all that sometimes grief turned to anger. And when a man such as Beobrand was blinded by drink and grief-ire, it was best not to stand too near.

Beobrand spoke little. Athelstan seemed content to match him cup for cup and did not seek conversation. The hubbub of the feast rolled over them. Food was served. Anhaga, who knew his master's tastes well, brought Beobrand a large slice of roast pork. The meat was succulent, the skin crisp. Despite his dark mood, the rich flavour brought a smile to his lips.

When all had eaten their fill and men had set to boasting and riddling, the king rose from the high table and held out his arms for silence.

Calm fell slowly on the hall.

"Welcome to my hall," said Oswald. "Feast well, my friends, my comitatus. You are my most trusted men." He cast his gaze around the men seated at the boards, seeming to look each one in the eye. "Those most valiant in combat." Beobrand believed that the king nodded at him with those words, though later, he wondered whether it had been his drink-soaked mind playing tricks on him. "Most proud. Most faithful. You are truly well come to my hall and it brings me joy to see you enjoying my table. Feast and drink. Tell tales and speak riddles this night, for tomorrow we travel south."

It took Beobrand a moment to understand Oswald's words. The rest of the men seemed to understand more quickly. They sat more upright. Leaned forward, eyes bright. Beards bristling from jutting chins. They were utterly quiet now, waiting for their king to tell them what enemy they would face.

"We journey, my most loyal men and I, to meet with Penda, king of Mercia. But we do not march to fight." A murmur from the gathered men. "Do not fear. You will have time to win treasures soon. We are surrounded by many enemies, but even the strongest of warriors must know when it is wiser to avoid a battle. We have destroyed Cadwallon and now Deira and Bernicia are once more united under one king. But the land needs time to heal.

"Penda, who was allied with Cadwallon against Edwin not two years ago, is no friend of Northumbria. He eyes this land with covetous gaze, and yet, he is beset on other sides. The East Angelfolc, the Waelisc to the west, and the West Seaxons to the south. All are pressing him. It is for this reason he has sent word that he wishes to meet with me."

Athelstan called out, "How do you know he does not mean to kill you, as Cadwallon did to your brother under truce?"

Oswald frowned and glared at Athelstan for a moment before replying.

"I am not Eanfrith. Many messages have been passed between Penda and I these last months before we have agreed to meet in person. We would both stare the other man in the eye and grasp his hand. Break bread and drink together. Only then can we be sure of the worth of the other's word.

"We are to travel to a place named Dor on the border of our two countries and we will each travel with five score of our most trusted men, no more. The terms are agreed and it is of the utmost import that none of you breaks the oath I have pledged. There will be no bloodshed. You are my escort. You will travel with all the finery of battle. Wear your most polished helms. Paint your shields afresh. Burnish your spear points. But there will be no battle. Any man who draws the blood of a Mercian will have broken his oath to me and his life will be forfeit. We cannot risk battle with Mercia. Penda must be allowed to turn his attention to his other borders."

Many of the men looked disappointed, but none spoke out against their king. Beobrand found it difficult to focus. Oswald's words washed over him and he felt his eyelids drooping. No fighting was good. He had had enough of killing. There was only one man he wished to kill, and he was not here.

"So, my brave men. We will travel to the border of Mercia and there I will meet with Penda. And there will be no fighting. I will find you treasures and riches elsewhere. Is what I say clear?"

A few men assented with a nod, or a word.

"Is that the noise made by my strongest warriors? You who strike fear into the foes of Northumbria. Those who have heaped the bodies high for the crows and the wolves?"

This time the amassed men let out a cheer.

Oswald nodded and sat back down. Slowly the noise in the hall returned as the men began to debate the king's words and talk of the journey ahead.

"Well," said Athelstan, raising his newly filled cup, "if we are not to kill, which is the one thing you and I do well, there is one good thing."

"What is that?" asked Beobrand, hardly caring, such was the amount of mead he had consumed.

"There will be more time for drinking!"

Beobrand watched as gobbets of vomit splashed into the churning wake of the ship. A white seabird shot from the hazy sky and speared into the water, evidently spotting something in the remains of his last meal worth diving for. The sight turned Beobrand's stomach again. The ship heaved and rolled on the swell. Beobrand leaned once more over the side and retched.

With a creaking shudder the keel of the sleek warship lifted on a wave. Beobrand lost his footing and would have tumbled into the cold sea had not a strong hand gripped his shoulder and pulled him back.

"I told you not to drink so much," said Acennan.

Beobrand groaned and slid down with his back to the strakes.

"When do I ever listen to you?" he asked. He remembered his first trip by ship from Cantware to Bernicia. He had not much liked it then. Now, with his head pounding and his stomach churning like the surf on the rocks of the Farena islands, he hated it. He wished he had heeded Acennan's advice the day before, but he would not admit as much.

He looked up and saw the concern on his friend's features.

"Do not worry about me. I've been drunk before." He forced a grin.

"I know," said Acennan. "Lately you are drunk all the time. It clouds your mind. It is not good for a warrior."

"The clouding of my mind is why I drink," Beobrand blurted out. Even he was surprised at the ferocity of his words. "Anyway, we do not go to fight," he said.

He pulled himself up and staggered towards the stern of the ship. All he wanted was some peace. The crowded ship was not a good place to find it. He clung to a stay that held the mast and looked back at the last ship in the small fleet of three vessels.

At the feast, he had thought they would be heading south by land. He would have been happy to ride. Sceadugenga was a good mount and Beobrand had looked forward to allowing the horse to carry him while he recovered from the mead.

But Sceadugenga had been left in the stables at Bebbanburg. The hostler remembered both horse and rider and promised to look after the stallion.

It turned out that Dor was on the river Scheth, tributary of the Dun. They would make better progress by water, but the constant motion of the Whale Road seemed sent to torment him. He closed his eyes. He prayed to the gods that they would not be long at sea. He did not wish to spend days emptying his guts over the side. He felt another spasm and retched again. Nothing came. He blinked away the dots of light that flickered in his vision. Were they elfs? Some magic of the sea? His vision cleared. There was nothing there.

"Here, drink a little water."

Beobrand turned. Coenred stood at his side, his woollen robe flapping about his slim form in the wind. Beobrand took the flask from the monk and sipped. He rinsed his mouth, spat, then drank a couple of mouthfuls. The cool liquid soothed his throat.

"Thank you." Beobrand handed back the flask. The sea breeze blew his blond hair into his face. The water, cool air and empty stomach all went some way to settling him. Perhaps he would be able to endure the voyage after all.

"So," he said, "Oswald means for you to write down what is agreed with Penda? To what end?"

"It is the way of great men. When words are written they become stronger than mere word sounds."

"A man's word should be enough. A king's oath is like steel."

Coenred nodded. He brushed his hair away from his face with his long fingers. "This is true. But spoken promises can be misremembered. Or ignored. The writing of them will always show the truth, no matter how many days or even years pass. Oaths can be forgotten. A written oath will live on forever."

Beobrand thought on this. It sounded like magic to him. He could see no use for the scratchings of the Christ priests on their parchments. But he did not have the energy to discuss it further.

"To live forever," he said and hawked into the sea. "The Christ god promises everlasting life. And his holy men scratch words that can live on forever. With such strong magic, it amazes me there is so much death on middle earth."

27

O swald looked up at the sky. There were grey clouds brooding in the west, but with God's providence it would not rain. He turned in the saddle and looked back to where men struggled with one of the two carts. They had already managed to get the other one up to the brow of the hill. There they had secured it, unhitching the mules and adding them to the team pulling the cart that was now wallowing in the shallow valley. Rainfall would hold them back even more.

He was glad he had listened to Oswiu's counsel and brought the ships. They had made good progress down the coast and then striking into the huge estuary of the Humber. They had navigated as far up the River Dun as they were able before it became necessary to disembark. They were near to their destination, but now they needs must rely on the few steeds they had brought in the ships. And of course, the brute strength of his warriors.

Oswiu, grim-faced as usual, rode up the hill to where Oswald watched the beleaguered cart. Oswald's mount shied away, skittering nervously to the side. Oswald almost lost his seating, only just preventing an unseemly fall by clutching the saddle. The horses were still unsettled after travelling over the water. Perhaps it felt to them as if the ground moved, as it did to him when he dismounted.

He soothed the horse, patting its neck.

"Well, brother," he said, "how do they fare?"

Oswiu reined in and expertly turned his horse to stand beside Oswald's, facing the same way.

"The men are tired and not happy, but the cart is undamaged. The scouts say we are close, this is the last major hill. After that, I suggest we ready ourselves. We should rest. Have the men clean and don their arms. We would have Penda see us in all our glory."

Oswald nodded.

"Thank you. I agree. We will rest and prepare to meet Penda. Even now," he scanned the horizon, searching for signs of movement or the glint of the sun on metal, "I expect he has men watching us. I feel exposed here. I can feel eyes on me."

"I sense it too. Let us hope all our plans and messages have not been for naught. I have sent one of Beobrand's men, Attor, out to scout while we wait here. But we do not have enough horses to properly survey the area."

Oswald bit his lower lip. He would not show his fears to the men, but a nagging worry gnawed at his insides. They were vulnerable here. Had he made a terrible mistake? He had prayed long on this; sought the counsel of his most trusted ealdormen. And his brother. And the priest, Gothfraidh.

Yet in the end, it was his decision alone. He led these people. He had chosen to come here. To make this pact with Penda.

Once more, he prayed that he was right to do so.

The sun broke through the clouds and a ray of light washed the site of the meeting in a golden glow. The Mercians had arrived some time in advance of the Northumbrians. Tents, some leather, some of cloth, were arrayed in an orderly fashion. The wolf banner of Penda stood erect and imposing before a large fire that was surrounded by men.

It was a wide, flat expanse of land. There were trees in the distance, but not dense enough to hide a sizable force. It was as they had agreed. A good place to talk. On the border of their two lands.

Oswald crossed himself and offered up a prayer of thanks that they had not been ambushed on the journey here. Perhaps his plans would bear fruit. He composed himself, setting his features into a grin.

He turned and waited until all of his men were in formation behind him. They were fine in their battle gear. Individual banners fluttered from spears. Polished helms shone. Burnished iron-knit byrnies gleamed. Arm rings and swords spoke of their prowess. And their wealth. These were the finest warriors in all of Albion. Despite his nerves, Oswald's chest swelled with pride.

"See how the Lord himself has brought the sun to shine upon us, that the Mercians may see us in all our glory?" Some of the men smiled. A couple laughed. But they too were nervous; uneasy at meeting a group of men in this field who were also bedecked with trappings of war. They all knew that this day could quickly turn from talk to sword song.

"Remember, my friends," said Oswald. "We come here to talk. Penda and I have shared oaths. No blood will be spilled here. To break oath with me on this, will spell your death." He looked along the line of men. None of them spoke.

From the Mercian encampment, two men mounted and rode to a point between the two groups.

Oswald looked to Oswiu, who nodded.

"Oswiu and I will meet with Penda," said Oswald. "Await for my signal before setting up camp."

Oswald and Oswiu spurred their steeds towards the two Mercians.

Beobrand watched as Anhaga helped to pull one of the tents into shape over its wooden frame. He seemed to know what he was doing, so Beobrand left him to it. He had no interest in tents.

He removed his helm and held it under his left arm. His shield rested on the grass. He stared intently over the short distance to where the Mercians were camped. There, with the smoke of the cooking fires drifting around it like wraiths, was Penda's standard, hung with wolf tails and crowned with a wolf's head. The sight of it made him catch his breath. His ribs had begun to ache. He rubbed with his mutilated left hand at the scar under his left eye.

Acennan stood beside him.

"You faced Penda at Elmet, did you not?"

"I did," replied Beobrand. "To see that standard again... I remember that day. The days that followed."

"Dark times," said Acennan.

"Are there any other kind?"

"Maybe not." Acennan sighed. He scratched at his beard, frowning.

"What ails you?" asked Beobrand, noticing his friend's discomfort.

Acennan sighed. "I have heard some troubling news. You are not going to like it."

"What?"

Acennan pursed his lips.

"What, Acennan? If you did not wish to tell me, you should have kept quiet."

Acennan sighed again. "Very well, but you are right, I should not have said anything, for it is of no consequence to us now."

Beobrand looked at him quizzically.

Acennan said, "One of the men told me that Nathair is dead."

"And his sons?"

"Not here."

Beobrand spat. He thought of the arrows over the Tuidi. The hatred in the eyes of Broden and Torran. He cursed.

"Tobrytan and Elmer are good men," said Acennan. "They will protect Ubbanford."

"They are only two men. And we both know that Tobrytan is as slow as a donkey. Thunor help me, if Nathair's sons raise arms against Ubbanford, I swear it will be the last thing they will do in this life."

"They will not dare."

"They will regret it, if you are wrong," Beobrand said. The events of the last days had all but driven thoughts of Nathair and his sons from his mind. Now uncertainty began to gnaw at him.

He looked once more to the tents and fires of the Mercians. There were many of them. Five score he supposed. The same as their own number. Two warhosts. Each capable of dealing death and destruction.

But they came not for war.

"I hope that Oswald and Penda can agree their terms quickly," said Beobrand. "I would be gone from this place. There is only so long that this many warriors can camp in sight of each other without bloodshed. Whatever their lords have commanded." He clenched his right fist, digging the nails into his palm. "And I would return to Ubbanford. Would that you had not told me of Nathair's death."

Beobrand cast his gaze along the Mercian camp. Most men sat or stood in groups around the cooking fires. The evening meal was being prepared. The scent of cooking wafted to him on the breeze.

Wardens were posted at intervals along the Mercian line. Each stood resolutely staring at the Northumbrian host as it readied its own camp. When Oswald and his brother, Oswiu the atheling, had returned from speaking with Penda, the king had informed them that in the morning the two leaders would meet in the centre of the field. Until then, the camps would remain separate. He had repeated once more his warning that no offence was to be given to the Mercians.

Beobrand and Acennan watched as men laboured in the centre of the swathe of meadow. An awning slowly came into being. Stout wooden beams were brought from the Mercian camp. Ropes were expertly tied to secure the wood in place. Strong cloth was lifted onto the frame and pulled taut.

The sun had dipped low in the sky now. The smell of woodsmoke and cooking grew strong, as the Northumbrian encampment settled in for the evening. The warriors were still on edge, but the tension had eased. Perhaps they would get through this meeting with a rival host without leaving corpses in their wake. Those with the sense of age, or the experience of battles past, hoped that the carrion birds would go hungry.

Beobrand willed himself to relax. He tried not to dwell on the events of the last weeks. Attempted to put from his mind the worry that Nathair's sons might still seek vengeance for their brother's death. He was far from home. There was nothing to be gained from fretting. He smiled absently, almost hearing the deep voice of Bassus saying those very words. Bassus. Hearth warrior of Edwin. And Beobrand's friend. He had not seen the huge warrior since Bassus had returned to Cantware, where Edwin's widow and remaining children had fled following the battle of Elmet. Beobrand wondered whether tales of his exploits serving Oswald had reached Cantware. Should he consider Bassus an enemy now? Edwin's queen must surely be an enemy of Oswald. But he could not imagine Bassus as a foe.

In an effort to follow the advice Bassus had often given, and not worry about the past or that which could not be changed, he focused on the building of the awning where the kings of Mercia and Northumbria would talk and agree the terms of peace. At first he found the construction conjured up memories of the new hall at Ubbanford. He shook his head. Memories clamoured for his attention. He looked into the setting sun, hoping that the burning light would sear the thoughts from his mind.

He returned his gaze back to the awning. Something caught his attention. The men were silhouetted now against the ruddy glow of the sunset. But there was something about one of the men that tugged at his memory. The man's gait was familiar. Beobrand watched as the figure stooped to help secure a rope.

Beobrand gasped, his mouth hanging open. No, it could not be.

Acennan turned to his friend.

"What is it?"

Beobrand seemed incapable of speech. He pointed at the awning. Acennan followed his gaze, but merely saw men constructing the shelter.

"What?" asked Acennan, puzzled.

Beobrand realised that Acennan would not recognise the man. He did not know him as he did.

How was it possible that he was here, one of the host that served Penda? Beobrand's head swam. He blinked. Perhaps the afterglow of the sun in his eyes was playing tricks with him. He looked back. Squinted into the bright light. There was no question. It was him. The gods were laughing at him again. Had Nelda's curse brought them together here?

"What?" repeated Acennan, concern in his tone.

At last Beobrand found his voice. It came rushing up from the depths of his being. Riding on a wave of anger and hate like flotsam thrown against a cliff in a storm.

He screamed the name of the man. The last person he had expected to find here. The man he hated more than any other who yet lived. And this man would not live for much longer. For Beobrand had sworn to kill him. And Beobrand's oath was as unyielding as granite.

"Wybert!" he shouted, and the force of his own fury ripped his throat.

All eyes across the field turned to find the source of the bellowing voice. Mercian and Northumbrian alike ceased their activities and stared. Cups were set aside. Whetstones faltered. Conversations died out.

The object of the ire-filled scream stopped fastening the line of cord to one of the wooden supports of the awning, stood straight and looked directly at Beobrand. The sun was at Wybert's back, making it easy for him to recognise the Cantware man, who squinted and shielded his eyes. Wybert stood there, as if pondering something for a moment, and then took a step toward the Northumbrian camp.

"Well met, Beobrand," he called out. "Are you hale? You look unwell."

"I will kill you, Wybert," Beobrand spat. He had no more words. Perhaps those were enough.

Wybert held out his empty hands.

"You would attack an unarmed man? Under truce-oath? I think not," Wybert sneered. "Perhaps one day we will fight, but not today."

Beobrand quivered with rage. His vision began to mottle, whether from anger or staring into the sun, he did not know. He made to step forward, hand on Hrunting's hilt. Forgotten were the words of Oswald. He cared not for the consequences. All he could see was the man who had raped Sunniva. He had not protected her, just as he had not saved Cathryn. All that was left for him was to exact payment for the crime in blood. He bared his teeth and pulled Hrunting silently from its scabbard. The sun caught the shimmering blade. It glimmered red as if with fresh slaughter-sweat.

Dozens of paces separated Wybert from Beobrand, yet he paled at the sight of the Cantware warrior and took a step backwards.

A strong hand gripped Beobrand's shoulder. Angrily, he tried to shake it off. It held firm, pulled him back. He turned to see who impeded his revenge. It was Athelstan.

"No, boy," the older warrior said. "Not here. Not now."

Athelstan turned to Wybert and said in a voice for all to hear, "Your sins are known to all, Wybert, son of Alric. I went to Ubbanford and offered weregild for your crimes. But Beobrand would only have your blood. I told him of what you had done and your life is his. But not like this. In this place kings must speak, not pus-filled maggots like you. Begone. Death will find you. If not from Beobrand, then from my own hand."

There was utter silence now. The sun continued to glide beyond the far horizon, gilding the land in gold and red.

"So you told him, did you?" asked Wybert, his voice quiet, but carrying to all who listened.

"Aye, and it pained me to tell of your craven act."

"Strange," said Wybert, shifting his attention to Beobrand, "that the Lady Sunniva did not tell you herself." He smiled. "Perhaps she enjoyed it. It could be that I gave her something you were unable to give."

Beobrand surged forward with a cry.

"I will rip out your guts and feed your eyes to the crows! By Woden, I will bleed you dry."

He was half-way to Wybert when hands again grabbed him. Acennan and Athelstan had both leapt after him and now, one clutching his cloak and the other with a hand on his belt, they dragged him spitting and fighting back towards the Northumbrian line.

Oswald stood there with his hands on his hips and face as dark as a thundercloud.

"What is the meaning of this?" he said. His voice was ice.

Athelstan uttered a few hushed words to the king. Oswald looked from Beobrand to Wybert and nodded.

Taking a step forward, Oswald, King of Bernicia and Deira, overlord of Northumbria, raised his hands and spoke in a clear voice.

"This is a matter of honour between two men. There has been an act committed which demands retribution. But blood will not be shed here. This feud will be set aside for another time and place." He cast his gaze across the Mercian ranks. They watched him attentively. "Go back to your meals. Tomorrow I, Oswald, will speak with your king, Penda, Lord of Mercia and we will swear oaths of peace. Let not any man break that peace."

For a long while nobody moved, then, when it became clear that no more was to be said, and no death was to be dealt, the warriors drifted back to their food. The sounds of conversation resumed. Though now there was a new topic to discuss over the mead that night.

Wybert, his bravado having fled under the withering gaze of a king, slunk back to the Mercian ranks.

"What is he doing here?" asked Acennan.

"I do not know," answered Oswald, "but you had best control your lord. I will not hesitate to take the life of anyone who breaks my pledge of peace. Do you hear me, Beobrand?"

Beobrand nodded. He shrugged off the hands on him, sheathed Hrunting. It took him three attempts to slide the sword home, his hands shook so. Oswald placed an arm around his shoulders and walked him away from the others.

"Beobrand," he said in a quiet voice, "are you able to control the blood lust you feel for this man? I know he has done you a terrible wrong and I understand your desire for vengeance, but I need you to hold back your anger. Can you do that?"

Beobrand sighed. His mind was in turmoil. Wybert here? He had been so close to killing him. Was it his wyrd to fail to exact vengeance for Sunniva, as he had failed her in so many other ways?

Oswald's eyes gleamed in the dying light of the sun. He was a good king. He had given Beobrand everything. How could he refuse?

Beobrand nodded.

Oswald stared into his eyes a long while. Then, seemingly content with what he saw there, he clapped Beobrand on the shoulder.

"Good. The ability to think beyond one's own desires is

what makes a leader. What makes a great man. Hold on to your ire, Beobrand. I will have need for it another day. But for now, we must let this Wybert walk free."

Beobrand swallowed. His mouth was dry.

He shivered, though the afternoon sun was still warm.

Beobrand knew that Oswald spoke the truth of it. A great man would set aside his anger. He would not act on the voice within him that screamed for revenge.

Beobrand clenched his fists against their shaking as he walked away.

He prayed to Woden and Thunor that he would be able to live up to Oswald's vision of him. That he could display greatness in this.

But as he trudged back towards Acennan and Athelstan, his thoughts were dark and filled with blood. For he knew, in the deepest part of himself, in a place where he seldom ventured, that he was not a great man.

The midden pit that had been dug to the east of the Northumbrian camp was already rank. The acrid stench of the waste of the warhost turned Beobrand's stomach. But none of the men would remain in this area for long. Which was just as he wanted it.

A blustery wind had come with the setting of the sun, and now a blanket of clouds rolled overhead, the silver light of the moon shining through, like a rush light behind thick cobwebs. Beobrand watched as the shadow of a broad-shouldered man stumbled from the camp. The large warrior made his way to the midden and there fumbled with his britches before pissing in a long stream that steamed in the cool night air. He let out a grunt of satisfaction and then staggered back to the camp.

He hadn't seen Beobrand. Or if he had, he would think the young warrior was doing the same as him. Why else would anyone be so close to the quickly forming quagmire of shit and piss?

Beobrand breathed through his mouth. He needed time to think. He knew what he must do, but it would bring death to him. If that was his wyrd, so be it. But what of his men? Would they be disgraced by his actions? He could not talk to anyone of his plans. They would seek to stop him, of that he was certain. But he might never get another chance. Wybert was there in the other encampment. Beobrand had watched intently as the last rays of sunlight showed which tent Wybert had entered.

It would not be impossible to sneak into the Mercian camp and find where Wybert slept. Beobrand had left his armour and shield back in the tent he shared with his gesithas. He had left Hrunting there too. Acennan would see that the sword would be passed to Octa. This was not the killing work of such a fine sword. There would be no sword-play. Beobrand would butcher Wybert with the seax that had been his brother's. Its blade was short, but wickedly sharp. It would gut Wybert well enough.

Beobrand took a swig of the flask of mead he had taken with him. He had drunk more than his fill since seeing Wybert and the world had taken on the soft-edged jaggedness he had come to welcome in the days following Sunniva's passing. Vaguely, through the fog of the drink, he wondered what would befall the men in this field after he had killed Wybert. Would a battle ensue? Perhaps Oswald would defeat Penda here, thus taking Mercia. It could prove to be the stuff of scops' songs.

The thought of scops brought back to him the face of

Leofwine. How was it possible that two brothers could be so different? Leofwine had been fair-haired, with a caring character. Brave and loyal with a voice like molten gold. Wybert was dark, angry, jealous and craven. He seemed to walk the earth seeking things upon which to focus his hatred. He had loathed Beobrand since the moment Alric and Wilda had taken him in and tended to his wounds after the battle of Elmet. His hatred had seemed to fester with every day that passed. For a long while, Beobrand had cared little for Wybert and his petty selfishness. That had changed now.

And there was only one end to this. Beobrand would wrest the life from Wybert, with a blade or his bare hands. It mattered not. It seemed it was Beobrand's wyrd to live his life seeking vengeance. Well, so be it then. He heaved himself up. If he survived the night, he would see what the day brought with it. But this night, death was stalking and he was its messenger.

Somewhere far off in the distance to the north, as if an echo from some half-forgotten dream, a wolf let out an ululating wail. Beobrand smiled thinly in the darkness. He felt wild. Reckless. He stifled the urge to return the beast's call and threw the half-empty flask to the ground. He had clearly drunk enough mead.

He made his way southward, away from the stink of the midden. Away from the tents and the guards. The Mercians had left wardens around their camp too, and he planned to walk south and then west. It should not prove too difficult to merely walk into their camp. With any luck, they would think him one of their own who had gone to relieve himself.

The thin light from the cloud-veiled moon allowed him to pick his way around clumps of shrubs and long grass. Brambles tugged at his cloak and leg bindings. The wind swung into the north and a murmur of rain followed. A light drizzle began to fall, and the grass was quickly slick, making walking difficult. Beobrand looked up at the sky. The clouds were thicker than before. He reached for Thunor's hammer at his neck. It seemed the thunderer god would once again provide him cover under darkness and rain. Perhaps he would send lightning too.

As if in answer to his thought, a flicker of light lit the clouds. Moments later, the rumble of the god's hammer reached his ears. He bared his teeth in a savage grin in the gloom. Thunor was watching over him this night. A storm would make it much easier to approach the Mercian tents and to find his quarry.

He cast his gaze back to the path before him, trying to gauge how far south he had walked. Another flash of light picked out the form of a warrior standing just paces before him. Despite himself, Beobrand let out a curse and took a step back. His feet slipped on the wet grass and he fell. He leapt up quickly, drawing his seax and brandishing it before him.

Thunder crashed, louder now. The storm was approaching.

The shadow of the warrior moved closer. Beobrand had not been able to make out the features of his adversary. It must be one of the Northumbrian wardens. They could not find him here. They would make him return to the camp. He would not be able to leave again. He was about to turn and flee when the warrior spoke in a hissing whisper.

"Beobrand, it is I, Acennan."

Beobrand let out his breath in relief.

"Go back to the tents, Acennan. I am well."

Acennan did not move. Beobrand could discern his form now, a darker shadow that blocked out moonlight and campfires.

"You cannot do this thing, Beobrand," said Acennan. "You will die. And many more might die too, if you break the truce."

Shaking his head, Beobrand wished he had drunk less mead. His mind was slow. He could think of no words to counter what Acennan said.

"I will die," he said. "Perhaps I will see her again…" His voice cracked. "I cannot see her face in my mind, Acennan. When I try, all I see is Wybert. I must kill him. I must."

"I cannot allow it," said Acennan.

"I am your lord," said Beobrand. "You will stand aside. Let me pass."

The wind shredded the words. Bitter rain began to pelt them from the angry sky. Acennan had to raise his voice to be heard.

"No! I am also your friend, and I cannot let you do this. Sunniva would not want it. You have a son. You must live."

Lightning flashed, a great forking streak of white fire in the heavens. The ground-shaking smash of Thunor's hammer followed a heartbeat later. In the moment of silence that followed the blast, Beobrand leapt at Acennan. He would not be deterred.

Acennan saw him late in the murky night, but he knew Beobrand and he was prepared for an attack. The stocky warrior stepped back, allowing Beobrand's fist to drift harmlessly past his face. Beobrand lost his balance and stumbled. But Acennan did not retaliate. He did not wish to raise his hands against his lord.

Regaining control, Beobrand spun to face Acennan once more. The cold rain went some way to clearing his head. He was still drunk; slower than he should be. But he knew he could best Acennan. He had done so before and he could do it now.

"Let me pass," Beobrand said. "I do not wish it to end this way between us. You have been the best of friends. Now step aside."

"We can find Wybert another day. In another place. Then I will watch as you gut him like a fish. Gods, I will help you do it! But I cannot let you throw away your life like this."

Around them the storm raged with renewed intensity. They abandoned all attempts at keeping quiet. They each had to scream over the cacophony of the elements.

"It is my life, not yours!" Beobrand spat.

He leapt for Acennan again. They grappled, Acennan seeking to restrain Beobrand. But Beobrand was larger and stronger. And as fast as a cat, despite the mead.

All about them lightning stabbed the sky and rain fell in sheets. The deafening roar of the storm was terrifying.

Beobrand's face was twisted with rage as he broke free from Acennan's grasp, pushing him away.

"Do not do this!" Acennan screamed. "You will bring about war and death."

"I'm sorry," Beobrand said, but Acennan could not hear the words. Lightning-glare lit Beobrand's features and Acennan knew then that he would not stop his lord. His friend.

Beobrand rushed in again. Acennan dodged to his left, again seeking to get a hold on Beobrand, to prevent him from his course rather than retaliate. Yet Acennan was not fast enough. Beobrand's right fist smashed into his face. All his weight was behind the blow and Acennan's head snapped back. His legs buckled as his senses left him. He slumped to the rain-soaked turf, his eyes glazed and unseeing.

Appalled at what he had done, Beobrand staggered away from his fallen friend.

His face was a mask of despair and anguish in the storm-flickered night. He squared his shoulders, flexed his fingers, feeling the sting of broken skin on the knuckles of his right hand. He made his way south. There was no need to worry about being detected now. Thunor's storm would provide him with cover.

It was all Wybert's fault. All this pain, the result of one man's actions. Wybert would die at his hand before the night was through. He would pay for everything.

Yes, it was all Wybert's doing. He was to blame for all of this.

But as Beobrand walked into the night, the rain running down his face stung like bitter tears of remorse.

28

The crash of thunder made Wybert jump up from where he lay. He groped in the dark of the tent for his seax. In his dreams Beobrand had been coming for him. Leaping from the shadows like a night devil. His blade had dripped with the blood of all the men he had slain. Wybert had seen him fight before. Beobrand was a born killer. Wybert had learnt much, perhaps even had natural skill. But he was no match for Beobrand's deadly ability.

In the gloom of the tent his hand found the wooden handle of his seax. He cast his gaze around, but there was no sign of Beobrand. Rain thrummed heavily on the taut leather of the shelter. Near where he sat hunched in the darkness, a stream of water poured through a leak. A flash of lightning lit the world outside and briefly, from the light that had shone under the edge of the tent and through the partially closed door flap, he could make out the forms of the slumbering warriors. None of them seemed to have noticed the tumult of the storm that raged outside.

Wybert flinched again, as another roar of thunder shook the world. He had always hated thunder and lightning. Leofwine had made fun of him about it. Just the gods at play, he had said. Well, they could keep their play. Their games had cost him his brother and father. His home. The gods must love to toy with him. He had found a lord in Bernicia. Athelstan had trained him in the way of the sword. Given him arms and a place at his benches. Then, as if they could not bear to see Wybert happy, the gods had thrown before him Sunniva, with her radiant beauty. How was it possible that he should lose everything he loved, yet Beobrand should gain riches and a woman of such beauty? The gods were capricious indeed.

How they must have enjoyed watching him telling Athelstan and his gesithas of his exploits. She was only a woman! What did they care? He had only swived her. It wasn't as if he had killed her.

At the far end of the tent, furthest from the draught of the door, lay Grimbold, sheltered under a huge bearskin. Wybert sniffed. Perhaps his luck was changing. Or the gods had grown bored of him. He had found Grimbold soon after entering Mercia. He seemed to be a good lord. And, having just lost three men to the red plague, was not one to ask many questions of a warrior who had his own horse and weapons. Wybert had kept himself out of mischief, being careful to befriend the strongest of the warriors. He trained with them and continued to pick up new techniques. His strength grew, as did his confidence.

Until he had seen Beobrand that afternoon.

He shivered in the dark and ran his hands through his hair. Grimbold had asked him about the confrontation with the thegn from Northumbria. Wybert had shrugged it off. It was a personal matter, but he would not break the truce over it. He would face his enemy at another time. Grimbold had raised an eyebrow.

"See that you do not break the truce," he had said. "Penda is furious that the peace may not hold. If you fight, he will have your guts as a belt and a saddle made out of your hide."

Lightning flickered outside again, followed by the hammer-smash of thunder. The rain fell in torrents, deafening within the tent.

Wybert had a sudden need to piss. The encounter with Beobrand had unnerved him. He had drunk too much ale afterwards in an attempt to rid himself of the gnawing sensation of impending doom that had descended upon him. He had hoped that fleeing to Mercia would be far enough not to see Beobrand again. He had thought that perhaps their paths would cross one day. If Mercia and Northumbria fought, they might face each other in the shieldwalls, but he had not thought to see him so soon. And the thought of meeting Beobrand in combat nearly unmanned Wybert.

The rain continued. Little rivulets ran through the tent. One of the sleeping men rolled over out of the damp and cursed.

The urge to empty his bladder was overbearing now. There was nothing for it but to venture into the storm. He sheathed his seax and stood. Wrapping his cloak about him in an effort to protect himself from the downpour, he stepped over the thrall who lay at the entrance to the tent, and pulled the flap aside.

He was buffeted by the wind, but the rain seemed less virulent outside than it had sounded from within the tent.

He walked a few steps away from the shelter, enjoying the sensation of the cold water running over his face. Perhaps it would wash away the fear-sweat from his dreams.

He glanced over at the largest of the campfires. Several men huddled there – the wardens, he supposed.

The white-light flicker of lightning shone on the world for less than a heartbeat, then all was dark once more. Images were burnt into his vision. The tents. The wardens standing by the fire. The distant woods. And the figure of a man, not ten paces from him.

With a start he realised he recognised the man.

The peal of thunder smothered the scream that left Wybert's lips. He fumbled for his seax. But his movements were sluggish. The shock of seeing the face in the lightning-glow had sapped him of his strength. How could he be here?

A moment later, the figure was upon him. Wybert felt a searing pain in his side. He felt the blade wrenched free from his flesh. The warmth of his own blood gushed over his stomach and groin, where it mingled with his piss as his bladder let go.

Wybert screamed again. His own voice seemed to break him from his momentary inaction. He grabbed the wrist that held the knife, stopping a second strike. He felt his adversary grip his own wrist, preventing him from stabbing with his seax. Without thinking, he drew his head back and snapped it forward with all his strength. His forehead connected with his enemy's nose, crushing it. Blood splattered in the rain. The grasp on Wybert's wrist loosened. He pulled his hand free and slashed at his opponent's midriff. The blade raked along the man's stomach and clattered over his ribs.

Wybert could feel his life blood pumping freely from the wound in his belly. His strength would be gone soon. He did not want to die like this. Killed in the dark.

How had his attacker come to this place? Wybert had recognised the face instantly. He should have killed the man when they had first crossed paths. He would not miss the opportunity again.

Wybert pulled back his hand for the mortal blow, when his enemy fell to his knees and flopped onto his back. Wybert laughed, the cackle of a madman in the storm. The man was pathetic. He had lost consciousness. Wybert gripped his seax tightly in his right hand and dropped to kneel beside the prostrate form. He raised the blade above the man's pale throat.

The rain lashed them both ferociously. Wybert could feel himself growing cold. The thin moonlight picked out the bleeding form before him. His vision blurred. He tried to focus, to will himself to draw his blade across the exposed flesh of the man's neck. But his fingers would not obey his commands. The seax fell harmlessly onto the drenched grass, where it lay like a beached fish, a-glimmer in the dark.

As he sank into darkness, Wybert sensed people around him. Was that Leofwine? His father? Why were they pulling at him so roughly?

And then, he knew no more.

"Get up," Beobrand hissed. He gripped Acennan's shoulders and pulled him into a sitting position. Rain still fell, but the lightning had passed. Thunor had grown bored with this small field on the frontier of Mercia and Deira. Or perhaps he had witnessed enough that night to amuse him and now moved on to watch other men.

Acennan was groggy still. He struggled to sit, was unable to focus. Beobrand shook him.

"Rouse yourself. We must return to the camp."

Slowly, Acennan regained his senses. As his strength returned, he pushed Beobrand's hands away.

"So, you have done the deed?" he asked, his voice as flat and cold as wet slate.

"No, my friend," answered Beobrand. "I do not know what has happened, but the Mercian camp is in uproar. We must get back to the tent before we are missed."

In the distance, the Mercian campfires were being stoked into life. Fresh logs were being thrown onto them, showers of sparks and smoke rising into the rainswept sky. The flickering light from the fires showed men running from the tents. The metal of battle gear glinted in the gloom. The sounds of shouts and cries reached them distantly on the wind.

"Friend, you call me?" said Acennan. He grunted as he rose to his knees. Beobrand reached out to help him. Acennan batted away his hand. "Friend?" Acennan repeated. "Is that what we are?" With a groan at his aching limbs, Acennan stood. Beobrand could feel the anger rolling off of him in waves. Or perhaps it was disappointment.

"You are my friend," he said. "I know that, for I see it in your actions. You are true. A better friend than I." He looked through the thinning rain to where the Mercian fires burnt high. The shade-like forms of warriors gathered there.

"If not for you, I would surely be dead now. And probably with nothing to show for it. Now come, I would not have your blood on my hands, and we will surely be killed should the Mercians find us here."

Acennan did not answer, but after a brief pause, he began walking slowly back towards the Northumbrian camp.

Beobrand trudged behind. The last vestiges of the drink-haze were melting from his mind like fog in the dawn. And he could see clearly despite the darkness. He had been a fool. Acennan was right to despise him. He would have his revenge on Wybert, but how had he thought it was worth breaking his oath for that worm? Did he wish to face Woden as an oath-breaker? A man who puts his own desires for blood before that of his lord and king? A nithing who cares not for his own gesithas and would be prepared to sacrifice them for his own ends?

Oswald's words came back to him then. A leader must look beyond his own desires. That is what makes a great man.

The words taunted him. Judged him.

And found him lacking.

29

The clouds had torn into rags as the sun crested the hills in the east.

Dawn would usually be a still, quiet time. Men would slowly emerge from their furs and blankets, disturbed by the light and the movement of others in the camp. They would warm themselves by the fires that had been newly coaxed into life after the long night. Smoke would drift like wraiths around the hunched forms of men pissing into steaming puddles.

This was not such a daybreak.

The night had exploded into a chaos of lightning and thunder.

And treachery.

Now, as the sun shyly peeked over the eastern horizon, stroking the scattering clouds with golden fingers, both war-hosts were aligned as for battle. They faced each other over the field, unsure of what the day would bring, but ready for the battle-play, if that was where their wyrd took them.

The shelter that had been erected between the two forces still stood, despite the ferocity of the storm. One corner of the awning had come adrift and now flapped forlornly in the morning breeze. The movement drew Beobrand's gaze.

Athelstan, beard bristling and brow furrowed, turned to Beobrand, who stood to his left in the line.

"What in God's name has happened? Last night we went to sleep all set for a quiet talk today, and now we wake up to find the Mercians as angry as a man who has bedded a beauty and woken with a sow."

Beobrand shook his head. He had no idea what had occurred. He shifted guiltily, feeling that somehow he was responsible for the change in the mood of the camp. And yet, Acennan and he had managed to get back to their tent without notice. It was not till morning that the others commented on Acennan's face. When pressed on how he had got the swollen-shut and bruised eye, he had refused to speak of it, but Garr had sharp eyes and noticed the split skin on their lord's knuckles.

"It would seem that Acennan has once again angered our lord Beobrand," he had said, laughter in his voice.

"Shut that gaping hole you call a mouth," Beobrand had snapped. "Unless you wish to know what it feels like to anger me."

After that, nobody else had mentioned Acennan's eye or Beobrand's hand.

Until now.

Athelstan shifted his position and looked to Acennan, noticing the angry bruising and swelling of his eye for the first time.

"By the bones of Christ, lad," he said, loud enough for all to hear, "did you use your face to hammer in the pegs for the tent?"

Oswald, resplendent in his purple cloak, sunlight glinting

from his burnished helm, turned to Athelstan with a frown. He was wound as tight as a bow string at full draw.

"Stop your chatter," the king said. "Someone approaches. Hold still and calm, my countrymen. I feel that one move out of place now and we will face battle where we only sought to exchange words and oaths. Come brother, let us see what they would say to us."

Oswiu and Oswald walked towards the awning.

From the Mercian encampment came a group of three men. Two were garbed in the finery of great warriors. The dawn sun glistened from polished metal. Buckles, brooches and belt-tips gleamed. They walked with an assured air, square-shouldered and confident. Behind them, stumbling and limping, came a bedraggled creature. His hands were tied before him and a rope was fastened around his neck. One of the warriors, his black cloak swirling behind him like crow wings, held the rope. The tied man was slow. His right leg was horribly twisted, and his halting gait must have infuriated the black-cloaked warrior, for he gave the rope a savage tug, sending the captive sprawling to the wet ground.

Beobrand's stomach twisted. There was something terribly familiar about the man being led on the leash from the Mercian camp. They were still some way off and he was hidden from view for much of the time by the two noblemen, but Beobrand had seen that limping walk too many times before.

Black Cloak righted the man, practically lifting him bodily from the earth, then, with a vicious cuff about the face, he sent the prisoner forward once more. The light fell squarely on the captive's features and Beobrand drew in a sharp intake of breath. The face was bruised and beaten, but there could be no doubt.

The man being led like a goat to sacrifice on Blotmonath was Anhaga.

The three men were approaching the shelter at the centre of the field now, where Oswald and Oswiu, not having been slowed by a tethered prisoner, already waited. The small group of five men – kings, noble thegns and one crippled servant – was watched by all. They were beyond earshot, but the onlookers strove to see a hint of the mood of the conversations; any sign that battle would ensue.

Athelstan raised his gnarly, ringed arm and pointed.

"Isn't that your man, Beobrand? The cripple?"

Northumbrian warriors peered at the men under the awning; flicked sidelong glances at Beobrand.

Beobrand said nothing. He clenched his jaw till his teeth ached.

The talks seemed to be getting heated. The Mercians gesticulated wildly. Anhaga received another slap that sent him to his knees. The report of the blow reached Beobrand's ears an instant after he saw the black-cloaked warrior's hand connect with Anhaga's cheek.

"By all that is holy, what has that cripple done?" asked Athelstan. "The Mercians don't seem to like him much."

Beobrand blanched as Oswald turned back and scoured the Northumbrian lines with his gaze. The king's eyes flashed with fury when he found Beobrand amongst the throng. Beobrand held the stare for a moment, then, with the sinking feeling that he knew all too well what Anhaga had done, he covered his eyes with his half-hand.

"Did you think to defy me so easily, Beobrand?" Oswald's tone dripped with venom. He did not raise his voice. There was no bluster. No screaming. He did not snatch up and throw the wooden cup from the small chest that rested beside the cot where he had slept.

He did none of these things.

Yet this quiet, icy intensity was more ominous. Beobrand had no doubt that his life hung in the balance of his king's judgement.

They were in the king's tent. It was bright outside, but they had closed the tent flaps, providing them with a semblance of privacy, though they knew that there could be no secrets when the walls were made of hide. Whatever was said within the confines of this space would be overheard and the news would travel through the camp and be known to all long before nightfall.

The air within the tent was still and hot. Sweat beaded Beobrand's brow.

Oswiu sat, brooding and silent on a stool, while his brother the king, paced.

"Do you think I am a fool? A witless animal?" Oswald asked.

"No, my lord king," answered Beobrand quickly. He thought the tent held only one fool, and it was not the king.

How could he have been so stupid? Acennan had warned him that his actions would lead to warfare. To the deaths of others. He had not cared, so blinded had he been by grief and the desire for vengeance. But now, the sweat trickling down his back, he understood.

Anhaga, it seemed, had had the same idea as his lord.

"You thought to send your man," Oswald almost choked on his own anger. He visibly fought to control himself, to keep his voice lowered. "You thought to send your crippled servant to murder your enemy? Is that how you keep your oaths, Beobrand, son of Grimgundi?"

"No, my king." Beobrand's face flushed. "I did not send Anhaga to do this deed." Had it not been for Anhaga he would now be either dead, or a prisoner awaiting execution. Anhaga had failed to protect Sunniva against the hate of Wybert and had perhaps failed to mete out vengeance for her violation. Though it would seem he had done a better job than Beobrand at both. His actions would surely now bring about his death. And disgrace would be heaped upon Beobrand, his lord, as manure is thrown into a midden. And yet, Anhaga's very oath-breaking had prevented Beobrand making a terrible mistake.

"You did not send him, you say? And yet he attacked this Wybert in the heart of the darkness of the night. Is Wybert not your sworn enemy? Did you not say before us all that you would kill him for what you say he did to your wife?"

At the mention of Sunniva, Beobrand felt the cold fire of battle fury beginning to take hold of him. His eyes flicked from Oswald to Oswiu.

"Wybert is a worm," he spat. "It is not simply my belief that he defiled Sunniva. It is so. He spoke of the deed himself before Athelstan and all his gesithas. Anhaga was there in my hall when the attack took place. He was beaten hard for it, but was no match for the attackers."

Oswald stopped his pacing. He looked Beobrand in the eye and when he spoke again, his tone was softer.

"Yet you did not witness these events?"

"I did not. I was doing my king's bidding fetching the bishop from Hii. And now my wife is dead and cannot speak for herself." Beobrand let the implications of his words hang in the stifling air of the tent.

King and thegn glared at each other. At last, Oswiu broke the tense silence.

"Could it not be that Anhaga, having been present at the horrendous attack, felt compelled to seek vengeance on behalf of the Lady Sunniva? Perhaps he felt it his duty as an oath-sworn man of Beobrand's. He must have believed he had failed to protect his lord's woman."

Beobrand felt the sting of those last words as if the atheling had struck him a blow.

"It was I who failed to protect her," he said in a small voice. "Anhaga is no warrior."

"He may not be," said Oswald. "But he has wielded a blade against a man under Penda's protection, so Anhaga must die."

Beobrand let out a shuddering breath. How had he failed so absolutely? Anhaga had shown nothing but a true heart and loyalty to him and Sunniva. And now he would pay the ultimate price. Beobrand clenched his fists. The skin cracked on the knuckles. He grimaced at the pain. How could he be so blind? Acennan too had proven himself time and again, and he had repaid him with violence.

He was no lord. Was he nothing more than a reflection of his father? A man who grasped hungrily at wealth and beat those who loved him?

"Yes," said Oswald, his voice flat. "The cripple must die. His treachery will cost me dearly. Penda has demanded blood. And treasure. He will have both. It may be as my brother says. Perhaps Anhaga saw it as his duty to seek revenge. But this does not matter. Anhaga's lord's oath to his king is stronger." Oswald stepped close to Beobrand. Light glinted from the golden cross pendant the king wore around his neck. Oswald's eyes were dark; his pupils great black pools in the gloom. "I do have your oath, do I not, Beobrand of Ubbanford?"

The temperature in the room seemed to drop as he stared into those unblinking eyes. Beobrand wondered if the king's

Christ god enabled him to see through his eyes and spy his thoughts. Oswald had given him everything: trust, riches, land. Beobrand had sworn his oath to him and he shuddered now to remember how close he had come to forsaking his vow. Riches, land, even loved ones could all be taken by cruel men and even crueller gods. A man's word was all he truly owned. He would never break faith with his lord again.

"My lord king," said Beobrand. "You are a good king. You are just and generous. I gave you my oath and my word is iron. I will not break my oath to you. You are my lord and I am yours to command as you will."

Oswald held his gaze for a long while, and then nodded.

"I told you what breaking the truce would bring, did I not?"

Beobrand assented with an inclination of his head.

"The price to pay for violating the peace is death," Oswald said. "Wybert's lord, Grimbold, also demands retribution for the injury to his man. I have agreed the price. You will pay it, Beobrand. And pray that Wybert does not die, or the were-gild doubles."

Beobrand stiffened his jaw and nodded. He did not speak. There was nothing to say. He would not pray for Wybert. If he survived the day, it meant little. Beobrand swore a silent oath on all the gods and on Sunniva's memory that he would see Wybert dead.

"You may go now," Oswald gestured towards the tent entrance with his hand. "And be ready at the midpoint of the day, when the sun is highest in the sky."

"Ready, lord?"

"Anhaga is to be slain at midday," said Oswald. "And to show good faith to Penda, you, as Anhaga's lord, will slay him."

30

"He's in here." The large, bearded Mercian, fearsome in his chain-knit byrnie, held aside the leathern flap.

Coenred waited patiently for Gothfraidh to shuffle past, then followed him into the murky interior of the tent. It stank of sweat and piss, the air heavy and acrid. Coenred wrinkled his nose at the noisome air, but he did not detect the sweet, sickly smell of the wound-rot that often came before the death of warriors.

Coenred allowed his eyes to grow accustomed to the gloom. The tent was a jumble of warriors' gear. There were furs of different kinds, bags, sacks, cloaks, a couple of wooden boxes, but there was only one inhabitant. It seemed the other warriors had no desire to be here with him.

The warrior pointed to the far corner. "Over there." The man hesitated for a moment as if unsure whether to remain or leave. Eventually he said, "Don't touch anything. Say your spells and then begone. I'll wait outside."

Coenred and Gothfraidh tentatively picked their way through the detritus on the ground, stooping beneath the low ceiling of the tent.

Wybert seemed to be asleep. Or perhaps death had claimed him already. His lips were pale and thin, his skin tinged with a grey pallor. Coenred stared down at the still form. He had known him for a long time, but they had never been close. Coenred had been a novice, studying under Fearghas and the other monks, Wybert was the son of one of the ceorls of Engelmynster. Coenred had never liked him. There had been a mean streak to him. Coenred did not understand why. Wybert's parents were loving and kind. His brother Leofwine was sensitive and charismatic. Yet Wybert had always seemed to be chasing something just beyond his reach. And his inability to grasp whatever it was he sought filled him with a deep-seated anger. That anger bubbled up and manifested itself in insults and petty vengeances for supposed slights. Coenred could scarcely believe this young man could have done the things they said he did.

Could it be that he had raped Sunniva? Coenred remembered Tata then. Her last moments had been filled with pain and terror as she was violated by Waelisc warriors. How could Wybert have done such a thing?

Coenred hoped he was dead. He deserved to go to hell.

At that instant, as if awoken by Coenred's secret thoughts, Wybert's eyes flickered open. Coenred started, drew in breath sharply. His thoughts were not those of a monk. God could see inside his soul and would know what he had thought. Coenred swallowed the lump in his throat.

"Coenred," Wybert said, his voice blurry and dull, "I seem to be meeting many old friends." He forced a smile, but it turned to a grimace, as he coughed.

"I am not your friend," answered Coenred. His tone was as cold as the tile floor of the chapel in Engelmynster had been when they'd found Tata's corpse. Wybert winced.

Gothfraidh shot a glance at Coenred, then cleared his throat.

"You asked for priests of the Christ? My name is Goth-fraidh. I believe you know Coenred. We are brethren of the Holy Church of Lindisfarena. Do you worship Christ? Do you wish to confess your sins?"

Wybert smiled thinly. "Why not? If I am to die, I would seek to soften the way as best I can. I have a knife here to hold when the time comes. They say Woden favours those who come to him with a weapon in their hand. But if the old gods do not welcome me, I hope you can smooth the way for me to your god's heaven."

"I see," said Gothfraidh, shifting his weight from foot to foot uncomfortably. "I understand there are no monks or priests of Christ in Mercia."

"Penda does not believe in your Christ," said Wybert, groaning slightly as he moved on the furs.

"Hmmm," said Gothfraidh, frowning, "we shall do what we can, but I fear that if you call Him our Christ, and not yours, your penance may not be well received by Him. Now, Coenred, fetch us something to sit on."

Gothfraidh sat on a small well-worn wooden stool. Coenred pulled a travel chest close to Wybert's cot. He hoped it did not belong to the warrior who waited at the doorway. Coenred did not think the man would take kindly to having his things moved.

Fixing Wybert with an unflinching stare, Gothfraidh said, "What are the sins you would confess to almighty God?"

Wybert stared back, but he could not meet the monk's gaze for long.

"All of them," he mumbled.

"You will have to do better than that," Gothfraidh said. "You must show yourself to be truly penitent. Only by describing the deeds you have done and seeking forgiveness can you be granted absolution. Do you understand?"

"Not really. I thought Christ offered life eternal."

"That he does, but you must truly believe in him and accept him as the one true God. And you must repent of your sins."

"Repent?" Wybert looked blankly from Gothfraidh to Coenred.

"Yes," blurted out Coenred, "ask for God's pardon for your sins. You must remember some of what you were taught at Engelmynster."

Gothfraidh held up a hand.

"Hush, Coenred." Then, to Wybert, "Let us begin by having you renounce all other gods. Renounce Woden, Thunor, Frige and the other old gods. Renounce them and give me the seax you clutch in fear. The old gods have no power over death. The blade will gain you nothing. Renounce them."

Gothfraidh held out his hand to Wybert.

Wybert looked down at his own hand, his knuckles whiter than his pallid skin as he gripped the hilt of his knife as a man floundering in a stormy sea would grip a rope thrown to him from a ship. He lifted the blade. His hand trembled. Coenred was suddenly fearful for the old monk. Wybert could cause him great harm despite the smallness of the blade. Coenred stood abruptly, ready to leap forward should the seeds of his fears bear fruit.

For some time, Wybert struggled, fighting a battle only he understood. Gothfraidh's eyes glimmered expectantly in the darkness.

Then Wybert's hand fell back to the furs of his bed, seax still firmly held.

"You refuse to renounce the old gods?" Gothfraidh asked, his voice not much more than a whisper.

"I cannot." Wybert shuddered and closed his eyes. "What if you are wrong and your god does not exist?"

"You are a coward," spat Coenred. He could not be in this place with this man any longer. He was surrounded by men who preyed on others. The world was a dark and evil place. He wished to be gone from this cloying murk, out into the sunshine where he could try to forget about Wybert, Tata, Sunniva and Cormán. "You attack women. You are nothing. God would not welcome you. You are damned!" He balled his hands into fists.

Gothfraidh stood and pushed himself between Coenred and the prostrate man.

"You forget yourself, Coenred!" he said, his tone stern. "We are men of God. We do not sit in judgement. Now go and wait outside, you are no use to me here."

Coenred gazed down at Wybert's pale face. So help him God, but he hoped he died.

"Go," Gothfraidh said.

Coenred turned and walked back towards the tent flaps. Light streamed in as they were thrown open before he reached them. The bulk of the warrior filled the doorway. Coenred blinked against the sudden brightness.

"What is happening here?" the warrior asked. He took in the scene with the practised eye of one used to making decisions quickly in battle.

"You have been here long enough. Leave now."

Gothfraidh said, "But I need more time to talk with Wybert. He has not yet carried out penance."

"And he will not, unless he can do whatever that is alone. You will leave now." The huge man placed his hand on the finely-worked pommel of his sword to press home his point. With the other, he held open the tent.

Gothfraidh hesitated, then nodded.

"We will pray for your soul, Wybert. May God have mercy on you."

Coenred did not look back, but pushed past the warrior, who looked surprised and a little amused as the young monk shouldered him aside.

He did not slow his pace as he walked back towards the Northumbrian camp. He could hear Gothfraidh puffing behind him as he tried to catch up. Coenred did not wish to speak to him. The old monk would ask him what he had been thinking and he did not wish to lie to him. To lie was a sin and he had surely sinned enough for one day. Abbot Fearghas would have been so disappointed in him.

He sensed Gothfraidh drawing near, so he sped up, almost trotting towards where the Nothrumbrian warriors looked on, anxious for the safe return of their holy men.

Coenred had a sudden urge to laugh. One thing that Gothfraidh had said was true. They would pray for Wybert's soul. Yet Coenred did not think God would be too pleased with his prayers. For a monk should not pray for the death and damnation of one of His flock.

Beobrand closed his eyes. The sun was warm on his eyelids. A light breeze pushed his hair back from his forehead. He could feel the eyes of two hundred men on him.

But only the eyes of one man mattered at that moment.

Beobrand looked down and stared into the face of Anhaga. His servant knelt before him. His face was swollen. Bitter bruises mottled his eyes and cheeks. His nose was twisted to one side and a gash had scabbed across it. His clothes were ripped and stained brown with dried blood and mud. His hands were tied. The noose that had been used to lead him still hung from his neck.

Their eyes met and Anhaga lowered his head in acknowledgement of his lord.

Beobrand said nothing. His mouth was dry.

So it had come to this. He was to kill the only man who had tried to protect his wife from attack and avenge her death.

A jackdaw hopped across the grass someway behind Anhaga. It looked at them, head jerking, eye prying, before spreading its wings and flapping away to the north. Its call was harsh in the hush of the midday sun.

A chill ran down his neck, despite the warm sun. Nelda had said he would die alone. Her curse was upon him.

"Oswald, is this whelp truly a thegn of yours?"

The harsh voice from behind broke into his thoughts. Beobrand turned to where his king stood with Penda. The king of the Mercians was broad-chested and fierce. His beard was combed to a fork. Around his shoulders hung a wolf pelt. His forearms were bare and displayed the criss-cross patterns of scars received in combat. He sneered at Beobrand.

Oswald replied in a cool tone, "He is young, but he is no whelp. Beobrand of Ubbanford slew the mighty Hengist and captured Cadwallon of Gwynedd."

Penda arched an eyebrow, but did not look impressed.

"He looks like he was sucking on his mother's tits yesteryear. Boy," he said to Beobrand, "you will have to learn to keep your men under control, if you are to be a leader of warriors."

Beobrand's face grew hot.

"And you, Penda," he said, his words dripping bile, "will have to stop housing curs amongst your pack of wolves, if you do not wish to see them killed like vermin."

Penda's eyes narrowed, his brow creased.

"Be careful how you address me, boy." He spat, and scratched his chin under his beard. "Remember it was your man who broke the truce, not I." He stared at Beobrand for a moment, and then, seeming to decide not to push the matter further, he turned back to Oswald. "Well, are we to settle this once and for all as agreed? I am growing hot and would rather we sat under the awning with some ale for our talks."

"Do not fear, you will have your blood, Penda," said Beobrand, who could barely contain his anger. It was bad enough that a good man would die, but for the warlord of Mercia to make light of it was more than he could bear.

Oswald stepped forward and held up a hand.

"It is time, Beobrand." His face was expressionless, but his eyes burnt with fury.

It would not do well to anger both kings more than he already had. Beobrand stifled a reply and walked to Anhaga.

He glanced over at the amassed Northumbrians. He recognised the faces. They were good strong men. His shield-brothers. Shame weighed on him like a physical thing as he recalled how close he had come to plunging them into battle. It should be him kneeling here preparing to die.

He took a deep breath. He knew what he must do and yet he hesitated.

Anhaga looked up at him. His body was beaten and broken, but his eyes shone brightly. His spirit was still strong.

Beobrand drew his seax from its sheath and offered the bone handle to Anhaga.

"Take it, so that Woden might see and welcome you to his hall," whispered Beobrand.

"No," answered Anhaga. "I am no warrior." He lifted his bound hands and brushed sweat away from his brow.

His fingers came away smeared red. "I wonder whether there are truly gods watching over us anyway."

Beobrand looked up at the tatters of clouds scudding across the dome of the sky. A red-feathered kite circled above them, its great wings outstretched to catch the zephyrs of the warm day.

Could the bird be one of the gods looking down?

"I do not know the ways of the gods any more than the next man," said Beobrand. "But you should hold the seax. Woden would surely wish to take one as brave as you into his hall. You have a warrior's spirit, Anhaga."

Anhaga reached out his hands for the blade and then hesitated. He dropped his hands back.

"The Lady Sunniva did not have a sword in her hand." Anhaga sighed. "I would go where she is. It must be a more beautiful place than Woden's corpse hall, if Sunniva is there."

Beobrand blinked back the tears that threatened to fall.

"I am sorry, Anhaga. I have failed you."

Anhaga shook his head.

"You have not. You killed Hengist when I could not." Suddenly, he gripped Beobrand's hand in both of his. Beobrand could feel the coarse twine that bound Anhaga's wrists.

"Promise me you will avenge us both. Avenge Sunniva and me, Beobrand. Kill Wybert, my lord."

Beobrand stared at him for a long while. He gripped Anhaga's hands tightly and nodded.

"You have my word. I will slay Wybert."

Anhaga nodded. The resolve was clear in his lord's features.

Beobrand's word was steel-hard, but when oath is piled on oath, the gods laugh.

Penda's gruff voice cut through once more.

"Come now. You have said your farewells. Be done with this. I am thirsty."

420

Beobrand squared his shoulders. His hand fell to Hrunting's pommel. For a terrible instant he pictured himself turning, leaping towards the king of the Mercians. Hrunting would find its mark, drinking deeply of Penda's blood.

Anhaga shook his head, almost imperceptibly.

Oswald's calm tone spoke from behind Beobrand.

"It is time, Beobrand. You must do as was agreed. Speak the words for all to hear."

Beobrand did not turn back to his king.

"Very well, Oswald King," he said, his words clipped like knappings of flint.

Beobrand took a deep breath and spoke in a voice loud enough to be heard by all present. Mercians and Northumbrians quietened in their ranks to listen to the words this huge thegn spoke from the centre of the meadow.

"This man, Anhaga, son of Agiefan, broke his oath to me and to our king." The words tasted like ash in his mouth. He tried to swallow, but his mouth was drought-dry. "He raised arms against a man while under oath-truce. All…" He looked to both sides of the field and hesitated. Acennan stared back at him; his bruised features an accusation. The stocky warrior made no indication of recognition.

Beobrand swallowed again against the dust in his mouth. He had done so much that was wrong. Made so many mistakes.

"All," his voice carried to each of the two hundred watching men, "knew the punishment for breaking this peace. The punishment is death. Let all behold justice."

Beobrand looked back to Anhaga. The man's face was pallid as bone beneath the blood, bruises and dirt.

"Make it quick," said Anhaga.

"You should not face death kneeling. Let me help you up."

"I do not think I can stand."

"I will support you."

Beobrand pulled on the wrist restraints and Anhaga staggered up. For a moment, he swayed there, like barley in a breeze. Then Beobrand clutched Anhaga's right arm firmly with his half-hand. For a heartbeat, their eyes met one last time. Lord and servant. Ring-giver and steward.

Death-bringer and victim.

Pulling hard on Anhaga's arm, Beobrand pushed the seax forward with the speed of a striking serpent. The blade was well-placed and true. It plunged through clothing, flesh and sinews, ploughing deep into Anhaga's chest. Beobrand felt a judder as the iron nicked a rib, before surging on, between the bones to reach the heart.

Anhaga shuddered. His eyes flared wide, but he did not cry out.

Beobrand wrapped his left arm around Anhaga's back, feeling the life and the strength leaving him as rapidly as a skylark flees a disturbed nest. Anhaga's legs buckled and Beobrand used all his strength to slowly lay him on the grass. Anhaga looked up at him with something like wonder in his eyes. He blinked twice and then his focus went beyond Beobrand. He gazed into the sky and his face relaxed, soothed.

Beobrand cast a glance into the sky. There, above them, circled the great red kite. It had flown higher, lifted on the warm air of the midday sun, but now it folded its wings and tumbled down towards them. At the last moment, with barely enough time before it came crashing to the earth, the bird let out a cry and spread its wings wide again and soared once more into the sky. What this omen meant, Beobrand did not know.

Looking back to where Anhaga lay, Beobrand could see that the life had left him. He pulled the seax from the wound.

Blood bubbled and pooled there, pumping feebly. Anhaga released a rattling breath and all was still.

Beobrand did not turn to acknowledge the kings who stood close behind him.

He turned to the line of Northumbrian warriors and walked, stiff-legged back to their ranks.

He saw where his gesithas waited. None would meet his eye.

All except for Acennan, who watched, unflinching with baleful stare, as Beobrand approached.

31

Beobrand patted Sceadugenga's neck. The stallion flicked its ears and nickered. It seemed they were both pleased to be home. Beobrand felt the knot in his stomach loosen slightly as he looked down into the bend in the Tuidi valley where Ubbanford nestled. The settlement was as they had left it. Smoke drifted and curled from the thatch. The unfinished hall presided over the rest of the buildings from its vantage point on the knap of the hill. They would be able to finish the construction now they had returned. With hard work and some luck, it could be finished before the season changed. They could winter in the new hall. Sunniva's hall.

Beobrand looked back to where his gesithas marched. There was a spring in their step now. Home and hearth awaited them. He frowned when he saw Acennan walking with the others. He led his mare, choosing to walk with the men rather than ride with his lord. He had barely spoken to Beobrand since they had left the frontier of Mercia. The men felt the simmering anger that lurked between the two, and they were uncomfortable when Acennan and Beobrand were in close proximity. Beobrand understood this. He knew he had done wrong by Acennan. And Anhaga. And Sunniva. So he kept himself apart from the men.

Oswald too had not addressed him directly since Anhaga's killing. The king had spoken to Penda for much of that day, the monks scratching away at their records of the decisions under the shade of the shelter in that meadow in Dor. The kings had parted on good terms it seemed, but when Beobrand had enquired over the outcome to Coenred, the monk would say little more than that decisions had been made and the kings were content. When he had pushed for more details, Coenred had snapped at him.

"It is not for me to tell you the words of kings. It seems to me that had they wished for you to hear, they would have invited you to sit with them." Coenred had not met his gaze and Beobrand had not attempted to speak with him again.

They had parted ways at Bebbanburg with scarcely a word between them.

For a moment his thoughts clouded. Nelda's curse seemed ever more likely.

The sound of the chatter of the men approaching reached him. He decided to wait no longer. They would arrive soon enough.

He touched his heels to Sceadugenga's flanks and gave the horse its head. The stallion sped forward and down the slope at a reckless gallop. A rare smile tugged at Beobrand's lips. The unseen fingers of wind pushed his hair back from his face. He clung to the reins and pressed his thighs in tightly to Sceadugenga. He cared not whether he would fall, which made the run all the more enjoyable. There was no time to notice anything untoward about Ubbanford as he careened down the hill. It was all he could do to remain in the saddle, but as he reined in his steed on the open ground before Ubba's hall, a niggling doubt prickled his mind.

Where was everyone? He looked up at the sky, gauging the height of the sun. The day was warm and there was much daylight left. There should have been men and women working the fields, tending the animals.

The settlement was unusually quiet.

Cold claws of dread scratched down his back. He leapt from the saddle and led Sceadugenga towards the hall.

Raised voices emanated from the open door as a tall warrior, shield and spear in hand, stepped out. The man carried his war gear deliberately, as one expecting violence. His helm half covered his face, but Beobrand recognised him.

"Elmer, what tidings? What is afoot that you greet your lord with arms?"

Elmer quickly pulled off his helmet.

"My lord," he said, his voice breathless, "you are well met." He cast around behind Beobrand, but could see nobody else. "And the others?" he asked, his jaw clenching against the possibility of grim news.

"They are following on foot. They will be here shortly. But tell me. What has happened here?"

Elmer grew pale. "The tidings are of the worst kind." He took a deep breath and said, "Tobrytan is slain."

"Who has done such a thing?"

"It was the sons of Nathair. Their father is dead and without the shackles of his will over them, they came seeking vengeance. Tobrytan and I stood strong. We turned them away."

Other figures came out of the hall into the afternoon sun. The Lady Rowena had a splash of blood on her mantle. Edlyn, all pale face and huge eyes, stood at her mother's side.

"Lady Rowena," said Beobrand, "are you hurt?"

"No," she replied, "the blood is Tobrytan's." Her face was drawn. The woman had endured much over the last year. It was good that she still had her daughter, she had lost so much else.

Elmer's wife, Maida, came out of the shadows of the hall and went to her man. On her hip, she carried Octa.

Beobrand's heart leapt in his chest. He was not alone after all. The boy was safe. Beobrand was shocked at the strength of his own emotion at seeing Octa. With force of will he turned away from the baby with his tuft of blond hair.

"How did this happen?" Beobrand asked.

Elmer did not answer, seemingly content now to defer the telling of the tale to Rowena.

"It seems," she said, "that after they had been turned back from," she hesitated, "your lands, Torran loosed an arrow which pierced Tobrytan's throat. We brought him back here. But we could not staunch the flow of his lifeblood."

Anger like a bitter winter storm filled Beobrand's being. He recalled the arrows whistling towards him as he fled along the bank of the Tuidi.

"This was a craven act," he spat. "Torran will pay for this. I warned them not to cross me again."

"There is more," muttered Rowena, her voice unusually tremulous.

"Yes? What? Speak then. Tell me all. I must hear."

"As they fled from Ubbanford, they found one of the thralls in the low meadow, near the river. It was Reaghan."

"Reaghan?" said Beobrand. The name was unfamiliar. A Waelisc name.

"She…" Rowena hesitated, clearly uncomfortable, then apparently deciding there was no alternative, she continued. "She was the girl who… attended you… on your last night here before you travelled to Bebbanburg."

Beobrand started. He had tried not to think of the slight girl. Her thick dark hair. The long lashes. Her pale, fragile body, that had trembled and bucked under his drunken thrusting desire in the darkness. Yet the image had come back to him again and again. He had scarcely allowed himself to think on her, yet he had been secretly looking forward to returning to Ubbanford. He felt so alone. He had hoped the dark thrall would be able to help him forget.

He gripped Sceadugenga's reins tightly. His knuckles whitened.

"Did they kill her?" he asked, dreading the reply.

"No," Rowena said. "But I fear it may be worse for her."

"Worse than death?" asked Beobrand.

Rowena nodded, her face grim with dark understanding of what befell women at the hands of men of war and violence.

"They took her with them."

A piercing shriek shattered the still of the night.

The men looked about nervously for some sign of the source of the scream, but they saw none. They touched amulets and weapons for protection from the evil things that stalked the night. They hoped it was an animal of some kind. The alternative did not bear contemplating.

They had walked in silence under the trees for most of the night. They had no need to talk. Their hasty plans had been discussed at Ubbanford and they had marched over the Tuidi with the setting of the sun. Their only sounds were the crunch of shoes on loose gravel, the jingling of war gear, the occasional clank of a helm against a low-hanging branch. And the dull thudding steps of Sceadugenga and Acennan's mare. The horses' hooves had been wrapped in thick cloths in the hope that the muffled sound would not travel far and alert their quarry.

Beobrand touched his hand again to Hrunting's pommel. The sword's presence reassured him. But with each touch his body thrummed with the pent up excitement of impending battle. He could feel the black coolness of battle lust pushing its way into his mind. He had felt such sorrow and anguish for so long, he welcomed the opportunity to unleash his anger. He could not fail again. Reaghan might only be a thrall, but she was his. He would protect her and return her to Ubbanford. And those who had taken her would pay.

He could just discern the shapes of those around him. The night was cool and quiet. A light mist had risen from the ground and the river and they passed like wraiths through the murk. They were shades lit by the dim glow of the half-moon that filtered through the leaf canopy. The broad, comforting form of Acennan trudged close by. As they had readied themselves to leave, Beobrand had approached him. He did not wish to force his friend to speak with him, but they could not march into danger as they had been. Without talking. Avoiding each other. When the sword-play began, chaos would reign and they would all need to depend on one another.

"We march to fight, Acennan," he had said.

Acennan had continued wrapping strips of cloth tightly around the branches they had cut for torches. These were then being passed to Attor, who soaked them in fish oil, so they would burn long and hot.

"Acennan?" Beobrand had said.

Acennan had looked up at him from where he sat. The skin around his eye still showed the yellow and green reminders of the bruise Beobrand had inflicted. Beobrand tried not to flinch at the sight.

"You can rely on me, Beobrand, if that is what you were going to ask." He stared at Beobrand for a time. "You have my oath and I am no oath-breaker. And besides," he had reached up and pointedly touched his bruised eye, "it will be good to have a fight where I can hit back."

That would have to be enough. Beobrand hoped that Acennan would see fit to forgive him, but for now, all he wanted was to know he had his friend's sword and shield protecting his flank.

The rest of the men had been grim-faced as they prepared. Elmer, who had not travelled south to witness the events at Dor, had spoken out.

"Are you sure of this, Beobrand?" he had said.

Beobrand had rounded on him. "If you have no stomach for the fight, Elmer, you can stay with the women. Help Maida with the children." He had regretted his anger the instant the words left his mouth. Elmer had stood before the sons of Nathair and seen Tobrytan killed. He was no coward.

"I know you are a brave man, Elmer. Forgive me. But we will do as I have said. I have spoken. The sons of Nathair will die and we will bring back Reaghan."

Elmer had nodded and spoken no more. The others, aware of Beobrand's quick temper, had bent their heads to the tasks at hand. Weapons were sharpened. The torches were prepared.

The women had brought them small parcels of food as they prepared to leave. Maida brought Octa to Beobrand. The baby was alert and wide-eyed, the light of the late afternoon sun giving his skin a ruddy, hale aspect. Beobrand had reached out and placed his hand upon Octa's tiny head. His wispy hair was as soft as goose down. He was so small. So fragile.

"My thanks to you for keeping him safe, Maida, Elmer-wife."

She had beamed and then gone to bid farewell to her husband.

The Lady Rowena had come to him as he tied the cloths to Sceadugenga's hooves. Her shadow had fallen on him and he'd looked up.

"Finish them once and for all, Beobrand," she had said, her voice hard and cold as the crag of Bebbanburg. "Finish this and then come back. Come home. Your son needs a father. And we need a hlaford." She had reached out and gently touched his arm before walking back into her dead husband's hall. She had not looked back.

They were close now. The misty glow of open land showing where the forest path ended.

"We halt here," whispered Beobrand. In the mist-shrouded night his voice sounded unnaturally loud.

They huddled close in the gloom to hear Beobrand's whispered words.

"Attor, you know what to do." Attor was the slightest of Beobrand's gesithas and he wore no metal armour, preferring instead to rely on his agility and speed. He could pass unheeded through the darkness like a nihtgenga, a dweller of the night forest, and he was deadly with the long seax he wore at his side.

"We will wait for you here, as agreed," continued Beobrand, "but we will be ready. If you need us, shout and we will be there in moments." Beobrand grasped the arm of the slim warrior. "Go silently and may the gods smile on you."

Attor showed his teeth, a dull gleam from his dark bearded face. "The gods will smile on all of us, but not on those Pictish bastards. I'll return shortly, be ready with the fire."

And with that, he slipped into the night and was lost to sight and sound.

They tethered the horses to branches at the edge of the path. They would not be needing them for what was to come. They had brought them to help carry back any injured. And Reaghan. They knew not if she would be able to walk.

"Aethelwulf," hissed Beobrand, "see to the fire, but have a care to keep it in the pot. The rest of you, ready yourselves and take the torches."

The movement of the men, rustling and stealthy, still sounded as loud as a shout in the hazy darkness.

From where Aethelwulf knelt, there was a sudden flare of light, gone as quickly as it had appeared. For the briefest of moments the men, the horses and the trees were illuminated. If anyone was watching in the dark, they would surely see the light.

"Position yourselves between Aethelwulf and Nathair's hall," said Beobrand. The men shuffled around.

Then Aethelwulf struck his flint again. As they watched, they saw how he captured the spark inside a large earthenware pot where he had already placed a small pile of dried fungus shavings. The spark rested on the fungus fleetingly and then dwindled to nothing, plunging them all into darkness again.

For a third time, he struck a spark. Again the spark fell into the prepared bed of tinder. Aethelwulf, his crooked nose and beard aglow from the tiny flame, leaned over the pot and pursed his lips. His breath brought life to the flame and he fed it with slivers of dry wood. The light grew from the pot and gave a warm glow to the faces of the men who looked on.

Another otherworldly shriek split the night and the men looked up from the warmth of the fire that called to them in the darkness with the seductive voice of home and hearth. A flash of ghostly white flitted across the path in the direction they had travelled.

"By the gods, it is a night spirit," said Ceawlin, terror in his voice.

Acennan muttered, "It was only a bird." And with those words, echoed from the darkness of a winter cave far away, the vision of Nelda's jackdaw, Muninn, came to Beobrand. The white-rimmed eye, twitching with a malevolent intelligence. Charcoal wings beating. Jagged talons stabbing at his eyes.

He glanced at Acennan. His eyes were like the embers of a funeral pyre in the flame-glow. Acennan met his gaze and nodded slowly.

"Only a bird," Acennan repeated, as if he knew what Beobrand was thinking.

Yes. Merely a bird. Muninn was nothing more than broken bones and feathers now. Beobrand raised himself up to his full height. The men looked to him for strength. He was their lord. He could not cower in the night, frightened of the calls of birds.

"Do not lose your nerve now, my gesithas," said Beobrand, forcing his voice to remain calm. "It is but a white owl. They scream to each other in the dark, but they are birds, nothing more." The faces of his men were strange in the trembling flicker of the flame in the pot. He was unsure his words had settled their fears. Ceawlin's eyes were wide.

"They scream, but when they hunt they are as silent as spirits, and so must we be. And as unseen. Now, cover that pot and get ready to move. Attor should be back soon."

Aethelwulf placed the lid on the pot, leaving a small gap for air to allow the flames to breathe. He took cloths from a pouch and wrapped the base of the pot with them so that he could carry it without fear of burning his hands. The smallest amount of yellow light seeped from the gap, lighting Aethelwulf from below and giving his face the aspect of a savage creature from legend.

They stood silently for some time then, each lost in his own thoughts in the darkness. Beobrand fought against the memories that threatened to drown him in their misery. Instead, he focused on his anger. He longed to feel the weight of Hrunting in his hand again. He recalled the sneering features of Wybert. He could scarcely believe the man had survived the attack by Anhaga, but such was what he had heard before leaving Dor. But Wybert would die at his hand. He had sworn it. And he had sworn to protect the people of Ubbanford. The sons of Nathair had awoken a bear by killing Tobrytan and capturing Reaghan. Beobrand stoked his fury. He was surprised to find he was thinking of the Waelisc girl. He remembered her hair. The touch of her skin. Her scent. And then, unbidden, his son's tiny features played in his mind. These Picts had sealed their doom when they had raised their hands to his people. His kin.

From the darkness, as silent as fog rolling over a fen, stepped Attor. The pale light from the fire pot picked out his face. His mouth was wide in a savage grin. In his hand he held his seax. It was black in the darkness with fresh blood.

"I was not seen," Attor said in a hushed voice.

"Wardens?" asked Beobrand.

"Only one at the door of the hall. He died silently. We should go now, before his body is found."

So the die had been cast. There was no more time for dwelling on the past, or what might be. The time had come to act.

Beobrand grasped Attor's shoulder.

"You have done well," Beobrand said, drawing Hrunting in a smooth motion from its fleece-lined scabbard. "Lead the way."

32

The seven men crept through the settlement towards the hulking shadow of the long hall. The houses brooded silent and dark in the night. After the darkness of the forest path, the moonlight seemed bright. They followed Attor, who had led them off the path to cross the stream where the banks were shallower, avoiding the wooden bridge and the noise they would make by crossing it.

Beobrand scanned the shadowy bulk of the buildings they passed for any sign of movement. But all was still. To his left he spied the glimmer of light from the fire pot. It glowed weakly on Aethelwulf's face, which was a mask of concentration as he carried the pot, careful not to let it drop.

They reached the hall. Its black shape blotted out the moonlight. They gathered in the moon shadow of the building and Beobrand touched Aethelwulf's shoulder gently. Aethelwulf set down the pot, took a cloth so as not to burn his fingers and lifted the lid. A dim red glow lit his face. He quickly dropped some more wood into the earthenware vessel. Within moments, flames crackled and yellow light flickered.

Aethelwulf stepped back and as one the warriors dipped

their fish oil-soaked torches into the pot's fire. The light dimmed, smothered by the torches. They were all suddenly blind again after losing their night sight from staring at the flames.

Beobrand's heart hammered in his chest. To be discovered now would bring disaster. He turned his back on the fire pot and the torches, looking out instead into the night.

The flames were evidently catching behind him, as the light expanded and cast his shadow, black and dancing before him. Still there was no movement from any of the buildings. Beobrand offered up silent thanks to Woden. Perhaps it was his wyrd to be victorious this night. He spun back to his gesithas. Their faces, lit by the guttering torches, were all ruddy cheeks, shadows and glinting eyes. These were his men. His gesithas. They had followed him here. They trusted him and he believed in them. They would fight for him. Kill for him. Even die for him.

But they would not die this night. These men were eager for battle. To hear of the abuse of Sunniva had dismayed them. They still felt guilty for their part in it, Beobrand was sure. The death of Anhaga had shaken them. And now they had lost one of their own. Tobrytan was liked by all, and had been murdered in a cowardly attack by Torran, son of Nathair.

Beobrand could feel his own battle fury threatening to blank everything else out, and he knew in that instant, with the clarity of the searing flames on the torches, that his men felt the same way. They had come to this place to rescue Reaghan. Yes. But more than that, they had come to satisfy their need for blood. They brought flame and sword in the night and they all now looked to him to give the command. To unleash their vengeance.

Beobrand nodded at Acennan. For a moment, he merely frowned back and Beobrand thought he would not respond.

Then Acennan signalled to Elmer and Garr, and like hounds released to the scent of a stag, they ran off, disappearing round the side of the hall. Propped at the edge of the porch, Beobrand noticed in the torchlight a slumped shape. The door warden's corpse. Attor was sly. The guard could have been asleep.

Acennan indicated for Attor and Ceawlin to watch the village huts, protecting their backs. Then, ramming his burning brand into the soil, he joined Beobrand and Aethelwulf to form a small shieldwall before the doors of the hall.

Beobrand hefted his shield, tightened his grip on Hrunting. It would not be long now.

He could hear the crackle and hiss of larger flames from the rear of the building. Elmer and Garr had brought flasks of fish oil to aid the fire and the night was dry. A red glow crowned the hall's roof as the flames began to feed hungrily off the wood and thatch. Beobrand looked up at the moon. Did the gods look down from there? He knew not, but if they gazed upon him, he would give them a night to remember. A night of fire, battle and death. A night worthy of the songs of scops. He hoped Leofwine was seated in Woden's corpse hall watching. The scop would revel in the telling of this night's tale. What a song he would sing.

And then Beobrand's attention was pulled back down to the hall.

Because the doors burst open.

The dark hush of the night exploded into light and cacophony. Flames leapt high from the hall, sending sparks flying towards the bright moon. Behind their meagre shieldwall, Beobrand heard screams. Shouts of fear. Cries of pain. The high-pitched wailing of children shaken from their slumber by frightened parents. He sensed Ceawlin and Attor readying themselves for any attacks from brave or foolhardy villagers.

The hall doors had been flung wide and smoke billowed forth as men tumbled into the night. The first man was large and clumsy with sleep. He was shouting over his shoulder, evidently to those yet to escape the burning building. He was close to Beobrand when he turned and saw the warriors, flame-licked helms and weapons gleaming. His face took on a comic look of surprise, his mouth a black circle. Beobrand recognised his grey-streaked hair and unruly beard, remembered how his toe had ached when the weather turned cold ever since kicking this same man in the teeth. The man had no time to recognise Beobrand, who took two steps forward and smashed his shield boss into the shocked face. The man went down hard.

The second man was fractionally more alert. He saw his friend drop from the shield-blow to the face and managed to arrest his forward motion. But before he could take stock, Acennan leapt forward and swung his sword. The blade sank deep into the man's shoulder. He looked down in absolute horror at the iron jutting from his body. He began to keen, an ululating shriek the like of which none had heard before. His hands flailed up, flapping like injured bats at the cold blade that had pierced him. Acennan twisted the blade savagely and pulled it free of the sucking flesh. A great gout of blood spewed forth. The man's keening turned into a grunting groan and he collapsed, face first onto the earth.

The other men who had begun to leave the hall retreated back inside. Behind them, flames and smoke were engulfing the wooden structure. They would not stay long within the hall. The heat would force them out soon enough.

Beobrand glanced back to where Attor and Ceawlin stood. As he looked, a man dressed in nothing more than a kirtle, bare legs pale in the night, ran at them. He was armed with a small axe. Attor let the man come. The hatchet rose high and the man screamed his defiance. At the last moment, Attor dropped his shoulder, slid harmlessly beneath the man's flailing attack, and lifted him with one fluid motion over him. The man crashed into the hard earth. Attor picked up the man's axe and turned away from him. It was only then that Beobrand saw that Attor must have driven his seax into the man at the same moment as catapulting him into the air. He lay there, mouth gaping and hand gripping at the bubbling hole in his stomach. His kirtle was stained red.

Beobrand turned his focus back to the man at his feet. The man was dazed, his eyes groggy. Blood and spittle flecked his lips and beard. His teeth were a jagged ruin of broken grave markers. Beobrand dropped to the ground beside him. He put Hrunting down beside the man and slapped him hard.

"Where is she?" he bellowed.

The man's eyes tried to focus. Flames and sparks reflected in the large pupils.

Beobrand took hold of his throat and shook him.

"Where is she?" he repeated. The fire was raging now. If Reaghan was in the hall as he suspected, she would die if they did not get her out soon.

"Who... what?" The man's voice was slurred.

"The girl? The girl you took, where is she?"

Recognition came then. He looked up at Beobrand and found his courage. He smiled through his bloodied mouth and broken teeth.

"She's inside. She was a tasty morsel. We all had her," he started to laugh. "She was a fighter. Made it more fun."

The words turned to burbling choking. Beobrand had taken up Hrunting and drawn its blade across the man's throat. It sliced deeply, through sinew and flesh, until metal rasped against bone, such was Beobrand's ire and Hrunting's sharpness.

Beobrand stood. Acennan and Aethelwulf shuffled close on either side.

"She's inside," said Beobrand. The rear part of the hall's roof was now a conflagration worthy of a king's funeral pyre. They could see the shapes of figures in the doorway, dark against the flames. The heat was increasing. It was getting painful to stand this close to the hall. Gods knew how long those inside could hold out.

From behind them came more sounds of combat. Another glance told him Attor and Ceawlin were still standing. More corpses had joined the axeman at their feet. Attor was mad with the blood lust. He grinned widely and screamed at the gathered villagers.

"Run now, or die! I have the taste for blood and I would have more! I will rip your guts from your bellies. I will fuck your women. Eat your babies!"

Beobrand turned away from the disturbing sight. Attor was like an animal. A wolf worrying defenceless lambs in a field.

The searing heat pushed Beobrand and the others back a pace.

"She'll die in there," Acennan shouted over the tumult of the fire and battle-clash.

Beobrand ground his teeth. It was true. If they did not come out, there would be none who could survive in that inferno much longer.

"Sons of Nathair!" he roared. "Come from your father's hall and fight me! You have killed my people for the last time. Come out and face your doom!"

He did not truly expect the men inside to react to his words. But his voice carried the force of his frustrations. His rage at the gods. All his sorrow. And his loss.

As if at his signal, the moment the words left his lips men rushed from the doors. They had used their time to prepare themselves for they now bore war gear. Blades flashed. Helms glimmered. Three men leapt from the doors and sprang forward, shields raised high before them.

The force and speed of the attack gave Beobrand pause for a heartbeat. It was all he could do to raise his shield against the sword thrust that whistled towards his chest. Then the man was upon him. Beobrand attempted to sidestep the careening run of his adversary, but he was not fast enough. The Pict collided with him and they fell to the ground in a tangle.

To Beobrand's left, he was dimly aware of the massive form of Broden, son of Nathair, smashing into Acennan. The huge man swung a deadly two-handed axe as if it was a child's plaything. Acennan was forced back by the onslaught.

On the right, a scrawny, wild-haired man spat and shouted in his native Pictish tongue, all the while trying to gut Aethelwulf with a short slashing blade.

Beobrand rolled away from his opponent, distancing himself from him and again stopping a blow on his linden board. He scrabbled to his feet, breathing hard now. Death was in the flame-filled night and Beobrand could feel its breath on the nape of his neck. He faced the man, allowing the battle-anger to fully take hold.

The man feinted towards his face. Beobrand didn't even deign to parry or block the blow. He merely swayed back allowing the feint and the follow up slash to his groin to miss him. Beobrand watched the Pict carefully. His eyes widened the instant before he lunged and Beobrand pushed the blow away with his shield boss. The blow was powerful, sending a jarring shock up his arm. He lost his grip on the boss for a moment, but the straps Sunniva had fashioned for him held firm. Another blow came swinging down towards his head. Beobrand batted it away with Hrunting's blade. Sparks flew. The Pict was tiring now, aware that he was outclassed by this tall thegn of Bernicia. Sweat poured from him, his eyes wild.

Around them the night was chaos. Aethelwulf still fought the slight warrior. There were more sounds of battle from behind, where Attor and Ceawlin stood. And Acennan was backing away from the power of the axe blows raining down on him from the hands of Broden. As he watched, Acennan's foot caught on the torch he had planted in the ground. His ankle turned and he fell. Broden loomed above him, axe raised.

"No!" shouted Beobrand, but his voice was lost in the madness of the night. He could not allow Acennan to die. But he was too far away. And there was another enemy before him.

Beobrand dragged his gaze away from Acennan's plight. He would be no help to him if he allowed this clumsy Pict to stick him with his blade. Time to finish this. He lowered his shield and took a step back away from the sweating, panting man. Just as Beobrand had anticipated, the Pict took a step forward and raised his sword. At the same instant, Beobrand changed his direction and sprang forward, Hrunting beating against the outstretched blade. Then, turning his back momentarily on his adversary, he spun on the balls of his feet. He felt Hrunting meet with resistance, then carry on through its arc. The man's head toppled from his body, even as his legs still carried him forward. Spouts of hot blood spurted into the smoke-hazed night. The knees buckled and the headless corpse flopped to the earth.

Beobrand did not falter. He used the momentum from his spin to send him flying towards Broden.

The night was ablaze, the hall fire adding its roar to the screams of the dying. Heat, acrid smoke, and the ring of iron on iron filled the night. But for Beobrand, that hellish night receded, pushed away by the intense focus he now brought to bear on a single point of conflict.

On a single foe.

Broden stood astride Acennan's prostrate form. As Beobrand rushed to his friend's aid, he saw the heavy axe head rise and fall. It chopped deeply into Acennan's shield, splitting it. The next strike from Broden would slay Acennan. There was no doubt. Beobrand would never reach them in time to prevent it.

"Broden!" Beobrand shouted, willing himself to move faster.

But the burly son of Nathair did not hear him, or was not so easily distracted, for he smashed the axe down. Acennan twisted and writhed, throwing his shield boss desperately into the path of the blade. Deflected, the axe slammed into his left shoulder.

"No!" screamed Beobrand. His shield boss caught Broden in the side. Beobrand's weight and speed shoved him clear of Acennan. Beobrand followed the shield charge with a slashing cut to the face and was surprised at Broden's speed. Broden regained his balance instantly and deflected Hrunting's serpent-like blade with the haft of his axe.

Beobrand took a deep breath and steadied himself. This man was a master of the axe. That was clear. He swung the weapon now in a flurry of intricate patterns. He wove a deadly thread with the axe, constantly moving. High and then low.

Left then right. The haft slapped against his meaty palms and all the while the iron head of the axe glinted red in the light of the hall's death throes. It would take a brave man to confront that wall of death. Or a foolhardy one. Beobrand's lips peeled back from his teeth in a grin. Men had said he was brave. He did not know whether that was so. But he was sure he was foolhardy. The hair on his right arm shrivelled in the heat from the hall. This man had watched Tobrytan die. And taken Reaghan. Now she must surely be dead within that fire. Beobrand had warned him what would happen.

Without more thought, Beobrand stepped into the axe's dancing death whir. Broden's eyes betrayed his surprise at Beobrand's actions. Beobrand had gauged his moment well. The axe was on a downward arc. He raised his shield, catching the axe head on the wood. Pain surged up his left arm, his fingers numbed by the blow. The axe broke through leather and linden, cutting deeply into his forearm. But Beobrand did not slow his advance. Even as the axe sliced into shield and flesh, Beobrand's right arm darted forward, a viper striking a rat. Hrunting buried itself deep in Broden's left underarm. Beobrand stepped in closer, lifting Hrunting's hilt and angling the sword downward. He pushed savagely. The blade vanished into Broden's flesh. A tremor ran through him as the steel point found his heart, and the huge Pict collapsed to the earth, an expression of shock on his dead face.

Beobrand stepped back. His arm throbbed with each heartbeat. He couldn't feel the fingers on his mutilated hand, but he clenched them into a fist and raised the ruined shield. It was so heavy. He struggled to lift it. For a moment he feared he had lost the strength in his arm, then he noticed the axe. Its head was still embedded in the board, its blade sawing into his arm with each movement. He lowered the shield so that the trailing axe shaft touched the earth, then, with a grunt of pain he pulled backward, levering the axe out of board and flesh. Hot, fresh pain rippled into his fingers as the blade came free and the axe fell, heavy and still, next to its wielder.

He felt his blood flowing freely now. He would need to bind the wound. He shrugged his arms free of the straps and allowed the shield to drop to the ground.

Turning, he hurried to where Acennan lay. He squirmed and cursed, looking up at Beobrand.

"The Pictish bastard has broken my shoulder," spat Acennan.

Some of the rings of his byrnie had split, but the metal shirt was well-made; the axe had not cut deeply. However, Broden was strong and the axe was heavy. Acennan's left collarbone had shattered.

"Thank the gods your byrnie rings are well-wrought," said Beobrand, shifting his sword to his blood-slick left hand and offering Acennan his right.

"Thank the smith," answered Acennan, grimacing. "The gods care naught for whether I live or die." He took the offered hand.

"But I care," said Beobrand, heaving him to his feet. Both men groaned with the strain on their injuries.

Their eyes met.

"I know," said Acennan. Then, his gaze flickered to something behind Beobrand. "Look out!" he shouted.

With no time to think, Beobrand took Hrunting in his right hand and spun to defend himself.

A dark figure flew out of the smoke-filled darkness. Screaming wildly, it came at him, red metal gleamed. A wicked knife shimmered in the night.

Beobrand stepped quickly to his right, at the same time

swinging Hrunting in a deadly arc to the left. The blade connected with the attacker's face, cleaving through jaw and nose. Bone smashed. Blood and brains splattered. The knife skittered harmlessly over the rings of Beobrand's byrnie. He hardly felt the glancing blow.

He looked down at the twitching corpse and the ruined face. It was a small figure, but with rounded hips and breasts that were all too evident under the night dress. It was a young woman who lay at his feet.

Another woman dead.

How many more would he see perish in his lifetime? He had already seen more than his share. His gorge rose. She had only been protecting her home. Perhaps Broden was her man.

What had he become? All he had wanted was to bring back Reaghan.

Reaghan!

He ran towards the hall. Oblivious of everything else. The flames were a yellow and red wall that reached the dome of the sky itself. He could not get close to the blaze. His eyebrows and hair began to singe.

A creaking groan emanated from the structure. Was that a scream he could hear? Could there still be someone living inside that bonfire? Then, with an almost animal roar, the roof beams collapsed. Flames and sparks sprayed into the sky like a message to the gods. The heat intensified. His face began to blister. Nobody could survive in that.

He staggered back. Away from the flames and the burning pain of his failure.

Tears burnt from his cheeks as they fell. He had lost Reaghan as he had lost all the others. Edita. Rheda. His mother. Cathryn. And Sunniva. Sweet, beautiful, brave, Sunniva.

If he could just have saved the Waelisc girl. Just one. But it seemed his wyrd was to always fail. He could kill, but he could not prevent those he loved from dying.

A sudden searing agony in his right leg brought his thoughts screaming back from where they wandered. He looked down but for a moment he was unable to understand what he was seeing. Something bright white was protruding from his right calf. A feather. The fletchings of an arrow. He had been shot and the arrow had passed clean though the large muscle below the knee.

Looking in the direction the arrow had come from he saw Torran, thin face twisted with fury, lit by the flames of his destroyed home. He was placing another arrow on the string of his bow, but he had no time to draw and loose. For Attor had seen him too and was rushing at him spitting a cascade of insults as he ran.

Torran stared at Beobrand for a moment, his baleful eyes full of loathing. He hesitated. Attor would be upon him in moments.

"I will kill you, Beobrand of Ubbanford," Torran screamed, before turning and fleeing into the darkness that shrouded the land to the north. Attor sped after him and both were swallowed by the night.

The flames still raged in the hall and some of the other buildings had begun to burn, whether from stray sparks or put to the torch by his gesithas, Beobrand did not know. All about him lay corpses and destruction. Those villagers who yet lived had fled. All this death and he had not saved her. How the gods must be laughing. His eyes were drawn to the woman he had slain. He shuddered as he recalled the destruction of her face. The image was etched into his mind and he would never forget it. So it was as he had feared. He had become just such a killer as Hengist.

Acennan came to Beobrand's side. Ceawlin joined them. They stared into the crackling, roaring doom of Nathair's hall in silence for a time.

"Lean on me," Acennan said, then winced as Beobrand put pressure on his broken bone. "But take a care."

"I have failed," said Beobrand, his voice as desolate as a winter wind.

"I don't know," Acennan said, a smile playing at his lips, "you seem to have done a good job of destroying this place."

Beobrand frowned. He was in no mood for Acennan's humour.

"I preferred it when you were not speaking to me."

In answer, Acennan merely pointed. From behind the hall came Elmer and Garr. Beobrand's heart surged to see them both alive. It must count for something that all of his gesithas had lived through the night. He had not led them here to their deaths. Then he noticed that Elmer was carrying something. At first, in the flickering light of the flames he thought it might be a child, but then, as they drew closer, he recognised the long unruly hair and the slender curve of the neck.

Beobrand took faltering, stiff-legged steps towards Elmer. Jolts of pain shot through his leg where the arrow yet protruded. He ignored the pain. His left arm screamed in protest at being raised, but he reached out and lifted Reaghan from Elmer's grasp. He felt her living warmth against his chest and let out a sigh.

He knew not how she was alive, but suddenly the night was not so dark.

Reaghan lived. And Beobrand had not failed.

33

The sun rose dim and dismal in the grey morning. Its rays failed to penetrate the thick fug of morning mist and smoke that curled around the settlement, instead lighting the scene with a diffuse dreamlike glow.

"That is the best I can do," said Ceawlin. He surveyed the bindings he had wrapped around Beobrand's arm and leg. Blood was already seeping through, but more slowly now. He had let it run freely from the arrow wound for a time to flush out dirt and any ill magic. Now that it was bound tightly, it throbbed constantly, but the pain was less acute than it had been.

Beobrand had sat silently as Ceawlin ministered to him. His face was pale, but a serenity had descended on him after the combat. Briefly his hands had shaken and sickness had churned his guts. But he had breathed deeply and drunk some cool water from the stream and the feeling had subsided, as it always did.

Reaghan was nuzzled against his chest, her head turned away from the world, hair falling over her face. She had not spoken since her rescue, but she seemed unharmed.

Around them, his gesithas moved through the dead and the buildings, taking anything they could find of worth. There was not much. The hall still smouldered and there would be nothing worth taking, unless Nathair had silver or gold, which would survive the fire. Still, they could not stay here. They had won, but they were battered and Torran had escaped. If he managed to elude Attor and rally the villagers, Beobrand and his small warband could be overrun.

Beobrand looked at the bones of the hall. Flames still licked at the pillars. Smoke billowed. He could scarcely believe that Reaghan had not perished inside. He cursed himself silently for putting into action a plan that had almost seen her burnt alive. Elmer had recounted what had happened, as they'd bound their wounds and cleared the ash from their throats with water.

Torran and some of the other warriors had broken a hole in the rear wall of the hall. They'd rushed out, but were waylaid by Elmer and Garr, who fought them. They had slain one man and Garr had taken a nasty slash to his head which did not stop bleeding for so long that they began to fear he would lose all his blood and turn into a ghost before their eyes. Torran and his warriors had fled. It was then that Elmer had noticed Reaghan. She had crept out of the hole into the cool night. The girl had fainted away then, and he had feared her dead, or dying.

Beobrand gave her a gentle squeeze with his right arm. Her shoulders were tiny. She trembled under his embrace, but he felt her arms tighten around him.

"Hail," came a voice from the smoky fog. The men lifted weapons. Elmer and Ceawlin stepped towards the voice. They needn't have feared. The shadowy form that walked from the mist was Attor.

"By the gods," said Acennan, "you look as tired as a dog who has smelt a bitch the other side of the world and run all the way to find her."

Attor could barely raise a smile. He took a cup of water from Acennan and drank his fill. "I was chasing no bitch. Though Torran does run like a wolf. I lost him. He's a fast one."

Beobrand broke his silence. "I am glad to see you return whole, Attor. We have been waiting for you." Then, to all of his warband, "Ready the horses and collect what you wish to carry. We are moving out."

Acennan helped Beobrand to his feet.

"You saved my life, Beobrand," he said. "Again."

"And you saved mine. Back at Dor. If you had not fought with me, delayed me from my quest, I would be a corpse now. And an oath-breaker." He sighed, remembering how he had punched Acennan in the lightning-glimmer of the storm. He had been stupid with drink, but that was no excuse. "And I only repaid you with violence."

Acennan's mouth twisted into a crooked smile.

"Do not worry about that. You hit like a girl anyway."

Beobrand did not smile.

"I will repay you, Acennan. I will be a good lord. A good friend, if you'll still call me that."

Acennan did not reply. Beobrand's heart twisted. Perhaps there was no room for friendship now. Had he beaten it out of their relationship, the way a smith beats impurities from hot iron?

Elmer fetched the horses. Beobrand's leg and arm impeded him from climbing onto Sceadugenga's back, but with the help of a log to stand on and Elmer's steadying hands, he managed to pull himself into the saddle. Elmer helped Acennan up to the mare. Then he lifted Reaghan up to Beobrand as easily as if she had been one of his children. She squirmed to find a comfortable position, and then buried her head once more in his cloak, hiding her face from the day.

From his new vantage point, Beobrand looked down at the corpses, still and broken clumps of cloth and flesh, wreathed in mist in the dawn light. His eyes lingered on the remains of the woman he had killed. The sight of her smashed face sprang into his mind unbidden. He shivered. Reaghan tightened her thin arms around him, as if she could protect him from his fears.

"What have I done, Acennan? What have I become? Am I no different from Hengist?"

Acennan scratched at dried blood on his cheek and surveyed the destruction around them.

"You are a warrior and you are a leader of men, Beobrand. It is no easy thing."

Beobrand recalled Oswald's words.

"I am no great man," he said.

Acennan snorted. "I never said you were. But you are no normal man. You lead and men follow." He swept his uninjured arm to encompass the village. "Even when you lead them into fire and death."

"Well, that is a good thing, I suppose," said Beobrand.

Acennan shook his head and looked at Beobrand sadly. "I am not so sure. I think perhaps it is a curse."

"Maybe it is my wyrd to be cursed."

For a moment he was sure he could hear Nelda's words echoing in that dank cave on Muile.

Acennan suddenly smiled. "Well, if such is your wyrd, you will not be alone, for the thread of my wyrd is woven with yours."

Beobrand nodded.

"Thank you, my friend. In some things at least, I am lucky."

He swung Sceadugenga's head towards the forest path, and Ubbanford.

Then, raising his voice, for all his gesithas to hear, he said, "Let's go home."

Historical Note

This is a work of fiction. It is historical fiction, not a history book. If I have to choose between history and story, story wins every time. I try very hard to stick to what is known from primary sources and archaeology and never knowingly include anachronisms in my writing. But when something is not known for certain, then I think it is fair game for a novelist to make something up, and that is where things get really fun. The excitement in writing a story set close to 1,400 years ago, is that the details are scant, leaving lots of room for my imagination to run rampant.

Beobrand and his close friends and enemies are all fictional, but many of the events and people that appear in this novel are real.

Cadwallon was defeated at the Battle of Hefenfelth (Heaven-field) and the king was slain at a place called Denisesburn. The exact circumstances of his defeat are not known, but primary sources (Bede and Adomnán), do talk of King Oswald attacking at night, following a dream vision from Saint Columba. Before the battle, Oswald had a cross erected and made his outnumbered warhost pray to God. They were victorious, and one would imagine that would be a pretty good selling point for the new religion. Victory when facing overwhelming odds against a foe who has already killed three kings (Edwin, Eanfrith and Osric) in the last year would be hard to argue against.

The importance of this battle should not be underestimated, despite it not being well-known to modern audiences. This defeat of Cadwallon's amassed native Britons (Waelisc, the Old English for "foreigners", leading to the name of the Welsh in modern English) at Hefenfelth paved the way for the total domination of England by the Anglo-Saxons.

Oswald was a devout Christian, having grown up in exile under the protection of the kings of Dál Riata on the island of Hii (Iona). He saw in Lindisfarne the chance to mirror the holy island of the west coast in his own eastern kingdom and so sent for a bishop. The first bishop of Lindisfarne is not named by Bede, but later chroniclers name him as Cormán. The fact that he returned to Hii is described by Bede, who says the bishop "reported to his superiors that he had been unable to teach anything to the nation to whom they had sent him because they were an uncivilised people of an obstinate and barbarous temperament". I chose to have his acts a little more deviant than merely being unable to teach the people of Bernicia. I apologise to the memory of the man.

The next, and much more successful and widely known, bishop of Lindisfarne is Aidan, and he will appear in later stories.

There are several mentions of different months in the book. Each month in the Anglo-Saxon year had a name that reflected the main events of that month. Blotmonath (Sacrifice, or Blood month) is November, when the animals that cannot be fed through winter are slaughtered. Solmonath (Soil, or mud month) is February. The climate in Northern Europe would certainly explain that name. Travel in winter, with heavy rain and most roads being simple earth tracks, would have been extremely difficult and taxing. One can easily imagine trudging through the cloying mud of rain-drenched paths without the protection of modern waterproof clothing or boots. Hreðmonath, is March and is the month in which sacrifices were made to the goddess Hreða, though little is known about her.

Sacrifice is a running theme in this story. Sacrifices of all kinds would be made to gods to appease them, to secure a good harvest, to improve the weather conditions, anything they could think of. Belief in gods and spirits was not questioned and the greater the sacrifice you could give to a god, the more likely they were to smile upon you and answer your prayers. Human sacrifice was probably not widespread, but there is certainly evidence that it did occur. This makes the idea of Christianity very attractive, with its god whose son was sacrificed so that mankind could live forever. In a world where sacrifice was very real and sometimes horrific, the promise of never needing to sacrifice again, must have grabbed the attention of the populace. Add to this monks and priests who were more educated in areas such as medicine, therefore helping the communities they served, and it is not difficult to see why Christianity won the battle for hearts and minds.

Of course, the old religion thrived in villages and far-flung areas for many centuries, so it goes without saying that at this time, when Christianity was just beginning to gain a foothold in Britain again after the Romans left centuries before, that there would have been many clashes between advocates of the two religions. Bede tells the tale of Edwin's pagan priest, Coifi arguing with the Italian Christian priest, Paulinus.

Coifi eventually capitulated and accepted Christianity, even going so far as to defile the grove of trees where he worshipped the old gods by throwing a spear into the sacred tree. This was the inspiration for the confrontation between Paulinus and Nelda, though here the outcome and the destruction of the sacred tree is more dramatic!

Historical data concerning death in childbirth is not available for this far back in history, but pregnancy and childbirth have always been dangerous. There are developing countries now, in the twenty-first century, where one in seven women will die in pregnancy or childbirth! That is a hideous statistic, but one that lends credence to a young, healthy woman dying of pregnancy and childbirth-related medical issues in seventh-century Britain. Birth must have been a time of wonder, but also of fear and uncertainty. A child would bring joy and another pair of hands to help in the fields, at the loom and the hearth, even in the shieldwall, but it also brought another mouth to feed and the danger to the mother's health.

There has been a lot of discussion over the years about the exact nature of the Anglo-Saxon conquest of Britain. It was once commonly believed that they came over from the continent in droves of ships and took the land by force, pushing all those who stood against them back into the west and settling the land they conquered. Later research makes it seem much more likely that the actual number of settlers was reasonably small. It appears obvious to me that the Angles, Jutes and Saxons who settled in the eastern edges of Britain took power from the native Britons by force of arms and superior strength, weapon technology and, perhaps, fighting ability. But once they had established themselves as rulers, they would allow the locals to continue tending the land as they had always done, as long as they paid tribute and didn't cause too much trouble. So it is against this picture of a multi-ethnic Britain, with different races and tribes cohabiting, that we find Bernicia ruled by an Anglo-Saxon king, but with many subjects who must have considered themselves of older native stock, whether Picts in the north, or Britons.

If we look at modern societies with different ethnic and religious groups living together, we can see the tensions that can quickly arise. I believe that one of the challenges for a king of Northumbria at this time would have been to keep the peace within his own borders between his thegns and those of differing backgrounds. Of course, this would be coupled with wishing to maintain peace with powerful neighbours, such as Penda.

The meeting with Penda described in this book is fictional. However, the leaders of the different kingdoms of Albion created pacts and alliances and Oswald had a lot to deal with without having to worry about Penda. Penda at this time is the warlord star of Mercia and his power is on the rise. He has already sided with Cadwallon and killed Edwin, the over-king, or Bretwalda of the Anglo-Saxons, showing the scale of his ambition. The truce between Oswald and Penda as I describe it will not last for long, and the future of the two kings will be intertwined, just as Beobrand's wyrd is linked to the royal families of Bernicia.

There is still much to tell in Beobrand's tale. More battles and death. More raven-feeding with the corpses strewn in the mud before the shieldwall.

And more love.

But all of that is for another day and another book.

Acknowledgements

First let me thank you, dear reader, for buying this book. I hope you've enjoyed it. If you have, please take a moment to leave a short review on Amazon or Goodreads, and also tell your friends about it, be they on Facebook, Twitter or even in real life! Word of mouth and positive reviews make all the difference in the crowded marketplace of the modern world and authors rely on the support of readers saying nice things about our books.

When I was writing this book, I had yet to release *The Serpent Sword*, so I was writing in a bubble. There was no pressure apart from getting the words down and moulding them into an interesting story. However, the subsequent publication and overwhelmingly positive reaction to the first novel in the series added an extra edge of anxiety for *The Cross and the Curse*. I know now that it is not as simple as just writing the story. Once a book is released it gains a life of its own and with that come extra expectations for its sequel. Will people like it as much as the first one? Will it do as well?

In the end there is nothing for it, but to trust that all the hard work agonising over the words is enough and let it out into the wild. Just like children, when they are ready to leave the nest, you have to let them go. And just as with children, you hope they do you proud. And so, I hope *The Cross and the Curse* does me proud as I move on to work on book three of the Bernicia Chronicles, *Blood and Blade*.

But before I go, I must thank all the people who have helped me to get this book ready.

First, thanks to the team at Aria for all their hard work adding some extra polish to the book.

A sincere thank you to my trusty beta readers, Shane Smart, Rich Ward, Derek and Jacqui Surgey, Simon Blunsdon and Mark Leonard, each of whom offered useful comments and spotted mistakes that helped me to improve the book.

Robin Carter, of Parmenion Books, kindly agreed to read an early draft and he provided a wealth of useful input.

I am thankful to Dr Christopher Monk for his help with the intricacies of Old English pronunciation.

My great friend Gareth Jones read multiple drafts and was, as ever, full of energy and good ideas.

Thanks, as always, go to Alex Forbes, who is not only one of my oldest friends, but also one of my strongest supporters.

To my agent, Robin Wade, thanks for the comments on the manuscript and your tireless efforts to get a publisher to see the light. We got there in the end!

Special thanks to Matt Bunker, of the living history group, Wulfheodenas, for again agreeing to let me take photographs of his amazing and historically accurate battle gear – this time with him in it! Stephen Weatherly took the great photo that is on the cover, so I am indebted to him for that and for all the lunchtime chats and games of pool!

My parents have always been supportive of everything I have ever done and my writing is no different. Both of them have read drafts and provided feedback, but my dad, Clive Harffy, has gone one step further and edited the novel too, spending hours going over each and every word. He is writing his debut novel now, so special thanks to my mum, Angela Harffy, for putting up with my dad and me talking incessantly about writing whenever we get together.

Despite all the help I've mentioned, writing can be a very lonely business. By definition you need to be alone with your thoughts for many hours to produce a novel. Being able to reach out to a friendly community of other writers online for help and inspiration when things get tough is wonderful. There are many authors who have offered me their support in the last couple of years, but the following all deserve a special mention for being brilliant writers and lovely people: Steven A. McKay, Angus Donald, Paul Fraser Collard, Carol McGrath, Justin Hill, Toby Clements, Michael Jecks, Giles Kristian, Martin Lake, Samantha Wilcoxson, Stephanie Churchill and E.M. Powell. Read their books!

And lastly, putting up with my absences when I am deep in the writing or editing process, and my moods when the writing is not going well, my eternal gratitude goes to my ever-supportive and lovely wife, Maite and our daughters, Elora and Iona.